Red Ochre Falls

Kristen Gibson

Publication Data

Red Ochre Falls/ Kristen Gibson. —First edition.

ISBN 978-0-9909058-0-6

eBook ISBN 978-0-9909058-1-3

1. Mystery—Fiction. 2. Romance—Fiction. 3. Self-defense—Fiction.
I. Title.

DEDICATION

To John, Abigail, and Connor for making every day a beautiful adventure. Thanks go to family and friends who helped create this book.

In every conceivable manner, the family is link to our past, bridge to out future.

—ALEX HALEY

CONTENTS

ACKNOWLEDGMENTS

Thanks to the following people who encouraged my writing career and helped shape this story: Susan Rose, John Gibson, Bev Gibson, Ron Gibson, and Debbie Sears for their belief, enthusiasm and/or editorial skills; to the officers, insiders, and krav maga masters who offered help and information; the many incredible teachers and writers who've inspired me to become an author; to my husband and children for cheering me on, and smiling despite the countless hours of work and convenience meals it took to make this book a reality; and to my mom and grandma for sharing their storytelling gifts. Hope you enjoy the book and will overlook any mistakes.

PROLOGUE

My hands were tied so tight there was no wiggle room. My desperate
wrist contortions only made things worse, and the strap dug deeper
into my skin. Breathing hurt and the pain seared from having my
hands bound behind my back so long. I needed to get out of here. I
tried talking, actually reasoning with him, but could only croak out a
weak appeal. He was in charge, and wasn't interested in listening. He
wanted the stage all to himself. Speaking was a performance to him,
like he held some imaginary audience captive, not just me. He moved
closer. My gut clenched as the smell of his cologne mixed with the
damp odor of the place. The single light bulb hanging from the grey
ceiling cast his face with monstrous shadows. I searched the room for
another way out. Nothing. Absolutely nothing came to mind. I
braced myself, closed my eyes and thought, we all come from
somewhere. Then he knocked me out. Cold.

CHAPTER 1

We loaded the last boxes into an el cheapo version of a U-Haul and I piled a bunch of clothes into our car. Being neat was the last thing on my mind. I'd had it with boxes, and packing, and moving. I just wanted to close my eyes and forget this ever happened. Unfortunately, this was only the beginning, if you could call it that. It felt more like an ending—a big, fat disappointment of an ending. I was getting mad again. I needed to keep my emotions in check if we were going to survive the long drive ahead.

I sucked in a breath and turned to look back at our home. Then it hit me. It's not ours anymore.

We loved this house. We worked hard to make it our own—from the pastel tulips and sweet magnolias in the yard to the sheer butterfly curtains in my second-story room, and the built-in shelves in mom's office filled with books. We made a good life here. Now, we had to leave. *Why us?* I wondered. Because it was what was best for now, mom had said.

Pressure rose in my head and I stopped breathing for a minute. The sky beyond the house glowed with pink streaks as day gave way to night. The light was so intense I could barely see anything for a while after.

"At least we'll have a roof over our heads, Mattie," mom whispered as she touched my shoulder. "We should consider ourselves lucky."

I wanted to resent her, and her comment, but I knew she was right. We were lucky. Other families didn't have half of what we did, even though it didn't feel like much right now. Mom had suffered a heart attack, we'd lost grandma, and our move felt like defeat to me. It would take some time to adjust. I didn't know if I could handle it.

Tears flooded my eyes as the hugs and goodbyes tore at my heart.

Once the send off crew started to wane, we prepared for takeoff.

My foot hit a crusty mat, and the truck creaked as I stepped up into the Faux-haul. The cab reeked of fast food, gas, and a few worse odors. At least it started.

Neither of us wanted to leave, so we took our time doing final checks. I programmed our destination into the plug-in navigation box my Aunt Eileen gave us. The note she included made us laugh, but it was a touching sentiment: *Never will you be alone; with this you can always find your way home.* We waved goodbye and headed toward our destination.

Mom drove the old beater, I got the rental. The truck shocks worked about as good as the as the old AM/FM radio—which came without knobs or power. If this was any indication of the trip ahead, I was in for a bumpy ride.

CHAPTER 2

After a couple hours, the rush of hitting the open road wore off. Driving felt like a chore—a tailgating Camry and a near collision with a semi didn't help. Plus, nature called, so I signaled for us to pull off the highway.

We stopped at a gas station. I nearly fell out of the truck. My legs reluctantly uncurled and a shiver shook me. I pulled out my phone. Another text from my friend Jocelyn.

I met Jos when we were kids and coveted her tan skin and stuffed animal collection. Growing up, we got into and out of tons of trouble.

Jos had been eager to hear about our new place, but I kept most of the details secret, even from her. I just didn't have the stomach to get into it with her over the phone. Honestly, I didn't know what to say to anyone about what happened and where we were headed.

Mom walked over as I finished texting Jos back. I told my friend I'd let her know when we got in, and we'd catch up later.

"You need anything from inside?" Mom offered.

"I'll go." I shook again and stuffed the phone back in my pocket. I'd make time to find a jacket after my pit stop. "How about some snacks?"

"Sure. Pick up a Lotto ticket while you're in there."

I would have said something, but she already knew my response. See, I used to think it was fun to pick numbers. We'd play our birthdays, and a few random numbers on a whim the years mom had a job. I think our biggest jackpot was fifty bucks—not bad, for a one-timer. We hoped to win enough she could quit her job, travel, and pay for college. Since mom got hurt, and left her job, money's been tight, so the lotto wasn't as much fun. Sometimes, I humored her.

"You never know, we might get lucky," she said and handed me a twenty.

I smiled. If it was one thing about my mom that stayed true through this whole mess, it was her belief something good would come of it. Despite her genuine concern about keeping us above water—doctors told mom to leave her high stress job, or risk another heart attack—hope remained. I felt hopeful too, but figured we needed more than a little luck to get back on our feet.

Guzzle Mart was bright and stocked with everything from donuts to shoe polish. They even had stuff I hadn't seen in a long time, like Corn Nuts, Big Slurps, and rotisserie hot dogs. I'd sworn off gas station meats ever since a finals week episode left me praying over a porcelain altar.

"Five on the Lotto." I piled everything, plus a car freshener on the counter.

The clerk looked as enthusiastic as a pit bull. He had dark hair, a bunch of strange tats and a nose ring.

"You wanna kicker with that?"

"No thanks."

He scanned the items, took the money then handed back my change, the tickets, and a bag filled with water, pretzels, and Corn Nuts. I couldn't resist. With food, drinks, and music, I felt ready to tackle the road again.

When I got back to the truck my phone buzzed. I was just about to turn it silent, when the text caught my eye. It was from Chloe, my college roomie:

M – seriously need UR help, call me soon – C.

I should have called, but changed my mind when I saw how tired mom looked. The purplish color under her eyes indicated we needed to finish this trip so she could rest. My phone went silent.

I crunched some salty Corn Nuts and plastered a smile on my face. Mom needed me to be strong through this, and that's what I intended to do. I hugged her and watched her get back in the car, then hoisted myself up into the moving truck.

The car freshener was so strong, even in the plastic it scented the cab. The smell wasn't great, but it overpowered the sweaty feet just enough to seem like an improvement.

Wheels rolled and we pulled back onto the highway. My thoughts focused on mom, then navigating semis and lane changes. The truck didn't have a working radio, and once I'd run out of songs to belt out a cappella, it was easy to get caught up in figuring out why Chloe texted me. Or why my ex had texted me the day before. It couldn't have been a coincidence. Like it or not, the people and past I tried to forget wanted my attention—I'd weigh the pros and cons, and maybe call them later.

Back in school, Chloe and I took a lot of the same classes, lived together in the same house, and shared a love of music. Between the two of us, and a great sound system, our room became a local hotspot. For a while, we were inseparable. Things changed when she met Tab, a nickname he earned in prep school because the guy never paid for anything. Tab made a habit of convincing people to pay his bills, college was no different. He thought he was God's gift, but he was less than average every way it counted. Once they started dating, Chloe picked up a lot of Tab's tabs just so we could keep hanging out at our favorite places.

Jos and I didn't like the way he treated her. It started with insults. Then he hit her. Chloe tried to convince us it was just one time, and an accident, but we begged her to leave him. She wouldn't. It damaged our friendship since I have a zero tolerance policy when it comes to abusive jerks, and she'd denied the problem for months.

One evening, Chloe claimed to need rest and backed out of dinner. Our friend Nina was really concerned because she'd overheard an argument, so a few of us went to check on Chloe. We approached the room and overheard a struggle. I tried the door, but realized it was locked. We never locked our room. The girls living there kept the house locked, and only our housemates had keys. I knocked on the door. Nina called to Chloe and we heard a scream. We banged on the door and warned Tab to stop. Nina begged Chloe to get away from him and unlock the door. I searched the hall table for the skeleton key to see if we could get her out. Then the door opened.

Chloe answered red-faced, hair a mess with a bleeding lip. She winced when she tried to smile. Nina and I forced our way into the room as Tab zipped up. He smiled and shrugged, barely able to stand. The jerk reeked of whiskey. We were pissed, and he knew it. If

I could have lifted his lousy butt, I'd have tossed him out the window. Instead, Chloe defended him. "We were having fun, things just got a little rough," she said. "I'm fine."

Nina and I looked at each other. We didn't believe it. Just then Jocelyn came back with the Resident Assistant (RA) who'd been cramming for a test in the basement while all this happened.

Our RA stood firm and told Tab it was time to go. He grabbed his shirt and, grinning, looked back at Chloe. "I'll see you soon." I hated him—we all hated him—for hurting Chloe.

Nina, Jos and I marched Tab downstairs. We shoved him out, locked the door and turned out the porch light.

After it was over, we sat down and talked to Chloe about what she'd been through. She wouldn't listen to anything we said. She made excuses for Tab even after we pleaded with her to see how dangerous he was and to cut him off completely.

Not long after that incident, Jos told us Tab and Chloe cozied up at the library. I'd had it. So, I made every excuse not to be in my own room until late nearly every night. My work suffered; I skipped classes just to rest in my own bed and try to take the edge off.

The whole thing strained our relationship. My life became about avoiding the people I called friends. So, I didn't tell anyone about leaving school until Ethan showed up to help me pack. I left and didn't look back. Couldn't look back.

Why Chloe would call me after our long silence eluded me. Maybe she wanted to talk about school, or friends, but my gut told me it centered on Tab. Whatever it was would have to wait, I had bigger issues to tackle right now.

After a few more Corn Nuts, and more butt-flattening time in the truck without a radio, we approached our exit.

Welcome to the jungle. I could see grit and guts in the dark corners and stone mammoths, icons from decades past, that contrasted hip, renovated establishments—signs of Cincinnati's revitalization.

There was something about coming back at night—lights shining over sleeping buildings, with buzzing pockets of energy below—it looked breathtaking. While we had a rocky past, the city felt familiar. This was the happiest I'd been about the move, or anything, in the past few weeks. I hoped the ending would be different this time.

We took 5th Street to Vine and wound our way though town until the voice on the Nav directed me to a side street. I made a series of turns and mom followed me uphill.

A mix of old historic homes and businesses, some still neglected, lined the street. The truck engine moaned. I hoped we'd make it where we were going soon. A guy in a red Beemer behind us must have felt the same, because he honked his horn like he was irritated. Guess he thought the truck would speed up if he annoyed it long enough. But it ignored him.

Mom and I passed a market, a few shops, a bar, and a bus stop— all the stores you'd need, and some you didn't. The bulls-eye on the screen showed we were close, so I slowed a little. The idiot in the Beemer laid on the horn, and made a hand gesture as he sped past. *Classy.* We'd almost reached our destination. We needed to cross oncoming traffic to park, so we waited for an opening. I cranked the wheel and pressed the gas to get up into the lot when a panel van nearly creamed me.

Two massive columns flanked the blacktop drive. A proportionately smaller iron lamp sat atop each painted white mass— I guess to light the way. Just to the side of one of them was a shorter marble sign etched with the business name: Mackenzie Funeral Home.

Above the columns I could see some parking spaces, blacktop, and the front steps. A newer, but slightly mismatched burgundy awning covered the entrance and two glass doors. As I gawked at the size of the place, the truck slowed. I hit the gas harder to get up the incline. The engine shift jolted me forward and the tires squealed. I pulled between two yellow lines near the side entrance and shoved it into park. "Good enough," I mumbled, and turned it off.

We parked at the side of the building in front of a massive brick wall painted white. Somebody really liked white. No windows on such a large wall made me think dark and mysterious stuff went on inside. It looked out of place, like a later addition to the main house. If you drew it on paper, the side of the house we faced would start from the left as a normal three story Victorian, with lovely windows and trim. Next, would be a standard-size door serving as the side entrance, followed by a white brick fortress plunked onto the back half of the house.

Welcome home. Only time would tell what the house had in store for us.

CHAPTER 3

Mom and I grabbed a couple suitcases and rolled them up the handicap ramp to the side door, not the front. It felt like the door was meant for the hired help—us. As soon as we got inside, my nose crinkled at the smell of new carpet and strong flowers. The inside was well lit, which helped reduce the spook factor.

Mom pointed left. "Those stairs lead up to our apartment."

The side door allowed us quick access, like a regular apartment building, instead of an entrance for the lowly help. I took a breath.

"The door ahead leads to the viewing room." She pulled a bag off her shoulder and set it down.

"Do you mean there are dead people here?"

"It's a funeral home, Mattie. Of course there are dead people. We discussed this already." Some days it was hard to be patient with me.

My eyes darted from the viewing room door only a few steps ahead of where we stood, then to the stairs leading to our place a few steps to the left. I'd figured it out. The viewing room sat below our apartment. "You didn't tell me we'd be living right above them!"

"At least they're prepped and dressed by the time they're under us," she said half-jokingly.

"And why wouldn't they be?" I was totally annoyed she left out that detail.

"Well," she paused, searching for the right words. "They aren't like that when they first get here."

"What do you mean? Don't they come dressed and ready to go? Are you telling me we've got random dead people lying around naked?" I couldn't believe we'd engaged in a conversation about dead people. I was too young for this! I needed to be shopping, and texting my friends about guys and classes, or complaining about work.

The problem since mom told me about our new "residence" was I'd been closed off and told none of my friends about our new living situation. Jocelyn and I hadn't talked much lately, and she should've been the first to hear news this huge. But I hadn't told a soul. It's a lot to keep inside and I really needed to vent about it, ASAP.

"Sweetie, this is a full-service business. They receive, embalm, dress, and prepare the bodies here. They also held viewings and services for the deceased."

"Eww, old naked people." I acted twelve, but it sounded gross. Was it too late to leave? Something moved and I screamed.

"Whoa, take it easy. Grandpa Stanley hardly ever runs around without his clothes, so all the old naked folks around here are dead." My heart pounded and my face flushed when he winked at me.

Mom put a reassuring hand on my arm.

He stood nearly a foot taller than me in dark suit pants and a white business shirt that hugged his upper body. He unbuttoned the cuffs and rolled up his sleeves. Who was this tall Romeo with a gorgeous smile, and…incredible blue eyes? Was I staring? Did anybody notice? He extended his hand. I tried to park a heavy suitcase, but lost my grip and the thing landed on my foot.

"Ouch!" I yelped then clasped a hand over my mouth. I tried to move, but tripped over mom's bag instead. Mom made a move to help; only he was faster. In one move he stopped me from tumbling head over rump and snagged the suitcase so I didn't klutz my way to the emergency room. I couldn't figure out what it was, but I couldn't take my eyes off him. He held my gaze for a second. Electricity shot through me. We walked to the nearest table and sat down in a couple of plush chairs.

"Are you okay?"

"Yes. I didn't mean to trip over my own feet, sort of a bad habit. Thanks for saving me."

"Anytime."

Maybe he was so focused on helping, he didn't catch me gawking at him. My face turned several shades of red. *Where is a rock I can crawl under?*

I was so busy worrying about my first impression I nearly forgot mom was still with us.

"You okay?" She brushed some hair from my face.

I was embarrassed at what I'd done, and wasn't sure if mom caught me staring at the guy. "I'm okay mom, just a bruised ego. Should be fine in no time."

He let out a laugh and I smiled back.

"Well, we've got more stuff," mom explained.

"I should be ready to unload in a couple minutes."

Since her heart attack, I hardly let her do anything. I felt bad she was alone when it happened. The school pulled me out of a history class when they broke the news. I was happy to get out of another one of Professor Conklin's Civil War lectures, but would have preferred it if mom had never been hurt at all.

I begged my ex, Ethan, to drive me home and he agreed immediately. Mom liked him—he was generally polite and a pre-med student. We made a go of it for a while, but it didn't work out. There was something about him that felt more like brother than boyfriend.

When mom got sick, it'd been a year since the break up, and Ethan moved on with a freshman or two. Despite our awkward end, he was a good choice to drive me home. He owned a car and lived close.

Being a nice guy, he helped me get home. We spoke with the Dean of Students, an awesome lady who looked like she could have walked right out of Haight-Ashbury circa 1960. Mrs. Thayer excused us from classes to make the trip. She told me to take as much time as I needed, and said there would be a place for me when I returned. It was a relief because losing scholarships would have made it impossible to come back.

We didn't have a lot of money. Most of the money mom made went to our middle-class home, maintaining a reasonably priced car, and keeping food on the table. She'd done it my whole life and part of me felt like she was left hanging when I went to school. I breathed a little easier knowing I was headed home to help. I just didn't know what it would be like when I got there. I had no idea she'd be in such rough shape.

Ethan took me straight to the hospital. Mom was asleep when we arrived. She'd had some problems during surgery, but the doctor said she was tough. He expected she'd recover, but with some limitations.

Mom had monitors taped all over when I finally got there. She looked pale and tired. Her breathing was ragged, but eased when I took her hand. I hadn't realized how much I needed her until then, so I held her hand and cried.

Mom raised me. Dad left when I was a baby, so she did it all. Played every role: mom, dad, coach, and friend. She fixed stuff around the house and knew her way around just about everything. What she didn't know, she learned. While we struggled during my high school years—what teenage girl and her mom don't have trouble then? —we reached a place where we could talk again without fighting about her being the head of the house, and me being old enough to make my own decisions. At least we were working on it and could survive under the same roof with minimal eruptions. It's tough having two strong personalities in the same house.

I knew she needed me. In the hospital room, before we even spoke, I resolved to help her any way I could. No matter what it took, so I left school and never looked back. The memory faded as I wandered back to the present.

"I'm almost good as new. Um…what did you say your name was?" I tried to stand and wobbled a bit until he caught me. He was younger than I expected a business owner would be. My mom mentioned their family ran the place when we talked about moving here, but I'd partly tuned her out hoping our problems would go away, and we could stay in our home. It didn't work.

"It's Garrett." He shook my hand as an official introduction. "Nice to meet you."

Since we were doing the handshake thing, I responded. "I'm Mattie."

"Your mom mentioned it. I just finished closing up for the night. Give me the keys. Been sitting most of the day and could use some exercise." He opened his hand. Was he speaking a foreign language? I tilted my head as if it would help me understand better. He chuckled. "Can I have the keys? Please?"

What was it about him that distracted me? I needed to shake off whatever I was feeling. Did I hit my head? It sure felt like it. I grinned like an idiot and got the keys out without looking away from him. He cupped my hands discreetly and took the keys. It happened so quickly only the two of us would have noticed. Was he flirting?

He turned and walked away. I hadn't looked before, but he looked good in his tailored pants and shirt. Okay, I did look, but his back was as nice as his front, and I really checked him out this time.

Was I drooling over mom's boss? I mean our boss? Our landlord, for cripes sake! *Stop thinking about it!* This was bad. Very bad. *Stop it now!* I tried to yell at myself in my head. I did it a lot. Only, it almost never worked.

I expected Garrett to shake his head, or run, at the site of our beat-up, brown sedan parked next to the Faux-Haul, but he didn't flinch. Not even when he saw the peeling paint and threadbare seats. Before he got to work, Garrett suggested we not draw too much attention to all the goodies we brought, so I told him to grab our bags out of the car. We didn't need much to get through the night. The big stuff in the truck could wait until morning when my cousin, Zack, and his buddy planned to help. They were coming up from Louisville and planned to crash at a hotel.

Garrett carried every bag upstairs. He insisted. Then he showed us the apartment and gave us our keys. Mom sat on a chair he brought up from downstairs while I blew up the air mattress. It wasn't an ideal bed for her, but it would be better than the hard floor.

"It's getting late. I'll let you two get some rest. If you need anything, just page me."

"Thank you," mom said.

Garrett walked me to the door.

"We've got people coming in and out of here all day and night." He showed me the keys and locks. "Just make sure you use the deadbolt and you should be fine."

"Thanks for everything."

"Sure." His eyes stayed on mine. "See you in the morning."

"Goodnight." I double-locked the door after he left and smiled. We'd see each other again, soon.

The owners stocked the kitchen with dishes, napkins, silverware, and towels. Mom got a glass of water from the sink. I unloaded the cooler and made her bed. We washed up and shuffled to our new, but nearly empty bedroom. I looked out the window and could see some of the city lights. We were on the second floor and without curtains it felt a little exposed. We'd take care of it tomorrow, either with actual curtains or pinned up sheets. She sank onto the mattress and yawned, I crawled into the sleeping bag beside her.

"I'm glad we made it. I love you, Mattie."

"Glad we made it, too. Love you, mom."

She sighed and drifted off within a couple minutes. I stared at the ceiling for a few minutes until sleep washed over me.

CHAPTER 4

The next morning we got an early start. I used a food finder app to locate the nearest breakfast shop and brought back a couple sandwiches and coffees. My cousin Zack texted me he and Tony were on the way, so I bought extra.

By the time I returned, they were already hard at work, and Garrett was there too. Huh. Maybe he noticed how tired mom looked, because I saw him take a box out of her hands. Then he pointed her in the direction of a lawn chair and told her to sit. She obliged. Interesting, she never listen to me that easily. But, he was bigger than me, and the boss, or one of them.

Sometime during the move-in, a long, black limo pulled into the driveway, and drove to the back of the house. The sun warmed up, so I went inside to take off my sweatshirt.

I noticed the vending machine and wanted a cold drink. It wouldn't take my dollar after repeated attempts to feed the machine. I went into the office to ask for change. No one was there, but I heard someone in the hallway. I hesitated, but didn't think anything much could be going on, so I pushed open the door. No one was there either, which seemed odd. Then I heard voices behind the door at the end of the hall. Determined to get a cold drink, I followed the voices.

I walked through another door and stopped short of a corpse. A blanket covered everything but his face and feet. I'd only ever seen the dead at funerals and on TV. This person looked completely different—he looked like he'd been doused by the sandman—both ends were covered in some kind of rust-colored powder. An antiseptic cleanser and something that smelled like the school Biology Lab hit my nostrils. My expression must have been something close to deer in the headlights shock. I heard the voices trail off and the door behind me closed. Garrett stood there dressed in scrubs. He smiled at me from behind his mask, but I panicked.

"He's dead, right?" I asked in a hollow voice.

"Yes," he spoke carefully. "How can I help you?"

I stared at the white sheet and the strange face, and wondered what the rest of the body looked like. Some of the powder rubbed off onto the sheet as Garrett tried to cover him up. Even then, I just stared. His feet still stuck out, the guy was dead. I shuddered and took off. Air. Must get air.

There were two doors between the nearest exit and me. I shoved one open quickly. The second door took longer, but once it was open wide enough to get through, I picked up speed and ran down the driveway. There was no traffic, so I didn't stop. I kept going and ended up across the street in another parking lot. Not knowing if I'd hurl or pass out, I bent over and clutched my knees. My lungs didn't burn, but I breathed hard. Hyperventilating, no doubt. A young guy about my age came toward me. He was medium height and build, wore a tailored dark suit, and carried a purple flag in his hand. He stopped near me and looked concerned.

"Are you okay?"

My head said no, so did my body. He directed me to sit on a bench near the edge of the lot. Brick pavers below it created a circular pattern around which, boxwoods and some late season yellow-orange marigolds were planted. I flashed back to the body and decided I should sit. He waved the flag to another guy sitting in a parked car, engine running. I noticed the lot was full of cars.

"Thanks, I think so."

"What were you running from?"

"A dead guy."

"Your first?" He smiled, more relaxed than when we met. His warm eyes looked inviting, a good asset to have in this business.

"My first, outside of funerals and crime shows. All he had on was a sheet, and it didn't cover everything."

"Oh, don't worry, you're not the first one to run, and you won't be the last." He looked at me with a pleasant and comforting smile.

The blood returned to my head and I blushed.

"I'm Derek." He put his hand out to shake mine. "Derek Davis."

"I'm Mattie. Mattie Harper." I shook his hand and my eyes wandered to the engraved stone sign on the driveway. It read: Davis and Sons Funeral Home. "Is this place yours?"

"It's our family's. We've been here almost as long as those guys." He pointed across the street to the other funeral home—my new home. "I noticed you moving in earlier. Are you new to the area?"

I nodded yes, and listened to him explain a little about himself. How he'd gone away to school, but came back to help run the business. He signaled the driver, in what I now realized was the hearse, to go get something. A few moments later, the guy brought me some water.

"Thanks." The water quenched my thirst. Things felt a little more normal.

"Your color looks better. Tell me something about you. Where are you from?"

Just then Garrett walked up in his street clothes.

"Derek," Garrett said curtly, and they did a firm, one and done handshake. Garrett stepped closer. His stance softened, but his eyes showed concern. "Are you okay, Mattie?"

"Sorry, I forgot that you sometimes have people, er, bodies in there. I was thirsty," It was all I could muster, and it was the truth. Both of them laughed at me.

"What are you guys, like thirteen?" My freak-out was embarrassing, but they thought it was funny? Maybe they were right to snicker. I couldn't help but shake my head and laugh, too.

Garrett inserted himself between Derek and me. He put his arm around my waist and helped lift me off the bench. "We should get back," he said.

"Yeah, we're just about to head over to the cemetery," Derek said. "Mattie, if you want to come over later, I can give you a tour. No dead bodies. Scouts Honor." He held up his hand, crossed his chest to indicate he meant it. I giggled.

Garrett stared him down. I wondered why, figured it had something to do with the family rivalry, and shook it off. Then we headed home.

The Mackenzie house looked different from across the street—it stood out as the highest point on the block. Framed by trees and flowers it didn't look so blank, and the trim was beautifully detailed—I made a mental note to read up on the home's history sometime.

Garrett walked me up the front steps through the glass double-doors. He made sure I was good, and left to get down to business in the back room.

After everything I saw, work could wait. It was time for a mental break. I let Zack and Tony know they could help themselves to the cold cuts in the fridge, and I crashed on the bedroom floor. My stomach felt uneasy. My head hurt. Reality set in. This business needed people—bodies, like the rust-powdered guy downstairs—to keep it afloat. It made sense, but I'd have to adjust to the whole bodies thing. I couldn't relax, so I washed up. The icy water hurt my skin at first, but I felt refreshed once I toweled off. After a change of shirts and a sandwich, I got back to work.

Mom called me over as she positioned a lamp in the living room. Even though we'd been unloading most of the day, and had a lot more to go, she wanted me to meet the other owners.

As we approached the back office, we heard someone on the phone.

"Yeah, Bert, I told you this weekend doesn't work. You have to cover. I already made plans." Garrett paused while the other guy said something.

We stopped in the hall and waited politely while they finished their call.

"Mom, didn't we do this last night?" I cringed at the thought of another introduction. It felt like I was being led to the principal's office at a brand new school. The new kid everyone would stare and maybe even laugh at.

My mom rolled her eyes, "Honey, it'll be fine. I told them I'd bring you down and introduce you before they left for the weekend. Sweetie, don't you want to meet the rest of the owners?"

Hardly, I thought. I really didn't want to be here at all. I couldn't act happy even though this job was the reason there's a roof over our heads. I still had a hard time with the fact that we lived above a funeral home. I was in hell. Or somewhere very close. Maybe I'd call it the 'gateway' until I found something better to call it.

"You're real funny, Bert. I'm looking at the calendar and you're name is written in bold across the entire weekend. You know, if you can't do it this weekend, then you're going to be on the hook for the next holiday. That's the deal. I'll give you your choice since your kid's in town."

It sounded curious. I thought my mom and would be working this weekend. The office was supposed to be closed for the holiday.

"Fine," the voice said curtly, "then write this down. You're working Labor Day weekend. I will be out of town and you'll be working, got it?" He laughed off something the man said and hung up the phone. I think he mumbled something else, but I couldn't quite hear it.

My mom took my hand and edged me forward. She dropped it when she saw the look on my face. Her look pleaded with me to behave. I stiffened up and faked a smile hoping this would be over soon.

"Hi, guys," she said as we stepped into the office. There wasn't a lot of room between the desks, but we squeezed in the best we could. "I wanted to officially introduce you to my daughter, Mattie," mom signaled for me to come into the middle of the room. It was a bit like being paraded on stage, but I was thankful to see pleasant faces. My eye caught Garret and I had to try and stop staring as mom got back to the intros.

Everyone stood up to greet us. "Hey, Nora," a salt and pepper haired man spoke. He looked from mom to me, "Hello, Mattie," he said and extended his hand. "Nice to meet you, I'm Hank." His smile was warm and he looked genuinely glad to see us. I could see where Garrett got his good looks. "Your grandma was a great lady, sorry for your loss."

Emotion welled up inside me as I fought back tears. Not long ago, we lost grandma. She was the kind of woman just about everybody knew and liked. Whenever I went out with her—didn't matter when or where—it was like watching six degrees of separation. She'd see someone who looked familiar, and with her soft curls styled into waves, make a beeline to talk to them. Sure enough, they'd turn out to be an old school friend, or the brother or sister of someone she knew years ago. If it weren't for grandma knowing Hank's wife, Sharon, we wouldn't be here now.

Sharon lamented that the Mackenzie family needed more hands to help with their growing business. Grandma knew just the person, and introduced mom. My grandma knew enough about them to know they'd treat mom right. It helped that the lovely old Victorian they operated out of had a couple vacant rooms. Mom needed a less stressful, work-from-home option so she could recover from her heart attack. Each family had something to gain. Grandma helped make the pitch, and it worked.

"I hear you're real smart and that you enjoy history," Hank's voice brought me back to the room. "We've got some really old books and blueprints of the house if you're interested in the history of this place. Old-timers, like me, can even tell you stories about the rivalry between us and the guys across the street."

"Rivalry? Sounds interesting." I was genuinely curious. "Thank you. I'll have to take you up on it once we finish moving in."

"And after you register for classes," mom nudged me.

Mom had checked things out before she made the decision to move us here. It helped there was a college nearby. Even though we had to watch our dollars, she encouraged me to get back in school right away, at least part-time.

"It's nice to have you ladies here with us. Is everything ok upstairs?"

"Yes, Hank. Everything is just about up and running. We have to finish unloading and unpacking, but all is well. Thanks."

"Glad to help. You should be fine. Just watch out for Stanley. My dad's a pretty good guy, but he's older and crankier than the rest of us. He likes to be involved and run things the old-fashioned way. I'm laid back, which is why we argue sometimes. I don't think you'll have any trouble, but we'll let you know if he's ever in one of his moods so you can steer clear." Hank laughed. Garrett shook his head and smiled.

Just then two more people entered the office. I noticed a large, chestnut-skinned woman with long brown hair streaked blonde. She'd curled it to frame her face and it looked attractive with her brown eyes and coral lipstick. A shorter guy about Garrett's age walked in behind her. He came up to me and tried to kiss my hand. I tensed and he dropped it for a less awkward introductory handshake. "I'm Ryder. Nice to meet you. I hear you almost ralphed when you saw Jimbo."

"Jimbo?"

The woman spoke with a deep Caribbean accent. "Ryder Mackenzie, where are your manners? Ya oughtta be ashamed talking to a girl like that!" I didn't know her name, but I liked her already.

"He's Garrett's younger brother, and sometimes forgets his manners. I'm Mildred. You can call me Millie." She shook my hand enthusiastically. "Or, you can call me Millie Dread, like those rascals in charge call me." She eyed Garrett. "What's da other one you guys use?"

It looked like he gulped before he responded. Maybe he wasn't sure if he should repeat it to her face.

"Dread of the Dead," he said quietly. Her response looked like it could go either way—rage or humor. Then she broke out laughing and hugged him. Everything on her body jiggled.

"You know we love you Millie, no matter what we call you. It's just more fun to call you Dread of the Dead sometimes. This business makes people crazy, it's our way of dealing with it," he told her.

She laughed a hearty laugh. Her whole frame shook with the effort. "You know I like you best Garrett, just don't tell the others." She pretended to whisper and winked at him.

"Not as much as me, though," Hank laughed. Ryder looked hurt for a moment then his green eyes were back on me like he wanted something.

"You boys are all my favorites," Millie said. "Now let me get on poor Mrs. Wood, before she crumples up and I can't fix her face no more."

"I worked on Mrs. Wood, you shouldn't have any face crumpling issues," Garrett said. The idea of face crumpling sounded interesting, but I wasn't sure I could handle the truth yet.

After the introductions, I went back to help Zack and Tony. Garrett tagged along, not saying much. Maybe he was worried I'd run off again.

My phone buzzed as I carried a chair upstairs, so I hustled the rest of the way up and sat the chair inside the kitchen to grab the call.

"Mattie," Chloe sounded anxious, but glad to hear my voice.

"Hi, Chloe," I said not knowing yet why she wanted to talk to me. "I got your text, but things have been so crazy. Sorry I haven't responded."

"It's okay. I'm just really glad we're talking now." She sounded relieved, and went on to explain she was working on a big case and needed help.

Good for you, how can I possibly help? I thought sarcastically. What came out of my mouth sounded something more like, "Cool." I heard her take a heavy breath. Okay, so maybe she sensed my tone.

Chloe apologized for the way we left things. She stressed her need for help, said it was important enough the legal case was being heard at the State Supreme Court. Chloe said my expertise could help them win, and set an important precedent. She sounded like she needed a friend. I felt the same way. Only she was smart enough to reach out, I just kept things bottled up. I softened and agreed to meet her when she hit town in a couple days. She thanked me a third time and hung up.

I sat in the chair and wondered how I'd manage to unpack, register for classes, find a job, and help solve Chloe's problem. I had my work cut out for me, so I stood back up and kept going.

We unloaded a ton more furniture than we has space for, and worked to make everything fit. When we'd just about finished moving stuff into the apartment Garrett found my bat. An old Louisville Slugger. Black painted wood with frayed tape from years of practice and pickup games. He looked it over and ran his hand over the silver logo etched in it, part of it had smeared from repeated hits.

"Looks like you got some use out of this."

"It's been around a while."

"Have you swung at anything lately?"

"Just her ex," Zack laughed. He and Tony carried our mattress upstairs while Garrett and I stayed to talk.

"Really?"

"Yup. He deserved it."

"That's harsh."

"I was angry, but I didn't hit him. He just happened to be standing a little too close to the fence I did hit."

"Remind me never to get on your bad side."

"Don't get on my bad side." I winked at him.

"Ha ha. Maybe you just need a release."

"Excuse me?"

"It might do you some good to swing at something you're allowed to hit."

"I'm listening. What do you have in mind?"

"Batting cages. Interested?"

"Very."

"Good, let's unload the rest of this stuff and take a drive. I know a place."

"I can't tonight. I promised to make Zack and Tony a thank you dinner for helping us. Can I take a rain-check?" I wasn't sure if it was a one-time offer, but I asked anyway.

"Sure." He sounded disappointed. I couldn't see his reaction because bent over and lifted a box of books. He walked them over to the steps and turned back. "Only if I get a thank you dinner in return." He smiled and walked away before I could answer.

As we finished, I put a rope knot doorstop behind the door and turned to look back at our new place. The heavy ball was a relic grandma gave me. She willed it along with a bunch of other old stuff to me, and I haven't been able to go anywhere without it. It's just so easy to leave by the door and forget about it. But, it gave me a sense of security. As though some part of gram was still around watching over us.

Mom came in from the other room and hugged me. It felt good to be finished, but it was going to take some time before anything felt like home again. I hugged her back and told her to settle in, I'd run to the store for groceries.

When I left, Zack and Tony were moving the couch, again. Mom wasn't sure if it should face the fireplace, or the TV. At least I had an excuse to take a drive.

"Oh, Garrett." I noticed him looking over some paperwork. "Thanks for your help. We couldn't have done this without you."

"Anytime. Glad you're here now." He looked at me for a long moment then headed back to the office.

Thankfully, the store was close. If the car crapped out, I could walk. By the sound of the engine when it started, that day was coming sooner, rather than later.

I shopped, and brought back all the fixin's for my famous spaghetti dinner. Dinner conversation was lively. We laughed as Zack and Tony recapped the most interesting parts of the move, like finessing the mattress around tight corners, and moving the world's heaviest couch a million times. I looked at the kitchen/dining area. The cabinets, windows, and sink were new to us; but mom's antique china buffet had been around for years. The smell of garlic lingered as we sat at the small table laughing together—it felt more comfortable now, like home.

CHAPTER 5

The next morning, mom and I ate and cleaned the kitchen. My phone screen showed a bright, happy-looking sun and a summer forecast of hot and muggy. I showered, and then put on a turquoise tee, white shorts, and sandals.

The dryer came on, and I used the roller brush to style my hair. This time of year, after a good dose of sun, the platinum and auburn highlights showed in my sandy brown hair. Come winter it would darken again. The idea of winter at a funeral home sounded so dreary. Bursts of bright sun shined through the upper half of the bathroom window. Gauzy sheers dotted with pink and green flowers covered the bottom half. They reminded me of my butterfly sheers back home, and it was enough to forget about colder seasons. Today was warm, a perfect day to run errands and get the lay of the land.

I clicked off the dryer and sat it beside the brush on the marbled laminate counter, which actually looked nice next to the dated pink sink and backsplash. My hair looked ready, so I added some waterproof mascara and a little sunscreen. I was good to go. Mom planned to spend the day unpacking, learning how to operate the phones, and promised she'd even rest a little. The Registrar's office opened early enough I could make it there, then the campus bookstore, and be back by lunch. I kissed mom goodbye and locked the door on my way out.

I flew down the stairs, but heard someone as I hit the first floor.

"Hey there," a balding man in a brown suit told me. "Slow down, we're running a respectable business here."

This must be Grandpa Stanley. His eyes were dark and harsh, but his comb-over distracted me enough to give him a half-smile. He leaned over and scowled. I wondered if I had done something wrong.

"C'mon Grandpa Stan," Ryder said as he walked past us with some flowers. "She's new here." He gave me a smile and nudged his grandpa. I returned the smile as he passed by, but got uncomfortable again when his grandpa just stood there. Next came Garrett with a larger arrangement of yellow roses. He caught my eye as soon as he came to a stop in the hallway.

"Grandpa." Garrett stopped near us. "Don't you remember? This is Evelyn's granddaughter, Mattie." He got Stanley's attention long enough for me to think about how to apologize for going too fast down the stairs. Was that it? "You know, Matilda."

How did Garrett know my given name? I haven't gone by Matilda since birth. Mom told me she and dad realized it was a big name when the nurses tried to use it. She used the nickname Mattie. I guess it fit, because the nickname stuck. *How did he know my name?* I struggled for a minute. Just stared at the pretty flowers Garrett had set down. My eyes lifted to his. He smiled at me and my anxiety eased. My grandma must have used my proper name when she told them about me.

"Oh, right. Nice to meet you," Stanley finally moved. He placed a hand on my shoulder and extended the other to shake. "Just remember, don't run and don't make too much noise." I think he smiled, but it was hard to tell. I smiled as best as I could and for some reason felt the urge to bow my head, although I didn't. Weird. I waited for Stanley to leave before I flinched.

"Thank you," I told Garrett.

"I think you just got your first speeding ticket." We laughed and I watched as his baby blue shirt practically split when he lifted the flowers back up. Sure, Ryder was kind of cute, but he wasn't the one I had flutters over. It was Garrett. There was something about him— the way he looked and carried himself, how easily he joked with me, and those deep blue eyes of awesomeness—everything attracted me. I sighed as he turned to leave. He probably had the same effect on lots of women, and our situation didn't make it easy to find out if he felt the same about me.

Even though the car screeched at start-up, it ran. I turned red when Stanley peeked out the window at me. My exit went as quickly and quietly as possible.

The car cooperated long enough to get me to campus. Sure, I wanted to finish college, but didn't look forward to the late nights and homework, or the questions I might get asked about moving. I tried to think of our situation as a reason to hit refresh and make friends, but knew it wouldn't be easy. Mostly because I live with my mom above a funeral home, a fact I hadn't even shared with my best friend. Not yet, anyway.

Jocelyn could be supportive, if I gave her a chance. Since we were back in the same town together, it was time to have a talk.

I breezed through registration—there was one spot left in the English class I wanted to take, so I snagged it, along with a spot in a Chemistry class I needed for a Gen. Ed. requirement—then headed to get my books.

A couple hundred dollars later, I piled the books on the passenger seat and headed home. The car sounded angry before it started, so I patted the dashboard to help it along. Between the cost of living, classes, books, and the car repairs we most likely needed done yesterday, my bank account wasn't going to hold out for long. Getting a day job just became my top priority. Before we moved, the job search had been limited to online sources, and phone interviews. The net result was zip. It was time to meet Jocelyn, and see if she had any contacts that might help me get an interview. I'd text her to meet up tonight just as soon as I parked Old Bessie.

The Mackenzie lot was empty, but Davis & Sons had a packed lot. I parked at the side by the stately Mackenzie house without incident. Just as I got in the side door to the funeral home, I heard laughing. Hopefully, it was from humans. Being so new to this place—not knowing much about funerals, or dead people—I felt like anything was possible.

Thankfully, a large dark-haired guy pushed his way through the viewing room door. His moustache served as proof of life—hairy-faced ghosts don't exist, right? He was a few inches taller than me and stout. He'd rolled his sleeves up enough for me to see "THUG" tattooed on his arm. Not a ghost, but I should still be careful here.

"Hi."

Before I answered him, another guy pushed his way into the room and nearly ran the big guy over. "What the—?" The second guy was shorter and paler than the first man. The shorter guy stopped and looked me over. Something must have pleased him because he started grinning. "Who's this?" he asked the big guy.

"I dunno," the dark-haired brute said. "Let's ask her." He stood up tall and brushed his hands down the front of his shirt leaving rust colored marks. "I'm Sledge," he said with a smoke-and-whiskey voice. "This here's Manny." He put his hand out to shake mine.

"Hi, I'm Mattie." Sledge withdrew his hand when he realized there was stuff on them. He had knobby knuckles and coarse skin, but his smile seemed welcoming.

Manny pushed his way forward to shake my hand. "Are you the new girl?"

"That's me."

"We're the dead guy disposal team," Manny laughed.

Sledge gave Manny a sideways glance. "Don't mind him, he has the manners of a goat. We're glad to meet you. When things are hopping, you'll see us a lot. We're the body guys."

I could see him do something that looked like he was shaking off what he just said, like he wanted a do-over.

"I mean we're the removal service. We bring the deceased here for proper preparation and burial." It almost sounded rehearsed, maybe the work of his boss, or Grandpa Stanley.

"Ahem," Manny cleared his throat and waited.

"You may already know this, but we get a call when a person dies," Sledge explained. I shrugged to indicate I didn't know. "Then we show up at the location of the deceased and bring them to funeral homes around town. The rest you'll mostly learn from the Mackenzie family."

"Thanks, for the heads up. I'll try to remember."

"You got a pickup, just call us." Sledge and Manny departed.

I had a lot to learn about this business. Not sure I was psyched about it, but this work beat life in a cardboard box. I carried the books upstairs. Mom greeted me with lunch.

"Looks good."

She'd placed a couple turkey sandwiches and a salad with cucumber and tomatoes out for us. It looked good, so we washed up and dug into the food.

"How was registration Miss College Co-ed?"

"Fine." I told her and took a bite of the sandwich. It was quiet for a moment, but she kept here eyes on me. She wanted details.

"Okay, campus is cool, parking tough, and I picked up two classes. Thanks for the encouragement, mom."

She smiled at me and enjoyed a few bites of salad. We washed our food down with some lemonade she'd made from scratch, better than any stuff you could get from a packet or restaurant dispenser. It hit the spot.

"Zack and Tony head back to Louisville?"

"Yes. Zack wanted to take you out for some fun, but he had to work. He and Tony said they'd come back in a few weeks to check on us, and move the couch again, if needed." Mom laughed. Stress was noticeable around the crinkle in her forehead, but it was such a relief to see her joking.

"How is Stanley?"

"He's fine, but we have a lot to discuss. I'd like to unwind a little before we get into it." Her smile faded and I knew she needed some rest.

We finished with a couple wafer cookies and I helped get her set up on the living room couch with some books and magazines. She propped her feet up on the ottoman and put on her horn-rimmed glasses. They looked nice with her creamy skin and short reddish bob.

The window air conditioner kicked on and cooled the room fast. I put a lightweight blanket over mom and headed back to the kitchen then cleared the table. Mom was zonked, so I went ahead and balanced the checkbook, paid a couple bills, and scanned my textbooks. I was searching jobs online when Chloe's mom called.

"Hi Mrs. Ellis. How are things going?"

"Hi, Mattie. I'm doing all right. How's your mom?"

"Doctor says she's doing better since surgery." I thought about how far mom really had come the past few months. "We're trying to make sure she rests and keeps her stress levels down. It seems to be working."

"I'm glad she's improved. Give her my best, would you?" Her voice sounded off.

"Are you okay Mrs. E?"

"Actually, I called to ask about Chloe. It's been a couple days since we spoke. Have you heard from her lately?"

"We talked a couple days ago," I answered. "She sounded fine to me, just busy with work."

"Chloe mentioned working on a case when we talked, but I haven't heard from her since. It's starting to worry me, Mattie."

"She's probably just busy," I reassured her. "We're supposed to meet up tomorrow. I'll see if I can find anything out, and let her know to call you."

"Thank you, I really appreciate it. It's probably nothing. Maybe I'm being an overprotective mom, but it's always best to check things out."

"No problem, Mrs. E. Take care."

"You too. Thanks." She disconnected and I started to worry.

Chloe and I hadn't talked in a long time, but she reached out about an important case. Next, her mom called to ask if I've heard from Chloe because she hasn't talked to her in a few days. Something about the coincidence unsettled me. Hopefully, there'd be a good explanation for it all tomorrow. Maybe I couldn't solve the Ellis family problems today, but I could work on my own. It was time to talk with Jocelyn and let off some steam.

Jos and I finalized plans to hit a couple hot spots. I threw on my best going out clothes. I'd been a social hermit most of the summer and wanted my debut to be a good one. I pulled on a soft pink top dotted with sequins and a black skirt, then styled my hair with sparkly clips and dabbed on some perfume. I sighed. It'd been a while since I really looked at myself in the mirror. I cleaned up pretty good, but seriously needed to relax. Tonight was the night to slip away and feel like my old happy self again.

"Hey, girl!" Jocelyn called from the parking lot. She wore a short denim dress and wedges. We met at Granger's Pub. My idea since I owed her an explanation about our new living situation before she saw it first-hand.

We ordered appetizers and drinks. I'd twisted up my napkin until it started to fall apart, then summoned up some courage and told her where we moved. She looked at me like I had horns coming out of my head.

"Is that why you've been avoiding me?"

"Kind of. Yeah."

"We've been friends forever. Do you think I care where you live?"

I shrugged.

"Your family hit hard times and did what was necessary. That's smart. Besides, I'm glad you're there."

"Why?"

"It means we get to hang out again." Jos knew just what to say.

By the time we made it to the dance club, we'd caught up on everything and were invigorated to be out on the town.

"I just want to dance, it's been so long." I followed Jocelyn inside The Boxcar and she found us a spot near the dance floor. Drinks flowed under the neon 80s Night sign, so we grabbed a couple and hit the floor right away.

The club was fairly clean, but it's mostly a meet market. Tons of students and young execs, with some random dance-hungry girls like us thrown in the mix.

"I love this song! It's Howard Jones." Jocelyn shouted as we got to our spot on the dance floor. It was crowded, but tonight crowded felt energizing. It was time to shake off anxiety and have fun.

On campus, Jos and I got a reputation for dancing. We didn't dance for anyone but ourselves and we never held back. People used to stop and stare, while others joined us. Tonight was no different—dancing was our workout and tension reliever rolled into one. A couple guys approached us, but we weren't here to snag dates. Jos and I just needed to unwind, so we ran interference for each other.

A young looking banker-type and his wingman approached us as we made it to the bar for another round. They bought us drinks and we thanked them, but made it clear we were here for fun, not hook-ups.

After the second round, we felt pretty good. The vibe was electric and we danced out butts off for a while. Sweat beaded up on my neck while we kept up with a thrumming bass. I moved my arms under my hair to flip it up and get some air to my skin. As I let go my arms caught someone on the way down.

I kept dancing and turned to apologize for slapping the innocent bystander when his eyes meet mine. He looked amazing—clean-shaven and lightly tanned, dressed in a casual t-shirt and jeans. He smelled even better—a crisp, musky scent mixed with his body heat and pheromones. I could've eaten him up, but I needed to maintain my composure.

Someone bumped me from behind and I stumbled into Garrett. He steadied me at the waist and gently placed one of his hands on the small of my back. So much for remaining composed. His blue eyes mesmerized me. Heat shot into parts of my body I didn't know existed.

"May I have this dance?"

"Yes," I whispered. He pulled me close to dance. My heart fluttered when I placed my arms around his neck. Our eyes locked. His blue pools of awesomeness looked darker than usual. I hoped it was a good sign. As he pulled me even closer the whole arm-flexing thing distracted me. I didn't know how much more of this I could take before I completely melted into him. This was bad. Very, very bad, but felt so very, very good.

He leaned in and gently pressed his lips to my ear. I felt his breath as he whispered, "Nice moves."

He made me feel really good. Better than I should have felt, considering the desire to do more with him was overriding my common sense. I shivered and he pulled back. My attention moved from his soft, decadent lips to his gorgeous eyes.

"But, you hit like a girl." His lips pulled up into a sly grin. I knew he referred to the hair flip-and-slap incident from a minute ago, but it took a moment for me to respond.

"Very funny." I playfully punched him in the arm, a little harder this time.

"Umph. Just kidding, there's no need to get testy. Although, I like the feisty side of you." His comment shocked me enough my mouth may have dropped open. He placed his hand under my chin as if he was going to close it. Or, was he going to kiss me? I felt breathless. What's he waiting for? I'm here! Take me now! It got really loud in my head.

"Don't let me stop you, big guy," Jocelyn must have decided it was time for Mr. Handsome to get the once-over while I stared at, no, drooled over him. "I just wanted to see the first person to ever render my best friend speechless." Jos was a great friend. She came to make sure I was ok, and not getting hit on by a crazy stalker. This is not a crazy stalker guy, Jos. Really. I hope she read it in my expression and got the hint.

"Jocelyn," I said, a little disheartened she was still standing there because I really wanted to dance with him again. "This is Garrett."

"Nice to meet you, Garrett. I'm Mattie's best friend. We're dancing tonight to help her forget her troubles."

"Troubles?"

"Yeah, she's had a tough year. Her mom's been sick, they lost their house, and they just moved into a creepy new one."

I wanted to crawl under a table. Was there one around here somewhere? No? I had to face this head on. Only, Garrett beat me to it.

"I'm Garrett," he shook her hand. "Owner of Mattie's creepy new house."

"Oh, really?" Jocelyn eyed me as though I owed her a long and detailed explanation. I wanted to argue, *I just gave you an explanation even if I left out some of the good parts.* Jos smiled at Garrett. Did she just bat her eyes at him too? OMG! What level of hell was embarrassment? "She never told me you were so…young." At least she didn't say hot. "And hot." Jos nodded in my direction.

I guess I deserved that. Not only had I kept my address quiet, I kept the hottie boss a secret too. I had a lot of explaining to do.

"Thanks for the compliment," Garrett said to Jos before he eyed me. "So, do you think I'm a hottie, Mattie?"

Did he really want my answer? Could I give him an answer? What would happen if I told him he was hot? I grabbed him to steady myself.

"Whoa, there. Either it's the answer I hoped for, or you're a lightweight." He held me and I wanted to say something, but couldn't.

When I looked to Jocelyn for help, her face went blank. I followed her eyes over to a dark corner of the bar. It was Tab. He saw us, and walked over to where we were on the dance floor. Even over the booze of the bar and a hundred sweaty co-eds, I could smell him—drunk, again.

"Hey ladies," he flashed a greasy smile at us. "Looking good Mattie." He took a step, but Garrett stopped him.

"Garrett Mackenzie," he shoved his hand out to block Tab and shook his hand, firmly. "And you are?" Garrett did not sound happy. Tab must have picked up on it. He eyed me then Garrett and decided to play with him.

"Oh, I'm here for Mattie. Didn't she tell you?" He smoothed out his voice. "Sweet little Mattie used to be jealous of what I had going with her college roommie. She decided she wanted a piece, so I'm gonna take her back to my place and—" Tab raised his hand to touch me, but Garrett twisted it back so swiftly we barley saw it happen before Tab yelled out. "Ow!"

Garrett applied more pressure judging from the pained look on Tab's face. Even with his hand incapacitated, the drunk lashed out. "Hey man, don't start something you can't finish." Tab wriggled to free his hand, but Garrett held tight.

Knowing he had no place to go, Tab stopped moving. "I was just having some fun with the ladies. You like having fun. Don't you, girls?" He reeked of booze and violence, and it scared me.

Then, in a low, calm voice Garrett said something, and Tab went white.

"Tab's going to leave now." Garrett pulled Tab's arm tighter, not caring whether he broke it off, and walked him out the front door. Whatever Garrett told him must have been meaningful, because Tab didn't bother to resist or come back.

"What a creep!" Jos spoke first. She crossed her arms. Chloe's ex-rattled us both.

"Hasn't changed a bit, has he?" I jabbed.

The guy was bad news. I didn't like the fact he showed up just as Chloe and her mom seemed to be reaching out for help. "I've got a bad feeling about this, Jos. I heard from both Chloe and her mom this week."

Jos looked at me and I shared the worry in her expression.

"I know, I think Tab may be up to his old tricks. I'll know more after I meet with Chloe tomorrow." It was all Jos needed to hear.

We headed to our table and ordered waters. Jos described a couple recent incidents between Chloe and Tab. He supposedly looked her up to apologize for hurting her. Something about making amends in his effort to get sober. She must have loved the guy, or the sex, because he ended up charming her into bed, again. They went public with the relationship, and it seemed fine for a couple weeks.

Jos told me he showed up drunk at her house one night when she and a co-worker were going over a case. Tab went nuts, and started beating Chloe. When her co-worker tried to stop it, Tab started beating him. The guy ended up in the hospital, but was too afraid of Tab to press charges. Chloe told the police, who recommended she get a restraining order. Instead, she called Tab's father and they took him back to rehab.

Apparently, he'd gone off the deep end without Chloe. This was worse than I thought.

When Garrett came back, I didn't know what to say. How do you tell a guy you and your mom work for, but you barely know, a) Thank you for getting rid of the threatening lunatic we attracted, and b) You smell good, I want to be more than friends—what does one say in this position?

Garrett came back to check on us. He helped me off the stool without saying a word. He didn't look mad, but he kept quiet. We walked Jos to her car and made sure she drove off safely before we headed over to my car.

I reached for my key to unlock the door and started to shake. Garrett put his arms around me. "It's okay, I'll make sure you get home safe." He squeezed me tighter. "You don't even have to give me your number—I already have it."

It made me laugh, which was good because laughing seemed a lot better than crying in front of him right now. He opened my door and went around to the other side of the car. He got in the passenger seat and told me where to find his car.

I dropped him off next to a gorgeous black Maserati. If my car could blush from embarrassment, it would. Instead, it made a metal screech, kind of like an angry cat. When Garrett looked over, Old Bessie shut-up.

"Follow me. You're parking in the garage tonight."

I didn't know what that entailed, but I trusted him. Sure enough, he drove up on the other side of the funeral home and stopped in front of the garage. He pointed to the second of four bays, then got out and raised the garage door. I pulled in next to a black hearse and cut the engine. He parked outside in one of two spots near the garage entrance and came inside. Then I watched as he pulled down the garage door and locked it.

We walked through the hallway, past the room where I saw Jimbo the body, and into the office. Garrett stopped me.

"Are you okay?"

I nodded 'yes', but it must not have convinced him. He led me through the office and to the stairway leading to my apartment. "Everything's going to be okay." He gave me a reassuring squeeze. I smiled and went upstairs. After I reached the landing at the top, I peeked down to see if he was still there. He waved. I got inside safely and double-checked the locks.

Mom was asleep, so I did the bare minimum to get ready for bed, and hit the sack.

CHAPTER 6

The smell of toast and eggs woke me before the alarm. Mom must have gotten up before me. I met her in the kitchen and poured us both some orange juice. She asked about my night on the town as we shared breakfast.

I ate a forkful of eggs and tried to decide how much information to give mom. We're pretty close. Sure, we've had our disagreements, but we depended on and trusted each other—the way it's always been. She needed to know what happened, so I drank some OJ, and gave her the details. Not to worry her, but to make sure she stayed alert because I didn't know what Tab might do. I may have left out the part where I drooled over Garrett, but she knew he helped Jos and me.

As soon as we cleared the breakfast dishes, I grabbed a few things and stepped into the shower. I put my head under the hot water and waited for it to perk me up for the interview, errands, and meeting with Chloe I had planned.

I hoped it would be easy for me to find work since most college interns and part-timers would be headed back for fall term. Being young and eager should help me land something, right? Trouble was, I wanted a job that paid well with flexible hours—to leave early on class days, and take off whenever mom needed help. Basically, I needed a miracle. Jocelyn helped set me up with an interview at a local law firm. Maybe I'd get lucky.

I dressed in my best navy suit mom bought me for college interviews. It still looked new, and was the most professional clothing in the closet. The tailored skirt and jacket paired well with a white blouse, nude pantyhose and heels. I tied on bright scarf with yellow flowers for some added color, then spritzed my hair and brushed on some blush and mascara.

Not only did I look sharp for the interview, but I also felt better since our run-in last night. I might even see how Garrett responded to my polished look, although, it didn't matter because I felt good all on my own. My confidence soared as I grabbed my bag to leave.

"You look great," mom said when I stepped into the living room.

"Gee, this old thing." I twirled. "Wish me luck."

"Good luck, sweetie. I know you'll do great. If they're smart, they'll hire you on the spot."

"Thanks, mom. See you later." I leaned over, kissed her on the forehead and headed downstairs.

The car was in the garage, so it was necessary for me to walk to the back office and through the back hallway in order to leave. Unfortunately, I didn't see Garrett, but got a nice compliment from Hank on the way out. The garage door gave me trouble, but after a little nudging it flew open. My car didn't screech at startup this morning, which was a pleasant change. I backed the car out, and left it running while I got out to close and lock the garage door—no remote openers in this old place—and drove to the interview.

The office was impeccably decorated. The receptionist sent me back through a set of mahogany stained wood doors inlaid with glass. A woman with short black hair and a chic grey dress looked up at me over a large desk. The light from two overhead chandeliers reflected metallic flecks on her lips and nails—not what I expected in a conservatively decorated law office, but she made it work.

"Mr. Myagi is expecting you." She pointed toward a row of conference rooms. "Second one on the left."

They must have recently remodeled because the fresh paint smell overpowered my senses—I thought she just called the guy Mr. Myagi. "Excuse me. Who?"

"Mr. Myagi."

"You know Mr. Myagi is—" I started to say it, but a short grey haired man stepped up and shook my hand.

"Yes. I get that a lot, especially since I'm Asian. At least it gets me free coffee every now and then. So, I've learned to own it." He smiled. "Well, grasshopper. If you're ready, I'd like to ask a few questions." I chortled at the grasshopper comment, and sat down to talk with him.

After about thirty minutes the interview was almost over. I wasn't sure the questions he asked me really highlighted my strengths as much as they pointed out my inexperience. So, I took the opportunity to reiterate my dedication and drive—it might have been better to call it desperation, but I didn't want to scare him and ruin my chance to land this job.

He made some more notes before the interview concluded and I went on my way. Overall, I thought my chances were pretty good, and the Jocelyn connection could only help.

I had to book it out of there in order to meet Chloe, but was going to be late, so I texted her. When I finally got there, a number of people posed by Fountain Square and shot pictures, probably to share with family, friends, and social media followers. It looked tempting, but I'd have to find Chloe first.

I scanned the crowd on the south side then moved clockwise until I'd covered the whole area around the fountain. She wasn't there. Something felt off. She asked me to meet her. Sure, I was late, but I'd sent her a text to let her know it. She should be here. I sent another text and paced back and forth while I waited for a response. By the time twenty minutes had passed, I took another pass then ducked into a hotel café nearby. She didn't appear to be there either, so I ordered a soda while I decided what to do next.

I paid for the soda and left some change. As I hurried out, eager to do another search I noticed one of the pedestrians from the fountain at the café. Not Chloe. I tried looking again, but got frustrated and walked to my car.

The entire way things played out in my head. Chloe's sudden call after a long hiatus, and the call from her mom seemed explainable, but the visit from Tab bothered me. Footsteps followed, and they shared my pace. Usually, foot treads sound different until the person tailing you slows or passes you. It wouldn't have been weird except it sounded like they'd been there for more than a block. I sped up slightly and the person behind me did the same. My car came into view and the keys were already in my hands. As I put the key in the lock someone grabbed me by the shoulder.

"Mattie," he said.

"Ack!" I turned and saw Derek. My heart pounded in my chest and I was about to keel over.

"Oh, my gosh. I didn't mean to scare you. Are you okay?"

"Yeah, you scared me." I breathed hard.

"I'm so sorry. I saw you and thought I'd say hello. I tried to get your attention, but you seemed distracted and kept speeding up."

Of course I was distracted, I really needed to get to the bottom of this. I needed to find Chloe. "I was supposed to meet a friend and she ended up being a no show. I guess she got so busy at work she forgot to cancel."

"Her loss is my gain." Derek smiled. "Do you want to grab a coffee?"

"I should get back home, I've got to find out what happened to my friend." I looked at him and noticed the chiseled features of his face. He was handsome, but I had other worries.

"How about another time?"

Derek seemed really disappointed. I caved.

"Sure." I didn't know what else to say. He seemed nice. I figured one coffee couldn't hurt. I could maybe pick his brain about the business and learn more about the Davis and Mackenzie families.

Derek helped me into my car and waited while I got it started. My spotted chariot decided this, of all times, to crap out. Even though I cranked it and pushed the gas, the car made a chortling sound and died. My face went beet red. Derek held back laughter.

"Can I give you a lift?"

"Please." I made sure to slam my door shut before locking and leaving it. There was no way this could be good. And it was most likely going to cost a lot to get my car fixed. It'd take a lot of work to earn enough to pay for repairs. I figured Derek and I could make the most of the ride, and I'd tell mom all about it right after I took a nap.

Turns out, Derek had pretty good instincts. Having been around the funeral business his entire life, he said he noticed how bothered I was by it when we met. Not hard to miss a panic-stricken girl bolting across a busy street and nearly running a guy over just to get away from a dead guy. He was able to put me at ease about the whole living and working with dead bodies issue I seemed to be having this week.

He pulled his Lexus up the driveway and parked. When did we get here? It didn't seem like we'd been in the car long enough to already be home. Oh, well, I thought. As I unbuckled, my car door opened.

Garrett extended his hand to help me out. I didn't notice him when we pulled into the driveway. When did he get here? My brain must not have been fully functioning today—my interview felt a little flat; I couldn't find Chloe; and guys were magically appearing before my eyes. Maybe a nap wasn't the only thing I needed.

"Is everything okay, Mattie?" Garrett sounded concerned.

"I'm fine, thanks."

"Just some car trouble." Derek walked over to us. "I saw her downtown and offered to give her a ride."

"How nice of you." Garrett's voice had an edge to it.

"Yeah, my car bit the dust. I'd have had to call a tow service, and cab it back here if Derek hadn't been there to help." Then I turned to thank Derek only he hugged me instead. I don't know if I was more uncomfortable or Garrett, but we both thought Derek's move was a little over the top. I didn't hate it, but it felt weird with an audience. I stepped back. "Thanks, Derek. See you soon." I did an uncomfortable wave at the elbow because I wasn't sure what else to do besides wave goodbye.

Garrett gave him the stink-eye to indicate it was time to leave. Derek smiled. He got in his Lexus and we watched him drive across the street and go inside the house.

"I'm hungry," Garrett said out of the blue. "How about you?"

"Me too." He might have noticed the hesitance in my voice.

"Sorry, Mattie. I'm glad you got back okay. There's just something about the guy I don't trust."

I tried to analyze his expression—was it a mix of concern and regret? I couldn't tell—but decided to leave it alone for now and get the lunch I'd missed. I'd search for Chloe and deal with my broken car later.

"I could eat. But, I need to check on mom first."

"Sounds good. Think you'll be ready in twenty?"

I smiled and nodded.

"Mattie? You'd better change and bring your bat." He winked. "I'll meet you in the front office." I watched him turn and walk away before I ran up the stairs.

Mom was fine, disappointed our car broke down and that Chloe stood me up, but happy to hear I made it to the interview, and got a ride home without much trouble. She reminded me Aunt Eileen planned to visit, something I'd forgotten about until now. I mentioned Garrett's offer for food, and she told me to go ahead. There may have been a slight hesitation when she said it, but it was hard to tell. This didn't need to be a big deal. My plan was to play it safe: we'd eat and we'd talk, nothing more. Easy, right?

I changed into khaki shorts, a light blue t-shirt and tennis shoes. After a quick touch-up, I stuffed my ID case in my shorts, hugged mom and grabbed my bat on the way out.

"Wait here, I need to check something in the back room," Garrett told me when I reached the front office. "It shouldn't take long." He put his phone in his pocket and jogged out the door.

I hadn't been here, except to peek when we took our first tour of the place a few days ago. The front office, located just inside the glass doors at the front of the house, looked more formal than the back office. The guys planned funerals with grieving families in this office. The room projected style and professionalism, and a designer's touch ensured it felt like it belonged in a grand old Victorian home.

The focal point of the room was a cherry stained writing desk framed by two large cherry bookcases that stood against the wall a couple feet behind the desk. A deep burgundy leather chair sat empty at the desk. Opposite the desk was a floor lamp and a small round-top table situated between two Queen Anne chairs. Large windows behind the chairs and table let in an abundance of natural light. Beige sheers covered the windows.

I peered out one window for a few minutes contemplating the day. When Garrett returned, he had on shorts, a t-shirt and tennis shoes, like I did. Only his t-shirt hugged his upper body muscles like nothing I'd ever seen. I swallowed hard and he smiled.

"You ready?"

"Ready for what?" I had some idea, but at the rate my day had gone, asking seemed like a smart move.

"A stress reliever." He took my hand, then lead me out the front doors. This was not the Maserati from the other night. It was a big Ram truck, and looked newer than any car I'd ever owned. He opened my door and helped me up. He got in on the other side and started it up. Can trucks really look this good? I ran my hands all over the inside to find out. He made a couple noises and handed me a granola bar.

"Here, you look hungry."

"Sorry, I didn't get lunch and I have major truck envy." I ate the first part of the granola bar. He pointed to some water in the cup holders so I could wash it down.

"Hopefully, it'll tide you over until dinner." He started the truck and we took off.

Dinner? Who said anything about dinner? I would've been happy to get a snack bag of chips, and a little chitchat about the weather. This ran dangerously close to actual date territory. I got nervous so I devoured the rest of the granola bar and went along for the ride.

When we got to the batting cages, he directed me to an open one on the end.

"I like to be on the end. It's less distracting."

"Huh. Me too."

Although he brought a shiny new bat out of his trunk when we arrived, he reached for mine.

"Do you mind?" he asked permission.

"Go ahead." I shrugged and gave it to him. As he walked over to feed the machine, he handled the bat almost with reverence.

"Not a lot of bats like this around these days."

"I know. Metal is king, but it's a little too shiny for me. Plus, metal bats just don't sound the same as wooden ones."

"I know." He turned and smacked the crap out of the first ball that came out of the machine.

Impressive, I thought. Let's see if it was just a lucky shot.

He swung again. The bat extended out, then up and over as he sent the next one flying. It was a nice shot, too.

"Do you play?"

"Not for a long time." He popped the next one foul.

"Why not?"

"Just haven't had the time. Or the desire."

"Yeah, I can relate."

He cracked another, and another. Then he turned the bat toward me.

"Wanna try?"

"Sure," I said. Not sure how this would go, I started to get antsy. Once I had the bat, though, things calmed.

"Just pretend it's your ex," he joked.

I turned my head to glare at him and missed the first ball. "Very funny." I settled back in, more determined than ever to whack the snot out of the next ones. Crack. Crack. Crack. I hit them one after the other. Then started to pull my hips too much and hit a couple fouls.

Garrett put his hand up for me to stop and walked closer to me. "You probably know this already," he said, and put his hands at my hips. I gave him a death stare.

"Easy now." Garrett pulled his hands up then motioned to see if I would let him put them back. I didn't think I needed a baseball lesson, but it felt nice having him try. I gave him the okay nod. "You're trying too hard. Relax and wait just a second more before you swing." He was right. My body was tight and it messed up my swing. But, was he really talking about batting, or was it something more? I wondered.

I tried to remain calm, but Garrett used his hands to steer me through a slow-mo swing. He looked and smelled so good I almost dropped the bat. He pushed my arms into position and slowly moved his hands back down to my hips. So much for food, talk, and nothing more. This felt thrilling and dangerous. I needed to get a grip. Only, he did it for me. He backed away and motioned for me to swing again. "Go on."

Another ball went by as I regained my composure. I listened for the whirring sound and then the thump as the machine launched the ball. This time I was ready and hit it right on the sweet spot. Much better.

We traded off a couple more times before we left.

"Are you hungry?"

"I could eat." I really could eat.

"I feel like Italian. How about you?"

Boca is known for really good food, and I was seriously hungry after our workout. But, I barely had twenty dollars to my name, and really good food costs money. So, I wasn't sure if I should say yes, but I really didn't want him to leave.

"Sounds great." I'd either eat breadsticks, or forgo food for a while to afford dinner. It didn't matter. I just wanted to find out more about him.

We talked about the day's events and ate a good meal. He seemed interested to know more about Chloe and Tab, and had a few words about Derek showing up out of the blue. I got the distinct impression he and Derek had a problem with each other, not sure what the problem was, but it may be part of the rivalry Garrett's dad, Hank, mentioned when we met. I would've prodded, because it's my nature, but he was already doing me a favor helping me unwind and paying for dinner—he told me during our early dinner we'd also stop by and check on my car, which was still downtown, probably racking up parking tickets.

The city started to glow from sunset and evening lights when we got to the contraption I called transportation. He parked behind it then held is hand out for the keys. I obliged since they were on the ring with my house keys, and wished him good luck because he was going to need it.

We exited the perfectly polished truck. I stood next to the decaying car as Garrett got inside and turned on the ignition. It made a feral noise, like it might start, but then stopped. It wouldn't even turn over on his second attempt. He shook his head, then patted the dash and pulled the keys out. We went back to the truck and climbed inside.

"What?" I tried to sound defensive, but it was hard to sound tough when he looked at me like that. "I know it's not the most stylish, but at least it's paid off."

"I didn't say anything," he defended.

"You didn't have to. I've seen your gorgeous cars. The Maserati you drive to work, and now this new Ram."

"You noticed that, huh?"

"Hard not to notice." And it's not just the cars, it's you. I thought to myself. You're a hard guy to miss. I had no idea if it was only in my head, or if he'd really set his sights on me, but the way he acted had me excited and anxious. Why couldn't I keep things straight when he was around?

"Good. Now that we've established you noticed the cars. What do you think about the guy?"

Gulp! This guy was direct. *Um, where to begin? Your charm and wit, your gorgeous eyes, or maybe it's your superhero biceps?* I went to la-la land for a minute as I contemplated his good qualities.

"Speechless is good, right?"

"Most of the time," I blurted. My smart aleck comment made me feel a like I'd regained some self-control. Only, it didn't take long for his warm scent and blue eyes to distract me again. I exhaled long and slow. Self-control around him was difficult to maintain.

"Oh, is that so?" He raised an eyebrow at me. I tried to be calm, but shifted in my seat instead. "I didn't mean to make you feel uncomfortable. I was just having some fun," he said.

What was I supposed to say now? Seriously?! Whatever I hoped we might talk about, or do, appears to just be playful banter. The conversation circled back to my crappy car, and my desperate need for working wheels.

"While it may not be your favorite car, it does run, although not right now."

I felt a little embarrassed. *Oh well, what can you do?*

"I can recommend a good mechanic. You should have the engine checked. Hondas are generally reliable, but I think this old model had transmission or ignition problems, and there could be a fix."

"Great," I said half-heartedly when I really just wanted to cry. We didn't have money to fix problems, especially not big ones, like a transmission. And how would I pay to get that hunk of junk hauled away? He picked up on my anxiety—it was kind of hard to miss.

"Don't worry about the cost of the tow, or the work. This particular mechanic owes me a favor."

"Is there anything I need to know? Like, is this some kind of a Godfather thing?"

"No, it's not some Godfather thing." He leaned closer and used his husky voice. "But you will owe me a favor."

Yikes! It was a Godfather thing. I wasn't sure this was a good idea. I had a really hard time knowing whether to run, or stay and pull him closer. The look in his eyes warned me I was playing with fire—the dangerous, seductive kind—and already in way over my head.

"Okay," my voice crackled. I thought it over, and then in my best South Jersey accent said, "You want I should whack somebody for you?"

He laughed at my attempt at humor. "Unh-unh. Nope." Garrett waggled his finger at me. "The favor comes later, and it'll be a something you can't refuse." He finished the last part in his best Brando Godfather voice.

My phone buzzed. I figured it was mom, probably worried about what we might be doing for so long. I'd kept her in the loop up until we stopped for the car, but got busy wondering what a brave woman would do with this hunk of a man sitting beside her. I'm usually much stronger, and more in control when it comes to feelings. Okay, so I cried to chick-flicks, and anything involving animals and kids, but I sort of felt like a tough girl. Not totally hardened, but picky when it came to my time and my heart. Maybe it was just the way I'd insulated myself over the years—hurt has a funny way of working on people like me. Instead of being logical when it came to our situation, and remaining friends in light of the fact he was one of our employer landlords, I struggled against the desire for more. The way he acted made me think he might have felt a similar conflict.

When I checked the display, it was Chloe's mom. Did they not talk? I thought my previous message to Chloe was clear: Call Your Mom!

"Excuse me, it's my friend's mom and I really should take this call," I told Garrett apologetically.

I started the call upbeat, and slightly perturbed, but felt heavy with guilt when Mrs. Ellis mom broke down. "She's gone. Chloe's dead."

At first, I couldn't believe it—we'd talked just a few days ago, and were supposed to meet up to discuss her case. Mrs. Ellis said she was dead. Suicide, the coroner had ruled.

There was no way, I thought. Chloe told me once she'd dreamt her whole life of becoming a judge. Chloe had so much going for her as an up-and-comer in the legal world—working on a big gambling case, being heard by the State Supreme Court. The case would have bolstered her career and put her on a fast track to the bench. *Why would she kill herself before it was even heard?* No way she'd miss the opportunity of a lifetime. She didn't commit suicide. Chloe's mom didn't think her daughter had either.

"I'm so sorry, Mrs. Ellis, so sorry to hear about Chloe. What are you going to do?"

"I don't know, Mattie. I want to get a second opinion, but don't know if I should."

"Maybe I can help."

"Doing what, dear?"

Garrett sat patiently, absorbing at least the half of the conversation.

"Well, mom and I work at a funeral home now," I admitted, and blushed even though she couldn't see it through the phone. Then my eyes went to Garrett and back to the dash.

"I know a guy in the business who may be able to help." I waited for her response.

"Do you think he'd look into it?"

"I trust him to find out what really happened to Chloe." At least I hoped so. I looked at Garrett and he politely signaled me to hand over the phone, so I did. I blew out a breath and waited for them to discuss the next steps.

"It would be best. If you released the body to our funeral home, so I could take a closer look. We don't want whoever may be behind this to know we're investigating."

This scared me. It all seemed too real, and wrong. I had no idea what really happened. But, we intended to find out.

"I'll do whatever I can to help you, Mrs. Ellis. I'm very sorry for your loss," Garrett told her sincerely. He handed me the phone and waited for me to finish.

"Thanks Mattie, but please be careful. I couldn't stand it if anything happened to you or that nice young man because you helped me."

"Mrs. E., I promise we'll do whatever we can to figure out what happened to Chloe. Once we know more, we'll call you. Just hang in there." I disconnected and quiet shock took over for a few moments. My breakdown would have to wait. Could Chloe have killed herself? If she didn't, then she was murdered. That made everything much worse. Who would kill her and why? Could it have been a colleague, or even Tab? My head spun.

Garrett knew about Chloe and Tab's rocky relationship. I'd told him about it after our run-in with Tab the other night. It made sense to fill him in on the rest. I told him about Chloe's call to me for help on a case; her mom's call for help getting in touch with Chloe; and how odd it all seemed for them to contact me considering we hadn't kept in touch much after I left school.

He listened intently then drove back to the funeral home. We'd both been lost in our own thoughts on the ride home until he pulled in a parking spot near the garage doors.

"I've got a friend who might be able to help. Calvin's a detective, and we go way back, so I trust him. He may be able to help us, but we won't know if it's worth pursuing until I take a look at Chloe." He sighed. "Mattie, I've seen cases like this where family, or friends, can't come to terms with a loved one's suicide. It can be a real mess of grief and guilt. I just want you to be prepared in case she did take her own life, and to know you're not responsible."

Garrett unbuckled, and signaled for my phone, which I still held in my hands. I handed it to him and he typed in his contact information. "As for your car, someone will pick it up tonight. Text me at this number when you're up and running tomorrow. I'll text you back and let you know if I can drive you over to the garage, or not. Ask to see this guy." He handed me a business card and continued. "If I can't make it, I'll leave some keys in my top desk drawer so you can drive over and check on your car. Leave my car there, they'll get it back to me later."

"Thank you." He was going out of his way to help with everything. Filled with so many emotions, I didn't know what else to say.

"Anytime. I know living here has to be an adjustment for you and your mom. These other problems are only making life more complicated. Let me know if you need anything."

Before I could say anything more, or hug him, his phone rang. It was my mom, and it was quick. It took a moment for me to register what they discussed.

"We've got a body. Sorry, a customer. We'd better get inside."

The wind gust had a cold edge to it when we hopped out of the truck. He led me inside, closed the door and watched as I ran my fingers through my hair to calm it back into place. He shivered, probably from the wind. He stepped close enough I could feel his body heat. Maybe not the wind.

"Mattie?" Garrett looked at me so intently I felt a shock wave. "Can I ask you something personal?" I kept quiet and said yes with my eyes.

Just as he opened his mouth to ask, Sledge and Manny burst through the back door.

"Got another dusty one," Manny called out casually as if he'd said, 'Honey, I'm home' while he and Sledge rolled the latest body, um, customer inside. I didn't run this time. But, I did avoid looking directly at the black bag for the first few moments.

"Easy guys." Garrett pushed open the door to the holding room while maintaining my gaze. "If they're right, and it's the same stuff found on the last one, we'll be talking to Cal about more than just Chloe tomorrow."

Sledge and Manny went inside and Garrett's voice softened.

"We'll pick our conversation up where we left off soon. Okay?" He smiled warmly. I smiled back and let him get to work.

When I got upstairs and locked the door, mom greeted me with chocolate chip cookies and milk. The warm vanilla and gooey chocolate welcomed me to sit and unload my worries. I let mom have it, the good, the bad, and the ugly. Well, most of it. I left out the part where I felt mixed emotions about Garrett, and volunteered us both to look into a possible murder. No need to worry her unless something more happened with either situation, right? Maybe nothing would.

Mom expressed her sympathy over Chloe's death then reassured me we'd be fine, that the car and our finances would hold up. Despite the fact I didn't get the job I'd interviewed for recently. The office left a voice message and said they'd keep my resume on file a while longer—I wasn't going to hold my breath. Picking up some kind of work remained a priority. Garrett offered to take care of the car repairs, and to help look into Chloe's death. I didn't want to be in his debt any more than I already was.

"You two girls all caught up?" Aunt Eileen surprised us in the kitchen. My aunt's autumn print dress and cropped red hair reminded me of my third grade English teacher. The look suited her.

"Yes, thanks. Everything okay with the arrangements?" Mom looked at me and brushed a bit of hair behind my ear the way she had since I was a kid. Something was up. She looked back at my aunt.

"I'm taking your mom on a little trip," Eileen said.

"Is everything okay, mom?" An impromptu trip worried me.

"I'm fine, honey. But grandpa's hit a rough patch and we thought a visit might cheer him up." Mom sounded concerned about grandpa. "Eileen will do most of the driving, I'll annoy her with advice and help out if needed. We'd be gone a few days. I hate to burden you with extra work, but I need you to answer the phones and cover any office requests while we're gone. I wouldn't ask unless it was important." She looked worried, and it was the last thing she needed to feel right now.

"It's no problem. Just get me up to speed and I'll handle it. Aunt Eileen, please make sure she gets some rest, too." Mom and my aunt hugged me at the same time.

We visited a while longer. They went to the bedroom to pack mom's things while I polished off another cookie and packed the rest in two containers, one for me, one for their trip. I took one final swig of milk then washed the glass and put it on the drying rack. As mom and Aunt Eileen got ready for bed, I grabbed a pillow and blanket from the bedroom closet and put them on the couch in the living room. I rinsed up, said goodnight, and crashed.

CHAPTER 7

I woke up to mom and Aunt Eileen singing in the kitchen. They used to break out singing a lot when they cooked with grandma. I'd almost forgotten how much I missed hearing them harmonize. We ate oatmeal and chatted some more about the trip. After breakfast, I walked a couple bags downstairs and loaded them into Aunt Eileen's burgundy sedan. We exchanged hugs and they left.

I sprung up the walk and into the back office. Fran, an assistant funeral director in training, told me Garrett was at a graveside service and would be back this afternoon. Ryder was meeting a family, and Hank had already left to begin his holiday weekend. She had no idea where Stanley was at the moment, although I thought I heard her murmur something about a coffin.

I snagged the keys and headed upstairs. My to do list was pretty long, so I texted Garrett to say I picked up his keys and planned to stop by the garage later. My instincts told me Garrett would find something, so I got started on Chloe's case early. I called her mom who was understandably distraught, but helpful. She gave me a contact number for Chloe's office, and her address.

A clerk at the office I called didn't help much, but only because he didn't know me, and claimed he couldn't give out confidential information. The clerk did, however, slip and tell me the name of a lawyer working the case with Chloe, Ted Oxley.

Mr. Oxley, a practicing attorney, headed the college Law Club, although not a professor. I knew him from a mock trial Chloe and I participated in a few years back. His business was listed online. I figured there was no sense in letting the Maserati sit around all day, so I headed over there to ask Ted about the case.

As soon as I parked, I texted Jos and told her we needed to meet ASAP. A guy got out of a car near me and went inside the office building. I didn't recognize him, but he looked like he belonged there. Suit and briefcase.

The elevator dinged when it reached the third floor, my stop. The doors opened, I stepped off and looked at the black lettering on the marquee to see where Ted Oxley's office, suite 307, was located. His assistant notified me he was in conference with a client, offered me a beverage and a magazine while I waited.

I glanced over the headlines, but decided to check messages and play with my phone instead. The messages indicated mom and Aunt Eileen were making good progress; Jos would be spending the weekend with her family; and Garrett wanted to catch up before he left for the holiday. While everyone else had Labor Day plans, mine looked to be pretty quiet. Maybe I'd unpack, curl up with a book, or watch chick-flicks and eat popcorn until Tuesday. Three days is enough for a person to binge on whatever they wanted. I'd have to decide later because Mr. Oxley's client left, so it was my turn to see him.

"Good to see you." Mr. Oxley shook my hand and walked me into his office. He signaled for me to take a seat then walked around to his desk and sat in an expensive looking leather office chair.

"Sorry to hear about Chloe."

"Me too. I wondered if you knew anything about her recent cases."

"Well, we did work together on a couple cases, but I hadn't talked to her much lately. From what I understand, she'd been given some clerk work on a high profile case to stop a casino build. Normally, you can't stop a build like this once it starts, unless you've got a pretty strong case."

Oxley lifted his arms off the chair. They came to rest on the desk and he pulled his hands up until only the fingertips touched. From the way it looked, he was either going to pray, or tell me more bad news. "Chloe had come to me for help, but I'm afraid I couldn't offer her much. The next thing I heard, she...she'd killed herself. Maybe she couldn't handle the pressure. Mattie, you know what it's like." He threw that last part in unexpectedly. I was a bit shocked by it, but answered quickly.

"Yes, I do know the pressure can be overwhelming. But Chloe was different, she didn't bend to it quite as easily as I did." I felt my statement was a good recovery considering it sounded a lot like he was taking a jab at me. He knew pressure was part of the reason I left school and hadn't been back, before now. The college work wouldn't have been so bad, but financial pressures and family health issues, made it unbearable. I couldn't handle it all at the same time, and I broke. Remembering it saddened me, but not as much as it used to. "I thought she worked with you some on the big case."

I noticed him stay in control, except for the tension in his hands. "True, she was helping me with a case. It was just a small family land deal, nothing big though. I wish I could help you more."

Almost as an afterthought Oxley told me something about a recent run-in between Chloe and Tab. "You know, they were volatile together. Maybe she just wanted off the merry-go-round." It devastated me to think she could have taken her life over that jerk. She seemed stronger than that, but Oxley had a point.

I left the office in a crabby mood. The Maserati was a seriously awesome ride, but it wasn't mine. Time to face facts, and find out what was up with my car.

I drove to the garage listed on the business card Garrett gave me. When I pulled up a heavy man covered in tattoos and grease was working on an old Dodge. He finished and closed the hood. He wiped his hands on a blue shop towel and came to greet me.

"Hello, there. You Mattie?

"I am."

He shook my hand with a hearty welcome. He was even larger than he looked under the hood. Still, I wasn't without my manners. "Are you Garrett's mechanic?"

"That I am. Hear you're old Honda's giving you trouble."

"Yeah, it used to make a loud noise at start. Now, it doesn't even start. Can you take a look?"

"Sure thing, but we're backed up right now. Why don't you leave me the key and I'll look her over this afternoon?"

"I would, but I've got things to do today. Is there any way you can give it a quick check while I wait?"

He eyed me for a minute, then the corners of his mouth turned up in a smile.

"Garrett didn't tell you?"

"Tell me what?" I was totally clueless.

"He made arrangements for alternate transportation."

"What sort of transportation?" I said suspiciously.

"Take your pick." He tipped his head sideways to indicate a row of cars near the side of the building.

"Are you serious?" There were half a dozen cars, all brand new, except one.

"Just pick one. You can head inside and sign it out." He paused and smiled. "I may not get to your car today so you can keep it through the weekend if you want."

If I want? Yeah, I want. But, what's the catch? Am I going to have to whack someone to pay for this? He must have read my mind.

"Don't worry about money. Garrett's got it covered."

I shivered wondering what I might owe Garrett for this one. Mysterious? Sure. But, I didn't have the luxury, or time to ask a lot of questions. Granny always said, "Never look a gift horse in the mouth." I'd taking her advice on this one. Besides, he didn't have an air of superiority about working on my crap-mobile or giving me a loaner. He just acted like he was doing his job, which made it easier to accept the gift.

"Thanks."

"Sure thing. I'll call you when your car is ready."

I took the apartment and storage locker keys off the ring and handed it to him. I briefly glanced at the new cars and headed inside.

A woman in a tight red shirt, and an even tighter black skirt met me. Her brown hair was pulled up, and she looked striking. The only thing that looked out of place was the small black skull tattooed on her neck. A part of me winced thinking of the favors she must have owed Garrett, and what he actually did to earn them.

I swallowed my pride, stiffened up, and extended my hand. "Hi, I'm Mattie."

"Garrett said you'd be needing some help." She didn't roll her eyes, but it wasn't hard to hear the tone in her voice and see her disappointment. "I'm Bianca. I see you already met Dawes."

"Is he the mechanic?"

"Yes, he's the mechanic. His name is Billy, but he goes by Dawes."

She eyed me for a few moments. I'm pretty sure she just checked me out, and not in a good way.

"So, how do you know Garrett?"

"Work," I said, not wanting to get into the details. "Billy, I mean, Dawes said you had keys?"

She kept her eyes on me as she rounded an old metal desk that looked like it belonged in an institution. She swiped a hand on a computer screen and typed something. The laptop was new and looked out of place.

"Well, which one?" She huffed. Not much for chitchat I guess.

"Car?"

"Yes, which car did you want?"

It wouldn't have been a big deal, but I'd about had it with rude people. I didn't do anything to her. I just wanted to get the keys and get out.

"Hello...Car?"

That's it. I don't like rude, and I don't like being rushed. I was perfectly happy to take the Mini, but now it seemed too...mini. So, I did what any self-respecting girl in my position would do. I didn't back down.

"I'll take the Hellcat." Definitely not mini.

"Huh, I didn't picture you as the American muscle type." She grabbed the keys out of a lockbox and dangled them in front of me. "It's pretty powerful. Think you can handle it?"

"Absolutely." I snatched the keys from her hand and left without another word. When I got out the door I growled. Her comment about me handling 'American Muscle' went beyond the car. And there was no way she and was going to intimidate me about anything. Including accepting a better-than-I-could-ever-afford car, albeit a loaner, and repairs to my current rust bucket from a guy I barely knew, and she apparently knew intimately. She irked me on a day I didn't need it. Best to get out before I said or did anything stupid.

When I got to the car Dawes stopped what he was doing to walk over. He whistled through his teeth and leaned into the window. "Nice choice. Just make sure you watch the throttle, it'll kick you in the a—" he caught himself before he finished. "Just make sure you take it easy the first few go-rounds."

"Thanks." I put on my shades. "I appreciate the advice. Call me when you know more about what's going on with my car."

"Will do."

The Hellcat growled extra loud as I pulled out. Probably because I wanted to let everyone, including Bianca, know I was leaving.

It took moments for me to hit the road home. It had been a long day, and it was only half over. I planned to stop at the bank and the store before I went home, but I was hungry and agitated. Errands could wait. I headed home to grab a PB&J instead.

My phone buzzed just as the engine stopped. Garrett wanted me to meet him at the police station. Talking with the police didn't sound fun, but answers were more important than food and comfort right now. I texted that I'd meet him, turned the car back on, and rumbled out of the parking lot. There was enough power to easily beat out a hatchback and head downtown.

CHAPTER 8

Garrett told me to wait inside until he, or Detective Calvin Bateman showed up.

I arrived a couple minutes early, so I took the opportunity to check on mom. When I called she sounded good. Mom told me she and Aunt Eileen were doing fine, and she promised a more detailed update later because they were discussing grandpa's latest run-in with the nurse's aide who came to help him each week. I hung up and wondered how things were really going, but was glad mom had someone with her. Lord knows they'd have their hands full with my grandpa.

About the time I finished checking my news feed and the ten-day forecast, Garrett sat down beside me. We only waited a couple minutes before a light-haired man about an inch taller than Garrett walked in with two teenagers in handcuffs.

"I picked up these two thieves and brought them here for booking. These geniuses tried to swipe a Sonicare toothbrush, shirts, and some kind of book reader thing from the department store. I was picking up socks on my lunch break." He sounded humored and annoyed. It was hard not to laugh, but they looked every bit as dumb as their attempt at shoplifting sounded.

"I didn't get to finish shopping," Calvin said. "And I really need socks."

I laughed imagining the guy trying solving crimes without socks.

"I'll hand them off and take your information here in a few," he said to me. "You can sit by my desk. The coffee is free, but it tastes like crap. Garrett shook his head to reinforce the point. If you want something else, the vending machine's that way." He motioned to an area past the front desk. I really just wanted to get down to business, so I followed Garrett to Cal's desk and we waited.

When Cal was finished with dumb and dumber, he met us. We talked over Chloe, Tab, her mysterious casino case, and anything else that seemed out of the ordinary, like the calls she and her mom made to me this past week.

Going on my assumption that Chloe wouldn't commit suicide, Cal said there was a real possibility the Tab or someone from the case she was working had a part in her death. Garrett and Cal talked about the autopsy, which they told me would have been standard in a case like this. Something I hadn't known before.

Garrett looked at me cautiously, then at Cal and described the things he noticed about Chloe. Garrett told us he discovered some scratches, bruises, and a tiny needle mark on Chloe that must have been made by an especially small needle. The mark was made by someone who knew what they were doing because he almost missed it. I wasn't sure if it there was a mix-up at the Coroner's office, or not, but something about it bothered Garrett. It bothered me, too. If he hadn't been looking for something, it might have stayed hidden.

Originally, Chloe was found with a nearly emptied bottle of sleeping pills by her bedside. Garrett's new information made Calvin wonder if the killer used some kind of poison, then staged the scene to make it look like Chloe did it herself. If we were correct, then we'd eliminated one unspeakable act and replaced it with another. Maybe Chloe hadn't killed herself, and someone else was responsible. It was difficult to process, and I couldn't imagine how Chloe's mother would react to this news.

Cal thought Tab was a good suspect since he'd abused her before—Chloe had fresh bruises—but Cal didn't think a fake suicide fit Tab's profile. Tab seemed more impulsive, not methodical enough to pull off something like this.

Cal stopped the conversation and looked directly at me. He asked me if I understood violence was unacceptable. He quoted domestic abuse statistics, so I'd understand how easily things could have escalated. It was scary to hear him talk about it. Scary enough, my mind started to wander back to some of the things I'd seen.

While I was distracted, they started to discuss the dusty bodies that were coming to the funeral parlor. Apparently, the local police were trying to keep the details under wraps. They didn't want to alert the public until they knew what was really going on. Calvin spoke quietly as he told Garrett the bodies were covered head-to-toe in what the lab determined to be some kind of pulverized rust. Probably the reddish powder on the first dead guy I saw at the funeral home.

I didn't totally understand, but it seemed significant that the two bodies were also discovered near a known mob hot spot with what Cal described as native artifacts. He didn't give more detail, but told Garrett to watch out for anything suspicious. Basically, he told Garrett to double check the bodies as they came in for anything that the Coroner may have missed. When Cal said the last part, Garrett stiffened up and looked more serious than before.

"Easy, now," Cal said to Garrett. "I'm just saying what you already know. I trust you better than her. If you notice anything that could be useful, give me a call."

It was apparent Garrett was still tense, but he smiled at his buddy. "Of course, I'll call you with any news," Garrett said.

Cal told us he'd look into Chloe's background and see if anything popped. He expressed concern, and warned us not to mention either case to anyone before he could get more information. Cal said he'd make it a priority and keep us in the loop, and he was sincere, even though his desk looked like he had plenty of cases to handle without mine.

After we finished Garrett walked me out. "See you back at the parlor."

"Sure. I'm just going to grab a peanut butter sandwich, or some crackers first if it's okay."

"I'll grab some sandwiches and meet you there." Garrett turned to leave.

I walked toward the Hellcat, which was parked down the street. My thoughts went all over. This whole thing with Chloe was crazy. Why did she waste her time with a jerk like Tab? Why didn't she leave when he hurt her the first time? How could the normal girl I spent practically every day with in college end up dead like this? It didn't seem possible to have a murderer invade our little part of the world. Was it Tab, or her work that killed her? I had to find out.

My distracted brain registered a noise behind me. I walked faster and pulled out my keys. If there was enough distance between us, I'd make it to the car and get safely inside, but there wasn't. I knew it and started to run.

A large man grabbed me from behind and lifted me off the ground—his chest and arms were huge. He turned me to face the closest brick building. I struggled to hit and kick him, but he had me locked down so tight, I could barely move.

"You can have my purse." Terror shot through me and tears welled up in my eyes, but instead of crying, a little whimper escaped. "Take the money. Just please, don't hurt me."

He covered my mouth with one of his hands then squeezed tighter. It hurt to breathe. I wiggled in an attempt to free myself, but I was only able to move just enough to get a tiny gasp of air. The guy waited for me to waste some more energy trying to escape. My arms started to feel like fire, and my mind raced with thoughts of what he might do to me. Maybe someone would see me in distress and come save me. No one came.

"Are you listening?"

I hesitated, then shook my head yes.

"Stop poking around other people's business, or next time you won't be so lucky." He squeezed tighter until my bones and cartilage started to grind. "This is your only warning." He let go.

My body shook. I nearly collapsed, but I was too afraid to move. Not knowing what to do, I stood there for a minute and kept my eyes focused on the weathered bricks in front of me. When my instincts kicked in, I turned, grabbed my bag and keys off the pavement, and ran for the Hellcat. I didn't stop until I was locked inside with the engine running. My fight or flight instinct yelled at me to get as far away as possible, so I pushed back the tears, shoved the car into drive, and zoomed off.

By the time I got back to the funeral home, I was one hot mess of tears, mascara smudges, and panic. Garrett's truck was parked next to the garage, and so was his Maserati. I punched the gas and squealed the tires coming up the driveway. It didn't matter if the Hellcat crashed through the building, I wanted everyone to know I was here. Mostly so they could help me in case the crazy guy came back.

I flew in the back door, through the hall and into the office. Apparently Garrett was unable to hear my entrance because he had his hands full. With Bianca. I nearly ran them over. They stood lip-locked. I stopped short and stared in shock. He pushed her away just as I bolted through the office. He caught me halfway down the hall.

"Mattie," he said firmly. "It's not what you think." Right, and I'm a brain surgeon who moonlights as a Victoria's Secret model. Not buying it bud! I turned to dart off again and he grabbed my arm.

"Hey!" I protested still wounded from the psycho encounter. It must have taken him by surprise, or he noticed my panicked look. He let go. I started off again when the door to the viewing room opened. I freaked and tried to move left, only my foot caught part of the doorway and I went flying. Gravity brought me down with a thwump. Crap! Crap! Crap! Crap! Crap! "Ouch!" was about all I could manage with my face to the floor. I was going to have bruises and rug burns, or worse.

Mille and Garrett both ran over to help me.

"Walk much." I heard Bianca say as she came toward us. She was on my last nerve and I was going to give her an attitude adjustment. I tried to get up on my feet, only nothing worked right and my foot slipped and landed me back on the floor.

"Stop movin' girl," Mille told me. "Or ya gonna hurt somethin' even worse." She put a hand under my right arm and one on my back. "Garrett, help me move her over." He got in position on my left side then stopped.

"Wait. Mattie, are you okay to move? Does anything feel broken?" Only my ego, loverboy. Only my ego. I lifted my face off the floor and rested my chin on the carpet while the rest of me was pretty much flattened.

"I don't think so," I said. They turned me over; I wasn't much help even though I tried. I lay flat on my back for a minute looking up at Mille, Garrett, and Bianca who stood over me in a skirt so short I could see up to her neck. I gave her a dirty look, which turned to a death stare when she smirked at me.

Garrett must have noticed because he stood up and told Bianca it was time to leave.

"Sure, babe," she told him. "You know how to reach me, day or night." She rubbed up against him, gave me a look, and sashayed away.

Garrett got right back down beside me. "Are you alright? Can I get you anything? Do you want to try and sit up?" He nervously fired off questions as he stroked my hair. I wasn't expecting it, considering the whole Bianca thing, but it softened my anger a little.

"I'm hurt. Still breathing. I could use a stiff drink, but I'd settle for whatever you've got. As long as it comes with some kind of pain reliever." Millie and Garrett supported me as I sat up and only yelped once.

"Garrett, go," Millie said. I watched Garrett as he quickly disappeared into the back hall. Millie held one of my hands and used her other arm to keep me from falling backward.

"There, there, now. Don't ya worry about 'dat girl,'" she said. "Bianca's nuthin' but trouble—a whole lotta trouble. Ya got to do your own thing. He'll come 'round."

"What do you mean, Millie? I—"

"Ya can't fool me, neither one of ya. I know what I see with my own eyes and hear with my own ears. Ya got some kind of animal magnetism. Heat has been comin' off ya both since ya met."

I blushed. There was absolutely no comeback for what she said. I didn't know whether to deny it or give in to it. Situation: hopeless.

When I didn't respond, she continued the conversation. "Mattie, I don't know what ya been through today, but it looks to be somethin' more than tripping in the hallway." I was scared, but felt safer than before.

"It's been a tough day, but I'm okay."

"When Garrett gets back, I'll give ya somethin' to help the pain. Made in my own shop."

"Shop?"

"Yes, I sell natural herbs and medicines made the old way." Something about her brown eyes told me to trust her. "And if ya need to talk, I'll listen. I got big ears. See?" Millie pushed back her hair to reveal large dark lobes decorated with beautiful wood-carved earrings. She was right, the ears looked big even on her frame.

Garrett hustled back with a glass of water and a couple pills, which Millie waved off.

"Oh." Recognition crossed his face. "She's gonna give you some of the good stuff. It'll definitely make you feel better, but watch out for the kick that comes later."

"After the morning I've had, I'll try just about anything." I tried to move. It took the three of us, but we managed to get me upright. Garrett hesitated to sit me in the grieving area, so we headed to the office.

I sat at the desk opposite Garrett's before Millie got on her way. This seating arrangement meant he could keep an eye on me while she left to get her special herbal painkiller. When she left, I wondered if I should have asked for a mind eraser to go along with it, so I could forget the madman from earlier, and Bianca, too.

Garrett sat down. My chair was really low and the light from the desk lamp made me think he was about to interrogate me. I had no energy to fidget, so I left the lamp alone.

Garrett started with his explanation for the whole Bianca incident. She came by to drop off his car, blah, blah, blah, and ended up kissing him just as I walked in. He was, apparently, not kissing her back, and had to pry her off his face using some amount of force. Their kiss was the last thing I wanted to think about, but he felt it needed cleared up. What Garrett told me sounded like the truth, but irked me anyway. He noticed and changed the subject.

Garrett offered up a plain white food bag on his desk. After he handed me a club sandwich with pickles, I took a few bites and practically moaned it was so good, or maybe I was just extremely hungry. Fear can make a person ravenous, right?

He asked me point-blank what happened. I took a huge bite and smiled while contemplating what to say.

"I was threatened by a lunatic." I bit off another corner of the sandwich and chewed.

A flash of hurt or anger crossed his face. His jaw tightened and he glared at me. He sat his sandwich on a wrapper and leaned forward. "I need to know everything."

"Everything?" I asked hesitantly.

"Everything."

I filled him in on all the details I could remember about the super strong and scary guy. The way he easily grabbed and lifted me off the ground, and how I couldn't see him because of his sneak attack from behind, and my absolute fear and inability to defend myself.

As Garrett listened, his jaw clenched and a big vein popped out on his neck. I stopped, but he signaled me to continue. I explained that I offered the guy my bag, but he refused, and instead threatened me to stay out of other people's business, or else worse things would happen.

Garrett stared silently and let everything sink in as I finished. He looked angry. Maybe I'd said too much. Retelling the ordeal hit me hard and I started to cry. He came over right away and reassured me things would be okay.

"Mattie," he softened. "You've been through a lot today. You need to eat and drink something. When Millie gets back we'll give you whatever pain reliever she thinks is best and we'll get you upstairs so you can sleep." He gave me a reassuring touch, but my body hurt so much I winced. He pulled his hand away and pushed my sandwich toward me so I'd eat. It smelled good, like fresh baked bread and deliciousness. I took a bite, but was so tired it took me longer to chew the crusty bread. I washed it down with a cold soda, and went for another bite.

"You know, I've been in some pretty bad situations over the years, and I think I can help you through this." Garrett pulled up an office chair and sat next to me. "If you'll let me." He looked hurt or maybe just tired, like me. My eyes drooped. I could have fallen asleep right there at the desk. When my head snapped back, I sipped some more soda and tried to look awake.

"I appreciate it." I was reluctant to feel anything about him, or his generous offer, because it would mean feeling pain, and I just didn't know if I could handle more pain than I already felt. He probably offered help just to be nice, or because he felt guilty and wanted to reassure me. Probably nothing more would come of it, I thought.

What he said next surprised me. "After you get some sleep, we're going to hit the gym."

It didn't make sense, maybe he worked out to let off steam. Judging by his massive arms he looked like he did it a lot. But, I was far from functional, in case he'd missed it, and not in the most physically capable condition. Going to the gym seemed like a really bad idea. When I gave him a look to that effect, he shook his head to indicate we were going to hit the gym even if he had to drag me there. Fine. Whatever he thought best, but only after I'd slept a very long time. Only, I didn't know if I could sleep through phone duty.

Phone duty was part of the work we did for the Mackenzie Family. As the answering service, we fielded after-hours business calls. All. Night. Long. And these business calls were not just, "Hi, thanks for calling. I'll take a message," mind you. These were death calls. Not from actual dead people, but from loved ones, nursing homes, physicians, caregivers and friends. These were some truly hard calls. I thought getting yelled at over the phone for late or burnt pizzas was bad, this was worse.

The people who called us were in all sorts of moods, mostly sad, shocked, or crying. It's not the time to fake a good mood (grinning wildly), "Hi there, how may we help you?" Here we needed to be serious and alert. You couldn't give callers what they truly wanted— the return of their loved ones. It's tough to deal with such raw emotion: regret, anger and sadness. Mom told me to listen and be sympathetic to callers because they probably lost somebody they loved.

A funeral home gets all kinds of calls: calls about flower deliveries, caskets, obituaries, and people asking for viewing times and directions. The list goes on, but the most difficult calls are death calls. Sometimes a caller will get right to the point, but sometimes they can't. You listen, let them grieve, and when it's really bad, cry along with them. It happened to me once already.

I hated death calls because it meant the end of a life. I hated that we moved here, and we had to be alert when most normal people slept. Mostly, I hated death. Spending a prime part of my life in a place of death sucked. But at least I had him…

I must have looked ridiculous staring at Garrett, because he laughed. What? Did I drool? He smiled as I came back from la-la-land. I ended up there a lot more than usual. We ate quietly for several minutes. Shortly after, Millie opened the door.

"All right, girl. I got what ya needed to get rid of that fiery pain. Here. Drink this." She pulled a small vial out of her purse and handed it to me firmly. The dark blue vial must have been a little smaller than my finger.

"Before I take this, I need to know if it'll make me drowsy." Millie laughed a big belly laugh and Garrett nearly fell off his chair. I took it as affirmation that the super pain killer, potion, or whatever she called it would knock me out. "If so, I'll have to pass because it's my night to man the phones." I was too chicken to go through with it, so I milked it. "I promised mom."

"Don't worry, I've got the phones tonight." Garrett pushed the vial up toward my mouth. "Drink 'da potion," he tried do his best impression of Millie.

I twisted off the black cap, did an air 'Cheers' and drank it down. My mouth puckered and I would have spit it out except Millie and

Garrett were staring.

They helped me upstairs to the apartment, it was the first time either of them had seen it fully furnished, but only partially decorated. We had more to do. A couple stacks of unpacked boxes sat in a kitchen corner near the table, but most everything else was put away. My legs felt heavier as we walked through the kitchen, past a table in living room and into the bedroom.

The medicine hit me fast, but I was awake long enough to remember Garrett and Millie tucked me into bed. My body shivered when it hit the cool sheets then I crashed hard. I didn't notice them leave.

CHAPTER 9

Sometime through the night I found myself dreaming of a grassy field. Along the edges of the green field were some hills, grassy knolls, which didn't look like much at first. Once I stepped closer, they grew ten to fifteen feet around me. I heard a female voice nearby say something, but I couldn't make out the words.

I turned to find a young girl. She was in her late teens, or early twenties, and wore clothes of another era. She had on a long powder blue dress with a lacey white petticoat paired with white gloves. The girl searched for something. As I turned to face the direction she looked, I noticed a young native boy about the same age as the girl dart behind a tree. The tree was huge, and loaded with branches full of deep green foliage. As the wind picked up, sunlight glimmered through the leaves and hit the ground all around us. I looked back to the girl. She must not have seen the boy, or maybe he wasn't what she searched for, because she kept looking. She threw her hands up and walked to the tree and sat down. I tried to speak, but I couldn't. My mouth opened wider, but no matter how hard I worked to make a noise, nothing came out. I tried harder to push out anything, even a breath, and panicked when my air supply cut off. My voice and breath were lost. I started to choke. I ran to the girl for help, but the scene went black before I reached her under the tree.

I woke up choking and gasped for air. A coughing fit took over my body for a couple minutes until I realized my breathing was difficult because of an anxiety attack. I didn't understand where the anxiety came from, except the weird dream, or the encounter I'd had with Mr. Crazy. Slowly, and with some concentrated effort, my breathing regulated.

As I sat up in bed, a huge sigh escaped. The day had started without me, my clock showed it was after nine, but I didn't feel as much pain as I expected considering I got threatened and nearly crushed yesterday. I ran my hands through my hair and felt how desperately I needed a shower, but realized it was important to first find out how the business end of things went last night. I hit the office button and buzzed downstairs. Ryder answered.

"What's up?"

"Um." I didn't know what to say. Did he know about what happened, or that Garrett covered the phones for me while I was passed out on Millie's super-healing buzz-berry juice?

"Phones?" was the most I could manage.

"Garrett said he came in early," Ryder told me. "So we've already got the phones. You know, you sound weird. Is everything okay?"

Since Garrett covered for me, I tried to pull it together and act like everything was normal.

"Yeah, just had a long day yesterday," I said, and found a good reason for my call. "Hey, I'm in the mood for coffee and pastries. Just called to see if you know of any good places." Whew, hopefully he bought it. I really was hungry, so it wasn't far from the truth.

"Yeah, there's a place not too far from here. Come on down when you're ready and I'll give you the address." We clicked off.

I planned to check in with mom after breakfast, so I jumped in the shower and did my best to wash off the leftover fuzziness from heavy sleep. Who-knows what herbs and other assorted things Millie gave me to induce such rest and healing, but the pain was a tiny fraction of what it felt like yesterday. After a good cleanup, I got dressed in khakis and a t-shirt then motored downstairs.

I needed some coffee, but the black stuff I saw in the pot downstairs looked and smelled like it had cooked for a few hours. Besides, I'd already asked Ryder if he knew of a good coffee shop. I walked past the dual burner coffee maker, some old news clippings hanging on the wall, and met him in the office.

"Hey, I thought everyone was out enjoying the holiday weekend."

"Would be nice, except we got two in last night," Ryder sounded miffed.

"Oh." I remembered nothing about last night except some details from my dream. "Why did you have to come in today?" It was Saturday of the holiday weekend.

"See this calendar. We use it to divvy up evening, weekend and holiday coverage. It's my weekend to cover family appointments." Ryder pointed to a calendar pinned to the wall. It showed a lovely field of summery flowers, and the name Batesville Casket Company written at the bottom, the kind companies give their clients for the holidays and New Year. Each of the calendar squares had lines or names written in red. It was the same calendar Garrett used when he argued about holiday coverage several weeks ago, and the one mom showed me a few times since we'd been here, so I'd know who to call with questions and business emergencies.

A typical end of day transition at the funeral home went like this: mom and I'd get an intercom call from downstairs, or get asked to come to the office; we'd review the client list; and get a business update before the office closed and everyone, but us, went home. We'd then answer incoming calls from a business phone in the apartment until the office opened up the following morning during weekdays, and for viewings, services, and special appointments on evenings and weekends. Each rundown included a quick bit about contacting them through the night or weekend, but the calendar was there in case anyone forgot. It was also on a server or the cloud, but not everything had gotten hooked-up, yet.

These guys were on call, like doctors, and they were generally consistent, although Bert threw an occasional wrinkle in the calendar plans. I'd caught on to some areas of the business, but wasn't totally clued in on why it was so urgent to hold meetings today. My hesitation must have shown.

"We can't have funerals unless clients or families make funeral arrangements. Since we have some new customers, I'm on the hook to help each family set up the funerals."

We heard a noise. "Sledge and Manny just brought in the second customer this morning, and Garrett's taking care of the other preparations in the back room." Ryder meant Garrett was embalming the bodies. It's what they did to preserve them before viewings, funerals and burials. I'd learned Garrett embalmed bodies in addition to his normal funeral director duties. They hired Bert, a local embalmer they knew well, to help when business got busy. I wasn't surprised Garrett was here, he'd offered to answer the phones, and I took the darn medicine before I asked any questions. Had he been here all night because of me? I felt bad it. Now, Garrett was taking care of Bert's bodies—Bert left Garrett hanging last holiday, and was supposed to make it up this weekend—I wondered what happened to Bert.

"Anyway," Ryder continued. "We can't wait to have the family meeting until Tuesday—while I enjoy my holiday weekend—it would push the funerals further into next week, and bodies don't stay fresh for long."

I winced at the though of ripened bodies, because it's what he implied.

"Oops, didn't mean to gross you out. It's not too bad usually, but we are on a timeline out of respect for the dead and their families."

Just then Sledge and Manny came into the office laughing about something. When Ryder asked what was so funny, Manny spoke up. "I got a joke. Wanna hear it?"

Ryder looked at me then we both looked at Sledge who shrugged. I thought his response meant 'proceed with caution', but before we could say anything, Manny told the joke.

"There are these two funeral directors standing over a full casket prepping a body for burial. One funeral director sees the other tying the dead man's shoes and asks, 'Why are you tying his shoelaces together?' The other director looks at the first and says, 'So that when the Zombie Apocalypse comes, I've got a better chance at getting away.' Hah-hah-hah!" Manny burst out laughing like a hyena and the rest of us laughed just hearing him.

After a pause, Sledge stepped forward and nodded. He was dressed in heavy overalls and big black shoes.

"Boss," he said to Ryder. "Wanted to make sure we settle up before the holiday, if you know what I mean."

Ryder looked around and found a standard white envelope sitting on Hank's desk. He picked it up and handed it to Sledge. "Here you go."

"Thanks," Sledge responded as he peeked inside. "Appreciate the business." He nodded to Ryder then spoke to me. "Got any plans for the weekend?"

"Actually, I'll be here. I'm answering phones while my mom is visiting grandpa." I regretted it as soon as I'd said it.

Manny stepped close to me. "Need any company?"

Garrett pushed through the door, maybe he heard us laughing and wondered what was happening. "Off limits, Manny," Garrett said firmly.

Sledge grabbed Manny by the scruff of his shirt, pulled him backward and gave him a scary look.

"Hey, c'mon, I was just kidding guys." Manny looked at me. "Sorry, didn't mean to disrespect."

My lips tightened into a half smile as I accepted his apology. It still made me uncomfortable to think he knew I was going to be alone here for a couple days.

"It's just you're kinda hot, and all," Manny no sooner go the words out when Sledge slapped him on the back of the head and shoved Manny toward the door.

"Look, he's mostly harmless, just not the sharpest tool in the shed. We'll get out of your hair now. Call us if you need anything," Sledge said trying to recover. Garrett gave a nod and they left. We heard them bickering on their way out the back. Hopefully, Sledge was right and Manny was just awkward, not harmful.

"He may have something with the whole shoe tying thing," Ryder broke the silence. We laughed. "Okay, maybe not, but a little humor every now and then never hurt anybody."

Garrett seemed to loosen up a little, but tension remained in his shoulders even after we started joking about Manny's Zombie Apocalypse.

We talked briefly about the weather before Ryder mentioned the coffee shop. Somehow I offered to pick up coffees for everyone. It was okay though, because Ryder gave me cash to pay for all our goodies, and I really didn't mind helping out. The phone rang and Garrett offered to walk me to my car while Ryder stepped into the back hall to take a phone call.

"It's his bookie." Garrett smiled for the first time since he walked in on Manny's inappropriate comments.

I didn't mind being considered kinda hot, but it wasn't Manny's attention I wanted. Besides, it was intimidating since I barely knew the guy, and he and Sledge came here a lot.

Garrett sensed my uneasiness. "Look, you're safe, he's gone. I'll have a talk with him, and it'll be okay." Muscles tightened in his neck, and I wondered if he really planned to talk to Manny, or do something worse.

When we got outside by my car, Garrett's eyes were trained on me. I didn't think they could get more beautiful, but the sunlight made them glow. I blushed and looked toward the car.

"I mean it. You're safe here." Garrett started to move forward until something stopped him.

"Mattie," Derek said. "I hoped to find you here." He beamed at me then eyed Garrett. There was a brief stare down before I spoke.

"Hi," I responded, eager to break up the testosterone match. "I'm here."

"Good, are you free this weekend?" Derek asked.

"I…um…"

"Actually, she's booked." Garrett answered for me and I'm fairly sure he mumbled 'forever' under his breath.

"I didn't ask you," Derek went beet read. He was noticeably ticked off as spoke to Garrett. "I asked the lady, if she was free this weekend." He did his best to smile at me. "Mattie, are you busy?"

"Actually, I have to work this weekend, so I'm mostly busy."

"Mostly? Are you free for lunch today or tomorrow?" Derek was not going away easily.

"Maybe, can I get back with you on that question?" He seemed nice, and it would be good for me to meet more people, but I was uncomfortable standing in the middle of whatever was going on between them.

"Let me give you my cell number," he said. I pulled out my phone and added his number. "Call me if you want to go out. I could show you how to have a good time in this town. Unlike this guy, with his head stuck in the business, and his—other parts stuck in, what's her name? Bianca? Or maybe the chick from the morgue? I guess it runs in the family, huh Garrett?" Derek crossed a line, and we all knew it. Garrett got up in Derek's face. "Leave. Now." They were obviously worked up, and I got nervous when I saw Garrett's fist curl at his side. Derek grinned. He pulled up my hand and kissed it, then saluted Garrett and left.

I didn't know what to make of the scene. One minute Derek seemed polite and warm, the next he stirred up trouble with Garrett.

When I knew he was out of earshot, I decided to ask Garrett. "What's up with that guy?"

"It's a long story," Garrett said as he opened my car door. "One I promise to tell you, someday, but there's not enough time to get into it now. I've got to work, and you promised coffees. The least you could do for making me stay here all night long answering phones."

I felt a pang of guilt and worry about crossing lines and asking Garrett for too many favors. I stiffened and clicked on my seatbelt. Garrett leaned toward me with the door still open. "I think a coffee run is a pretty fair trade for you."

I studied his face, and was distracted by his lips when he gently moved my chin so my gaze met his. He had my full attention.

"Unless, you want to owe me more favors." He brushed his hand past my cheek and I swallowed hard. "I'd keep a running total for you, Mattie, but someday I'm gonna come collect, and you will make good on your debts." It sounded a heck of a lot like a proposition. While my body may have been eager, my head was confused. Pursuing any kind of relationship outside of business seemed dangerous, and he was probably just being playful, but he sure knew how to tempt a girl. It took a second, or ten, before I could figure out how to respond.

I leaned toward him and smiled seductively. "You can collect anytime you think you can handle it big guy." It caught him by surprise, so I grabbed for the door. He backed up so I could close it. The key turned and the engine revved. I flipped my hair, winked at him and left to get coffee. My heart pounded in my chest, I might want to avoid caffeine. Pastries. They'd be enough to balance everything out. My smile widened because the thought of a speechless Garrett pleased me.

CHAPTER 10

A wave of freshly brewed coffee hit me when I walked into the shop. There's nothing like that smell. It'd been an interesting night, and this morning was shaping up to be just as interesting.

One barista took orders at the register while another made coffee. The grinder sounded above the low chatter of people. A young couple in the corner looked cozy together, a businessman worked on his laptop while three older women in spandex stood ahead of me. The ladies took turns ordering nonfat mochas, scones, and a Soy Chai. I ordered two large coffees, a regular latte, and three slices of coffee cake.

When I got the order, I sugared up my drink and hit the road. The barista gave me a cup carrier, but I was too nervous it might tip over in the car, so I put two coffees in cup holders and the third between my legs then drove at a snail's pace back to the parlor.

Ryder was in the middle of meeting a family and Garrett had nearly finished his job in the back room when I returned.

I put one coffee and a pastry bag on Ryder's desk and another coffee and pastry bag on Garrett's. Curious to try out Garrett's chair, I sat my latte and coffee cake on his desk and plopped down. It rotated and rocked and did all sorts of cool things. When I went to adjust the height, it slammed me to the lowest setting, just as Garrett walked into the office.

"You don't do well with hydraulic things do you?" He laughed. He'd nailed it because the exact same thing happened the last time I sat in Ryder's chair.

"I just wanted to see what it could do."

Garrett showed me how to use it correctly. Then he grabbed his stuff and sat across from me at Hank's desk. I watched as he inhaled the coffee cake and took a few swigs of hot coffee. He seemed ready to talk after all that, so I asked him how things went overnight. We talked a few minutes, he told me everything went fine and tried to make me feel better by saying he would have been here through the night anyway. He could have waited to work on the bodies until today, but needed to get finished early to make it to an important appointment this afternoon.

The thought of him leaving made me a little sad, but I wasn't really sure where things stood between us. There was an attraction, sure, but we had business and families depending on us not to screw things up. A relationship seemed impossible. I couldn't risk getting mom fired and both of us kicked out, and he couldn't risk getting fired and kicked out by Grandpa Stanley either.

"How are you doing today?"

"I slept good, had a crazy dreams, but I feel pretty good considering yesterday's surprise attack." My brain flashed back to the guy lifting me off the ground and nearly crushing me. I shuddered.

"That's what I wanted to talk to you about."

"I told you everything I could remember."

"I know. It's time to get ready."

"Ready for what?" I wondered if it was related to working the phones this weekend. Maybe he was ready to leave and wanted to give me the updates I missed last night.

"Time to hit the gym. Why don't you change into something more comfortable and meet me back here in fifteen."

Surprise and maybe even fear crossed my face. I figured he just wanted to talk about Chloe's case or grill me some more about what happened yesterday while he did push-ups, pull-ups, and squats holding thousand pound weights, or whatever guys did at the gym. I shrugged and left to change.

Once I got upstairs and locked the door, it didn't take me long to freak out. What would I wear? Why was he taking me to the gym? What did he expect me to do? If it involved pull-ups, I was doomed. I'd missed doing laundry last week, because I hated going into the basement and traipsing up and down stairs a bunch of times to switch loads. My closet offered really limited options: no gym-worthy spandex, and a few other potentials that were either too baggy, or had holes. I found a pair of pink lounge pants, basically my pjs, but they fit and were flexible. I put on a sporty tank, layered a t-shirt over it then pulled on socks and tennis shoes. The look didn't convey hardcore gym rat, but it should get me through the front door alongside Mr. Universe. The ponytail was last. I grabbed my keys and ID case then locked up and ran down the stairs to meet up with Garrett. Maybe he's Superman because he was already changed and ready to go.

"Ready for a workout?"

It really was time to hit the gym. *Oh boy!*

"You'll see." We sped away in the Maserati. We traveled less than ten minutes. Long enough for my stomach to churn acid thinking about hitting the gym with a guy who looked like he spent every day working out. I'd worked out before, but something bugged me about not knowing what to expect at his gym.

Only it was unlike any gym I'd ever seen. We parked by an unmarked industrial building off of the main road. There were a few other cars and trucks in the lot, most of them looked just as nice as Garrett's—Porsche, Land Rover, even a Ferrari.

Garrett waved a card across a reader and the door unlocked. We entered a darkly lit nondescript hallway then turned right to head further inside the building. A neon green and black snakehead stuck its tongue out at us from behind the reception area. The main desk was wrapped in black suede-like material, and the glass top was up-lit with green and yellow neon lights. The receptionist was not there at the time, maybe because it was lunch, or maybe the snake ate her. I hesitated. Garrett reached for my hand and pulled me further into the lair.

Garrett stopped at the second door and opened it for me to enter. As we walked across the gym there were several guys training. Seriously training.

"Is that guy holding a gun?" I whispered.

"Yes, but the short guy standing with him is about to take it away." Sure enough, the short guy took the gun in a couple swift moves.

"Wow."

"Yeah."

"Are these guys training for anything in particular?"

"Life after service. I know plenty of guys who served. All of us came back changed. Some are still wound so tight they can't find peace unless they remain trained and ready for anything—prepared to defend themselves and their families against all enemies. It's how they cope. Many are still fighting, even though the war is supposed to be over."

"Really?"

"Yeah. Pros and mercs come here to train."

I gulped thinking of mercenaries running around our town.

"Normally, I go to a different place, but too many prying eyes there tonight."

Was he worried about being seen with me? "Do you think they'd tell your grandpa?"

"I don't want to take the chance right now. He might use it to make a point. Not worth the chance."

It was polite of Garrett to be concerned. If his grandpa was trying to give us trouble like he seemed to do with everyone else, I should be more careful, too.

We wound our way through the maze until we reached a dark hall. There were no windows on any of the walls as far as I could tell. It felt very private and I wondered what happened in rooms with no windows. Just about then I heard a pop and jumped.

"Easy."

We went further inside the building. The pop turned to bang and I stopped moving. When he looked to see why I wasn't moving, he saw the fear on my face.

"This is a turnkey training facility," he said, like it meant something to me.

My feet didn't move. I just shrugged.

"This is a full-service training facility. They have rooms for hand-to-hand, and a few areas laid out for munitions training."

I knew he meant guns, and by the sound of the 'munitions' we heard, probably very big ones. His military training showed in his stance and his word choice. I wondered what he was trained to do, and what he must have had to do to serve our country. More loud noises sounded off, and he pushed me to get moving again, this time I walked faster. I'd ask questions another time, right now we needed to get where we were going, hopefully far away from here.

It only took a couple turns for the bulk of the gunshots to fade into popping noises again. Garrett stopped at a door, used his key card again, and walked inside. I followed as he turned on the light and closed the door. It was just the two of us. He put his hands on my shoulders. A mixture of excitement and fear shot through me like electricity.

"Relax. You need to take a few breaths and get ready to learn."

Right, training. The problems facing us brought my anxiety back. I tried to shake them off before we started.

"What exactly are we doing here?"

He had a serious look on his face I couldn't figure out. I had a bad feeling.

"I'm going to teach you self defense."

My stomach flip-flopped. *Was he kidding?* Nope. He cocked his head and directed me to stand opposite him. I didn't move. My feet wouldn't budge.

"Mattie, you were threatened by a lunatic in broad daylight. You have to take this seriously."

Garrett took it seriously enough for both of us. But, it was Saturday, and I had nothing better to do. Speaking of Saturday, I thought he had plans. Were these his plans? When did he decide to bring me here? I shrugged it off then got into place and waited for his instructions. I watched as he moved. He wore a black tee with grey sweatpants and looked prepared. My pink pants and pussycat top made me look like an amateur.

Garrett got into place to teach me whatever self-defense moves he thought might help an uncoordinated wimp like me defeat a crazed lunatic I'd somehow managed to piss off. This ought to be good.

"What do you know about self-defense?"

"It can be used to ward off an attacker?"

"Good." Next, he set his legs slightly apart and pulled his arms up as if he was going to launch into fight mode.

"Are you kidding about this?" I asked in disbelief. Not exactly what I hoped we'd be doing when we were alone.

"Look, it's not a question of if, but when. He's coming for you and you need to be prepared. You need to learn close quarters combat." Garrett paused. Probably to make sure it registered.

He is totally serious. My thoughts ran wild. We're here, together. Just us. And Garrett wanted to teach me close quarters combat because I went an angered some guy who had no idea hurting people was a bad thing. My attacker must be crazy and desperate. I managed to get in his way.

Garrett whistled and waved his arm in from of my face and pulled me out of my trance. "Are you with me Mattie?"

"I'm...uh...I'm here."

"I need you to pay attention because your life depends on it. Are you ready?"

"I'm with you, but I'm telling you now, you've got your work cut out for you." And he did, because I hadn't totally mastered the whole balance thing. I'm a certified klutz. But, a determined klutz, which is a dangerous combo.

"First, you need to learn how to stand."

I looked at my legs and noted I was already standing.

"You've got to work on your fighting stance. So you're prepared to defend an attack, or fight."

I swallowed hard.

"You're right-handed, is that correct?"

"Um, yes?" What did it matter?

"You are right side dominant. So, stand with your left leg, the non-dominant leg, forward. Let the heel of your back leg come off the ground a little. This will help keep you balanced and ready to move. Tuck your chin down, lift up your arms, and bend your elbows. Hold your hands out about 8-10 inches where you can use them to grab weapons or fight."

No way I'd get all that right.

"You're not very big or powerful, so you need to learn to parry a strike."

"What?"

"Some mercs call it hand to hand. A few might describe it as fighting in a phone booth—up close and personal."

"Mercs? Personal? What's happening?" My legs felt wobbly. I started to go down, but Garrett held me up.

"Mattie, get a grip. You can do this. I've seen your determination, and stubbornness first-hand."

I stood there dazed and confused.

"Sorry for the lingo, sometimes it slips out. Mercs are mercenaries, and with our guy it's definitely personal, so he'll try to catch you off-guard. You need to prepare to fight this guy one-on-one. Any situation at any time. That's why I want to teach you Krav Maga."

"Krav-ma-what?"

"Krav Maga. It's a type of self-defense used by Israeli commandos."

"Commandos? You think you can turn this—" I waved my hand across my frame to indicate the lack of muscles, "into a commando?"

Garrett laughed. "Mattie, I'm not trying to turn you into a commando. I'm just trying to teach you some techniques for defending an attack. This kind of defense is helpful for anyone who needs to get out of a bad situation. The military and police use it. Heck, some war-torn regions even teach these moves to little kids. I think you can handle this."

Great, kids do this, now I felt like a total wimp. It's sad any child has to become skilled at fighting to survive. I figured I should give it a try and learn some moves to fend off my one, silly, crazed lunatic. "Okay, I'm ready." I swallowed hard enough you could hear it.

"Good. Now, I want you to stand here." Garrett came in close, really close, and positioned me across from him. I inhaled his warm scent and drifted off. He said something else, but I was way too lost in thought to hear what it was.

I wondered what he was thinking. I wondered if he thought about me. Was he as lost as I felt? Did he know my heart raced being in the same room as him? Was love supposed to be like this? Did he have any clue how much I wanted him to kiss me? I really wanted to know what it felt like to kiss him.

Wait...

Slam!

What happened? How did I end up on the floor? Was this part of the lesson? Why did my back hurt?

Garrett stood over me and breathed as hard as I did. It felt warm and a little muggy in the room. I wondered if that's why we're both breathing so hard. My heart wanted to jump from my chest. He loosened his hold on my arm, but lowered himself until his face was close enough I felt his breath on my lips. He moved his arms around my back, grasped my waist, and slowly lifted me. With his face still dangerously close, I felt when his lips gently brushed by my ear. "Are you okay?"

"I...I'm fine. Just not coordinated enough to handle your moves yet." I was weak, but tried to make light of the situation. He looked a little confused. "What I mean is I'm not quite ready for the Ultimate

Fighting Championship."

Garrett cracked a smile and pulled my hand to his chest. It felt like it belonged there. "I don't want to hurt you." His expression was eager and intense. His muscles were taught. I felt the hardness through his shirt. He looked ready to pounce. Did it mean he was going to pounce on me? Oh, I hoped so. I looked into those big blue eyes then got distracted by his mouth. Waiting felt like agony. But, I wasn't moving. I couldn't. I stayed there, drawn to his heat. He kept his hand around my waist and my breathing pattern matched his. I wanted to lean in, but I was terrified he'd pull away. It would have devastated me. I just wanted to be close to him right now. He looked at me as if he was figuring something out. Like he wasn't sure what to make of me. Was I sweating too much? Did I smell? What was he thinking?

"Are you ready to go again?" He helped me up and moved away.

Darn it! I put my hand up to my hair and pushed back some loose strands. Enough of all this, it was time to get serious. "Yes." I brushed myself off and asked him to repeat the instructions.

"Stand across from me. I'm going to come straight at you. As soon as you see me move, take a step forward."

"Forward?"

"Yes. You want to close the gap between us. Once you step forward, and I'm within arms-reach, pretend to thrust the heel of your hand upward as hard as you can into my nose." Garrett put up his finger to say hold on. "Pretend like you mean it, but you don't actually want to do it. Okay? Otherwise, you'll be driving me to the hospital."

I had serious doubts about how things might go down. Hopefully, he had good reflexes just in case my pretend thrust actually made some kind of contact.

When he came forward, I let him get too close and couldn't get my hand up in time. My timing improved on the second and third tries.

"Good," Garrett said. "Let's continue until you're comfortable with it." We practiced a few more times then moved on to a new skill.

"The next one has more steps, but it shouldn't take you long to learn." At least one of us was confident in my abilities. "Stand over there. This time I'll grab at your shoulders. When I do, bring your arms up through the middle then back down over mine and use them to break my hold. Like this." He showed me what seemed like a simple, but effective move and indicated he was ready. I nodded then Garrett came toward me. He grabbed my shoulders so fast it shocked me. I got my arms tangled up and he pinned me from there. We stopped while he showed me what he wanted me to do and we tried it again.

Garrett came at me, I put up my hands. He got my shoulders then I extended my arms up and over to break his hold. It worked!

"I think you got it."

Learning these defensive moves made me think I might have a chance if the bad guy came after me.

"Thanks."

"No problem. I'm just trying to make sure bad things don't happen to you."

My energy and enthusiasm surged. I had a thousand questions for him. I needed to learn more, but I wanted to understand why he was doing me all these favors. It would be a bonus to find out about the rivalry between the families, what exactly his deal with Bianca was, and if there was any chance...

"Are you ready for the next one?" Garrett's voice brought me back out of my head.

"Sure." The answers would come, I told myself, and prepared for the next skill.

"This one takes a little more coordination," he paused and smiled to himself. "So it might take some time."

Ha! If it required coordination, it might take weeks, or years. I gave Garrett the floor. He planned to come after me from behind, like my attacker, and face me against a wall. He continued by explaining how I was supposed to use my ninja skills (my words, not his), to climb the wall—while being held from behind—flip over him and escape.

"Seriously?"

"Let's just try it okay?" We moved over to a wall. He walked behind me and asked if I was ready. I eyed him over my shoulder for a second and nodded for him to start, then turned my attention to the wall ahead and waited.

Something strange happened when he grabbed me. He had control, all I saw was wall—it was panic, the same reaction I had to my assailant. This time I didn't try to ask him if he wanted my bag, I just started kicking and screaming. As loud as I could. "No! Get off me! Let me go!" I cried.

Garrett put me down and turned me toward him. "Mattie, it's okay." He spoke, but I couldn't hear him because I was louder.

"Leave me alone!" I yelled some more.

"Mattie! It's me!" This time loud enough I could hear him over my own voice.

"Please! Leave me alone." I collapsed onto the floor and started to hyperventilate. Garrett got down next to me and held me gently. I looked at him, clutched his arms, and buried my face in his chest. Recognition and relief overcame me. We stayed there until I calmed down.

When I started to move, he stood and helped me get up on my feet. "It's me," he said softly. "Are you feeling okay?"

I looked at Garrett then smiled as I nodded to let him know everything was normal. At least as normal as it could be at this point. "I don't know what happened."

"You finally let go of the emotions you held back from the attack—fear, anger, pain—they all just came to the surface. It's actually a good thing."

"How can it be good? I just freaked out and collapsed onto the floor." I didn't mean to sound defensive, but might have.

"You needed to deal with your feelings. The longer you bottle it up, the worse it gets. I speak from experience."

It caught me off-guard. He seemed like a guy who had things pretty much in order. What would he know about bottled up feelings?

"I've had my share of setbacks, and it's okay to shrug most of them off and keep going. Something as big as a threat to your life, though, you can't ignore. You have to admit how it made you feel then move forward." What he said sounded smart. But, it still took me a minute to figure out what really bothered me.

"Okay, it made me feel really scared and vulnerable." There, I'd said it. "What can I do about it now?"

"You can start by leaving any feelings of guilt behind. You are not responsible for what happened, the bad guy is. Next, you can let me help you move past it." I believed he meant it.

"How do we do that?"

"We practice some more, and head home to discuss what I found out from Cal today."

"Why didn't you tell me sooner?"

"I needed you focused on training, for your own good."

"My own good?"

"Your body may have felt better after Millie's magic serum and a good night's rest, but you needed to deal with the emotional pain that guy caused you. I thought bringing you here would make you feel safe and strong enough to let go."

"You brought me here to break down?" I got mad and backed away.

"No, I brought you here to help you feel strong and in control again."

"Did you just see me in a puddle on the floor? I don't think it worked. Besides, what does it matter to you?" I was still deciding how mad I wanted to be at Garrett.

"What does it matter?" He looked at me in disbelief. "I care," he stopped and blew out a breath. I wondered what he meant by care, and why he actually said it. Were we about to get into full-on confessional mode here? "Can't you tell?" Now he sounded mad.

"I guess. I mean, yes. I appreciate all you've done to help mom and me since we moved in, and maybe I should have thanked you sooner."

"I'm not fishing for a thank you, although, it's nice to hear. I care about what happens to you." He moved close enough I wondered if he was going to kiss me. But, he hesitated. It confused me. "It's important you understand how much I care." Maybe he cared, or maybe he just liked me as a friend, I was too drained to think about it.

"It's nice to know someone cares." It felt weird when I said it.

"Look, you don't sound like you want to talk about this right now. Let's just get out of here and head back to the parlor. I can explain what Cal told me, and you can decide what you want to do." Garrett picked up a gym bag, and signaled for me to head out. What didn't I want to talk about; being attacked, being friends, or just being confused? Was this all in my head?

We left without incident, except I jumped because we heard gunfire on our way out. It sounded like the bullets would come through the walls, so we moved faster.

When we got to the car, he opened the door for me, even if there was still some tension between us. We drove through the rough streets in silence and headed back to the funeral home.

"I'm sorry, Mattie."

"You don't need to apologize. I know you were just trying to help." I'd softened up a little bit, too. Maybe it had something to do with putting distance between us and fight club. If he meant to help me regain some control by going there, it worked. Although, it wasn't much, it was a start. "What happened back there?" I asked.

"I don't know," Garrett admitted. "There are some things we need to discuss before things go any further." His serious tone startled me.

"Did I do something?"

"No, why do you say that?"

"I don't know. I'm confused about all this."

"Me too. Look, my car may not be the best place to talk about this, but it's private."

"Is this about Chloe?"

"Some of it." Garrett's eyes were forward, but he glanced at me briefly then told me everything. "When I examined Chloe, I found a couple things."

"Besides the needle mark?"

"Yes. It looked like a hasty job determining cause of death. She had some bruising, faint scratches, and the needle mark didn't have a bulls-eye on it, but it shouldn't have been missed in the exam."

"Why didn't you tell me this yesterday?"

"I wasn't sure it was relevant."

"Relevant?" I had anger on my lips. "Why didn't you think it was relevant? I'd say anything that has to do with the murder of a friend should be considered relevant!"

"I guess it was just hard for me to believe there could have been any wrongdoing." Garrett sounded hurt. "I wanted to ask some questions on my own before I started pointing fingers."

"And what did you find out?"

"Something big is going on, Mattie."

"Bigger than a fake suicide?"

"Yes."

"Like what?"

"Like the cover-up of a fake suicide." He stopped at a traffic light and looked at me intently.

"What? Why?" I couldn't believe it. "Who would do that? I'm having a hard enough time understanding why someone would want Chloe dead, much less kill her, and now, you're telling me someone is trying to hide the murder?"

"I think so." The car started moving again.

"How do you know?"

"I know the examiner. She wouldn't have made these mistakes." He made a turn and we were nearing the funeral home.

"What if she was having a really bad day?" Anyone can have them. I'd been having more than my share lately, and this news didn't help today's outlook either.

"She still should have caught these things. We're going to find out what happened when we talk to her in person."

"We?"

"Yes. I spoke with her over the phone. She tried to give me a story about botched paperwork, but I didn't believe her. I want to ask her in person, to see if she'll lie to my face, and I need you to be there."

"I'll go because I want answers as much as anybody, but why do you need me there?"

"Because we have a history." Garrett gave me a quick glance before his eyes moved back to the road. "I don't know how I'll react if she lies again." As his words escaped, they weighed like storm clouds.

"Is she the woman Cal mentioned yesterday? The one he didn't trust?"

"Yes," Garrett sighed. He needed me there, even though I wasn't sure I wanted to see him in the same room with his old girlfriend who might upset him by lying to his face. Made more complicated because I'd brought the case to him, not the other way around.

I blew out a breath. "When do we see her?"

"3 o'clock. It gives us time to change, eat lunch, and come up with a plan."

"Do we need a plan?"

"Afraid so." He pulled into the driveway and groaned.

"What is it, Garrett?"

"Grandpa's here."

"Ugh, you can pull over to my side of the parking lot, if you want to drop me off." I wasn't happy about it, but it was better to sneak in quietly than to let Grandpa Stanley think we'd been up to something other than training.

"No, I won't. You don't need to worry about it. Just let me do the talking."

I fidgeted with my hair then looked in the mirror. My pink flushed cheeks and messy hair would definitely give Grandpa Stanley the wrong idea. Hopefully, Garrett had an idea for how to play this. If things went south, I planned to ask Millie for some kind of potion to make Grandpa Stanley forget whatever happened.

"Look, before we go in there and get sidetracked, I want you to know one other thing Cal told me." He looked intense. "When they went through Chloe's things, they found a business card for some lawyer named Ted Oxley. There was a number scribbled on the back of it. Cal said he'd look into it, but didn't know if he could get to it today."

It couldn't have been a coincidence she had his card. We needed to figure out if he knew more than he'd admitted to me, and we needed to find the owner of number on the back of Oxley's card. Maybe the person had some idea of who killed Chloe and why.

"She worked with Ted Oxley. I paid him a visit after we found out Chloe was dead."

"Why didn't you say anything?"

"I didn't think it was relevant," I said it the same way Garrett had.

"Not relevant, huh?" I think we both believed we did what was best at the time. If we were going to find the truth out about Chloe's murder, we needed to be honest about everything.

"I thought so, at first. Now, I'm not sure. He told me they worked a small case together, but he seemed more abrasive than I remembered. Maybe he's hiding something."

"Everybody's hiding something."

"Well, what he said and how he said it didn't seem significant, but circumstances have changed since then."

"We can look into him, after we see what's going on here." Garrett helped me out of the car. We got inside the door and headed toward the office. I stopped. He signaled for me to get moving.

"Unh-unh. No. Can't do it." I shook my head.

Garrett reached for my hand and pulled me reluctantly to the door then wham! Garrett bumped into his grandpa.

"Umph, watch it," the dark voice said. Grandpa Stanley. He quickly turned away from us and stuffed a paper in his jacket. I wondered if Stanley was ever in a good mood.

"Better watch your step." Stanley turned back and eyed Garrett over his glasses. He must have been reading whatever paper he tucked away before we came.

"What's that supposed to mean?" It sounded harsh, but I knew where it came from. Besides, from what I'd seen and heard, Grandpa Stanley had a bad habit of putting people on edge.

"You know what it means," Stanley responded, then noticed me staring at the paper sticking out of his jacket pocket. He shoved it down further. "Hello, Mattie," his voice sounded silky sweet when he spoke to me, like I was an old friend. "How are you ladies getting along up there?" It was really strange to hear him sound so nice.

"We're doing fine, thanks," I responded carefully.

"Glad to hear it. You let us know if there's anything you need." Stanley gave me a polite nod and smile.

"Will do. Thanks for everything." It didn't matter how nice Stanley sounded, there was something about him that made me suspicious. I turned to see Garrett, and he told me to head upstairs. Even though we needed to talk about strategy before heading to the Coroner's Office, this seemed like a good time to leave the two of them alone.

Before I got all the way down the hallway, I heard them get into something heated. I guess Grandpa Stanley's good mood had faded. Garrett was a grown man and he could handle himself, so I stepped up the pace until I reached the apartment door. The air on the landing felt warm and stale, but cool relief hit me when I walked inside.

The locks clicked into place. I headed straight for the bedroom. I'd find some clothes, freshen up, and check in with mom and Jos while I waited for Garrett to give me the all-clear signal. Whatever we wanted to accomplish had to happen while Ryder, or someone else, was around to man the phones. So, I needed to be ready for just about anything.

Late-summer heat had baked everything around us the past few days, but rain was headed our way, so I planned for sun and rain and changed into a sporty skirt, tank and tennis shoes—because walking in drenched sandals, with mushy wet feet and squeaking noises, annoyed me.

I fixed up my ponytail since the humidity was high, and there was no sense trying to compete with Mother Nature. Once I felt somewhat put together again, I grabbed a glass of lemonade and flopped on the couch. The window air conditioner kicked on and drowned out the traffic noise. Pretty soon I relaxed. The outside air smelled slightly damp—maybe the weather forecasters were right about the rain.

I sat the glass down on a photo coaster sitting on the coffee table. It was a photo of mom and me. It reminded me to check-in. There wasn't an answer, so I left a message telling her to enjoy her visit and to give everyone my love. They were probably eating lunch. The thought of food made my stomach growl.

Jos texted me about getting together once she returned from her regularly scheduled mandatory family visit. She sent a series of emoji—everything from annoyed to crying faces—at least she got to visit her family. I felt stuck at work, and stuck on what to do about Chloe's death. Even though we hadn't spoken until very recently, I felt guilty for not making the effort to stay in touch with Chloe after college. Maybe if I had kept in touch, or texted her sooner, or arrived at our meeting earlier, she would still be alive. I started to go down the rabbit hole and needed to stop.

I sent back some heart and family emojis with a smiley face ☺. Jos responded with a smiley face ☺ and a martini glass Y indicating she was ready to find her happy place. I sent her a clock and asked if it wasn't a little early for drinking. She responded with, 'it's five o'clock somewhere'. I knew she was kidding, there was no way she'd risk getting caught drinking this early, so I texted 'Cheers!' right back to her. We signed off. I stared out the window for a few minutes and watched as clouds rolled in and nearly swallowed the sky.

CHAPTER 11

I saw a flash of light and returned to the green field of my previous dream. The light of day was dim, maybe fading into night. I could just make out the same young girl in her dress as I had before. This time we stood nearer together. Her mouth moved, but I couldn't hear her, so I inched closer.

Next to her, an old native man crouched over something on the ground. I watched as he pulled a small brown satchel off his belt. The man's calloused fingers untied a leather strap that held the bag closed. He said a few words, but I couldn't hear much because the wind whistling past us.

The old man said something else then reached inside the satchel and pulled out a handful of a reddish-orange powder. He began chanting and let the dust fall from his hands to the ground. The wind blew it around, but I looked down to where he wanted it to land, and saw a body. The person was unrecognizable. I watched as the powder cover the body. The old man rubbed his hands together. More dust fell and stained the grave.

The girl in the dress caught my attention. She tried to tell me something. I still couldn't hear because of something now buzzing in my ear, but watched as she mouthed the same thing over and over. I stepped toward her again—was it one, or won, no. Then a switch flipped off the buzz and I could hear.

"Run. Run. RUN!" She screamed at me. I turned to see what she wanted me to run from and everything went black.

BEEP! BEEP! "Hello?" The intercom sounded distant. BEEP!

"Mattie, are you there?" Garrett's voice pulled me out of the dream world. I must have drifted off a bit.

"Yes." It felt like my body was nailed to the couch. It took me a minute to move and pick up the phone.

"Stanley's gone, and Ryder's covering. Come on down, we'll grab lunch, and review the plan."

"I thought we didn't have a plan."

"We don't," he admitted. "But we've got a little bit of time to make something up before the meeting."

"Sounds good. I'll lock up and meet you downstairs." I checked outside. The sky had turned grey green, so I grabbed a jacket and an umbrella, just in case. Then padded downstairs, determined to get some answers about Chloe's murder.

We agreed to grab a quick lunch so we could spend some time reviewing the information we had and preparing questions. The problem is, I'm short on cash and bills don't pay themselves. Wouldn't that be nice? Before I could say much of anything, about lunch or questions and murders, Garrett pulled up a chair for me and asked me to sit.

"Can you help me with something?"

"Sure, I guess," I answered him.

"I planned on picking up lunch, but we have some paperwork to submit and Ryder is tied up right now. It isn't a job requirement, the pay isn't great, but it would really help us out. Would you be interested?"

Would I be interested? In my head it sounded desperate and sarcastic. "Of course," I said in a normal voice. "What do you need me to do?" I figured they'd give me some mundane job like stapling papers, checking e-mails, or making coffee.

Turns out the guys hate writing obituaries. Obits are informational paragraphs, sometimes stories, about a person who died. They typically include the deceased's name, a bit about their family, what type of services would be held, along with the where and when. They're needed for practically everybody who comes through here. If I worked it right, this could turn into a nice side-job.

The problem was I had no idea how to write, format or even submit an obit. Garrett agreed to teach me. I grabbed some paper and a pen to take notes. He handed me a newspaper with some obits circled in red. He gave me a slip of paper with a website and login information, and some paperwork for Harvey Glump.

I eyed Garrett because he knows this one wasn't going to be easy.

Harvey Glump came in with his wife a few weeks ago to make a down payment on his funeral in advance. He was a real jerk to his wife; criticized the way she walked, corrected nearly every comment she made, and pushed her when she didn't move fast enough out the door.

The only reason I knew it was because mom and I happened to be waiting for a tour of the casket room at the time. Hank asked us to wait in the parlor next to the office up front, so we heard a lot of what he said. Afterward, Hank told us Glump was the guy on the news connected to a real estate scam. Glump had 'allegedly' conned a bunch of old folks to invest in a Florida retirement community with the promise of timeshares in winter and profits from managed rentals the rest of the year. I could see how it might be an easy sell; especially since we lived in the snow and ice belt.

Maybe Glump got what was coming to him, or maybe he was innocent, but he seemed like a jerk. Like Tab thirty years from now. Ok, it was harsh, but I did not like mean people.

"How much does this pay?" I wondered if it was worth it.

"We can negotiate the fee, but I will make it worth your while." He knew he had me hooked. "I'm heading out. Will bring back food, then we can go over some paperwork to prep for our meeting."

"Okay. I'm pretty sure I'll need sustenance if I'm going to negotiate with you, so bring me one of whatever you're having and a soda."

He left. I sat there looking at Harvey Glump's file. What should one write about a person they didn't know, and certainly didn't like? I read a few of the obits in the paper and scanned a couple more on the computer—you can look up everything online these days. After reading several examples, I stared at a flashing cursor.

In some article archived in my brain, I'd read that the best way to tackle a blank page was to just let it rip—write anything and everything down and edit afterwards.

Here goes: Harvey Glump. He was a real jackass to his wife, rumors around town said he swindled old people out of their life savings in a fake real estate deal, and probably no one will miss him much. It was a rough draft, but it had potential.

Second draft: Harvey Glump lived a corrupt life. He stole from the elderly, treated wife poorly, and was an all around jerk. His death will be celebrated Tuesday from 6-8 pm with a Mass and party to follow Wednesday at 10 am. Donations to the people he swindled and his poor wife for enduring 35 years of his crap will be accepted in plain envelopes anytime between now and Thursday.

There, I felt better already. Too bad I couldn't use any of it. Although it was creative, I needed to start over. This was harder than it appeared. I wondered if a drink would help.

No one was around. I thought about raiding the desks for a bottle of something mind-altering, then decided against it. I didn't need a shot of whiskey to do this. Harvey Glump may have been a tool, but he was dead. No sense in putting his wife through any more heartache. Maybe Glump was having a bad day when we saw him. Maybe a bad year. I shouldn't judge. He'd meet his maker, good or evil, and get back what he gave. The fact remained: I needed money. They needed an obit. Time for a new approach.

Stick with the script. Include the basics: name, age, surviving family members, and details of the service.

Harvey Glump was a walking, breathing person—a good start, I thought. Then my fingers flew across the keys writing stuff about a guy I never knew. After inserting some details about his family, and his businesses I'd finished. That ought to do it. Where's the next one? I was ready for more. *Show me the money!*

CHAPTER 12

Garrett walked in with lunch. Good thing I didn't scream out loud or try to jump up on the desk. I smiled, made a mental note to ask for more obit work and got ready for lunch.

We laid out our sandwiches and split a bag of chips. Garrett told me it was some kind of tuna with peppers and I turned up my nose. There was no way I was going to eat it, except I was really hungry, and I didn't want to insult the guy who provided the meal. So, I picked up one of the triangles bursting with tuna, mayo and peppers, and nibbled on the end. It was surprisingly good.

While we ate, Garrett told me about his history with the pathologist we were meeting at the Coroner's office.

"I met Tess in college. We both wanted to work in medicine. But we'd been raised around family businesses. The expectation was for us to follow our parents' footsteps—I'd become a Funeral Director, and Tess was supposed to become a Pharmacist. Only Tess had other ideas." He paused to take a bite.

"What happened?"

"Tess and her family had a falling out when she informed them of her interest in Forensics. Her father planned to have her take over a small chain of independent pharmacies when he retired, and if she went into Forensics, she couldn't take over and he couldn't retire on schedule. He got mad. Apparently, mad enough he stopped funding school."

Garrett had a faraway look in his eyes for a moment. "We were dating at the time, so I offered to let her move in with me while she sorted out her family issues. Things got serious. Then Tess took a job to help pay for school. The problem was her employer was a mobster. I asked her to quit. Tess insisted it was legal, and refused."

Whoever the mob guy was, and whatever work he had Tess doing must have been pretty bad if Garrett insisted she stop. They broke up over it. I could tell she meant a lot to him, and the way things ended was rough. This meeting could get messy.

We talked it over. Since we didn't want their past to cause problems, we decided to take this approach: Garrett would explain that I brought Chloe's case to him, and I'd explain the reasons I did. We'd ask questions about the exam Tess performed as politely as possible. If I had trouble, Garrett could back me up and diffuse Tess, if needed. He didn't think she'd react as badly to me asking questions as a concerned friend, as she might react if he came out and accused her of missing something important. We agreed to the strategy then cleaned up our sandwich wrappers and drinks before we left.

The atmosphere was so dense sweat beaded up on my skin as soon as we walked outside. Thankfully, Garrett's Maserati was right outside. He opened my door and let me in before he walked around and got in the driver's seat. He was polite and sweet as well as handsome, and I liked that he opened doors for me.

The new car smell, and the rumble of the engine followed by the blast of A/C made me want to stay there all day. Sitting next to Garrett didn't hurt either. His strong hands steered through turns and I watched his sharp facial expressions when one guy tried to cut us off. All of it changed as we came to a stop outside the Coroner's Office. He looked glum.

Our plan to finesse information out of Tess better work. The sooner we got out of here, the better.

We checked in at the front and were issued Visitor IDs. We swiped the badges under a red scanner until the light turned green, and we were cleared. I followed Garrett through a turnstile and down a corridor. He looked at me and tried to smile as we approached the conference room. I smiled back and hoped for the best.

Garrett knocked, even though the door was open. A woman in her thirties sat behind a desk eyeing a monitor. She finished typing something, clicked the screen and turned her attention to us. When she stood I noticed she was a couple inches taller than me, with tan skin and striking brown eyes. She wore a grey power suit, which looked mostly business-like. But I wondered about the revealing blouse and black stilettos. Her rich, warm perfume floated near us. The twisted up hair, dangling earrings and expensive manicure looked out of place at the morgue. Was this all a seductive show for Garrett? She extended her hand and let it linger in his. "It's been a while, Garrett." She looked perfect.

"Sure has." He responded with quick words and one firm shake before he broke free.

"And this is?" She turned and looked me over.

"Mattie." I shook her hand.

"Hello, Mattie. You can call me Tess. Would you like to see our research library?"

"Maybe another time." We needed to get to the point and get out.

"I like to offer it as a courtesy, although not many people take me up on it. Usually it's limited to students interested in forensics. Anyway, we've got some remodeling projects going on, so there's not a whole lot you can see." She signaled us to sit. "Garrett tells me you are looking into a friend's death. I'm sorry for your loss. How can I help?"

It was weird to be in the room with both of them, knowing personal details about their relationship. It was also awkward because Garrett had already asked Tess about Chloe, but he wasn't satisfied with the answers he got, so we were here to investigate. He sat stiffly and stayed quiet while we discussed Chloe.

"I wonder if you can help us answer some questions about the way she died." I used my polite voice.

"I'll do my best," Tess said, and offered a genuine smile. "Why don't you tell me a little bit more about your friend?" She appeared sympathetic to my case even though I was a stranger. Perhaps, she was doing this as a favor for an old flame, or she could have had other reasons, it didn't matter. This was our chance to find out more about the way Chloe was killed.

"Well, she lived in the area for several years. We went to school together and she just started her law career."

Tess leaned forward and I got a closer look at her face. Her complexion looked nearly perfect—uniformly tan, slight blush on the cheeks, and deep red lips. Either she was gifted with good looks, or she worked very hard to look polished for our meeting. I could see how Garrett could have been attracted to her. I studied the woman he'd once loved, took a heavy breath, and explained Chloe's situation.

"When my friend was found," I did my best to sound informational, "there was a bottle of prescription pills near her. Her mother told me it was a recent script written to treat anxiety. As far as I know, someone at the scene had my friend transported here, so the cause of death could be determined. She was examined, and her death was ruled a suicide."

I noticed a change in her expression when I made the last statement. It was slight, but easy for me to spot since I was analyzing her so closely. I'm sure Tess had seen a few cases like this before, but I couldn't help but wonder what she was thinking about right then. She paused before she spoke.

"When I spoke with Garrett," she glanced at him when she said his name. "I told him I conducted the examination on your friend. I noted she was young and healthy. By our accounts, the evidence indicated your friend ingested a number of pills and died as a result."

I needed to know more. "I understand, but what about—"

"What about the bruises?" Garrett broke his silence.

"They looked old, and the police noted she'd been in an altercation with her boyfriend a week prior." Tess sounded pretty sure.

"*Ex*-boyfriend," I added.

"What about the scratches? And what about the needle mark? Why weren't they noted in her file, Tess?" Garrett asked the questions I hoped we wouldn't have to ask.

"Listed in my notes, but they didn't make the final report," Tess answered.

"Why not?"

"Because they weren't direct contributors to her death."

"But why did you choose to leave them out of the report?" Garrett sounded upset.

"Look, obviously the girl was into something more. Drugs are more common for people in high-stress jobs."

"Drugs?" I asked in disbelief.

"The needle mark on the neck is typical in addicts who want to hide their drug use."

"But, Chloe didn't use drugs. She had nothing to hide," I insisted.

"The police report indicated Chloe was an abuser. She had prescriptions for several anti-anxiety and depression meds over the past couple years. The needle mark may have been her new way to get high, but the facts were clear—she overdosed on the pills.

"The facts?" My anger flared. "Chloe wasn't a druggie, and there is no way she did this to herself. No way!"

"Looks like you left out some facts," Garrett told Tess. "It seems to be a regular occurrence with you these days."

"This has nothing to do with my past mistakes, Garrett." Tess fidgeted. She was definitely uncomfortable. "Besides, I told you over the phone it was a cut and dry case. The report Detective Marlucci gave me backs it up."

Tess got beet red, like she was upset or said something she didn't mean. She immediately fired back at me. "Your friend, Chloe, took enough pills to put down a horse, I didn't think it was necessary to smear the girl's reputation any further."

It must have been what Garrett wanted to hear because he softened. "I just thought you might have gotten caught up in something."

"Chloe had her problems, but she would not have given up like this. You have to believe me!" I pleaded with Tess, but I really wanted Garrett to believe me and help me find the truth.

"Garrett," Tess ignored me and reached for his hand. "I'm past it, now. Ruggiano was a long time ago. Please don't hold it against me any more." She squeezed his hand and he let her.

Garrett stood, so we all stood. He walked over to her and took her hands in his again.

"I'm sorry, Tess." Garrett said it like he'd hurt his best friend, or lover. I wanted to barf. In fact, I contemplated launching my partially digested tuna all over the both of them. Why was he apologizing anyway? She was the one accusing my dead friend of being a drug user, which was insane.

"I understand. We had a great time together, but we didn't exactly end on the best of terms." It was clear she was using their past against him.

This was why I came—why he wanted me to be here. I did the best I could to keep it together and press her for more information.

"We appreciate your discretion Tess," I said in my most annoyed voice laced with sweetness, "but in the interest of truth, it would really help us if you shared your notes." Garrett told me at lunch this was what he really needed to get out of this meeting. I guess he knew exactly what he was doing by bringing me here.

"I'd love to, but I can't share them at this time. Perhaps, I can run them by your office Garrett?" She batted her eyes and started to stroke his hands.

No. Way. No way! Give us the exam notes now, or else! I wanted to yell at her, but I took a breath instead, because I was about to lose it.

"Of course, Tess," Garrett said all syrupy, like he liked her. "I'll be back in the office next week. Stop by and I can show you the new equipment." Was he talking about his equipment, because it sure sounded like it? Did he just give her his 1000-watt smile? What was happening?

Confusion and rage shook me, so I walked out. Just like the time I left college. I kept going and didn't look back, even as Garrett called to me. He only tried twice, so I figured he wasn't really trying. Anyway, he must have gone back inside to ask Tess to marry him, or whatever, because I made it all the way to the turnstile and there was no sign of him.

I gave my badge to the guard, walked out the front door, and called a cab.

The cab smelled like stale smoke and a bunch of strange things I didn't want to think about, but at least it was a ride. I noticed the driver's card and a couple photos of his kids posted up front. The cabbie, his name was Harry, asked me to repeat the address a couple times—he seemed a little anxious by the whole Coroner to funeral home drop-off, but money is money, and he drove me anyway.

Harry the cabbie tried to ask me about stuff. I gave short answers until he got the message to leave me alone. I stared out the window wondering why I let things get to me so easily. Tess and Garrett had lived together, and I wasn't dating him, so I had no right to get upset over their closeness. Except, I really wanted to have something with him, and we needed to find out what happened to Chloe. Their reunion was interfering with us finding answers.

Call me an amateur, but I had no idea what to do next. The investigation wasn't going well, and my hasty exit would make the next conversation with Garrett awkward.

Oh well, nothing I could do to change it now. I needed to get back to the apartment and figure things out. An old blue truck almost crashed into us, but the cabbie made it back to the parlor in good time. I paid the fare and tipped the guy a few bucks. No sense taking my bad day out on Harry.

CHAPTER 13

It started to rain, and I'd forgotten my rain gear in Garrett's car. Today was not going my way. I could run inside and curl up in a ball, but I thought ice cream might help me feel better. Ryder's car was still there, so there was time for a grocery run. I pulled my keys out and rumbled off to grab something to satisfy my need for sweets.

The grocery store was parked up. Probably full of people buying goodies for their Labor Day celebrations—I was going to need a lot of chocolate sauce and whipped cream to get through the weekend alone.

By the time I got inside the store, the rain had soaked me clear through. I dripped and squeaked my way over to the freezer section. My outlook improved as I scanned countless varieties of frozen pies, cakes and desserts until I found what I wanted—jackpot. I opened the freezer door and a blast of icy air hit me. I tried to move quickly, but my hands were frozen as soon as they grabbed the container. Carrying ice cream in already cold hands was painful. I should have picked up a basket. The freezer door slammed shut as I turned to leave. One step, and I bumped into Garrett.

"Planning a party?" he sounded friendly.

"It's not a party unless there's chocolate," I said, and brushed past him.

"You look cold. Can I carry that for you?" He took the ice cream and we walked over to the toppings. I may have drooled over the chocolate, marshmallow, and caramel sauces, but it was hard to tell since I was still dripping wet.

"So many choices," I searched for the right one, and waited for him to explain himself.

"I like the milk chocolate, or hot fudge." He grabbed them both. "What do you think?" He held up both jars for me to choose.

Things could get ugly if he expected me to share after what happened earlier. I gave him a sideways look.

"Why don't we get both?" Garrett started walking toward the dairy case. He seemed to have a plan, so I followed and watched as he poked around the cooler. After he picked up some whipped cream, he turned and looked at me. "You know, we really ought to have dinner first."

"This afternoon hasn't gone too well, and I'm soaking wet. Ice cream was going to be my dinner." I sounded pathetic.

"I have something else in mind. Let me grab a few more things. Then we'll get out of here and get you out of those wet clothes."

I raised my eyebrows at him.

"Don't worry, it's just food…for now." He flashed a warm smile my way, so I did the same for him. It was hard to stay mad when he was obviously trying to make amends.

Garrett proceeded to snag a cart and filled it with our goodies, then added cheese, bread, salami, grapes, and wine. We checked out and he walked me to the car.

"Nice ride. Can I borrow it sometime?"

"It's a loaner. But I know a guy who knows a guy." We both laughed.

"See you back at the parlor," he winked and took the groceries with him.

We parked next to each other back at the parlor. Ryder was in the back office when we came in. He looked at me and did a double take.

"Lost a fight with a fire hose," I joked. "I'll change and come right back, so you can give me the rundown and get out of here."

"Cool."

I sloshed down the hallway from the office to the stairs then squeaked my way upstairs. I was drying out, but would need a hot shower to ever feel warm again. All I needed was a quick shot of heat, so I threw off my clothes and jumped in the shower. For five minutes, the water beat on my back and neck. I quickly washed then dried off and got dressed.

I got back downstairs and noticed Ryder had left.

"Did I make him mad?"

"No, I just gave him a hint and he took it."

"You shouldn't give Ryder the wrong idea, I don't want to get in trouble. I acted weird earlier, but it was because you were busy getting cozy with Tess instead of getting answers about Chloe's death. Whatever you two had or have going, is up to you. I just want to find out what really happened to her and put it to rest." It was mostly true.

"I was trying to get answers."

"Look, this isn't a game. My mom and I need this job, and we need a roof over our heads." It needed to be said.

"I'm not playing," he looked serious. "I didn't tell you Tess could be manipulative, but I expected she might try. I cared about her before, but even then she had her faults. It was important for you to be there not only to ask questions, but I needed to see how she responded when you prodded, unrehearsed, about Chloe's death."

"Oh," I said quietly.

"Having you there to ask questions gave me an opportunity to watch her respond. The more you pushed, the more uncomfortable she appeared."

"I caught her fidgeting. She sure poured on extra sweetness for you, though. You noticed all that?"

"Yes, of course. I played into it to find out how bad she wanted us out of there. She only got sweet to distract us from the real issue—something doesn't add up about the exam, or the report. I thought you could tell."

"No. I thought you still cared for her. I—I feel terrible for walking out like that." I sank thinking of how childish it must have looked to him.

"You may not have understood, but it worked like a charm."

"What did?"

"The plan."

"It did? You mean you got the information?"

"Not exactly, but I have a good idea of where to find it."

Garrett picked up the sack of groceries and walked me to the back hall. He put the ice cream in the freezer above the fridge used for keeping lunches and drinks cold then took me out the back door where we parked our cars. The rain had cleared, although everything was still wet.

"It's nice enough, I thought we could eat out here."

I looked at the paved driveway and our cars and wondered if he meant for us to sit on the side porch. A puzzled look crossed my face.

He held up a finger, "Stay here, I'll be right back."

He came out with a large plaid blanket and shook it out over a spot near my car. "It gets boring eating inside all the time," he said. "I got this to sit outside and catch some actual daylight on slow days."

My eyebrows raised, impressed by his impromptu picnic. The blanket had a backing, so we wouldn't get wet.

Garrett ran back inside and brought out some plastic cups. He used a pocketknife combo to uncork the wine then poured two glasses and handed one to me.

"Cheers."

"Cheers." We clinked glasses.

Garrett sat down with his drink and patted a space near him so I'd sit. As I sat down, he pulled out paper plates and filled them with bread, cheese and other foods. He gave me a plate and we started to eat.

"Thanks, this is nice."

"My pleasure, I thought you could use a change of scenery. I did a lot of work on that apartment, so I know it's nice, but it's small."

"It is smaller than our old house, but at least it's a roof, you know?" I sighed when I looked at him then took a drink of wine. "Besides, I like old homes like this. They have a lot of history and character."

"And a lot to repair and replace," he chuckled then made a sandwich out of some salami, bread and cheese.

"I appreciate this…picnic." The tension I'd felt since he told me we were going to see his ex-girlfriend eased.

"No problem." He clinked my glass again before he took another drink from his. We ate, drank, talked and watched the sky clear enough the sun burst through high clouds over us.

At one point, he caught me staring at him. I sat up straight and tried to act like it hadn't happened. Instead, I just blurted out what I'd been thinking. "What's going on with you?" It came out too abruptly, so I tried to cover. "I mean what's going on between you and Derek." It was a fair question. Derek acted strange around him and I wanted to know why.

Garrett shot me a sly smile. Even though he didn't owe me an explanation, I hoped he'd let me in on the big secret.

"You know there are a lot of stories to go with this old place. And since we're in the business we're in, there are even some pretty good ghost stories."

I figured this was a stall tactic, but a ghost story sounded interesting. He watched to see if I was receptive to hearing it, or maybe he was hesitant to scare me since I'd be alone tonight. Thinking about being alone made me hope Garrett would have a reason to stop by tomorrow. Although, I didn't want to wish people dead just to see him, I sure thought about it.

"This used to be ancient Indian land. The heads of many tribes would assemble near an old ceremonial tree that sat on this very property." He pointed to the corner of the parking lot.

There was no tree that I could see, just asphalt and a dumpster.

"People came from all over to discuss leadership appointments, land disputes and other important issues. This was a gathering place, and a place of ceremony where the ancient people danced, celebrated, and gave thanks to the Great Spirit."

Garrett settled in and told me more of the story. "Sometime around 1865, a wealthy tycoon named Samuel Davis made a deal to take over the land. He agreed to split some of it with several businessmen he knew."

I leaned in, grabbed a couple grapes and snacked on them while Garrett told more of the story.

"Davis made plans to clear most of the land and build Amelia, his bride-to-be, the finest Victorian home in the area. This home. And if that gesture wasn't impressive enough, he planned to build another home for her sister over there." Garrett pointed across the street to the Davis and Sons Funeral Home.

"Just before the land was taken over by Samuel Davis and his cronies, an Indian Shaman came and warned the men not to tear the trees down. Davis agreed, but later found out Amelia had secretly met with a young Indian near the great ceremonial tree. When Davis found out, he didn't ask questions. He just bulldozed the lot, trees and all, as a symbol of his power and dominance."

"What happened to Amelia and the young man?" I pulled my

knees up to my chest and wrapped my arms around them. I had to know more.

"Amelia claimed they were just friends, but Davis called off the wedding. He kept his promise to give Amelia's sister the house across the street, partly to torment Amelia. Considered tainted by scandal, Amelia's sister took her in, and she lived there the rest of her life."

"Did anything happen to Davis?"

"The way I heard it, the Shaman paid Davis a visit and told him, 'It is one thing to take a man's land, and quite another to take his heart.' The Shaman told Davis that he, and anyone who owned the home would be haunted by ancient spirits until they made amends for the offense." Garrett eyed me. I sat mesmerized.

"But, if Samuel Davis lived here, why isn't this place named Davis and Sons Funeral Home?"

"Because Samuel Davis found out the Shaman was right. Davis's old journals give accounts of the house's first ghost sightings. Davis feared he'd go insane. He swapped houses with his ex-fiancée and her sister. The women moved here, and Davis settled in with one of Amelia's cousins over there."

"He doesn't sound like a very nice guy." I wondered if Samuel Davis was a distant relative of Derek Davis.

"He wasn't a good guy, and his offspring didn't turn out much different, in my opinion." Garrett took a drink of wine and looked distant.

"Is Samuel the one behind the Davis and Sons Funeral Home?"

"He's ancestor to our very own Derek Davis. Although, Samuel didn't start the funeral business, that happened after my Great-great Grandpa Mackenzie, a cabinetmaker by trade, took over this house in the 1920s when Amelia's family vacated.

Back in the day, a number of cabinetmakers made caskets for burying the dead. Grandpa had the idea to create a formal place to hold funeral services, and found this old beauty. The business was such a success, a few years later, one of grandpa's school friends—a member of the Davis Family—copied his idea, and opened Davis and Sons Funeral Home."

There was bad blood between the families, but whatever was on Garrett's mind went beyond an old rivalry. I searched his face for answers, as if studying Garrett would provide more insight into what happened between him and Derek. Garrett caught me looking and he loosened up. The distant look was replaced by a focused energy on me, and telling the story.

"I don't think Grandpa Mackenzie knew about the curse until after he turned this place into a funeral home. There were stories, even articles, about the place being haunted, but as far as I know, we haven't had a ghost around since my crazy Grandpa Stanley claimed to see one at his grandma's funeral. He told us the ghost chased him to the third floor where he hid under a chair for a couple hours until his dad found him." Maybe Grandpa Stanley had seen a ghost, it would explain a lot.

"When we were little, mom warned us to be kind to others and pray hard that the curse would miss us." Garrett looked at me and smiled, only I was not smiling. "Don't worry, you should be fine. The whole story was probably made up to keep us all in line and in church."

Garrett lowered his voice. "I think, if you look up," he leaned me back onto the blanket then stretched out next to me and stared at the sky, "on nights like this, you can sometimes see the Great Spirit keeping watch overhead."

My eyes practically popped out of my head as I searched the chaos above looking for some sign of ghosts, or the Great Spirit.

Garrett let out a hearty laugh. "I was just kidding about the Great Spirit in the sky thing. You just looked so intense, I couldn't help myself."

"Ugh!" I rolled onto my side. "I cannot believe you. You really had me going."

He laughed and put his hands behind his head. I reclined and felt flush thinking of this strong, beautiful man beside me. Garrett turned onto his side, leaned his head on his hand, and looked deeply into my eyes. My heart fluttered. I did not know what to do.

I wanted him to kiss me, but was afraid I might jump his bones if given even the slightest opportunity. What was he going to do? So many thoughts raced in my mind. Now if I could contain my excitement and my desire, I'd be fine. Get out of your head, girl! What was that? Get out of your head and look at that fine man staring at you right now!

Our eyes locked, and I felt a fiery urge. My breath caught as Garrett leaned closer. I contemplated what I would do if he actually kissed me, only, he pulled back.

"Are you going to be okay here tonight?"

Wondering if he was up to something I stuttered, "I—I think I'll be fine. Why?"

"No reason. I just wanted to make sure you could handle staying here since I told that story." Perhaps, he realized it might not have been a good idea to share a ghost story with me when I'd be alone again tonight.

Stung a bit by the concern and not a romantic advance I huffed, "I can handle myself."

"I'm available in case you need anything." He obviously didn't buy my act for a second. "You've got my number and I can be here as fast as you need me." He smiled and turned to get up. His hand reached out to help me up, so I grabbed it and stood up with to him.

Being near Garrett warmed me even though the temperature outside felt like it had dropped thirty degrees. I shivered at a cold breeze. He moved the bag, lifted up the blanket and shook it out. Then, as he wrapped me up in it his body tensed. I waited for him to make a move, hoping he would grab me and kiss me passionately, just so I would know what his lips felt like. Paradise. I imagined paradise. The electric charge we shared lasted a few seconds, but felt like the heat of an eternal sun.

He leaned closer and pulled the blanket tighter around my shoulders. "It's getting late, let's clean up and head inside."

"Mmm-hmm," and head nodding was all I could muster.

We got inside and sat for a while. We talked almost an hour before a call interrupted us. We reached for the phone at the same and laughed. I used one of my standard greetings and took the caller's questions while he listened. I stood up to grab some paperwork, so I could give the caller details about a viewing. Garrett walked over by me and waited for me to put the phone down before he touched my hand.

"Mattie. We need to talk about what's going on here."

He could have been talking about Chloe's case, or work, or us. It made me nervous to think about the last part.

"What do you have in mind?"

"We need to talk, but I'd feel better knowing there won't be any interruptions—phones, deliveries, or anything else." He pulled my arm into his and walked me to the stairs leading up to the second floor. "Get some rest. We'll pick up where we left off tomorrow.

Buzz me when you're in safe, okay?" He squeezed my hand then let go.

Why didn't he kiss me? Should I kiss him? I didn't want to leave, but willed myself to walk upstairs and into the apartment. The locks clicked into place. I leaned against the door for a moment and let out a sigh.

After I buzzed down, and we said goodnight, I crashed onto the bed.

I counted plaster flower patterns on the ceiling for a million seconds and wondered how my life got to this point. My eyes moved from the ceiling to the windows that flanked the bed. Darkness was settling around the house. I remembered I was supposed to call mom.

When she answered, I felt relieved.

"Hey, Mattie," she sounded muffled.

"Hey, mom. Is everything all right?" I could tell something wasn't right.

"Things are fine, but I won't be able to come home for a few more days." She sighed and my heart sank. "Grandpa admitted he missed his last two doctor appointments. Your Aunt Eileen and I want to take him for a check-up next week. I think he really needs to go, he fell twice since we've been here."

It was important for mom to help grandpa. I didn't need mom as bad as he did right now. Even though I enjoyed being independent, I missed mom and needed some advice. Maybe Jocelyn was a better person for the kind of advice I needed, anyway. "Take whatever time you need."

"Will you be okay about handling work, and school?"

"Work is going pretty well, Hank and the guys are helpful. School starts up soon, so I don't expect any major projects for a week or two. Do what you need to help grandpa, I'll be fine until you get back." It was hard to sound convincing, but I tried.

"Thanks, Mattie. Make sure you keep the doors locked, and call if you need anything." Mom and I talked a while longer. She told me grandpa snuck a cigar into the house and tried to smoke it near a window so no one would know. Except, Aunt Eileen could smell it when she got back from grocery shopping, and she let grandpa have it. When he did see his doctor, he was given strict orders not to smoke, or drink, or have any fun, according to my grandpa.

"Sounds like you have your work cut out for you. I miss you, but it's good you both could be there for him when he needs you."

"He can be a tough customer, but it's a blessing to get time with him. I love and miss you, Mattie May." Mattie May was one of the nicknames mom gave me when I was little. I still liked hearing it.

"I love you too, mom. Take care and remember to rest when you can." We signed off of our call and emptiness filled the room.

I never got to eat the ice cream we brought home earlier, but it would take an act of God for me to open the door and go get it. I walked to the kitchen and checked the fridge and cabinets. A bag of M&Ms caught my interest. I poured some milk and took the bag with me to the bedroom.

The phone was quiet, so I munched a little candy then picked up a book and read for a while.

Part of my bedtime ritual included washing my face, brushing my teeth and reviewing my to-do list. Writing things down helped me unload what was in my brain, to help me sleep easier. I added milk to the grocery list then paged over to the section dedicated to Chloe's case.

There were notes all over, and a suspect list in the left margin. I scribbled some notes about our meeting with Tess, and made a note to research Ruggiano. My mind wandered to the story about Samuel Davis. I wondered what it must have been like to be Amelia—first engaged to Davis, then kicked to the curb, then shuttled from house to house with her sister while her ex-fiancée made a life with her cousin. What happened between Amelia and the Indian boy? I started to contemplate it when the phone startled me.

My hands searched the nightstand for notes on our current "guests" while I did my best to politely greet the caller.

"Did you forget what I said?" I froze. It was the same hard-edged voice that warned me before. "If you need a reminder, look out your front door. It's just a little something to show you that I can get to you anywhere."

I stifled a cry.

"If you don't stop asking questions, you'll be next," he threatened me, and then the line went dead.

Dial tone changed to annoying beeping, followed by a recording of an operator asking me to hang up and try again. I dropped the phone. My arms clutched my waist. I bent over to get air, and tried not pass out breathing heavy for a few minutes. After some slower, longer breaths, I calmed down enough to walk over to the window. There was no indication a maniac stood outside, but I couldn't see much. I walked back to the bedroom and reviewed my options. Hide under the covers until someone found me, or go out swinging.

I was scared, but needed to find out what the crazy guy left. Plus, I only noticed one phone line lit up when I answered the stalker's call—an indication that the bad guy was outside the building, otherwise, two lines would be lit. Good news. So, I grabbed my Louisville Slugger from under the bed, slipped on my tennis shoes and walked from the bedroom to the living room, and over to the front door by the stairs.

My hand grabbed the doorknob. I exhaled every ounce of breath I could, looked up to say a quick prayer, and turned the knob. I opened the door slowly. It creaked, so I stopped.

I pushed it open even slower. I don't know why, but being quiet seemed like it might protect me somehow. The door opened enough for me to peek out. I still couldn't see anything. I stuck my head and shoulders out as far as possible, without actually stepping out of the apartment. Nothing happened. A good sign, I hoped. The house sounded quiet, so I put two feet out the door. With one hand on the curved railing, and another on my wooden weapon, I moved down the staircase.

Pound, pound, pound, pound, pound!

"Ack!" I jumped. He's trying to get inside! Should I run upstairs, or stay still and hope no one hears me? I couldn't decide.

Pound, pound, pound, pound, pound! It came again as my heart thudded. I turned to run when I heard him.

"Mattie! Are you in there?" It was Derek. I reversed and took a few hesitant steps toward the bottom of the stairs. "Is everything okay?" He sounded worried out there. Maybe he'd run into the freak trying to scare me to death. I should let him in for his own safety.

Two enormous wooden doors were closed in front of me. Beyond them were the two outer glass doors, locked for extra security, and beyond that was Derek. He'd been friendly to me and was concerned now, so I responded in kind.

"Yes," my voice cracked. 'Yes, I'm here. Give me a minute." I set my bat down and worked the locks. As soon as the first set of heavy wooden doors opened, I saw him.

Derek stood on the front stoop holding a huge floral spray of dead roses. I had to will my eyes back to Derek, so I wouldn't go catatonic thinking about the dead flowers, or the bad guy who brought them to my doorstep.

I twisted the metal key inside the lock until it clicked. Derek helped open the door, and stepped inside. He stood there with the flowers and looked at me intently.

"I saw a strange van pull up. A really big guy in a ball cap got out and put these on the front stoop. He got back in the van and left, which was when I noticed the flowers were dead. Something didn't seem right, so I came over to check on you."

"Thanks. How did you see all that?"

"My dad had me taking care of some last minute details for a viewing next week. We needed to restock some supplies." He looked around and shifted uncomfortably for a minute. "Actually, I was unloading toilet paper from my car when it happened."

I stifled a laugh. Derek turned three shades of red. "I figured you were over here, and might need help. The look on your face when you opened the door says I was right."

"Yes," I admitted. "I'm glad you came. I got a strange call. Some guy told me to look out my front door for a package. I guess he left these." I took the flowers and looked them over. No card, no note, just dead flowers and a black ribbon.

"If you want, I can help you look around and make sure everything is secure." Derek seemed harmless, and I wasn't about to do it myself, so I invited him the rest of the way inside. "I can pitch those, unless you want them for something."

"I don't want them." They were dead, they stank, and it scared the crap out of me to look at them. I gave them back to Derek. The stranger who left them knew exactly what he was doing, because there wasn't a note, and who would question dead flowers at a funeral home over a holiday weekend anyway? I'd make sure to tell Garrett and Ryder, but there didn't seem to be much else I could do.

"Let's get rid of these and then make our rounds," he suggested. I walked him all the way through the funeral parlor and out the back door.

"It's over here." We headed over to a large metal dumpster.

Derek lifted up one of the rubber lids and tossed the flowers in with the rest of the garbage. "All gone." He brushed his hands off.

"Now let's check out the rest of this place."

CHAPTER 14

We went through each room. Derek helped look around and made sure the doors were secured.

Derek asked me how I liked living here. I told him it was an adjustment, but something I could handle. I went with him everywhere except the prep room, which he quickly checked for me. "So far, so good," he announced as we finished locking up the back. "Let's go through the rooms to the front then check upstairs."

We were near the fridge when it hit me—ice cream. For Derek's courageous efforts, I promised to share some with him. I took the ice cream and my baseball bat as we finished the first floor lock-down. Derek followed carrying hot fudge and whipped cream.

"I planned to have this for dessert but was too chicken to come and get it after everyone left."

"Understandable."

Soon, we reached the top of the stairs. The apartment door was open, and I couldn't remember if I left it open, or not. I eyed the door and then looked at Derek.

"Why don't I go inside first, and take a look around," Derek suggested. I was nervous about bringing a guy I barely knew up to the apartment when no one was home, but a stalker was running around, and I wasn't about to go in alone. I nodded quickly. May as well rip the Band-Aid right off! I thought.

Derek entered the apartment carefully, with me right on his heels. He looked alert as he moved around inside.

We worked our way from the front to the back of the apartment, going through every corner of the bathroom, living room, bedroom—it was only slightly embarrassing when he noticed my jammies and M&Ms—we reached the kitchen, which is where the reconnaissance ended.

"All clear." His shoulders relaxed and he smiled at me. "This is a nice place."

"Thanks. We tried to make it as much like home as possible. We even have a wall clock and a plant." I pointed them out to him, like they were game show prizes. "I appreciate you coming to my rescue, and making sure everything was safe."

"Anytime, Mattie. I'm happy to do it." When he smiled, I blushed. His black t-shirt looked good against his light skin, and there was something that almost glowed in his eyes. He was attractive, but this was not what I expected to be thinking about after everything that happened with Garrett tonight.

"Ice cream doesn't seem like the right way to thank you, but would you care to join me?"

"Only if you're sharing the fudge and whipped cream." He said seductively.

I tried not to think about it too much as I made us a couple sundaes. I topped his with extra whipped cream, just to have some fun. I poured extra chocolate on mine—it'd been that kind of a day. "We can sit at the table, or in the living room, if you want."

"How about outside?"

"Come again?" I didn't think it was such a good idea to leave the apartment, but he sounded confident enough for the both of us.

"Don't worry, I'll protect you." Derek walked to the door. He picked up my bat from where I'd left it on the living room chair. "Here, you can take this in case I'm not enough." Then he winked at me.

Derek seemed brave enough, so I went along with him. We walked back downstairs and opened the heavy set of wooden doors. After I unlocked the outer glass doors, we stepped onto the porch and sat down. With the awning, and my Louisville Slugger, as our protection we ate ice cream and watched the cars drive by.

"How are you feeling?" he asked after a few bites.

"I'm doing a little better. This was a good idea. If we hadn't come out now, I would've probably hid inside until the crew came back next week."

"Coming into this business as an outsider must be difficult for you. I had a lot to learn when my dad first showed me behind the scenes." He took a big bite of ice cream and looked over at his family's funeral home.

"There sure is a lot more to it than I thought," I admitted, and stirred fudge into some of my melted ice cream. "Dead bodies, strangers and coming in at all hours of the day and night. Some callers, like tonight, bother me more than anything."

"I've had those. One night, this guy called in hammered and asked if we'd let him take a peek at the bodies."

"Eww, I hope you told him no!"

"I did, but he cursed me out. It was hard to understand him what with all the slurring, but I caught on pretty quick." We laughed.

"There was a woman," I told him. "She called to say her husband had died. She was so choked up, I could barley understand her when she started. Even when I helped her calm down, it took a while to get all the information. All she wanted to do was talk about him." I stirred my chocolate soup for a moment and looked back at Derek. "I listened to stories about how they met, and what a great husband he was. It was so sweet and sad, but I was happy to talk with her. And then, of course, there are the real crazies." I stared beyond the buildings into the sky.

"Do you want to talk about what happened with that guy tonight?" He poked his spoon around the bowl a little.

"It's a long story. I think it has something to do with a friend of mine." I wasn't sure where to start or how much to tell him. "She died recently, and I'm kind of investigating it."

"What do you mean?"

"Someone said she committed suicide, but it just didn't seem like something she'd do to herself, or her mom. I started asking questions. Now we think she was killed."

"We, meaning you and Garrett?" Irritation showed on Derek's face and in his tone.

"Yes. Why don't you two get along?"

"Long story."

"You can tell me if you want." He didn't make a move to speak, so I kept talking. "We talked to a woman at the Coroner's office, but she was adamant my friend killed herself."

"You guys saw Tess?" he sounded surprised.

"Yeah, why?"

"Because Garrett and Tess were pretty serious a few years ago."

"He told me," it felt weird to talk about it with Derek.

"The break up was pretty ugly."

"She seemed okay, but I don't think she's over him completely."

"Probably not. Garrett broke it off."

"That's what he said, but there was something else. Tess mentioned somebody named Ruggiano. It sounded like a sore spot between them. I was about to do some online research on the name when I got the bad guy's call."

"I can save you some trouble." Derek put his bowl down and turned toward me. "Ruggiano is bad news. He deals in all the illegal activities around here, and has for years."

"You mean he's in the mob?"

"Ruggiano is the mob." Derek was serious. "A few years ago, when Garrett and Tess were together, she got involved with Ruggiano. She claimed everything was legal then, that she was just helping him out with some personal business, but something didn't jive. Everything with him is illegal, and Tess was getting paid for whatever she was doing. Garrett told her to stop, but Tess is something of a hard head. When she refused to stop, Garrett ended their relationship."

"Wow. How do you know so much about it?"

"Tess told me." I tried to think of reasons Tess might have opened up to Derek about something so personal, but could only come up with one. Then he confirmed my suspicions.

"We started dating a little after Garrett broke things off." Derek looked at me intently, like he was studying my reaction. I didn't say a word. I just sat there and wondered what I thought about Derek. So far, he seemed to be both interesting and complicated.

"Look, I had a thing for Tess way back, and she knew it. She was fun to hang out with, but it became obvious she just used me to make Garrett jealous. It worked. He's pretty much hated my guts since then, but I give the guy credit. He didn't budge and he didn't go back. I heard him tell her once it had something to do with protecting his family. I don't know much more, we didn't date long."

My brain was trying to catch up with all this Garrett, Tess, Derek and Ruggiano stuff. Once I thought about it, the questions came. "Tess gave the impression her work with Ruggiano was in the past.

What do you think?"

"Maybe she thinks so, but once you're in business with a guy like him, I think you're in for life."

"Do you know if her work with the mob could be linked to my friend's death?"

"Anything is possible. I'd be careful if I were you, Mattie." He reached for my hand. "I heard Tess wasn't the only one working for Ruggiano. The guy still has a lot of players in the game—doctors, lawyers, cops—and he's hand-picked most of them. Rumor around town was Garrett did something big for him about a year ago."

"How big?"

"Like get your license revoked and end up in jail big. Just watch out, Garrett may not be the guy you think he is."

"Thanks for the advice. It's nice to have someone looking out for me." I meant it even though I was stunned by the information.

Suddenly, Derek leaned forward and kissed me. His lips tasted a little like chocolate, which wasn't what I expected, but definitely not bad.

"I'd like to do this again sometime. Are you interested?" He smiled. I had no plans on doing anything with anybody until I found out if Ruggiano was connected to Chloe's death, if Garrett was connected to Ruggiano and the mob, or if any of these things were connected at all. Derek had been nothing but nice to me, so I left the door open for the guy.

"Sometime." I began to stand. "I should head in and lock up."

"Sounds good. Do you need me to stay and make sure you're okay until morning?" Derek smiled and helped me up.

"I appreciate the offer, but I'll be fine." I hoped the scary guy was long gone.

"Just thought I'd offer. I'll stay here. Get inside, lock these doors and get upstairs. Then call me on my cell so I know you're locked up safe." Derek gave me his business card and waited.

It seemed odd to leave him standing here while I ran like crazy to the apartment, but I didn't have any better ideas, so I followed his instructions. I locked the outer doors while he smiled and waved goodbye. Next, I locked up the big wooden doors then high-tailed it up the front staircase and into the apartment where I slammed and locked that door, too. I ran through the apartment and checked the back door—it was locked tight. I grabbed my cell and called Derek.

"All good," I said to him, and almost meant it.

"Good, now I'm heading across the street. I'll be there a while, and I'm not far from here, so call me if you need anything."

"Thanks, Derek. I appreciate the help. Talk to you later."

"Later," he said, and hung up.

Everything in the apartment seemed to be in order except the stillness of being alone. Something about it felt overpowering. I took off my shoes, shucked off my clothes and put on my jammies then jumped back into bed. I moved my notes and stuff to the other side of the bed and clicked off the light. The uneasy knot in my stomach was either from the massive sundae I'd just eaten, or from the fear someone was keeping tabs on me.

It had to be more than just coincidence that every time I asked questions about Chloe's death, I got threatened. I tossed and turned until the phone rang sometime after midnight.

I froze. It took me a couple rings to get the courage to answer. I slowly reached for the phone, picked up the receiver and let the business greeting crackle out. It turned out to be a man—calling from the West Coast—to ask viewing times. I turned on the light and read the information off the info sheet. He thanked me, apologized for the late call and hung up.

This time after I turned out the light, I pulled the covers up to my neck and prayed for sleep to take over. Once it did, I slept hard, and long.

CHAPTER 15

The sun wasn't out the next morning, so it didn't have a chance to wake me. I finally rolled over around 8, but it took a little time to untangle myself from the covers. I sat up and scanned the room. When I noticed the phone, the memory of the crazy threatening caller startled me.

I tried to shake it off then fumbled around for my cell and checked messages. One of them was Chloe's mom. I cringed thinking I'd have to tell her we had no luck convincing the Coroner's office to reconsider her daughter's cause of death. Even worse was the thought that someone actually believed Chloe could be involved in drugs. Not the girl I knew—even if she had changed—I couldn't believe she'd be addicted to anything except hard work, and maybe Tab. I really didn't want to have to tell her mom any of it, but she deserved to hear the truth, at least the parts I could stomach telling her.

First, I needed some fuel. Maybe I'd call my mom, Jos, and then I could stall a little more by doing laundry, or cleaning the fridge and freezer. Excuses came easy when I dreaded doing something, but the feeling would probably pass, eventually. Anyway, I needed more time to figure out what to tell Mrs. Ellis.

I made the bed and sorted out some thoughts. Chloe's mom would find out, whether I told her or not, the Coroner's office hadn't changed the cause of death, yet. Given a little time, they might. Just not before Chloe's funeral. Did Mrs. E need to hear all the lies about drug use? Probably not. Just to be safe, though, I made a mental note to ask her about Chloe's prescription meds. If there was a reason to poke further into her anxiety diagnosis, I would, but it wasn't likely to come to that. At least, I hoped not.

The kitchen was my next stop. I opened the fridge then went to the pantry to find something resembling breakfast. A small box on the shelf caught my eye. I opened a box and snagged a pack of toaster pops out of it. The foil crinkled as I opened the package. Both pops went in our cheap, old two-slice toaster. It took a couple tries to get the lever to catch and the heat to come on, but when it did, I clapped. The scent of pastries warming was high on my list of favorite things. Usually, I tried to eat a balanced breakfast, but this was quick, and satisfied my need for a sugar boost.

While waiting, I tried mom. My call went to voicemail. Maybe she was finally getting to sleep in, or maybe Aunt Eileen got them to Sunday service. She attended church regularly.

Mom and I stopped going to church when I was a teenager—life got too busy. After grandma died, we went to service a few times after, but still felt lost.

My family would probably be tied up a while. At least until after service and some congregational lunch, they were always having at Aunt Eileen's church. Part of me wished I could be there with them, even if it meant listening to grandpa complain about being last in the food line because 'his legs didn't move so fast these days.'

I left a quick message and decided it was time to hit up Jos. I tapped her name and hit the call button. The toaster popped just as Jos picked up the line. So much for a hot breakfast, I thought, and flung the scalding pastries onto my plate.

"What's up girl," she sounded chipper.

"Hey. Just hanging out here all by myself and wanted to find out how everything is going. Are you heading back for the funeral?"

"Things are good. No big fights, only a couple disagreements. I think we're heading back an hour. Why? Is everything okay? It's not your mom is it?"

"No, everything is okay. Although she and Aunt Eileen are extending their stay at grandpa's. Just needed to chat about some stuff." I avoided specifics.

"Guy stuff?" Jos always did get straight to the point.

"Yeah, and some Chloe stuff."

"What time do you want me to come by for the service?" Getting through Chloe's funeral was not going to be easy for either of us.

"Come over whenever you can. Just make sure to be here by noon, so we can talk before the visitation." I hoped Jos would be back sooner, so we could talk about Chloe long before we buried her.

"Okay. Hang in there, okay? I'll be back soon and we'll get through this together." Jos was a great friend.

"I will, just be safe coming home. See ya."

"Later," she said, and disconnected.

Just about the time I finished selecting the dress and shoes I planned to wear to the funeral, Garrett called up.

"Mattie?" I heard him on the intercom then walked from the bedroom to the living room to pick up the phone.

"Hey Garrett," I said in my reserved tone.

"Everything okay up there?"

"I'm fine, just had a long night."

"Anything you want to share?"

"Not over the phone."

"I brought donuts." He knew exactly how to tempt me. "Holtman's. Made fresh this morning." Holtman's has been in business since the 1960s, and they make donuts to die for—even the custard and cream fillings are made from scratch, they don't scoop it from some bucket, like other donut shops. And I've been to a lot of donut shops. I eyed the toaster pops then thought about Holtman's with a side of Garrett. Yum! My body craved both. Although, I promised to be cautious and reserved until the whole Ruggiano connection was clear, donuts were fair game, in my opinion.

"I'll grab my shoes and meet you downstairs."

If I could take stairs two at a time, I would have, but I didn't want to risk missing out on donuts because I got hurt tumbling down the stairs. I guess it's possible to eat while on a stretcher, so I said 'screw it' and jumped over the last few steps. It took effort to act composed before Garrett saw me. I pat my hair into place and walked calmly down the hall and into the office.

My eyes widened. Garrett stood there holding open a box of Holtman's donuts. I could die happy right now. Well, maybe after I ate some donuts. And maybe after I worked them off doing something with Garrett I'd only dreamed of doing.

Man, I couldn't tell if it was the scent of sugary decadence that had me all worked up, or Garrett in his Sunday best. The man looked fine. I wanted to rush over and touch him. I mean touch it, the suit!

I planted my feet for a second and tried to stop the overwhelming feeling I had of going full throttle toward him. Whoa girl! As bad as I wanted a donut, and the other stuff, self-control was important.

"Uh, Mattie?" Garrett's expression changed from a smile to confused. "Donuts?" He shook the box a little at me.

Good Lord! I know there are donuts! I yelled in my head. Can't a girl have a moment to get it together before you tempt her any more than she is already?!

I took a deep breath and exhaled before moving again. By the time the donuts were within reach, I made my move.

"Thanks." I reached in for a cream-filled donut. "What brings you here this morning? Checking up on me?" I stuffed the donut into my mouth so I wouldn't say anything else. The fresh dough, the cream, and the chocolate blew my mind. I had to sit down.

"I guess you like donuts. Do you want me to leave you and the box alone for a while?" He let a little laugh escape.

I gave him a sort of evil eye look, only it probably looked freakish with my mouth stuffed so full of donut. I couldn't talk, so I just shrugged and enjoyed breakfast. I kept my eyes on him and the box. He set it on his desk and took a chocolate one out for himself.

It was hard enough to remain calm when Garrett did normal things—like, walking, talking, and conducting business—but seeing him in action at the gym, and watching him eat that donut would undo me.

I understood some of my feelings stemmed from my own hormonal reaction; maybe another part conjured in my mind, but this...what existed between us felt like more than just those things.

He smelled good. He looked good. But, was he good? Or at least, was he good in the ways he should be? He'd been nothing but nice, and flirtatious with me, but was it his personality? Did he behave this way with everyone? Or was there anything special about the way he behaved around me? In the time it took me to analyze what was happening in my head he'd finished his donut and grabbed a second.

"Mmm, these are so good!" He took a huge bite.

"Hey!" I yelled and grabbed a second. "Save some for me!" It wouldn't be hard for me to get a second one down, but it would probably be my last for a while. My body could only take so much sugar before I needed coffee. About the time I had the thought, he moved something on his desk and revealed the coffee he'd brought along.

"Goes better with this."

A handsome, intelligent man armed with pastries and coffee had just stolen my heart. I gave his cup a "cheers" clink and tipped it back. Hot and sweet, just like I like it!

"To what do I owe this pleasure?" I sank into the desk chair.

"I thought we should celebrate," he sounded pleased.

"Celebrate what?"

"I got the notes." He smiled at his accomplishment and took another bite of donut.

I sat stunned by what he said. It sounded like good news. I mean he wanted the autopsy notes, after all, but for some reason I didn't take it well.

Garrett beamed with pride at retrieving vital information in Chloe's case, but all I could think about was last night. While I was getting threatening calls and dead flowers, he must have seen Tess. How else could he have gotten her notes so easily? She made it obvious when we met that she really didn't want to share them. Then changed her mind when she thought she could use them to get close to Garrett. It seemed like a logical assumption, anyway.

"Yay," I raised my hands for a half-hearted cheer.

His confidence flickered. "I thought you'd be happy."

"I am happy, and also nervous." There was a whole lot behind the nervous part. Such as, did Tess come to see him, or did he go to her? It really wasn't my business, except I wanted it to be my business. But, more than that, I wanted to trust him. If Tess was still tied up with Ruggiano, and Garrett had done something for him once before, could they both still be involved with the mob? What did he do for Ruggiano anyway???

"Why are you nervous?"

"I'm scared of what we'll find, or what we won't." It went way beyond Chloe, but I didn't share that part with him.

"You're worried the evidence points to suicide?"

"I'm worried the evidence is wrong, or tainted." There. I'd said it. He was going to come down on me for sure, but it needed saying.

"I don't think it's tainted. But, it might not add up yet." His brow crinkled, he was contemplating something. "I couldn't sleep, so I looked it over last night."

Hey, a crazed lunatic threatened me again last night, so sleep didn't come easy for me either. Maybe Garrett didn't need to know that part just yet.

"Did you find something new?" I hoped it was something to contradict the Coroner's ruling.

"It's not new, but a new way of looking at what happened."

We both sat forward in our chairs as he opened the file. Before he showed me, he asked for permission. "Some of this isn't for the faint of heart. Do you want to see what I found, or would you rather skip this part?"

"Let me have it." I didn't want to back down.

Garrett pulled out some photos of Chloe. Post-mortem photos. I wanted to look away—the images didn't look like anyone I knew. The girl in the photos was discolored and lifeless.

"I knew as soon as I found the needle mark on her neck, something was wrong." Garrett pointed to a photo in front of me and explained his theory. "This injection mark was hard to find, and it was very precise. It may have been made with a small gauge needle. But it's still not the kind of mark a newbie drug user could make easily, and certainly not in a place someone just hoping for a fix might think to try. Too many things could go wrong—she could have easily missed, punctured an artery, and bled out." He stopped while I tried to catch up.

I stared at the photo. It made me sad and angry. Tears welled up until my eyes could no longer hold back the weight of them. My head sank and I sat there crying. Garrett grabbed a tissue box on his desk, they were in all the offices and rooms, and handed one to me. I gently patted the tears away and my gaze met his.

His warm hand brushed my cheek. I felt a shock of heat, and then embarrassment. We were discussing my dead friend, after all. Garrett stroked my cheek until the comfort and strength he radiated reached all the way to my heart. He was trying to help me get through this. The least I could do was pull myself together enough to finish what we started. I looked at him and reached up for his hand. He moved toward me as our fingers intertwined.

"Mattie," he leaned into me and whispered. "Do you want to talk about this?"

"Which part?"

"All of it." He tightened his hand around mine. "I didn't mean for it to happen like this. You just looked so sad, I couldn't help myself. I didn't want you hurt."

"I—I—think some air would be good." But I couldn't move.

His breathing quickened. He scooped me up out of the chair and led me through the back hall and out the door.

The wind gusted and forced air into my lungs. It might have knocked me over if Garrett hadn't been holding me steady. "Can you breathe?"

I took several deep breaths. "It's okay. I feel better now." I breathed in and out for a few beats and smiled. "I usually do around you."

"Mattie," Garrett beamed and set me down carefully. He looked conflicted, but overcame it and settled his hand comfortably around my waist. My heart raced being this close to him—staring at his gorgeous blue eyes and wild hair.

We locked eyes—and felt the soul lasers, cutting away fear and reticence. Garrett pulled me tighter against him. He leaned in, gently brushed his hand across my cheek, and touched his lips to mine. I put my hands around his neck to pull him closer, if it was even possible then he opened my mouth with his.

Our kisses intensified as I ran my hands up into his hair. When he reached my neck, I let out a little moan. He pressed himself against me and kissed me so deeply my entire body shook. Then he stopped. He looked at me for a moment, gave me another soft kiss and grinned.

"Just checking to make sure you could breathe normally."

"All clear here," I croaked. "Why did you stop there?"

"Like I said before, I didn't mean for it to happen like this. I just can't help myself around you."

"I've got no complaints." I smiled.

He came close and my temperature rose several degrees again. This time, he left some space between us. "I want to do this the right way," he said urgently.

"Oh, you're doing it right," I giggled.

"Not what I meant." He sounded flustered. "Let me take you somewhere—"

Just then, an unmarked cop car pulled up and stopped near us. Cal got out and walked directly over to us. He looked mad—all crossed arms and anger—and I wondered if he was about to ticket us for kissing in public. Maybe not. After analyzing his expression, it looked nothing like I'd seen before, and I'd seen his serious cop face. You know, when we went in to discuss Chloe's case and he gave me 'the talk' about domestic abuse—this was worse. He stared at us intently.

"I gotta call about a threat made here last night."

My heart sank, my face flushed, and I stood there dumbfounded. I was brave enough to look Garrett in the eye, but only for a second.

"Mattie?" Garrett and I both knew he wasn't here last night, so he looked to me for an explanation.

"What?" I shrugged, and tried to play it off, but then I huffed and got on with it. "Okay, I got a threatening call last night. Not totally unheard of in this business, right?"

"I heard it was more than a call," Cal retorted.

Garrett's eyes were still trained on me, indicating he wanted the whole explanation.

Oh! You didn't want me to skip over stuff; you wanted to hear about everything. Right. Silly me. The voice in my head could be pretty sarcastic every now and then.

"A guy called. He told me to stop asking questions, or else. Then he left some dead roses on the porch." I gave them the short version, but that along with my plastered on smile did nothing to fool the two men staring me down. I was in big trouble.

"How come I gotta hear about something like this from those guys?" Cal said sternly, and he pointed to the Davis and Sons Funeral Home.

"Look, I didn't want to trouble anyone with it this morning. It would have come up, eventually."

Hurt and anger flashed across Garrett's face. With his eyes still on me, he asked Cal about the call. "Who called it in?"

Cal didn't want to answer Garrett. I tried to wish myself out of this situation, but it didn't work. I pushed my shoulders back and stood straighter.

"Derek. Derek called it in because he was here." Then I thought about how it sounded and corrected myself. "After it happened. And just long enough to make sure the place was secure." And to have some ice cream, and try to kiss me, but there was no way I was telling that to Garrett right now, or maybe, ever.

Dark clouds hovered above us—the sun had disappeared behind

the mass. A wind swirl rattled the trees and carried Garrett's scent my way. I inhaled his warm blend of masculinity and passion.

A minute ago, we couldn't keep our hands off each other, but now seemed so far away from then. Now, I was in big trouble. I wanted to explain, but figured it might just make things worse. Instead, I waited for his response then anxiously waited some more.

Garrett had me locked in his sights, but his eyes wouldn't divulge his thoughts. I tried to look innocent, which I mostly was, except for the part about not saying anything. Guilty by omission, I suppose. Why hadn't I told him about last night's threat? Was I too preoccupied to bring it up, or was I afraid of what he'd do when he found out the scary Hulk-man was still after me? Or could it have something to do with Derek? The answer was all three.

Just when Cal couldn't take the silence any more, and started to speak, a sleek blue Cadillac screeched to a halt near us. Tess got out and bounced directly over to Garrett. She tried to lace her arm through his, but he shrugged her off.

"What are you doing here, Tess?" Garrett asked brusquely.

"I figured we could pick up where we left off last night," she answered, all shmoozy standing right across from me in her barely there sundress and heels.

"Last night?" I was the one in trouble, but I couldn't help but sound accusatory.

"Yeah. Didn't Garrett tell you?" She acted like I should know something so obvious.

My mood could change quickly, especially when people copped an attitude. This was one of those times. My mood wasn't great, but Tess's arrival was like pouring gas on a fire.

"He's been so busy, I guess it just slipped his mind." I batted my lashes at her then eyed Garrett. Cal cleared his throat, and tried to hide a smile. We waited for an answer.

Garrett put his hands up, like a perp. "It's not at all what you think, Mattie." He tried to reach for me, but I moved.

"You have no idea what I'm thinking," I fired back.

"You haven't told her what we talked about?" Tess saw our friction as an opportunity to sweeten her voice and inch closer to Garrett. If she got any closer they'd be conjoined. Seriously!

"I shared my notes with Garrett."

Really? Is that all you shared with Garrett last night?

"I told her—" Garrett started.

"Did you tell her my theory?" Tess sounded enthusiastic.

"I hadn't gotten to that part yet."

My fury simmered, but a new theory could be good news. No telling what it might be, but anything was better than nothing. Right? I forced myself to suck it up and listen to what Tess had to say. Cal crossed his arms. Maybe he was skeptical too.

"Chloe didn't do it," Tess said.

Hallelujah! Finally, she believed it wasn't suicide! Now let's get the report changed and tell Chloe's mom!

"At least not on her own," Tess added.

I stood silent. Okay, thought that part was obvious, but the way she said 'not on her own' sounded wrong.

"Tess thinks she had help," Garrett said.

"Wait? What?!" I stammered. The 'help' meant something other than murder. Garrett stood still even as my fists clenched. Cal stepped back.

"I read the notes. Tess thinks someone helped Chloe kill herself. But, she has no evidence to prove it."

Unbelievable! The hope bubble burst, and I was back to thinking Tess wasn't being totally honest with us.

"Ridiculous!" I shouted. I didn't care how badly we wanted each other, or even that he was the boss, Garrett and everyone here was going to get a piece of my mind.

"This is absolutely crazy! First, Tess tries to convince us Chloe was doing drugs, and now, Chloe had help to end her life?" I had no patience, and no reason not to lunge at Tess and do some damage, except I didn't need to fight that way—and there were still so many questions that needed answered. "Why?" I asked Tess. "Chloe's ascent to stardom in the legal world stressed her out too much?"

"C'mon," Tess spoke up. "It makes perfect sense. She had a demanding job, relationship troubles, and she'd been on pills. She might have wanted a way out. Maybe she turned to someone for help."

Standing still was impossible. I shifted my weight from one leg to the other. My hands automatically moved to my temples. I closed my eyes and tried to rub out the nonsense for a few long seconds.

"Easy, Mattie," Garrett tried to calm me down. "This is what Tess thinks."

I may have missed the part where he emphasized what Tess thinks. Either way, I took exception to the fact he hadn't come right out and told me earlier. I also got mad that Tess stood there so plain as day, after having spent some, or all, of last night "discussing" ideas about my friend's death with Garrett. Why not include me? Didn't I have a right to be involved? Or was something more personal going on between them?

"It might be easy for you to believe your ex-, but I don't." I was far from calm. "This feels like a big cover-up, Garrett. You noticed a needle mark. Tess came back with an answer that backed up her decision to rule Chloe's death a suicide. When questioned about the likelihood an "inexperienced druggie," as Tess has wrongfully labeled my friend, could inject her neck so precisely, Tess's answer is "someone helped poor Chloe do it." I was over the top dramatic and whiny when I said the last part.

"Mattie, you've got it all wrong," Garrett argued. "Tess was just making observations based on the things she saw. If you had evidence of multiple prescriptions for treating anxiety, saw the pills, and the needle mark, you might come to the same conclusion."

Was he really sticking up for Tess? Of course he was. Why didn't I see that coming?

"Listen, Garrett. I respect your position, and your knowledge. You and Tess both have impressive backgrounds, but you also have a history. Do you think, maybe, it's clouding your judgment?" I was angry, but tried to sound calm. Cal kept his eyes on us, like watching a train wreck.

"That's not fair," Garrett fired back. "There is nothing between Tess and me, and my judgment is just fine. You need to listen."

Tess shifted uncomfortably at Garrett's comments, but stayed close to him. I didn't wait for her to respond, even though she looked like she wanted to say something.

"Listen here," I waved my finger at the three of them. "Do you guys know why I'm so confident my friend didn't commit suicide? The same way I knew she wasn't injecting drugs into her neck. Because she wouldn't!" I was agitated—shifting back and forth waving my hands to make my point.

"While in college, Chloe took a few of us to her older cousin Patrick's lake house one summer. He'd inherited property near Whitefish Point in Michigan's Upper Peninsula—one of the most beautiful places I'd ever seen.

Patrick and I spent time partying and flirting. Things got a little crazy one night when everyone was hanging out around the campfire. When I saw Patrick head into the house, I waited a few minutes then followed him inside thinking we'd have some private time."

I eyed Garrett for a second. He had a past and so did I, but it didn't matter. Things needed to be said so they'd understand; I continued.

"My stomach did flips when he wasn't in the living room. I proceeded toward the bedrooms. I knocked and tried the handle of one door. Someone shouted 'occupied', so I moved down the hall and opened the next door.

Instead of finding Patrick, I found Tab. He was sitting on a bed with a needle in his hand. He had just injected himself with what I later found out was heroin. Tab downplayed the whole thing, told me things were cool, like it was no big deal. He even asked me if I wanted to join him.

I told him 'no thanks,' it wasn't a good idea, and that he should get help—Chloe had told us his brother was an addict—Tab didn't seem phased. He got up, walked over to where I was and tried to kiss me." I had flashbacks from that night and shivered involuntarily.

Garrett stared with his jaw locked tight. Cal and Tess even watched intently. Everyone was listening, so I kept going.

"I pushed at Tab, but he grabbed me and kissed me anyway. When I asked him to stop, he just laughed. He said I should loosen up and have a good time. We exchanged words, but he kept coming.

He backed me up until I tripped and we fell onto the bed. I wriggled and flailed, and screamed to get him off me, but he wouldn't move. I felt claustrophobic and sick as his hands wandered. We struggled until Chloe came into the room.

Tab got up. I backed away. He and Chloe argued. The next thing I knew, he swayed and passed out.

We tried to wake him, but he wouldn't budge. Pretty soon he went pale. We thought he was dying. Chloe rushed to check his pulse. I went to get help while she gave him CPR.

When I came back, I watched as Chloe breathed and pushed until she could barley move. Exhausted, she slumped over him and started to cry. I was torn between anger and fear. She knew what had happened, but Chloe pulled herself back up and did the breath and chest compressions harder until Tab finally breathed again. He was back, just barely. Chloe saved us both that night." If only it had lasted.

"I'm sorry," Tess interjected. "How does it relate to Chloe's death?"

Tess may have been a witch with a capital B, but I wasn't going to let her stop me.

"After several months trying to get clean," I sighed. "Tab decided he couldn't do it. He left a note and shot himself up with enough heroin to stop his heart." My energy drained until I looked at Tess standing there. She didn't know Chloe was the one carting Tab to rehab, and back home. She didn't even know about the nightmares, or how the situation with Tab brought him closer to Chloe. My anger resurfaced.

"Chloe saved Tab only to watch him turn around and try to kill himself. Chloe loved Tab. She found him nearly dead, again. And she saved him, again. She checked him into rehab, over and over trying to get him clean, and stuck by his side to show him his life meant something—but for every time she picked him up, he fell harder, and got meaner."

I got worked up, but made sure everyone heard the next part. "Chloe did everything she could, but it wasn't enough as long as he didn't care. She broke up to force him to get help. She vowed never to do drugs, and she meant it. She threw herself into her studies, and became a lawyer to put dealers behind bars. So she could save people like Tab. She wouldn't have done this!"

"Mattie." Garrett reached for my arm. "I believe you, but—"

"But what? You still believe Tess's drug addict story?" I shook him off. "Look, I should have been there for her, only I was too involved in my own problems. Whether you want to call it intuition or stubbornness, I don't believe Tess. Now, if you'll excuse me, I have to bury a friend." My voice was acidic. All the happiness I'd felt earlier with Garrett evaporated. My heart fractured. I barely looked at them as I turned and left.

When I got to the door, I heard Cal mumble something. He sounded concerned, but I didn't bother to ask him to repeat it. The door clicked closed behind me.

I shuffled my way through the house. About the time I reached the spot outside the viewing room, Millie startled me. She just appeared there and started talking. "You got to stop being so tough on that boy," she scolded.

"Why? What did you hear?" My cheeks flushed.

"Enough to know he didn't deserve 'dat. He only got your best interests at heart."

"If he did, then he'd believe me."

"He does believe ya girl. You just need to stop talking long enough to hear it," Millie pointed and chided me like a child.

"He took her side," I protested.

"From what I heard, he didn't get a chance to take nobody's side. Ya talked all over, but did ya listen? Did ya?" Millie may have been right. My emotions may have got the better of me, but it wasn't just jealousy over Tess. Something else didn't add up.

"Look, ya been working hard, and your mama's been gone. Ya aren't thinking clear right now. I can tell it from the muddy aura surrounding ya. What ya need is some time to rest and think. I got just the thing." Millie dug deep into her purse, which could have fit a side of beef. She pulled out two small vials and handed them to me. I half expected the bottles to start glowing and levitate, but they didn't. They clinked together in my hand.

"What are these?" I jiggled the colored liquids inside.

"Special herbal remedies," Millie said with a sly smile. She pointed to a blue one. "Take a drop a this one later tonight, when ya get tucked in and are ready for sleep. It'll help ya calm down and dream, which is important for the mind and body. Take one dose every night for the next week."

"Okay."

"This one," She pointed to the green bottle. "Will help ya with balance and clarity. Take it after the first bottle is empty, but not before."

"Why?" I was worried it might turn me into a frog or something.

"Because I said so, that's why!" Millie eyed me hard for a moment. She laughed a hearty laugh. "Ha-ha-ha! It won't turn ya into a frog, oh no! It's because ya shouldn't mix them or else ya might get sick." She smiled at me.

Could she read my mind? I didn't know, but I liked Millie even though her intuition scared me. My first experience with one of her lab experiments had been good—I hardly felt like a human accordion after taking her first potion—a little extra help in the clarity department wouldn't hurt either, so I kept the bottles.

"Thanks," I said, gently tipping them up and down.

"Get some rest and feel better. I gotta leave now. But remember, Garrett is only looking out for ya. Keep that in mind before ya open your mouth next time."

I slowly nodded in agreement. She left and the house was quiet. I figured Garrett, Cal and Tess were probably outside discussing my mental health, so I inched my way up the stairs and locked the door behind me.

Jos would be here in a couple hours. My overloaded brain screamed for me to rest. I walked through the apartment and crashed on the bed. But sleep just wouldn't come.

I checked my phone. No new messages. I wrote about the crap day I was having in my journal, got a drink of water, and ended up back on the bed. I tried to read, but couldn't concentrate, so I sorted laundry. It was piling up, but I was in no hurry to descend into the dank basement two floors below for a few clean t-shirts.

About halfway through the mound, I glanced at the bed. Suddenly, I didn't like the clothes I had picked out for the funeral, so I immediately tore through my closet.

Three dresses, a pep talk in my bathrobe, and two pantsuits later my phone buzzed. It was Jos. Crap! She was less than an hour away, and I still needed to get ready. My body ached. My head hurt. I went to the kitchen, grabbed some Tylenol and rushed back to the bedroom to get dressed.

I slipped on a deep plum dress, decorated it with the tasteful fake pearls Chloe always liked, and pulled my hair up. Something was missing. Shoes! I slipped on a pair of dark grey pumps and stood a couple inches taller than usual. I fussed in front of the mirror for a while covering a small blemish, and the circles darkening under my eyes. I added a touch of tinted moisturizer then powder, blush and lipstick. I stopped mid-mascara stroke when my reflection startled me. It was a grown-up I didn't recognize. A lovely woman full of strength and sorrow.

A text from Jos snapped me out of my trance: 'Almost there.'

I moved back to the bedroom and scrambled to stuff everything from my regular purse into a smaller one that matched my outfit.

When everything felt put together, and there was nothing else to do, I locked up and headed downstairs.

CHAPTER 16

Since Garrett was doing so much to help investigate Chloe's death, the Ellis Family decided to hold Chloe's viewing and services at the Mackenzie Funeral Home. No one from the family was here yet, but they would arrive soon.

Close family members often arrived before the visitation to prepare and have private time with the deceased. There'd be an open casket today. Everyone would see Chloe in her restful slumber. I cringed thinking about what she must look like dead. Although, the work Millie and the guys did was so good, I swore some of the bodies looked like they'd wake up and talk. Imagining Chloe's posed corpse gave me the heebie jeebies. I moved past the viewing room door without peeking.

The "cookies and mourning" tables—what I call the break area folks went to have a snack, and sometimes, a good cry—were empty. I went to the office to offer help, even though Garrett might still be mad at me for earlier. Surely, we could put aside our differences long enough to help Chloe's family say goodbye.

Ryder whistled through his teeth. "You clean up nice, Mattie."

"Thanks." I blushed.

Garrett looked up from his computer and smiled. I felt relieved. Maybe he wasn't as mad as I'd thought. He came over and asked if I was okay.

"I'm good." It was sort of true. "Thought I'd come down early and help."

"The viewing room's ready," Garrett said. "We just need to set up the coffee and cookies."

Since we moved in, mom and I helped set up a number of funerals. "I'll do it."

"Sure thing," Ryder answered.

Garrett got a serious look on his face. "I'll help her. Let me grab the cookies. Meet you at the tables."

"Sounds good." Garrett's expression looked troubled. Maybe he was mad after all.

I pulled some coffee out of the cabinet, placed filters in the baskets and emptied the foil packets into them. Water went in the top, the regular and decaf carafes got placed below, and I flipped the switch. It reminded me of the first funeral I worked.

A young girl was struck and killed by a drunk driver. The entire community came to pay their respects. The parents had their hands full with the crowd. I noticed her younger sister crying alone in the back of the viewing room.

She had on a soft pink dress and black patent shoes. Her hair was full of brown curls, which fell forward as she hung her head and cried. It was so sad to watch this girl who could have been dressed for a celebration sit alone crying.

Thinking it would help, I gave the girl some tissues. I let her wipe her face and told her, 'So sorry for your loss...time should help ease your pain'. I actually thought I was doing a good job comforting her.

Then this child, no more than seven, told me something that sounded so grown up, it shocked me.

"I'm sad she's gone, but all the love and fun stuff we did stays forever. I cry because I'll miss making new memories with her."

She was young to sound so wise.

The nutty aroma shook me out of the past. I watched coffee stream into the first pot when Garrett found me.

"Wanna help me with these?" He shook a bag of chocolate mints at me. We expected quite a few people, but one person could have easily set up the refreshment table. He wanted to talk and wasn't going to let me off the hook.

Not knowing what to say, or even where to begin, I just shook my head and quietly followed him.

I resisted making eye contact as Garrett opened the bag. My eyes followed a vintage floral pattern up the wall until it met the ceiling. He cleared his throat, and I traced some leafy vines back down.

When he finally caught my attention, he signaled me to give him a small crystal bowl, one reserved for the special mints. I slid it his way and returned my gaze to the wall puzzle.

"You know, you can try to ignore me, but I don't give up."

"Easily," I said instinctually, and pulled my eyes from the wall. He caught my glance and I had a hot flash.

"What?"

"Sorry. Don't you mean you don't give up easily?"

"No. I don't give up."

"Oh." It was hard for me to decipher his meaning because I was starting to feel all jumbled up. Upset about how I stomped off earlier, and unsure of his response.

It didn't help that I was well aware of our physical attraction. Keeping my eyes off him in his dark tailored suit, and crisp white shirt was difficult. We were close enough I could smell his clean, sexy scent, which tempted me as much as looking at him. I wanted to flirt and joke with him. I wanted to do even more, but I was too unsettled. Chloe was dead in the next room. We still had the viewing, and services—and little time left to say our goodbyes, because in just a few hours she'd be gone. Forever.

"I don't give up. But I can be patient." Garrett stopped working, and I noticed he had set everything out on the table. I had done nothing except reluctantly passed him a candy dish and deliberately ignored him. Why couldn't I be normal?

"Sorry. It looks nice." Our eyes met, and kept focused until the stare turned intimate. There was no denying it. I felt another heat spike through my entire body.

"Mattie," Garrett stepped toward me and I inadvertently pulled back. My eyes darted away. First, finding the visitation room, then the floor. "You're allowed to have feelings."

"Pardon me?"

"It's okay to feel confused." Garrett took my hand. "Do you want to see her?"

I was shocked. What did he say? What did he mean? What was happening right now? How could so many feelings—anger, avoidance, confusion, lust, fear, and sadness—pass through me at once? Maybe it was grief. I wasn't sure how to handle the flood of emotions. But, I did think seeing her might help. I nodded fast and hoped if anything strange happened, it would be during a private moment before Chloe's family arrived.

My pulse raced, but my legs felt trapped in sludge as Garrett walked me to the casket. The room was quiet. It was just the three of us, or two and a corpse. I stood there and looked her over.

Blonde waves framed her pretty face—Millie had outdone herself, and so had the guys—she looked dead, but still a lot like Chloe. She wore a tasteful floral dress. It was probably something her mom brought in because it was a lot nicer than the dressing gowns I'd seen before.

It's shocking how much a person can look asleep, when they're really dead. Her hands and arms didn't have a rubbery sheen, but I knew they'd be cold. I started to cry. After staring some more, my chest and lungs tightened. Feelings overwhelmed me and I bawled. Garrett put a hand on my arm to reassure me, but my head sank.

"Can I have a minute?"

"Sure." He squeezed my hand then left.

The place felt emptier than when he was here. Alone with Chloe's body, I cried until the tears burned, then started mumbling.

"I'm sorry. I should have stayed. I should have tried to help you more. I'm so sorry, Chloe!" Clutching the edge of the casket, I cried and explained.

"Jos, Nina and I tried to help, but you wouldn't listen. You know I couldn't stay and watch him hurt you, not after what he did to me. Mom needed me. She did, but I used it as an excuse to run far away. I abandoned you." The irony was not lost on me. I'd run away from this place, this town, and everyone in it, only to end up right back where it all started. And in what seemed a deeper mess than I'd left. My head pounded, and I was starting to sound crazy—justifying my actions to a dead girl. It was time to say a proper goodbye, and get myself cleaned up before her mom showed up.

"I'm sorry. I know you didn't do this. I promise I'll find whoever did this, and make sure everyone else knows it too. Whatever it takes." I patted her cold hand, said goodbye, and walked out of the viewing room.

Glad for tissue boxes, I snagged a couple and dried my tears.

"She feels guilty," a female voice said.

My brain didn't register it until I got near the office. Jos. The door was partially open and Jos was talking with someone. My head bobbed left and saw Jos talking with Garrett. Curious about their conversation, I took a few steps forward and to the right then hid so I could listen.

"Mattie felt responsible for all of us," Jos said. "When she left, things got worse between Tab and Chloe. Even though Mattie managed to avoid most of the bad stuff for a while, she felt guilty about it. She tried to keep in touch, but had her hands full at home."

I wondered why Jos was telling all this to Garrett. Maybe my hysterics in the viewing room had led to more discussions of my sanity.

"When Chloe reached out recently, Mattie hesitated. She was just overwhelmed with this move and helping her mom. She didn't have the time or the energy to get involved right away. But they did talk before Chloe died. I don't know. I guess Mattie feels partly responsible."

What? I wondered what she meant.

"You mean for Chloe's death?"

"You know, for not helping her sooner. Mattie probably thinks she could have done something more. We all do."

A knot moved from my stomach to my throat. My vision blurred as I fought the urge to cry.

"She is not responsible for Chloe's death," Garrett's voice had an edge to it. Similar to the edge he had when we argued with Tess about the suicide.

"I know it," Jos said. "And I think she knows it. But, maybe Mattie believes she could have saved Chloe. It's what they had in common."

"The need to save people?" Garrett understood. I'd told him about the night at the lake.

"Yeah. Mattie's been saving people since we were kids. Chloe helped save her from Tab. But Mattie couldn't save Chloe. Even though she wasn't responsible, I think she wishes she could have done something more. It's crushing her."

The wall couldn't hold me up. I started to sway, but made it to a chair. I laid my arms on the table, dropped my head, and let the tears flow.

Garrett and Jos found me crying. I wasn't in a chapel, although, it was near a casket room. A lot of people cried in this place. This was the mourning area Garrett and I had set up earlier.

Jos was the first to say anything. "Cookie?" She held out an oatmeal chocolate chip. I looked up and laughed. Garrett smiled thinly. He looked worried. I lifted my head and shoulders off the table and bit into the cookie.

"Didn't mean to mess things up," I apologized.

"You didn't mess anything up," Garrett said. "You can hardly tell anyone's been here, except for the missing cookie."

"I could put it back if you want."

"Customers don't appreciate half-eaten cookies."

"I guess I'll just have to finish it then." For a minute I forgot Jos was standing right there. I tried to eat and flirt, but ended up with cookie crumbs down my front. Bet they looked awesome with my mascara stained cheeks.

"Girl, you're a mess. Let's get you fixed up before Mrs. E sees you." Jos and Garrett helped me up. Jos took my arm and walked me through the hall and up to the apartment. I let us in. We were in the kitchen, and I still had half a cookie, so I pointed to the cabinet where Jos could find the glasses. "Milk?" I asked.

"Sure. But only if you sit for a minute."

I pulled out a striped chair and sat.

"I like your place," she said as she sat at the table with me. "Want to show me the rest?"

I shrugged. Giving a tour didn't seem important right now.

"After you eat your cookie."

The apartment was small, and she'd see half of it walking between here and the bathroom anyway. Maybe showing her around the apartment was the distraction I needed. I drank the milk then showed Jos around.

We walked through the kitchen, the living room and into bedroom. Jos picked up a photo. It was taken before I left school, and sat in a collection of family pictures on the dresser. Nina, Jos, Chloe and I had gone out to dinner, which we couldn't afford to do that often, so it was special. It was kind of like a last supper, only none of us knew it then. The day after, I got the call about mom's heart attack—so, I packed and left.

I sighed and Jos put the photo back down.

"How about we freshen up?" She smiled.

I headed toward the restroom. She followed me in and leaned against the counter.

"You're a beautiful person, even without touch-ups. I just thought you might feel better if Mrs. E saw you without black streaks."

"Thanks."

"No problem. You wanna talk about it?"

"Not really." I rifled through my makeup bag.

"When you do. I'm here."

"I know," I wiped away the mascara smears under my eyes with a soft, wet cloth. "I'll come around, eventually."

"I know."

I dried my face and patted on some foundation to cover the redness. Jos handed me blush and lipstick. I swiped some on then made a dramatic air kiss to signify I was close to normal again, and ready to go.

"You know he's hot for you," Jos said. We walked out of the apartment and headed down the stairs.

"He's hot," I agreed. "But I don't know if it's for me."

"Oh, it's for you. But, you can't see it. You've got too much going on. Do what you need to grieve. But, when this is over, go after what you want. You deserve to have some fun."

"Thanks, Jos." We hugged each other at the bottom of the stairs, just outside the viewing room.

"Oh, that's beautiful. You two always did get me worked up. Can I get in the middle?" His voice made me sick.

"You're a slime," Jos said.

"Who let you in here anyway?" My voice was low with anger close to erupting.

Jos and I stood opposite Tab.

"I came in the back door," Tab looked amused. Must have thought is was a real accomplishment getting in here on the day his ex-girlfriend—the one he mistreated and beat—was being buried.

"The back door is for the trash," I spat.

"I don't mind back doors, or trash. Neither did Chloe. But you knew that already, didn't you Mattie?"

I lunged at him. Just before I made contact, Garrett grabbed me by the waist and whirled me around until I was out of harm's way. Garrett ended up between Tab and me. I began to protest, but Garrett raised a hand to stop me, and I shut my mouth. He turned back around to Tab.

"You need to leave now," Garrett growled.

"Hey big guy. Came to pay my respects. Thought this was a free country," Tab acted like he wasn't going to leave.

"It is a free country, but this is my house. You aren't welcome in my house, or anywhere else these ladies happen to live, work or play." Garrett got really close to Tab. Part of me wished he'd kick Tab to the curb. Heck, we'd be better off if he chased Tab out of the state, but I worried something really bad might happen, so I stepped out from behind Garrett. My plan was to ask him to leave, but I'd had it.

"I can't believe you had the nerve to come here. You abused Chloe—repeatedly—and now you're trying to intimidate us. On the day we're burying her, no less. What is wrong with you?"

Tab got within an inch of my face. I tensed and felt flush with fear, but stood my ground.

"Nothing wrong with me, just saying goodbye."

If it were anyone but Tab, I might have felt bad. "Chloe loved you once. If you ever loved her, for any amount of time, you'll leave. Right now. There are too many painful memories of her with you. Please, let her family...let us give her the sendoff she deserves."

"Yeah, I got somewhere to be anyway," Tab said. He put his hand up and tweaked my chin. "One of these days, Mattie. I'm gonna catch you. Maybe then we can have some fun."

Garrett moved forward and grabbed Tab's arm.

"I'll see you soon, Mattie." Tab's smile widened.

Garrett yanked Tab away from us and ushered him out of the building.

At this point, I didn't care if he stuffed Tab in a dumpster and left to rot. Tab had no right to be here. The guy had no self-control—he enjoyed liquor almost as much as he enjoyed toying with people. He'd been the center of Chloe's world until she broke free of his abusive ways. I began to wonder if he might have killed her just because she left him.

"Are you okay?" Jos asked.

"Sure," I said it too quickly.

"You're shaking."

"I'll be fine. Let's get in there. We can talk about this later."

I pushed the Viewing Room door open. Immediately, I caught sight of Chloe's mom. She was up at the casket, dressed in a dark grey suit. Her head lowered. She was crying over her daughter's body. It hurt behind my eye. Then I noticed tears beginning to form and tried to blink them away.

"Mattie. Jos," a deep voice called to us. It was Chloe's dad. He wore an expensive looking black suit and shiny shoes. We walked over to the first row of folding chairs to see him.

"It's good to see you girls." He leaned over and hugged us one at a time. "Wish it were under better circumstances."

"Good to see you too, Mr. E," Jos said.

"Sorry for your loss." In the short time we'd lived here, I'd heard the phrase uttered a number of times. This felt different. I was sorry for his loss, but it went beyond today. It was about the years Mr. Ellis spent away from his family, providing for them and working at his career. It seemed like the right thing to say to Chloe's father, but I wasn't sure it would help. He might have seen it in my eyes.

"Chloe spoke highly of both you girls," he said. "Mattie, I know you tried to help Chloe many times. And now, you're helping prove she didn't do this terrible thing."

Mrs. Ellis turned and walked toward us. It was obvious she was devastated. I'd experienced pain when we lost grandma, but I didn't even want to imagine what it was like for them to lose a child.

"We're truly grateful." Mrs. Ellis put her arms around me. We hugged each other tighter and tighter while we tried to hold back tears. At that moment, we shared the devastation.

Losing someone you know is never easy. This was much harder. Chloe was close with her mom, like I was with mine. Whatever mothers and daughters go through together in life belongs to them. If they have a good relationship, there's a bond no one can touch. Not death, or the threat of death, can take that bond away. Coming so close to losing my own mom forced me to think about what it would be like to have the physical link broken.

I spent days and nights praying that if my mom died, we'd still be able to communicate on some spiritual level—that maybe she'd see me, and help guide me with occasional signs, like wind gusts and beams of light. A storm might sway me against doing something, and a ray of sunshine might lead me toward a certain path. It seemed silly. But, the thought that it could someday happen gave me hope.

Thinking about mortality, and mother-daughter bonds fueled my need to find Chloe's killer. Whoever ripped Chloe away from her life would be brought to justice.

Mrs. Ellis eased up and we gave each other knowing looks. I

finally answered. "You're welcome. I just wish we could have prevented this. We'll do whatever we can to find out what happened."

Mrs. Ellis hugged Jos briefly and took a place beside her husband. Mr. Ellis gave his wife a squeeze and a quick kiss on the cheek. The family stayed close and awaited the onslaught of people.

Garrett walked in and surveyed the room.

"You did what you could," Mrs. Ellis told me. "Now, we have to make peace with what's happened. Maybe then we can move on." She was right. We needed to make peace, for me, it meant finding Chloe's killer and taking the bastard down.

My grandpa used to joke we came from a long line of Pugilists. This was one of those times he may have been right. Still, I needed to simmer down or risk another confrontation at my friend's funeral.

For the next fifteen minutes there was a steady stream of family, friends and acquaintances. The place filled up quickly. So, when it was appropriate, Jos and I split off from Chloe's parents.

"Want to start making rounds?" I asked Jos.

"Sure. You need a minute?"

"I want to talk to Garrett."

"Right," she said, and flashed me a grin over her shoulder as she walked away.

In a quick scan of the room, I saw Chloe's parents with another couple their age. Judging from their suits, they were bankers, or real estate moguls like Chloe's dad.

Beside them, a young man in his early twenties with slick black hair, and a baggy jacket that looked like it had recently been dug out of mothballs, rested his hands on wheelchair handles. He pushed it past a row of seats on the way to the front of the room.

An old woman wearing a rose pink sweater with taupe slacks and matching shoes sat in the wheelchair. Her white hair sat elegantly piled on top of her head, and she wore a gold and pearl pin that looked expensive even from this distance. Judging from her posture sitting in the chair she came from money. Polished and proper. Her features had aged, but there was splendor in her smile. She waved to another woman standing near Garrett at the doorway.

With a viewing this size, Ryder was most likely posted at the front door to greet people, which left Garrett in charge of Viewing Room #1. I passed by some lawyer types on the way over to see him.

"How are you?" Garrett asked.

"Doing okay. I guess. Hey, who is the lady in the wheelchair? She looks familiar."

"She's sort of our neighbor. Her name is Mrs. Jacobson. She's lived down the street from us for longer than I can remember. Being a long-time resident, she comes for viewings a lot."

I eyed her wheelchair, and looked over the driver. There was something familiar about them both, but I couldn't place what. Garrett must have noticed because he answered unprompted.

"Mrs. Jacobson comes to several visitations a year. She's old, but can walk, although, sometimes she uses the wheelchair. The guy is her nephew. I remember someone telling me his name. It might have been Craig? Anyway, he's been around the past two summers earning money for college. You might have seen them around." Garrett paused. I sensed he had another thought. "You know, she could probably use extra help when he goes back to school this fall…and the job probably pays better than writing obits."

I smiled. He was right. Obits didn't pay much, but I liked writing from the comfort of home. Even if it was a funeral home. My smile faded. We were quiet for a few moments.

"Looks like it'll be standing room only," Garrett broke the silence. "If you're up for it, keep an eye out…for anything unusual. It could be slight, but even small details could be important."

"Will do."

"The family knows you, so they might come to you if they want anything. Bring the requests to me. I'll make sure they get whatever they need. And the same goes for you and your friends."

"Thanks," I said, and noted his watchful gaze. He was carefully doing rounds with his eyes. "You're on high alert. Something up?"

"Still amped up from earlier. And I'm on watch."

"Is it Tab? Do you think he'll come back?"

"He won't be coming back," Garrett gave me a sly grin.

"Good news. But how can you be sure?" I worried until his look turned me happily suspicious. Maybe Garrett considered my garbage dump idea. "What did you do?"

"Let's just say his car smelled 100-proof. The police may have received a call about a suspicious man, possibly drunk, and they may have observed the same suspicious man throwing punches at me in the parking lot."

"What? Why was he throwing punches at you?" My voice was low, but serious.

"I may have said something derogatory about his shoe size."

"Shoe size, huh?"

"Some guys are really sensitive about that sort of thing." Garrett flashed me a smile. I tried hard to contain a laugh.

"They picked him up and took him downtown. He's so belligerent they'll probably throw him in the pokey until he sleeps it off."

"We should be so lucky."

"We should. But luck isn't going to protect you from him. You need more training." Garrett wasn't kidding.

"I know," I answered uncomfortably. He didn't blink or flinch. At all. "When?"

"Not this second, but soon. You've been threatened by more than one nut this week."

"I know. The rise of threats and nuts in my life started to freak me out." I swallowed hard and thought about my two loonies roaming the streets. The first was a guy with a penchant for hitting women. Tab hadn't done anything to me yet, but declared he would just as soon as the opportunity presented itself. The second—some horrible giant—scared me more with surprise warnings, and rotting flowers. He indicated we could be all square, if I'd just stop asking questions. Which wasn't going to happen as long as I was breathing. Something my giant made very clear he'd put an end to, if I kept poking around.

"You need to be ready in case someone decides to follow through. We've got to prepare you. Escape techniques and passive resistance could save your life."

"Passive resistance?"

"Don't look bad guys in the eye. Don't act threatening. Don't mouth off."

I took exception to his mouthing off comment, but only because it was spot-on. Even as a kid, I tried my best to be polite, but too many things got me riled up to stay quiet.

Either way, Garrett was right. I needed more training, or to leave the country, an option I wasn't considering, yet.

"Okay. Let's talk later. We'll find a time that works for us both, and you can help turn me into She-Ra." He chuckled. Ryder caught his attention. Garrett reassuringly squeezed my arm and excused himself.

Scanning the room again, I noticed two people texting, and a third making a call. Seriously. How rude. There were plenty of spots outside the viewing room to do that kind of stuff. I only hoped Mr. and Mrs. Ellis didn't see it.

Eyes peeled, I noticed them standing in the front row. They remained close to the casket, but slightly off-center near a large spray of brightly colored lilies. This left enough space people could still walk up and see Chloe.

Her parents were in the middle of a group, no doubt listening to more expressions of grief and sadness at their daughter's untimely passing. Mrs. Ellis looked like she could barely keep it together—red, puffy eyes, a red nose, and tissues crumbling in her fists—classic signs of distress.

I headed over to rescue her when someone called my name. The high-pitched voice came from behind. I pivoted to find Nat Peterson heading straight for me.

Nat was a bouncy blond with a nice build and a big mouth. She was a fun girl. We hung out our freshman year. But she gossiped way too much for my taste. I could only take so much of the latest school scandals. I thought passing Chem 101 and the History of Ancient Civilizations was more important than who-slept-with-who.

Most people found Nat easy to talk to, which made her the perfect purveyor of campus information. We mostly got along, but didn't stay close.

During a random party sophomore year, Jos and I were complaining about the dorms. We bumped into Nat. She'd overheard our conversation. She told us about an off-campus contact with a house for rent. We jumped at the chance, and rented it with five other girls our junior year. The year everything fell apart.

I took her arrival as a bad sign. Not because she was a shameless gossip, but because she was holding the arm of Ethan Cane—my ex. This was the first time I'd seen him since I'd left school. We'd ended on not so great terms—hence, the Louisville Slugger incident—but we had patched things together, somewhat. It was enough we could ride in the same car for the time it took to get me to the hospital, so I could see my mom post-heart attack.

Memories flooded my head, temporarily overloading it with thoughts and feelings I'd contained for years. It felt like a white hot flash, maybe something along the lines of peeking inside Pandora's box then slamming the lid shut before the ensuing chaos broke loose.

My eyes zoned out then refocused. Behind Nat and Ethan, I saw Ashley, Jeremy (Ethan's roommate), and some other girl I didn't recognize.

"Mattie!" Nat squealed. "It's so good to see you." She gave me a huge hug, like we were best pals. Everything felt a little over the top, but I let it ride and tried to put on my best smile.

Nat introduced everyone in the entourage and began to explain each person's role in her life. Ashley and Becca, the girl I hadn't recognized, excused themselves after ten minutes of yawn to freshen up. Jeremy left right after them without saying a word. They probably figured Nat would continue to tell me all about them indefinitely, so why bother trying to speak?

"Nice to see you. I wish I could say it was under better circumstances."

"Oh, I know. Can you believe what happened to Chloe?" Nat said it in her gossipy whisper. "Such a shame!"

I did a mental head thunk and decided to do my best to be nice. See, Nat and Chloe were competitive. Mostly, Nat was competitive. Chloe just ended up getting a lot of the awards, and guys Nat seemed to covet. Including Jackson Everett, the dreamiest guy in our class, according to anyone with a pulse.

I remember walking into American Lit class late one day, only to find Nat and Chloe drooling as he read a passage from Thoreau. Jackson had one of those captivating energies. He was tall, dark and handsome. His body was solid, his smile wicked, and his voice could enthrall a Siren, so I get why they crushed on him so hard. That day, he read a passage from Walden, "It's not what you look at that matters, it's what you see." It sounded so deep and intimate coming from him. The entire class fell in love. He was all any of us talked about for days. It became obvious Jackson was a charmer, fighting off many advances, but Chloe quickly became his favorite. They started dating a week later. Nina, Jos and I pegged them as the type of couple who would get married, have 2.3 kids, awesome careers, and a big house with the white picket fence.

It wasn't until months later, when Chloe met Tab, that she and Jackson broke up.

Time had passed. I was so out of touch with nearly everyone from college. Jos was my only real link to people I once considered close.

Last I remembered, Nat made a play for Jackson, Ethan had proclaimed his love for the freshman he'd been courting behind my back, no less, and Chloe needed serious help. I should have tried to get to her sooner. Guilt spread its razor-sharp edges and sank them into my core.

"Hey Mattie." Ethan came up and hugged me. It felt weird. Not just because we'd been estranged for so long, but there were no bells or whistles. Just a no-frills, lean-in-so-we-didn't-touch-too-much hug. Totally unlike the sparks we once shared. My mind flashed back to a memory of us when we dated, but it flashed forward when he spoke.

"Sorry to hear about Chloe, I know you two were close." He sounded sincere.

Chloe and I had been close, but we fell out of touch when I moved away. Mostly because she was going to school, making something of herself and I was tending to my own family problems. And because she wouldn't leave Tab's cruelty, but this didn't seem like the place to bring it up just to correct Ethan. "Me too," I said. We glanced awkwardly at each other and then around the room.

Sensing she was no longer the center of the conversation, Nat interjected. "I heard it was pills."

I made a noise, but resisted going off on her. My brain started picking over the statement. If she'd heard about the pills, maybe she'd heard more. I started to evaluate the possibilities.

I could do what I thought was right, and veer her off this topic ASAP, or dig for more details. Urgency and dread played leapfrog in my head and gut. What I was about to do went against my entire sense of decency, but it could lead to information about Chloe's death. I couldn't pass up an opportunity to get to the truth, so I played a little of Nat's game.

"It was?" I did my best to sound shocked. "Are you sure?"

"Yes. My sister's boyfriend heard it from a friend who works at the pharmacy Chloe frequented."

Even if she meant no harm, the way Nat said it made Chloe sound like a regular at a drug bazaar. Here we stood, gossiping at her funeral. I grit my teeth and pressed on. "Really. So, she had a prescription filled there?"

"Oh, I heard it was more like her third or fourth."

"Wow, I'm surprised no one checked into it." It was bait, hung out as far as possible.

"They were. This friend said his manager had alerted the police, and they were looking into her doctor. I think it was a Dr. Avanti."

She'd snatched it up. Now I had a new lead. It was time to pick a little further. "Gee, wonder what Dr. Avanti did?"

"They thought he might have sold prescriptions to a bunch of people. Something about owing a lot of money to some bad guy named Regina, or something. I guess Dr. Avanti liked betting on football, a lot."

"It sounds so crazy." I knew she meant Ruggiano. I also knew it wasn't totally far-fetched to think a doctor with a gambling problem might owe money to the mob.

"I know," Nat said. "Word on the street is this Regina gets his hooks in you, and he owns you. You either do what he says, or you die." She sounded excited to talk about the mob connection. It just made me ill.

Ruggiano was dangerous. I'd done a quick search before today's event, and found out Ruggiano was really Rocco Ruggiano, born into a family of seriously dangerous gangsters. Now, reportedly running the family of seriously dangerous gangsters.

Google, Wiki and a few other searches turned up information about all sorts of alleged criminal activity—gambling, prostitution, and drugs, to name a few—emphasizing alleged. The Ruggiano family appeared to be the fly-under-the-radar kind of mob. Until Rocco came along. One story reported he was the kind of guy to make a show—and wanted the Ruggiano name elevated to Capone status. If he had some connection to Dr. Avanti, and indirectly to Chloe, maybe he knew something about her murder.

I took mental notes, memorizing everything so I could write it down later. There would be time for me to do more research tonight. I just hoped the information would lead to something significant.

"Can we stop talking about this?" Ethan spoke.

Although, it was hard to stop pushing, I was ready for it to be over too. I followed Ethan's lead. "Maybe we shouldn't talk about this now," I said politely, keeping my investigation options open.

"Agreed." Nat played followed the leader and broached a new subject. "So, did Ethan tell you he's single?"

"No." I watched Ethan turn fifty shades of red. "We haven't exactly caught up yet."

"Oh, foo! You guys should totally get back together." She spent a long time telling us all about the relationship we had years ago. As if we'd forgotten the highs—and the lows. Was Nat playing matchmaker? Yikes! Ethan and I laughed off her attempts, and finally changed the subject.

"How's your mom?" Ethan asked.

"She's doing okay. Still working to feel normal again." Mom had a long way to go, but I planned to be by her side and help. The fact that the friends I knew so well in school had no idea I desperately needed a job, or that we lived above this funeral home, even though it was to help mom dial back the stress, was my fault. I still hadn't come to terms with it. It really shouldn't have mattered, but at a reunion where everyone else seemed to be doing what they wanted with their lives—working, dating, and getting their own places— details of my life fell short. I guess the omission was part of my effort to feel some kind of normal.

"That's good."

Ethan and I talked about my mom's progress, and our move back to the area. I kept the details private. Just that we moved recently, and I'd be finishing school part-time. Nothing about our home above the dead. Telling them my secret now might have garnered pity, or charity—and I didn't want either.

"If you need anything, just holler."

Not quite ready for Ethan's comfort, or a longer trip down memory lane than Nat gave us, my eyes darted away and searched for Jos. She should be around here somewhere.

Garrett came up behind me. "I need to talk to you. Would you excuse us?" He told the group. Ethan nodded, and Nat didn't say anything because her tongue was too busy wagging.

Garrett whisked me away before I could say anything. He took me to a quiet corner, and positioned me with my back to the main entrance of the viewing room. Garrett's expression was odd, something was wrong.

"Is everything okay?"

Jos found us before he had a chance to answer. She had a similarly strange look on her face. "Did you tell her?"

"Just about to."

"Tell me what?" I scanned them both for an answer. Neither of their faces said anything other than something was definitely wrong. "What's going on? Why are you two acting so weird?"

"Maybe I should leave you two alone," Jos said, like she wanted to be anywhere but here.

"It's Tess," Garrett blurted out. Jos sounded unhappy with his answer.

"What about Tess?"

"She's here."

"No way. Why would she be here?" It seemed odd that she'd come. Unless, maybe, Tess had a guilty conscience. Perhaps, she'd go straight to the front of the room, admit her egregious error, and explain to everyone that Chloe's death was not self-inflicted. It wouldn't bring back Chloe, but it might comfort the Ellis's. If they didn't have to listen to rumors and whispers, or answer questions about what could have driven their daughter to such a dreadful act, maybe they could make some sort of peace with all this.

Jos waved her hand to get Garrett to come out with whatever he still hadn't told me. Expecting him to explain, I was surprised when his expression turned hard. His eyes were trained on the doorway by the guest sign-in. I looked over there too.

"Mattie," he whispered by my ear. "That's Ruggiano."

I shook my head. "No friggin' way." My eyes adjusted, but the image was the same. "This is NOT happening."

Garrett sensed my need to move forward, and placed a gentle but firm hand on my arm to stop me.

Despite the Coroner's report and some real evidence, I didn't believe Chloe took her own life. The girl was smart, outgoing, and determined. She was driven to become a successful lawyer. Partly, because she wanted to help people, but also because she wanted to prove to her parents, mostly her father, she could do anything. I understood the need to help, and the need to stand out. Seeking parental approval was something we'd cried over many times. This was not the way she'd go out.

On the other hand, Chloe did have problems. But part of the evidence Tess threw in my face showed Chloe was getting help. Going to therapy, breaking it off with Tab, and contacting friends. She wouldn't have called me talking about a big case if she was severely depressed. I didn't think so. By my account, she was close to an important breakthrough—not something she'd give up willingly. Chloe was murdered. Because of someone she knew, or the work she was doing.

Now, a known mob boss was here. One tied to the doctor who prescribed Chloe's anti-anxiety meds—the ones responsible for her overdose. I had to find out how he knew her, and if he knew something about her death.

"Did I miss anything?" The voice was slightly Italian and the tone was completely annoying. He walked in and acted like he owned the place. Five-foot-seven, on a good day, wearing a shiny blue suit, slicked-back receding hair, and crazy gold rings that looked too cliché to be true. There he stood, plain as day—Rocco Ruggiano.

Tess was next to him. I had no idea why, except maybe they had an "arrangement." This did not sit well with me. Something about it felt wrong.

They made their way to the casket. Even from where we stood, it wasn't hard to hear Ruggiano. "Pretty girl. Such a shame, doing herself in like that."

The friggin' nerve! Did he even know Chloe? The viewing room suddenly felt hot.

I made a beeline for him. Knowing there was no way to stop me, Jos walked alongside me. Garrett was on my left, and tried a couple times to slow me down, but kept pace as I shook off his efforts.

Tess looked at me with a slight nod. Then Ruggiano turned and saw me. "Well, hello. Yet another pretty thing."

What? Did he think we were all pretty things?

"Hope you don't have the same problem this one had," Ruggiano looked at me then Chloe as he spoke. I wasn't sure what he meant by problem, but he was about to have big problems of his own if he didn't stop talking.

"Frankly, I never touch drugs. They can do such terrible things to a person. Like your friend here."

He didn't know me, but I'm pretty sure he recognized the daggers shooting from my eyes. My pulse raced and rage grew. It took all my energy to resist the urge to lunge at him. "Excuse me?"

"Ah, I didn't properly introduce myself. Rocco Ruggiano." He stuck out his hand. When I refused it, he turned his hand over, checked out his manicure, and let the hand fall to his side. "I thought Garrett told you I was coming. Good to see you again Garrett."

"What?" I looked at Garrett.

"I wanted to tell you," he confessed. "But, he came in before I could."

"You should have led with him, not Tess," I said noticing the look of insult on Tess's face.

"I understand you're upset, Mattie," Ruggiano said.

"It's a funeral, nearly everyone here is upset," I sneered.

Ruggiano laughed. "You're different than Garrett's other girls." He inspected me as he said it.

"How would you know anything about me? And how did you know the deceased?" I fired back, so much for a gentle approach to questioning.

Garrett gave him a displeasing look. I wasn't sure why he hadn't told me about Ruggiano, but I suspected his reason was only going to piss me off more than I already was.

"Tess here told me about you and Chloe."

Yet another reason to despise Tess. I narrowed my eyes at her.

"Tess also tells me you ask a lot of questions."

"I have an inquisitive mind." Absolutely true. "Mind sharing what Tess told you?"

He chuckled again then looked me over like a wolf eyeing a Porterhouse. "What's the saying?" He snapped his fingers at Tess for an answer, but she just shrugged. Either she didn't know what he meant, or didn't want to speak. "Oh yeah, curiosity killed the cat."

I was thinking how much I hate that phrase when his eyes hardened. They looked almost black, and truly frightening. As if drawing on some deep, dark power, his body drew in upon itself and his voice deepened.

"Poking around isn't going to bring your friend back. Reports say she was weak with addiction. Dosed herself into oblivion. Case closed. Don't be the cat."

My blood boiled. I was mad at him, mad at Tess, and I'd had enough of this.

"I don't know what you two have got going here." I moved my finger in a circle between Tess and Ruggiano. "But, I don't believe a word of your stories. You might be able to convince the general population the reports of suicide are true, but I don't buy it. I'm not scared, and I'll keep digging until I find something." Actually, I was very scared. It would have been smarter to keep quiet, but my mouth wasn't on the same page as my brain. Passive resistance be damned.

I knew Chloe was murdered, and I knew someone was trying very hard to cover it up—someone powerful. Ruggiano fit the bill as much as anyone. This wasn't the place to accuse him, not without proof, but he'd just made my short list of suspects. What was his motive? I hadn't a clue. I'd look into it immediately after the funeral. We needed to finish this "discussion" before the Ellis's got wind of it and intervened.

"Now, now, Mattie. Take it easy. I didn't mean to rub salt," Ruggiano said. Of course he meant to rub salt. He wanted to rile me up, but why?

"Tess pegged you for the smart type. Let's not start something at a funeral. It's not very smart. I'm sorry for your loss." His sorry sounded hollow coming from his mouth. Ruggiano turned to leave, but stopped, leaned in and whisper in my ear. "Be careful. There are a lot of bad people in the world. Would hate to see you, or someone else you love get hurt."

Was he threatening me? Or admitting some sort of guilt? Infuriated, my cheeks flushed, but I had no words. The weight of it all came crashing down. Hard. I stood silent for a minute too long. Ruggiano was gone.

Jos had to break me out of my daze. She probably knew my catatonic state could reach total implosion, or explosion at any moment.

"Let's get some air." Jos didn't wait for my response. She snagged my arm and said in firm hushed tones as we exited the room and out the building. "Are you crazy? Talking to Ruggiano that way? We've got to get you out of here before he comes back with an Uzi, or something bigger."

Her statement brought me out of the trance. "He wouldn't bring an Uzi to a funeral." How ridiculous.

"Girl, for you he might reconsider. You got in his face but good."

When we got to the office, I had to sit down and put my head between my knees.

I'd screwed up. If the rumors and online stories were true, Ruggiano was mean and deadly. There probably weren't a lot of people who looked directly at him, and I'd just mouthed off like I was invincible. Jos might be right about Ruggiano bringing an Uzi to take me out. Although, he could probably have any one of his thugs rub me out any way he wanted. The thought made my head throb. I leaned over, rested my elbows on my knees and rubbed my temples. Searching for an upside to our confrontation, I found none. What had I done?

I had to think of a way to calm down, and get answers, and figure this thing out. Presently, I was getting nowhere. More questions swirled, and more anxiety over the questions gave me heart palpitations.

"Take it easy."

"Sorry, Jos."

"Why are you apologizing to me? You're the one hyperventilating."

"I mean sorry for this mess."

"You may have just pissed off a mob boss, but you didn't hurt me."

"I shouldn't have done it. I wasn't thinking."

"Give yourself a break, Mattie. This whole thing is strange. I mean, who would have thought we'd be here talking about Chloe's death, or murder, or whatever? You're upset. I get it. But don't worry about me, worry about yourself. I am," her eyebrows were scrunched up in concern.

"I can't accept that she'd commit suicide."

"This is hard for all of us. I don't think she could have done it either. But, we have to accept that it's possible she did."

"Why?" I was exasperated. Why was anyone considering it possible?

"She had her share of trouble. Neither one of us kept in touch with her. She was on anti-anxiety meds, and you told me she called needing help. Maybe she really needed help."

"I swear it just sounded like she wanted advice on a case." My mind raced thinking of different ways I could have carved out twenty minutes to talk with Chloe sooner. Had I really been too busy to call back the first time she reached out? Maybe I was concerned she'd just break down in tears over Tab, or something I thought she should have under control. Things in her life might have actually been worse than they sounded.

"Mattie, you've been protecting us since we were kids—standing up to school bullies and taking on crazy relatives. She stood up for you, and maybe you thought you owed her, but you have to let this go."

"It's too hard to process. She did stand up for me. She could have left me at Tab's mercy, but she didn't. You know better than anyone, people don't do that enough these days. I can't stand to think she hurt herself because she felt alone. If I'd called sooner, maybe I could have saved her. And if she was killed...Jos, I have to find out what happened!"

We heard the door hinges squeak as it opened.

"Hey. Mind if we talk?" Garrett indicated he wanted to talk with Jos, not me. I wondered if Garrett heard our conversation. Great, I'd probably upset him too. I just hoped he wouldn't tell his grandpa about Ruggiano.

"Sure," Jos answered. I sunk into my chair when they left the room.

What if he told Grandpa Stanley? It wouldn't go well. Stanley being set in his ways, despised disruptions to the business. Like the time we accidentally set off the fire alarm during a viewing. He looked at us sideways for over a week, all because we overheated some oil trying to cook dinner one night.

The longer I had to think about, and replay today's altercations, the worse I felt about everything. And if Ruggiano complained and Stanley found out? Catastrophic. Mom and I could be out by sunset. My chances for a plea deal were slim to none, and mom wasn't here to defend us.

I kicked my shoes under the desk and curled up in the chair as much as possible trying to hide myself. My dress stretched over my knees and feet. It didn't help me think any better, but it gave me the illusion of disappearing, which was exactly what I wanted to do.

After twenty minutes or so, my legs started to cramp. I uncurled and decided a drink, or a cookie would help. I stepped back into my shoes, and walked to the doorway. When I peeked out of the office, I noticed a group chatting near the viewing door, but no one devouring sweets at the mourning table. After one step toward the cookies, a man came up and grabbed my arm.

"Ack!"

"Shh! I'm a friend of Chloe's," he whispered. My heart pounded at the surprise. "We need to talk privately." As if he knew his way around the place, he lead me back into the office and to a corner desk.

My heart was finding it's way back to normal speed, but I remained wary of him.

"I'm Tom. Tom Clark." Judging by his slightly doughy six-foot-

plus frame, and straggling brown hairs—part of a receding hairline—
he must have been in his late thirties. He put his hand out. I stood
dumbfounded shaking hands with this guy I'd never met. He seemed
nervous because the hearty handshake went on and on, until he
pulled his hand back.

"Oh, sorry. I used to work with Chloe. We worked on the Oxley
case. She might have told you about it, about me? We were together
the night her ex- came over."

Oh. Oh! He was with Chloe when she and Tab fought. For one of
the first times all day, I stayed quiet and listened.

"We were doing research on a case. Tab showed up, and went
nuts. Thought she was screwing around on him. With me. She told
him we were just working, and it wasn't his business because they
were over. He got so mad. He ripped into her. When I tried to help
explain, he laid into me."

"Oh my gosh. I heard about it. Tab's unstable." And an addict,
and possibly a killer.

"Anyway," Tom continued. "I'm okay now. That's not why I
wanted to talk to you. It's about Chloe. The night we were meeting,
we discussed a land deal.

Chloe met a young man named Walter Sigo, on one of her trips
north. Walter explained he was in some legal trouble, and Chloe
offered to help. She took him to meet Oxley. Oxley asked lots of
questions and took notes, but then assigned me to help." Tom
shifted nervously and checked the doorway twice during the time it
took him to get the first part of the story out.

"At first blush, it looked like someone wanted the Sigo family's
land. Walter said they refused, and pressure came from everywhere—
the buyer, a local politician, and even tribe members—to accept a
revised deal.

Chloe really wanted to help the Sigo's. She told me it wasn't fair
they were being bullied. Walter Sigo told her a lawman came to evict
them, stating the land belonged to the government, but he had no
paperwork, so Walter's brother was able to talk him into leaving.

Chloe became obsessed. She set up camp in Michigan to sift
through old court documents and conduct interviews, all to
strengthen the Sigo family's position."

It's funny, I thought of Chloe as he spoke. Imagining her going
after cases to gain law experience. It must have been exciting to help

people, and chase down leads. Lord knows, I'd thought a lot about being a lawyer to help people when I was younger. But, life blew up, so my plans changed.

"A couple weeks ago," Tom continued. "Chloe called me excited, but anxious. She'd uncovered information that would help Walter Sigo's family. We scheduled a meeting to review in person, because she said it wasn't safe to talk on the phone.

The night we met, she started to tell me about a deal between Ruggiano and some politician. Chloe had proof something illegal was going on—"

I heard Garrett and Jos coming up the back hall. Tom got so nervous, sweat beaded up on his forehead. "I should leave. I can't afford to get caught. Take this."

Tom handed me a small paper and a LEGO keychain. Dangling from the chain was one silver key. It looked like a hundred other keys I've seen that unlock various doors. His gaze shifted to the entrances and back again.

"This will get you into Chloe's place." Tom shifted nervously. "She found something big, and wanted to loop you in for some reason. We didn't get to that part before I was carted off in an ambulance because Tab used me as a punching bag. Last time we spoke, she told me she'd been threatened. Chloe hid her files. The next I knew, she was killed."

It was the first I'd heard someone confidently say Chloe was killed, not that she had killed herself. Confused, sad, and happy, I stood wondering if I should hug him or hide him. The poor guy looked shaken.

"The information you need is in her files. Maybe it'll help. I'd look for it myself, but they threatened me."

"Who threatened you?" I asked, but he just went pale.

"I can't take any chances." Tom grabbed my arms, and stared at me with desperate intensity. "I've got a kid on the way. Chloe was a nice person. She didn't deserve this. Please, get help and find out who killed her. But make sure the people you trust, are people you'd trust with your life."

The door swung open and he let go of my arms. My eyes turned to see Jos and Garrett walk in the room. By the time I looked back, Tom was gone. Poof!

I glanced at the clues in my hands then closed them up tight. I wasn't going to let them get away.

CHAPTER 17

The expressions on their faces made it hard to determine if they were about to ground me, or launch into a full-blown intervention.

"Who was that guy?" Jos asked.

"Somebody who worked with Chloe," I said, not knowing how much to reveal. Tom was suspicious, and he thought someone was watching him, so I explained he was a co-worker expressing his condolences.

I made an effort to appear relaxed, but if anyone looked closely at me they'd see cracks in the facade.

Garrett studied me briefly. "It's almost time for the service." For a moment there was a faraway look in his eyes, but there was so much noise in my head I didn't ask.

Jos knew I was a bundle of emotions. Heck, we all were. But having to bury a friend only 18 months after burying my grandma felt so tragic. Death wasn't supposed to make sense—the finality a mystery, maybe meant to remind the living to appreciate even the most difficult days.

We moved back into the viewing room and sat a couple rows back and diagonally from the Ellis Family: Chloe's mom, dad, and younger sister sat up front.

Ryder gave a brief welcome speech then yielded the podium to the minister from Chloe's church. He mixed religious scriptures with anecdotes in a personalized speech. He told us all how he'd watched her grow from a precocious child into an accomplished young adult. It sounded beautiful, but I tuned it out to avoid bawling.

I stared at the floor, at the decorations, the wallpaper, and the flowers. Everything looked opulent and polished, but Chloe looked like a plastic doll sleeping in the coffin, lovely and lifeless.

How could someone kill another person? This, in my mind, was how it boiled down. Someone had killed Chloe, and they must have had a reason. I couldn't imagine killing could come easily, so it must have been driven by fear, anger, revenge, or something big.

Chloe wasn't the violent type, so it probably wasn't done out of self-defense. In fact, it seemed more likely to be out of greed, or passion. Chloe was not the silent type. If she thought someone was doing something wrong, she would have spoken up. Maybe using her voice, or threatening to, was what got her killed. I needed to find out more about the secret files she hid, and how I figured into this mess.

A stifled cry came from Chloe's little sister, and sent the room reeling. Jenny was up at the podium sharing stories, and telling us Chloe was a great sis, and how she missed her so much it hurt.

My sadness morphed into anger for what Jenny had been through, and her unbearable loss. Jos squeezed my arm reassuringly, but bitterness and determination took over. It was a lucky thing the pastor stepped in and started the prayers, or I might have screamed like a banshee and fled out the back door before the service was over. Instead, I waited anxiously until Garrett and Ryder gave final departure instructions and dismissed us.

Jos was on my heels after I left. "I can drive." She wasn't asking.

I shook my head yes, grabbed my bag, and pulled out a couple extra tissues before heading outside. The storm that looked like it was directly above us earlier must have pushed east, because the air was calmer, and the sun peered through the clouds above.

The procession wove its way through the city and into a slice of adjacent country that looked like summer fields from another time. Chloe's messages started replaying in my mind.

Her first was an innocuous call to 'catch-up' then a text, and another call. Each time the urgency increased, which I might have noticed had I been paying any sort of real attention to her. To me, it seemed like her usual drama over increasing work pressures, or Tab—I'd seen the cycle of abuse and washed my hands of it when I left school.

I assumed Chloe was in the same cycle as before, so I dismissed her easily. *How could she complain about those things when mom was recovering from heart surgery, and neither of us had a job?*

Turned out she wasn't calling to go over her usual set of problems; she called to get help. How stupid and self-absorbed could I have been? I'd abandoned my friend and failed her.

The scent of late summer filled my nostrils as Jos put the windows down. We were almost there, wherever there was.

We hung a right near a creek. Then wandered back and forth until reaching the spot. The hearse pulled over, and the rest of us parked behind it half-on, half-off a stretch of dirt road adjacent to the burial plot.

The cemetery workers had been busy. The headstone was in place, and the grave dug. We watched as Ryder and Garrett unloaded the coffin and the pallbearers carried it to the site.

The congregation slowly made its way to Chloe's grave. A few chairs were placed up near the casket for the family, and the frail. Two vibrant sprays of flowers flanked the casket, and several buckets of yellow roses were placed around the site, while a tent covered the whole circus. More kind and spiritual words were uttered as she levitated in her wooden state above ground.

I stared into the pit. I'd never noticed it before, but there was a metal insert, the shape and size of the grave, in the ground. It dawned on me, the rusted iron was put in place so the weight of the earth wouldn't collapse the grave, or crush the casket before it was lowered. I wondered how many holes the gravediggers had dug. Looked like a lot from here.

What happened after we left and the dirt was replaced? It wasn't as if there were underground cameras or monitors to watch the dead. Although, I bet someone, somewhere already had that kind of hookup.

Occasionally, my eyes lifted to give a suspicious glance as relatives, friends, and acquaintances showered her casket with roses. How could this happen? Who did it? Chloe couldn't have. Was it someone she knew?

The trees stood tall and green, with hints of yellow and orange to signal the coming change. I took a final look at the casket then stepped forward to say goodbye. Before the tears could flow, I let the flower fall and turned to leave.

In slow motion, I walked past the graves of strangers and family members, past the cars, and back to the creek. Most likely a tributary from the Ohio. I sat down, pulled my dress over my knees, buried my head in the fabric and began to cry.

The pain was raw. Part of it remained from grandma's funeral, part of it was attributed to a very real fear over mom's condition— why wasn't she back from her trip yet? Most of it was overpowering guilt blotched with anxiety. Time ticked by while tears flowed and ebbed. I sat alone and cursed death.

"Wanna talk about it?" Jos sat down next to me.

I shook my head no, and we sat wordless for a while.

My eyes hurt from crying, but I could see, with some effort, this was a beautiful place. The sun glimmered through breezy leaves, and dotted the landscape.

"I called your mom," Jos broke the silence.

"You what?"

"Your mom, I called her. She needed to know you were hurting."

"But, Jos—"

"Lord knows you weren't going to tell her." Jos was right. I'd have been on the deck of the Titanic saying everything was fine, even as it sank, if it meant mom wouldn't have a reason to worry. We sort of played this game of stoicism from time to time. Mostly, it was just a delay tactic, because inevitably we'd break down and share whatever bothered us. It always made us feel better to talk. But, we had a habit of doing the same song and dance before we could get it out.

I smiled at her. "You're a good friend."

"Are you off duty for a while?"

"I think so, but I better check."

"Good, then let's go see Mr. Gorgeous. Be serious, or bat your eyelashes. Whatever. Just tell him you've earned a break, okay? Now, let's get out of here," she helped me up off the ground. "And I'm a great friend." No arguments there.

Garrett was concerned and already looking for us when we ran into him. There was no problem getting time to grab a bite with Jos. I thanked him, and promised to be back, and check in, by 7 pm. The tires kicked up stones and dirt when we pulled away.

Driving was a blur. Thank goodness Jos offered to do it. We headed toward the horizon with the windows down, listening to the air whipping through the car. There wasn't a coherent thought in my head for the half hour it took her to find a restaurant. She told me ahead of time she'd pay, knowing I'd worry about how to do it myself. Like I tended to do about so many things these days. Instead, my senses absorbed the scenery: glorious and bright, with the wood-smoke scent of harvest time.

Hitting a diner, in my opinion, was the perfect way to end a funeral day. Diner food is comfort food, and we needed a big dose of food and comfort.

I skipped my usual breakfast order, and opted for grilled cheese. Jos didn't have to twist my arm much to get me to order a shake, too.

We sat, sipped then ate. Nothing was off-limits. We talked about everything from families and school, to tragedies, and work, which was its own tragedy for me. As I lamented the short supply of high-wage jobs for people with my skills, Jos eyed me funny.

"Your mom is coming back in a couple days."

I gave her an incredulous look. "It would have been nice if she'd told me herself." I took a draw off my black and white, a divine concoction of chocolate and vanilla ice creams blended together then topped with a pile of whipped cream and chocolate shavings. The only thing that might have made it better was Kahlua. Only, I needed to keep a clear head if I was going to get any research done later.

"She'll tell you next time you call. You were sort of busy with the funeral. She told me when I called."

"When did you call her?"

"Right before I ran into Garrett."

"You mean when you guys were talking about my sanity after you spoke with mom?"

She laughed. "Mattie, he was concerned. You're a strong person, but sometimes even strong people need help. I only told him what seemed relevant."

I eyed her suspiciously.

"You know I'm right." Jos held her ground, and we both dug into the food as soon as the plates hit the table.

I was pleasantly full when the conversation picked up.

"Are you okay?" Jos asked.

"In what way?"

"Start at the top, and work your way down."

"I'm worried. Mom doesn't sound right, guys are stalking me, strangers are giving me clues into Chloe's death, but everything feels weird."

"Maybe it's the jalapenos you put on your grilled cheese."

"Ha, ha," I mocked. "Not what I meant. But they'll probably come back to haunt me tonight."

"So, tell me Indiana Jones, what clues did you get?" Jos sat up to sip her shake.

"Indiana, huh? I wish. Indy gets golden idols and global adventures; I got a LEGO keychain, and a crumpled paper with a Michigan address."

"Michigan could be interesting. What's the plan? Give everything to the cops?"

"There is an officer I trust, but I'm not sure it's a good idea to give these up yet."

"You aren't planning to investigate this yourself?"

"No, of course not." I feigned indignation, but secretly knew she was right, going it alone was exactly what I'd considered. Jos had been at the top of my list of sidekicks until she made that comment. I hadn't exactly made up with my friends since returning to the city. Who had time? We were settling into a new place and I had responsibilities.

So, I would do it myself, except it would be smarter to have back up. Someone strong, reliable, and available. Garrett was strong and reliable, I wasn't sure about available, but two out of three would do. Whether it was a good idea, or not, we'd find out.

Even with the key, it might not be totally legal, or safe to get into Chloe's. Maybe I could beg him to help me. No, lure him with a promise to train like a soldier—it shouldn't be too hard once he realized how much help I needed. Being a Special Ops guy, he'd be ready to poke holes in any plan I offered, so it needed to be a good one.

"You've got that look in your eyes," Jos said, and I snapped back to reality.

"What look?" I drank more shake.

Jos shook her head. "Whatever you're up to, make sure to keep me in the loop. You know, in case you need help, or bail."

I smiled and sat my glass down.

She paid, I tipped, and we left.

Jos told me all the ways she barely survived her family visit on our ride home. We wound through back roads as daylight slipped away. I laughed at the pranks her younger cousins pulled. The boys (now teenagers) couldn't get their grandpa to fall for the plastic wrap over the toilet seat trick, but they did get Jos. She wasn't happy they also froze her bras while she went swimming. She set them out to thaw. The boys found them and froze them again—she ended up in her bathing suit most of the weekend, to keep things G-rated.

Jos noticed my relaxed state just as we hit the city.

"You should come with me."

"Next year?"

"No, tomorrow."

"Where?"

"The farm."

"What's at the farm? All night euchre tourney?" I asked, knowing her family's most epic card games lasted for days.

"Hay Bales. Hundreds of 'em."

"What do I need with hay bales?"

"They need painted for the Harvest & Hayrides event."

My eyes rolled back into my head.

"It'll be fun. Besides, you need a change of scenery." This was true. "If it helps, it's a paying gig." She smiled then turned onto Vine.

Jos made good arguments.

"If someone's at the parlor and will cover the phones, I can do it."

"Deal," she said quickly.

"What did you do, Jos?"

"I already cleared it with Mr. Handsome."

"Jos!" Embarrassment lit my face.

"C'mon, he's totally cool with it."

If I was going to be taken seriously, I needed to calmly take back my schedule. "Jos—"

"It's settled then?"

"Do I have a choice?"

"Not in this matter," she said, and we both got quiet.

The 'home' was lit up the way it was every night there wasn't a late viewing. One spot lit the stone block engraved with the McKenzie name at the entrance, and several outside lights glared around the building to keep away the unwanted—most of them, anyway.

We looked at the lot surrounding the car. I noticed a lit cigarette in a group of nearby tenants, maybe co-eds, hanging out.

"You want me to go in with you?" Jos asked.

Everything else looked secure, and there were no ghosts or goblins I could see, so I told her no.

"It should be fine. I'll text you when I'm inside."

"Okay. Have a good night, and try to get some rest."

"Will do. You do the same. And watch yourself getting out of here. It's steeper than you think, and everybody speeds, so gun it."

"Got it. Hey, call me in the morning. I have some job ideas." My face crumpled a little thinking about work. "I'll bring coffee," she sang.

"Sounds good."

I got out with my keys ready. One of the parking lot crew let out a screech, which sent me sprinting to the door. The lock tumbled, and the door opened and shut as fast as my human body could make it happen. After locking the door, my heart thumped away. I pulled out my phone and texted Jos, but it took some effort to settle enough to type.

The next order of business was to grab the latest paperwork, and head upstairs.

That's funny. There was no paperwork on the stairs. Ryder told me there was a new one coming in from Hospice tonight. Usually, someone leaves us a copy of the information so we see it on our way up to the apartment.

I looked at the stairs again then at the floor to see if the paper had fallen. Nothing. My nervous energy was still elevated, but I figured Ryder ran out of time to do a formal write-up. I headed for the office to grab his notes.

Halfway down the hall, I noticed one of the desk lamps lit. I stopped moving. Before I could turn, Manny saw me. "Hey. You looking for something?"

It didn't sound like Sledge was in the office with Manny.

Alarm bells were going off in my head. "Yeah, um, yes. Paperwork on the new guy."

"I think there's some paperwork over here," he said, and started moving stuff around on the desks with his eyes trained on me.

I planned to run, but needed to get a head start, which I couldn't do with him staring me down.

"It might be on Hank's desk," I said, hoping he would move away from the doorway. Instead, Manny slithered toward me.

"You know, it could have been propped between the balusters. I'll go check." I turned to leave, but Manny ran up to block me. Even putting his arm on mine to stop me.

"Where are you going? I think what you're looking for is in there," he pointed to the office.

"It's time for me to leave," I insisted, wishing I'd never come this way. Why didn't I just go to the apartment and lock myself in when I got home?

"Nah, why not hang out with me?" He grinned, standing way too close for comfort.

"Manny, it's—"

"It's time to go," Sledge was stern. Relief washed over me when I noticed Garrett walking along side him. They came to where we were standing, and Sledge put his arm on Manny's shoulder, firmly. "C'mon."

Manny looked disappointed. "Maybe we'll catch up some other time." And like that, he and Sledge were on their way out the door. "She's looking for some kind of paperwork," Manny said over his shoulder, like he was trying to help all along. Not as if he'd just scared the crap out of me.

I steadied myself, and waited for them to leave.

"Sorry about them," Garrett said.

"Hazard of the job, right?" Trying not to sound shaken.

"Some days I'm not sure if he's psycho, or really that weird. You didn't text, and it's—" Garrett looked at his watch then blushed, "it's almost seven." He gently twisted his fingers around mine. "Everything okay?"

"Not really, but it's getting better."

He moved me to the office, where we picked up the paperwork on our Hospice client. He shared a brief overview of Mr. Newton, and a recap of the business.

"Can I walk you home?" Garrett smiled, and the day's worries washed away.

"Of course." I smiled back, and we headed down the hall.

It wasn't a long walk, but I told him everything about Tom Clark, the address, and the key. We stopped at the top of the stairs, on the landing out side my door.

"What do you want to do next?"

I trusted Garrett to help. It didn't feel right to try and trick him into going, so out it came. "I was hoping you might accompany me on a little trip."

He didn't answer right away. I briefly worried he might be upset, but I was going with or without him. Then it occurred to me we had work responsibilities.

"Look. I'd like you to come. But, I should wait until mom is back, so there is coverage on my end."

"What about school?" It surprised me to hear him ask.

"Class is Tuesday and Thursday. If mom is home, and well enough, we could go next weekend."

He leaned against the doorjamb and grinned. Just stood there grinning.

"What?"

"You've got this all figured out, don't you?"

"Not exactly. I don't know where we're going, where we'll stay, or what we'll find, but—"

"Mattie," Garrett said in a low, soft voice. "We'll figure it out together."

He moved in, and left no gap between us, but waited for what seemed like my approval. My expression warmed when I saw the look in his eyes. The seriousness was there, but so was desire.

Garrett waited no longer. He used his hands to pull my body against his and kissed me deeply. It lit a fire so urgent, I grabbed at him so he wouldn't stop.

We kissed and tousled until I paused just long enough to get my key. I quickly unlocked the door. Garrett hoisted me up around his waist, carried me inside then twirled me around to shut the door and we kissed harder. I pulled at the back of his shirt to get it off. It wouldn't cooperate. His hand worked its way under my dress and up my back. I clung tighter. Garrett started to unfasten clasps, but hesitated. He kissed me intensely then placed me on the ground. I protested. He pinned me against the wall and kissed me again, slow enough I knew how hard it was to stop.

Garrett took a reluctant step back, and my dress slid back into place. We looked at each other, and for a moment, I thought we'd start up again.

Then the phone rang.

I ran from the kitchen to the living room to answer it. As soon as I said the usual greeting, the line went dead. "Hang-up." I banged the receiver back down and cursed under my breath.

"Don't worry." I came back to Garrett. "Probably just a wrong number."

"Probably. Say the word, and I'll stay...to make sure you're okay."

"I'll be fine." I didn't feel like he had to protect me, but it was reassuring to know he would.

"I know, but lock up anyway. I'll be downstairs a while. Call if you need anything."

"Will do." Thinking of him working on Mr. Newton killed the mood initially, but somehow I was tempted to have him stay for reasons other than safety.

He headed for the door. Before he opened it, he turned and spoke. "I don't want to, but I have to leave."

"I know," I said, and gave him a soft peck on the cheek. "I'll see you in the morning."

"Good night," he said, and headed downstairs. He looked back and watched as I closed up behind him. I made sure to turn all the deadbolts so he could hear them click into place.

CHAPTER 18

Research kept me busy most of the night. After completing initial work-ups on Ruggiano, and Tab (aka Brant Thibodeaux), I started files on Chloe, Dr. Avanti, and even Tess.

Ruggiano had been in trouble with the law since he was a teenager, no surprise there. During his rise to the top, he was charged with assaulting a city council member. The charges were later dropped. After that, he spent a couple years out of the spotlight. One report hypothesized he was going legit while others claimed he had health issues. *He acted crazy. Maybe he really was certifiable?*

A few years ago, photos of him with key public figures started surfacing. The papers snapped pix of Ruggiano with a union leader, a few politicians, and a judge. His photo appeared nearly every week for a couple months, moving closer to the front page each time. It was as if it coincided with his rise in the organization. It looked like a PR stunt to me, but what did I know?

The latest headlines had him all but admitting the mob was in town, and he was in charge. Ruggiano apparently ruffled some feathers with this approach because, as one conspiracy blogger reported, he was at odds with other mob guys in the region.

Fascinated with the history and hierarchy of organizations like the *Cosa Nostra*, I read about them as a hobby. While the public heard stories of the most notorious gangsters, many lasting and prosperous gangs grew successful because they stayed closed off, and operated under the radar. Ruggiano seemed to be bucking those rules. A loose cannon? Probably. He worried me, but until there was more to tie him to Chloe, or the doctor, I had to move on.

Tab's family had been prominent in New Orleans social circles for decades. Beneficiaries of the oil boom, his family held wealth and power.

Scandal rocked the Thibodeaux family when Tab's uncle was jailed for bribing a judge to approve drilling in a protected area.

Tab's older brother struggled with addiction, and made front-page news every time he went to rehab. Their father Lawrence, a former city council member, was caught in the company of a prostitute, and arrested for assaulting her. No charges were filed. He claimed they were admiring his antique weapon collection when she accidentally ran into the butt of his gun several times, so he was released. Tab, raised by a cruel father, developed a penchant for fighting, and hitting women. Not exactly a wholesome clan.

The family had enough money to 'fix' most of their problems. But they sent Tab away to 'find himself', or more likely, to avoid authorities for boosting a car in Baton Rouge. He became our problem instead.

Every once in a while Mr. Thibodeaux, with or without his wife, appeared on campus. He'd deliver a huge check and some board members would pat his back and make a big deal of it.

Sophomore year Parents' Weekend mom and I bumped into him. By this time, mom knew Tab abused Chloe. She made no bones about bringing it up to Mr. Thibodeaux.

"Lawrence, don't you think you should talk with Tab? Mattie told me he's been hitting Chloe."

Mr. Thibodeaux assessed the scene to see if anyone was listening before he responded. "Nora, I appreciate your advice. We'll look into it." They exchanged a few words, but it was tense the entire time.

Mr. Thibodeaux stopped next to mom before he left. I overheard him.

"As a politician, I welcome the public's advice. However, I'd appreciate it if you'd keep your mouth shut about my parenting. We're huge donors to this school and everyone benefits from Tab being here. Let the kids work out their own problems." With that, Mr. Thibodeaux excused himself and schmoozed his way through the room.

Anger burned in mom's eyes. "That man is as rotten as his son. I'll have a talk with Chloe's mom. If it doesn't work, promise you'll stay away from them all."

I just nodded. Mom was right. I trusted her to let Mrs. Ellis know what was really going on with her daughter's boyfriend.

Chloe knew about Tab's past, and begged her mom not to interfere. Chloe was desperate to help Tab. She sympathized because his home life wasn't as nurturing as hers. I was less forgiving. This continually caused problems between us. Time to move past Tab's file before I got too angry to work.

There wasn't much new about Chloe, except she had been a talented cellist, and had recently received a Community Service Award. Grief felt too fresh, so I quickly put aside her file.

Tess was a bit of a wildcard. All the things Garrett had told me about her family were true, but there wasn't much else to find. She had two older sisters and a younger brother. Her parents owned a family business, paid taxes, and stayed out of trouble. I was curious to find out what was going on with Tess because she was Garrett's ex, and showed up with Ruggiano, but the Internet didn't have a lot on them, and my energy waned.

I'd nodded off when Garrett called and asked me to come downstairs. After saving my files, and plugging in my laptop, I made my way to him.

He met me in the back hall, outside the prep area. I stood in a stupor, listing slightly to one side. Moving with purpose, he handed me a clear plastic baggie.

"I hate to bother you this late. Do you recognize this number?" The only indicators of his fatigue were under-eye circles and some stubble. I focused on what was inside the bag. A white card with reddish smudges. It was a business card for Ted Oxley, Attorney at Law. The front listed his contact information. On the back, in writing I recognized, was the name C. Ellis with Chloe's cell number written next to it.

I took a deep breath and sat in one of the chairs outside the Prep Room. "It's Chloe's."

"I thought so," he said grimly.

"What's the stuff on the card? Is it dried blood, or something?" I had a bad feeling.

"It's the same powder we've seen on a couple other victims."

"Victims?"

"Long story."

"Well, I can't exactly leave now. Why don't you fill me in?" I sank into a chair and listened.

"Jimbo, the guy you freaked out about your first day here, and nearly killed yourself running away from?"

"Yeah." Unfortunately, I remembered.

"He had the reddish powder all over him, and so did another woman that came in around that time. Cal asked me to give them a once over."

"Why?"

"Gut feeling. He thought two people dead within a week of each other, both painted red, was more than a coincidence."

The way he said 'painted red' made me curious. Seeing Jimbo dead wasn't the only reason I ran. Sure, he looked like a cross between an Aborigine and a powdered donut, which was creepy enough on its own. What I couldn't shake was the thought he'd wake up at any moment. I knew he was dead. But he terrified me. It didn't help that we were alone with his dead body in the back room of a funeral home.

Since then, I learned others have had similar fears. The living, unless they're in the business, or exposed to it regularly, don't have a chance to get used to death. It can feel antiseptic and cold—far away from the make-up enhanced, tranquilly lit glow shown at viewings and funerals.

Garrett and Ryder grew up around the dead. By now, they'd seen enough to know what to expect, or maybe they'd become desensitized.

"We weren't supposed to see him like that. There was a mix up with the delivery, and we got him first. The Coroner's Office picked him up the same day. But not before I was able to do an exam of my own. He had the same needle mark as Chloe."

"What about the other lady?" The second 'dusty' one as Sledge called her.

"Another delivery mix-up. Someone wanted us to see those bodies before the Coroner. I know it."

Garrett sat beside me—tired, defeated eyes. "When I talked to Cal, he told me to keep it under wraps until we had more proof."

"Proof? Garrett, what's going on?"

I flinched when the back door opened. Garrett reached out for me. "It's okay, I called Cal."

"Hey man," Cal nodded to Garrett as he stepped into the hallway with us. "Hey Mattie. You doing okay? You look shocked."

"Fine. Just a little on edge."

"Do you want coffee, or anything, Cal?"

"Nah, wired enough because of this case. Did you catch her up yet?"

"We just got started." Garrett answered.

"Would someone please tell me what's going on?"

Cal stepped closer. "You were right. Chloe was murdered."

"It's what I've been saying all along!" I banged my hands on the chair and stood up.

"Take it easy." Cal's hands moved downward, like the motion could suppress my anxiety.

Garrett jumped in with a softer voice. "She had needle marks like the others. But they were covered in powder. She wasn't. The only other connection is the business card with Chloe's name and number. It appears to be smudged with the same powder."

"Our lab tested it," Cal explained. "They found out the powder is actually a pigment called Red Ochre. This particular one is used to make paint. It's sold by high-end art supply dealers."

"What does paint have to do with Chloe?"

"Well, we don't exactly know yet. Maybe she was involved with the other murders, or knew someone who was."

"Excuse me? How did we go from Chloe was murdered, to she was involved in multiple murders?" I bit at my lower lip while my fingers twisted the edge of my shirt over and over again.

"Hold up there. I said maybe she was. It may seem unlikely to you, but it is possible. I'm a cop, and doing my job means being thorough. I have to question everything—even people I know." He eyed me suspiciously, which was more annoying than anything.

"I thought it also meant you're supposed to also trust your instincts," I fired back. "Mine tell me she wasn't part of a double homicide."

"Point taken." Cal eyed Garrett. They kept me out of their telepathic conversation. But I knew there was something they weren't telling me. "You mentioned Chloe called you for help earlier. Did she say why?"

"She wanted to my help on a case." If they weren't talking, I wasn't either.

"Did she say what case?" Cal sounded annoyed.

Sorry Cal, if you want more, you're going to have to ask for it, I thought.

"I may take that coffee after all," Cal said. Surprised, Garrett went to get Cal's drink.

Cal waited until Garrett was through the office, and out of earshot. He leaned over me. Instinctually, I backed up a step. Cal shook his head, and dropped his stern expression.

"I didn't mean to be harsh, but you were pretty worked up." Cal looked over at the door, calculated something in his head, and got to it. "I wanted to talk to you alone. Tox screens aren't back yet, so I can't say if all the vics were injected with the same stuff, but the needle marks were nearly identical. When Garrett told me about them, I checked with the Coroner's Office. They weren't noted on any files I saw. Tess had her hands on all the cases."

"We questioned her—"

"I know. I'm worried she's given Garrett some excuse, and he's too involved to see through her BS." The realization she had some hold on him now, or ever, left me uneasy.

"Why are you telling me this?"

"You need to watch out for him. If Tess is involved in these murders, or covering them up, she may try and drag Garrett into it with her."

"How do you expect me to keep tabs on him?"

"You don't need to tail him or anything, Nancy Drew," Cal laughed. "It's just that he's been spending a lot of time with dead bodies lately. So let me know if you notice anything weird—"

I wondered how much time Cal had, because since we'd moved in I'd seen a lot of weird.

"Or if Tess shows up here again."

We heard Garrett get closer, so we nodded our agreement.

"We'd established the vics shared similar markings, but we didn't have much else," Cal spoke as if he hadn't just told me to keep an eye on Garrett. "Appreciate the cuppa joe."

Garrett eyed us both. It took a second for me to plaster an interested-in-what-Cal-was-saying look on my face. Hopefully, it worked.

"Brass wanted to keep it under wraps until we knew for sure it was a multiple homicide."

"What does Brass say now?" I questioned.

"They're getting on board. The first two vics were found in Ruggiano's territory, but management is hesitant to tip him off that we think he's involved. Besides, we're stretched pretty thin, and it'll take more than what we've got for them to assign resources."

"Any leads?"

"We're looking into the first two, and now Chloe as a possible third victim."

Garrett's eyes were on me as soon as he said it. My face showed everything—sadness, guilt, anger and fear. I'd been pushing to get others to look at Chloe's case as a homicide. Here we stood with a member of Cincy's finest telling us her case was unofficially, official. Relieved, a wave of exhaustion washed over me. Garrett propped me up, and I was able to manage a quiet, but heartfelt 'thank you' to Cal before Garrett turned me toward home.

"You need to sleep," Garrett said to me, and then told Cal he'd be back. Garrett escorted me upstairs and helped me inside. He left to finish up and head home.

I downed Millie's potion, crawled into bed and fell asleep. I don't remember much after, except a blip of a dream where the old native man dusted graves with something. It might have made sense, except it was a flash. When I awoke the next morning, it felt like a Mack truck had run over me, repeatedly. *So much for Millie's Magic Potions.*

Jocelyn had convinced me I needed a day away from dead bodies. So, I drove up to her cousin's farm with the promise of treats, and a paycheck, to help set up a Happy Haunted Harvest event at her cousin's farm. It was an autumn festival mashed up with a not-so-scary introduction to Halloween for kids and grown-ups, like me, who never got that into heart-stopping stuff.

I enjoyed suspense, but only if I knew I was coming out alive— these days, it was hard to tell. Years ago, I'd had a run-in with a guy in high school who took his night-of-the-living-dead role a little too seriously. After jumping out of a dark corner of a Jaycees haunted house, he moaned and grabbed me. It felt so real, I screamed like a baby and flapped my arms to get him off me. He thought it was funny and kept taunting me. Jos got scared and had to literally yank me out of his clutches. We freaked, ran out of the house, and never went back.

I guess the guy did his job, but he deserved a kick in the nuts for scaring us so bad.

Jos's cousin was part of the Ashfield family—corn tycoons, or something. They had an old farm between Cincy and Dayton, which they maintained and worked to this day.

The countryside stretched out ahead. The car revved and I let it loose. Jos was right, I needed a break.

A half hour later, the Nav system instructed me to turn right. The car owned the road until the dirt trail. Pockmarked and only about a lane and a half, the trail started low on the property. It curved upward through trees and land until I saw a large yellow and white farmhouse. An idyllic setting for a house with a generous front porch, and two old-fashioned rockers out front.

I stepped out of the car and inhaled grasses and woods. The switch had flipped from summer heat to autumn cool. When I got to the house, Jos's Aunt and Uncle debated Farmer's Almanac predictions of another harsh winter. The idea of a polar vortex was unsettling, so I stopped listening and hugged Jos.

She gave me a brief tour, and introduced her cousins. It happened so quickly—I remember meeting her Aunt JoAnn, Uncle Lou and a bunch of kids. The farm buzzed with activity, so we headed outside and got started.

"So what do you want me to do with all these?" I indicated the enormous hay cylinders that towered over us.

"Spray paint them with pumpkins and goofy Halloween faces," Jos said, as she crossed her eyes and stuck out her tongue. "We want to keep it PG so little kids can enjoy it, and their parents will want to bring them back. Stuff like this helps keep the family business going after harvest. They even host a sleigh ride with Santa."

"Why couldn't I have pulled that gig?"

"I know you aren't into creepy stuff, but you'll enjoy this. Think of when we used to go trick-or-treating at Crystal Creek. It was all about dressing up and getting candy, not being scared by disemboweled freaks."

"Okay, but I'm out of here if even one person jumps out at me. That includes you."

"I know, I know." Jocelyn handed me a cardboard box full of

random paint cans, with and without lids. "Just paint something. Painting hay bales is like tagging a wall, only it's legal."

"I never painted the school, Jimmy Peters made it look like I did."

"I know, but I already managed to help you forget someone wants you dead."

My stomach knotted up and I thought I'd throw up. My face must have shown it too.

"Too soon? Sorry. Let's get to work. We can have lunch, or at least some cider and donuts when we're finished with all these."

"Yum. How many of these things do we have to decorate?" You could see acres of harvested landscape, and eight-foot or taller rolls of hay everywhere.

"We only have to paint 50; half are yours. It's doable. I have to head up to the house and get a few things together for Aunt JoAnn. Will you be okay here?"

"Yeah. Even if I wasn't, I'd still do it to help Jos." I recited the words she used to lure me here, and she laughed.

"It won't be bad. Text if you need anything." Jocelyn hopped on a small utility cart. The motor buzzed as she drove toward the house.

I sat the paint box near my first victim and picked up a can without a lid—much easier than prying one off with a screwdriver. I shook the can and heard the metallic ball clanking around before taking aim.

Paint droplets misted the air. Some even hit the hay bale. I concentrated and hit the target the second time. The gold and auburn countryside was picturesque. I'd say it took my breath away, but it might have been the paint fumes.

Painting in this setting reminded me of the time mom and I completed a baby-to-big kid bedroom makeover. We painted an old dresser then she sketched lines on the walls. I had sky, and clouds, and a rainbow in my room when we finished painting. The sun burned away my tears so I could get back to the hay.

After the first couple not-so-scary bale-faces, I felt like I'd gotten the hang of it. I got more creative and ended up with a couple of purple-haired googly-eyed faces that looked almost cute. I bent to find a canister of orange when I heard something rustle in the field a few feet away.

This was it, I thought. After confrontations and threats, someone was going to get me. My heart pounded. I looked for a clear path to the house, but gigantic hay bales were all over the place. I prayed the noise was just some birds, or field mice running around the corn stover because my only weapon was spray paint. I wished for a lighter to make a paint can flamethrower—but I had no experience, and probably would have burned the hair off my arms and face if I'd tried.

The wind picked up. Some leaves flew by and the rustling started again. I aimed a spray can with one hand, and grabbed my phone to thumb text Jos for help with the other. Then waited.

My hand cramped around the paint can, and my knees locked up waiting.

And waiting.

Wondering if I'd turn to stone, Jos came to my rescue just as a cat ran out of the field. Whew!

"Probably chasing mice," Jos said, and stepped out of the Gator. There were plenty of animals running around here, but something didn't seem right. "I can stay and help."

Relieved, I thanked Jos. We stuck together and painted hay bales until they were all decorated as fun-not-frightening characters. The rest of our time at the farm, we talked with her Aunt JoAnn and stuffed ourselves full of donuts and cider.

After an hour, I checked my phone. Garrett and Ryder had been really flexible about phone coverage the past couple days, and I didn't want to take advantage of their kindness. I signaled Jos. She knew I needed to head back. It was critical I start my 'shift' on time. Saying thanks didn't seem like enough, so I hugged Jos and her aunt then headed back with cash and cider.

Country roads and yellow lines lay before me. I turned on the radio, cracked the windows enough to let in fresh air, then hit the road.

During the drive home, I wrestled with the idea Chloe could somehow be linked to a gangster. It began to appear as though everyone was tied to the mob. Chloe, Tess, and Garrett—claiming a one time deal. It was Garrett's only flaw, so far. I was curious about a lot of things Garrett-related, especially, what he did for Ruggiano. But first, I needed to figure out how Ruggiano fit into Chloe's world, or vice versa.

Ideas tumbled around upstairs. But what stuck out was the Sigo case. According to information from Tom Clark, a guy I'd met only yesterday, this was a big land deal, and probably Chloe's big case. Seeing Tom's strange behavior, I knew it was important to check out Chloe's place. Last night was too late, Jos and I worked this morning, and I was headed back to the funeral home to answer phones through the night. Finding answers would have to wait until morning. My new to-do list: work, sleep, snoop, and school.

CHAPTER 19

When I got home, clouds hung overhead. Ash grey saturated every detail of the funeral home. The place looked dull compared to the vibrant landscape I'd left.

My motivation waned. But I thought of mom, and the job, and pushed onward.

Everything looked secure from the outside. Everything will be fine, I tried to reassure myself. Crisp air whipped at my skin and I had second thoughts about this place. Once safely inside, I shut out the outside world.

"Hey there," Garrett said. I jumped a mile high. "Easy, I'm friendly."

I heaved a sigh of relief then giggled thinking of him as more than friendly. Getting close to him posed a major risk, but it didn't stop me from imagining it. A perk of doing this sort of work was I got to see him nearly every day. More frequently, since we had an influx of dead bodies. I cringed at the thought and pushed it to the back of my brain.

Garrett took my hand in his. "Nice paint," he commented on my purple, orange and black hands. He led me through the hallway, past the cookie tables, the coffee pot, and into the office.

"Are we discussing business?"

"Nope."

"Then what?"

"You."

"Me?"

"Yes, you. It's time you tell me what's really going on with you."

"With me? I have a few questions for you, mister!"

"Okay. I'll answer yours, if you answer mine. But first, I've got plans."

This sounded promising. I wondered if he wanted to order Thai, hunker down, and figure this mystery out, or if he planned something romantic. *A girl can dream. Right?* "What plans?"

Garrett stepped closer, which made me warm in all the right places. When he leaned forward, I got ready for a kiss.

"Training," he whispered across my lips then picked some hay out of my hair.

I huffed at him, and he gave me a peck on the cheek.

"But first, there is someone you need to meet."

I eyed Garrett suspiciously. He'd arranged for me to meet Mrs. Jacobson, the lady who lived down the street. He told her I was looking for work and said she was more than happy to interview me.

It sounded like a nice gesture, but I wanted to get the job on my own merits. He figured as much and offered to stay behind. He then pointed me toward the door.

"I have to clean up."

"Better make it fast. She's expecting you in fifteen minutes."

"But, how did you know I'd be here in time?"

"Jos. She called when you left, so I could tell Mrs. J."

First, Jos talks to my mom, and now Garrett? "Are you guys double-teaming me?"

"Pretty much."

"I can handle myself, you know."

"I know. Just trying to help."

"It would be nice if one of these days someone would talk to me before making decisions about my life."

"Very well. You get to pick what we do after practice."

"It's a start."

I hustled upstairs, and did my best to scrub the paint off my hands and run a brush through my hair. My jeans were dirty, so I pulled on a pair of black pants, added a grey shirt, and stuffed my phone and ID in the pockets. Satisfied, I grabbed a jacket and went back downstairs.

Garrett gave me the address. Mrs. Jacobson lived across the street—three doors down from the Davis Funeral Home.

Freshly painted, her house stood as a revived Victorian among other less maintained homes.

When I got inside, Mrs. Jacobson showed me around. She explained how she decorated it just the way she liked. The house featured antique clocks and wood trim, Queen Anne chairs, and a library of old books. I could have browsed the library all day, and not read the same title twice. Everything appeared well maintained, and there wasn't a hint of must or mothballs. I could definitely hang out here.

Mrs. Jacobson used a cane during the tour. She wobbled a bit, but shrugged off my attempts to help—determined to prove her independence.

She directed me to sit. The couch was covered in an expensive-looking brocade. She had a tea set on the long, low table in front of us. Alongside it sat a three-tiered serving tray. The top tier held fresh strawberries, raspberries, and pears. The second tier had dessert bites that looked like pecan brownies. Beside those were mini caramel apple tarts, and cranberry scones with a side of clotted cream. The bottom tier held sliced cheese, and cucumber sandwiches.

When Mrs. Jacobson finally sat, she smoothed out her dress and asked me to pour the tea. I was a little nervous about spilling it, so I made sure to focus.

She added two sugar cubes and milk to both cups then gracefully stirred and lifted her tea to sip. I mimicked her. The tea was the perfect temperature and sweetness. When finished, she placed the delicate cup back on the saucer. I did the same.

"So tell me, dear," she said in a slightly broken tone. "What are your skills?"

Even though I knew it was an interview, the question sounded abrupt. The dainty foods, and sweet tea led me to believe it might be more of a 'get-to-know-you-chat'. Instead of panicking, I took a breath and asked her what the job entailed, so I could best answer her questions.

"You'd do a little of this and that. I like the company, and it helps to have someone here in case I run into trouble. You know, the 'Help, I've fallen and can't get up' scenario."

Mrs. Jacobson made light of her condition, she wasn't bitter. I liked her.

She explained that the cook was expecting her third child and wanted to scale back on work. She'd like to have me visit a once a week and occasionally run errands.

"I'd have my nephew do it, but he's not always available," she sounded perturbed. "I love the boy, but he needs to mature."

In answer to her question, I listed a half dozen skills and traits to fit her needs. Really, I was overqualified, but the woman needed help. I assured her I'd be prompt and dependable.

We snacked and discussed the schedule and pay rate. She was more than generous, so it wasn't much of a discussion.

My phone alarm buzzed. "Sorry. I promised to be home soon," I told her. "Do you have anything else you'd like to discuss?"

"Not today."

"Feel free to call if you have other questions, or need anything."

"Thank you, Mattie."

We both rose. She grabbed her cane, and even thought she didn't need to, she walked me to the door.

On the way out, I noticed an unfinished painting in the solarium. The landscape was unlike anything I'd ever seen. She caught me hypnotized by it. I blushed. "It's striking," I told her.

"Thank you, dear. I think so too. Needs some work, though."

There was something about the way she said it. "Is this your work?" I was astounded anyone in her frail state could paint such a beautiful piece.

"Don't look so surprised. I may be old, but I'm not dead yet." She eyed the painting then me. "I look forward to seeing you again." That was it. She offered no other details, and let me out.

As if in a trance, I thought about the painting all the way home. All seven minutes of it. I crossed the street heading toward Mackenzie's driveway. A blue van that I thought was a quarter mile away gunned the engine. I had to run to avoid getting hit.

I turned to curse at the guy and saw brake lights. The van screeched around, doing an illegal U-turn, and headed straight toward me.

I sprinted up the drive. My body was moving, but outrunning the van was going to be a challenge. I'd had a couple of angry threats this week, and I did not want to find out what happened if the stalker caught me.

In my mind, I started going through scenarios of how best to get inside. Coming straight up the drive meant my side door key was useless. It wouldn't unlock the outer glass, or the cathedral doors behind it. If I went to my right, my key would work, but I was totally exposed. People came through this place daily, sometimes hourly, when we were busy. Where was everyone when I needed help? Probably seeking shelter to avoid the rain, which had started.

If I ran left, I might make it to the back delivery door. If my followers gained speed, I could be trapped.

Front door, banging to get inside=bad idea. Side door, exposed=bad idea. Delivery side, trapped=bad idea. So, I chose the best of the bad ideas, and prayed. My legs burned as I ran faster, slipping only once.

This competition was about speed. I didn't look back for fear it would slow me down, but I could hear the van's tire squeal to grip the asphalt. They were closing in on me.

The front of the building flashed past, then the side portico—I didn't know if my key would work there, so I wasn't going to chance it.

I got a few feet further and heard brakes. A door slid open. Three more steps, and…Whump! Someone took me down from behind. I braced myself for impact, but the massive beast somehow turned as we fell, so I landed on him. Not the other way around. I noticed a sword tattooed on his wrist as he rolled me over. Dazed and confused, I looked over to see a dark-haired guy, dressed in black, wearing a Zorro mask.

"Where is it?" he yelled.

"Where's what?" I had next to nothing. Why would some masked man be tackling me?

"They key! Give me the key!"

"What key?" I said, as the rain came down harder. It occurred to me they could be demented thieves who wanted access to the funeral home. "You want my house key?"

"No!" He was anxious more than angry. "The key you got yesterday."

This was about the key Tom gave me. This was about Chloe.

"I don't have it on me."

"Where is it?"

What I said next was either very smart, or very stupid. "It's inside." I wanted to take the words back as soon as I'd said them. But if these guys wanted me dead, they'd have hauled me away in that creepy van already. When this guy tackled me, he twisted so I wouldn't be crushed or crippled. They needed the key. And they needed me to get it. My only chance was to buy time, and hope for a miracle.

Zorro picked me off the ground and led me to the delivery door. The yellow lines were visible and rain puddled on the blacktop, which made me think no one else was here.

I inserted my key then twisted the handle. The masked man pushed me in first and followed. I turned to head further into the building when Garrett jumped out and punched the guy. He got another good shot in before the bad guy fired back and locked his arms around Garrett's neck.

I scanned the room for a weapon, and noticed an urn and an umbrella. With his back turned, I smacked fake Zorro upside the head with the umbrella. It was a nice hit, but it only stunned the guy.

Garrett got free and smiled at me. Fake Zorro came back and punched Garrett who stumbled, but managed to grab the guy's shirt. They struggled near the open door where Garrett swung him around and slammed him into the door. The creep dropped to the ground.

I ran over, pulled off his mask, and smacked him. It surprised the guy. He put his hands up defensively.

"Why are you doing this?" I yelled. "What do you want from me?" I kept slapping at him even though it wasn't doing anything other than irritating him.

Garrett caught my arms, and lifted me off Zorro, out of harm's way. I started back toward the guy, but Garrett stopped me then turned to deal with my assailant.

Garrett pulled the guy off the ground, slammed him against the wall, and with an arm at his neck, started firing off questions. "Who sent you?"

No response.

"Who sent you?!" He pressed.

Still, no response.

"Do you need an incentive to talk?" Garrett pressed harder.

No response, but I heard some gurgling. Then the guy shook his head 'no'.

"Then tell me," Garrett said. "Why are you here?"

"We were told to find her. To get the key," the guy struggled, but Garrett wasn't letting go.

"What key?"

"Some key she got yesterday." It was obvious by his helium-pitched voice the guy was losing oxygen the longer Garrett held him there.

"Go back to your boss. Tell him the girl is off limits. So is the key."

"Please. I'm just doing a job," the guy said, and I could swear there were tears in his eyes.

"No key. If it's so important, your boss should ask for it himself." Garrett said, and threw him out into the rain.

Zorro ran to the van, which was sitting at idle. The driver must have missed the show. The now unmasked bad guy yelled at the driver in a foreign language then they sped away.

"I can't believe Ruggiano sent his goons again."

"No," Garrett told me. "That guy wasn't part of his gang."

It bothered me Garrett had worked for Ruggiano. Even worse, he'd done something that required him to know members of Ruggiano's gang.

"Who do you think we're dealing with now?"

"I'm not sure, but I have a hunch it's someone worse."

"There's someone worse than him?" I started to shake. Garrett noticed.

"Are you hurt?"

"Not really, just wet."

"We've got to get you somewhere safe, and dry."

"I'm fine. Glad you were here. Where's your car?"

"Detail shop. They'll deliver it when the rain stops."

"We need to get into Chloe's. Tom said the answers could be there."

"It's too risky now. They may be watching it."

"But Garrett, there might be proof she didn't kill herself." He knew how much it meant for me to prove this for her parent's sake as much as my own—I wanted to make up for times Chloe was there for me, and relieve myself of the guilt I carried around for not helping her sooner.

"Mattie, there is no way to take away their pain. You can only help ease it. The best way to do that isn't by getting yourself hurt, but by staying safe."

I wouldn't budge.

When he shook his wet hair, droplets showered the floor. His blue eyes focused on me. I was just about to agree with him.

"Fine," he said. "The least you can do is try and be safe."

I shrugged. "I'll think about it. After we search Chloe's"

"Here's the deal. If you're that determined, you've got energy for a lesson. Dry off and change into your gear. We'll run to the gym, then go to Chloe's."

I didn't feel like defense maneuvers, but he'd offered to check out a lead. I wasn't going to argue.

I dried off quickly, changed, and made it back downstairs in record time for me. He was already waiting. Was he Superman, or maybe, he wore workout gear under his regular clothes? Although, his bulging biceps made me want to believe the Superman theory.

"Looks like it's the Hellcat or the hearse. Mind if I drive?"

"Go ahead." It wasn't my car, but since it was a loaner from his mechanic, at his request, and my car repairs were being paid on his dime (currently), he deserved a chance to drive such an awesome machine.

"We'll figure this out," he reassured me as we zoomed through the streets.

"I know." But these answers didn't come easy.

He slowed the car near construction. I reached up to grab something for support, but missed and cracked my knuckles on the glass. He gave me a sideways look.

I shook out my hand. As if it might make the sting or the embarrassment go away. No such luck. I looked back at him. "What? I never pretended to be coordinated. Besides, it hurt me not you."

"It never ceases to amaze me, the number of things you run into and yet you're still here."

"Stubbornness pays off." I rubbed my hand.

"I guess so. Maybe if we practice some usable skills, you'll outlast the bad guys."

"You think I'll have to outlast a lot of them?"

"From what I've seen, you attract trouble. So, yes."

"But, people like me...most of the time."

"Bad guys don't care if you're likeable. If you get in their way, they'll come at you until you get out of their way...or stop breathing."

"Sheesh," I grumbled as we pulled into a parking lot in an area of town I'd normally avoid.

It really was time to focus. This was a gym unlike any I'd ever seen. It was a hole compared to the last place we'd gone. No fancy reception area, no neon snake, and no scary guys with semi-automatics. All fine by me. I felt more at ease here despite the fact it was crumbling around us.

We entered a big room with an old boxing ring near the center. A series of training stations surrounded the ring. The place was drafty and smelled like old shoes, probably from years of intense, sweaty use, and old shoes.

We walked around the outside of the room past a big guy punching a heavy bag, and a woman working with a special bag that kept springing back at her. Garrett called it a reflex bag. He told me it was even harder than it looked.

We turned toward a partially mirrored wall—I guess boxers, like dancers, benefitted from watching their moves. We walked a few more feet and saw a speed bag hanging from a splintered wood disc. It was barely attached to the wall by a black bracket secured with only one bolt, where I think there used to be two, or even three. I saw another guy taping his hands. We set our gear down near the mat we'd be using. There were a few others working around us.

What really startled me was the kid across the room—his baby face looked about ten, but his emergent muscles put him somewhere around puberty. He morphed into and out of adulthood as he practiced.

The boy was scrapping with a guy in his late thirties, but the kid held his own. Garrett must have noticed my staring.

"They've been here a few times." Garrett noted an even younger boy standing along the wall near them.

I watched and wondered. "They look so young. Why are they doing this? Shouldn't they be playing soccer or something?"

"The first time I saw them here, the kid working out was beat up pretty bad. Someone had done a number on him. His friend's uncle brings them in a couple times a week."

My eyes focused on the older guy. Built like a tank wearing lots of black and a crew cut, probably military.

"They practice here. Sometimes they film the sessions then post the videos online." Garrett was beside me now. "They want to help other people deal with the bullies in their lives."

"Those kids are amazing and brave." I admired the kid as he broke free from a chokehold. "Bullies suck."

Garrett's eyes were on me now.

"Bullies do suck. But, killers are worse. It's time to get serious. Before the next guy comes after you."

We were all desperate fighters in this dark place—men, women, and children. We came here to learn how to protect ourselves from something, or someone bad.

I was in way over my head and had absolutely no idea what I would do if someone attacked me. Other than scream loudly, if I could even do that. A chill raced up my spine. I felt the urge to run away, but ignored it. I took a breath, clenched my fists and found my resolve. "Where do we start?"

"Remember your fighting stance," Garrett said. "Left leg out front. Right heel up, so you're ready to pounce, defend, whatever."

"Got it." My hands went up, my chin went down, and my feet bounced around to let him know I was ready.

"All right," he sounded impressed. "Let's see what you've got. We'll go over the stuff I showed you last time. Then we'll work on things, like choke holds and gun threats, if there's time."

That sounded intimidating, but I steeled my nerves and waved him on.

"Mattie, I don't want to hurt you, but I'm going to come at you harder than last time. You need to do your best to keep me away. Just yell 'Time' if you need a break."

We stood there. I looked at him and blew out a big breath to calm myself. "I'm ready," I told him, but didn't say anything about being worried one of us might get hurt.

Garrett came at me from the front, and reached me before I could think of what to do. He stopped when he realized I wasn't ready. He stepped back and awaited my signal.

My brain processed the exercise. This was 'hand meets face'. I couldn't remember the technical term, so I shortened it to something memorable. Keep it simple. It's what this type of training was all about.

We nodded at each other and started up again. He moved toward me, I closed the distance and put the heel of my hand up to his face. Only his chin took the impact, which was to say my effort did nothing to stop him. He grabbed me and put me on the mat before anyone could blink. I was flat on the floor, but at least I was trying.

Garrett helped pull me up. I shook it off.

"Okay, let's try again. Remember, close the distance. Thrust upward."

When he came at me, I bent my arm and thrust the palm of my hand upward. He managed to pull his head back just before the contact.

"Nice job. If I hadn't moved out of the way, you'd have busted my schnoz. One more time."

The same thing happened. I struck and he moved his face to avoid collision.

"That's it! Injure the nose. Distract the attacker. Get away." He sounded giddy about me almost giving him a broken nose. Strange, but I was excited too.

"Now, we'll see if you can break my hold. I'll grab you. Bring your arms up the middle then back down over mine."

I remembered this one. Garrett stepped forward and grabbed my shoulders. I pushed my arms up and over. My arms came down on his and broke his hold on me. *Yes!*

"Nice."

"Thanks."

"This time, come back with the thrust move after you break my hold."

We tried a couple times, but it didn't quite work. He stopped to show me in slow motion, and I did better the next couple times.

Garrett spent an hour teaching me ways to break free from an attacker. With each attempt, we moved faster, and breathed harder. Distractions fell away, instinct kicked in—and something sparked.

I tried to break free from his come from behind attack, but couldn't. Pinned in his arms, my adrenaline surged. So, I improvised. My body weight shifted, enough to get him off balance. Then I grabbed his thumb and bent it back to force him to let go, which gave me space to move. It was enough for me to grab his arm and twist it backward until he was on the ground.

"Okay, you got me!"

I let go and helped him up.

"Nice improv. You may need it when the time comes."

To hear him say 'when the time comes' like that shook me up. It would take a lot more practice for me to get comfortable with all this.

A lot. I just hoped my mind wouldn't blank out if my life depended on it. Bad things happened to more people than me. How did they handle this fear? He must have sensed my apprehension, because his serious face faded.

"I think we've had enough sparring for one night. Let's get out of here."

"Agreed." The workout made me warm, but everything got hotter when he grabbed me, and pulled me closer. I was ready for something other than fear of death; whatever he had in mind. My finger caught the edge of his t-shirt and played with it.

"You look hot," he grinned, picking up on my signals. "Maybe you need a cold shower."

"Not exactly what I was thinking, but I'm willing to listen."

"If you towel off, we can do some investigating before dinner."

Investigating. Right. I was definitely distracted. Did I mention it was hot? "All right, but I get to drive."

CHAPTER 20

Garrett and I went to Chloe's apartment. A place called The Reserve near Fourth and Race Streets. I'd heard about it. The 15-story tower was originally built in 1927 in Cincinnati's Fourth Street Historic District. A commercial builder converted the Federal Reserve Bank offices into high-end urban dwellings. The kind of place Chloe, or her parents, could afford.

I punched in the code Tom gave me to get inside. Polished accents lined the way to a sitting area decorated with luxurious chairs. There were fresh flower arrangements on several tables around the room. The place glowed and smelled slightly of wood polish.

We bypassed the elevators and took the stairs—Garrett said it would be good exercise. Sure, walking up fourteen flights of stairs was good exercise, but it meant I'd be starving soon. Having already burned a ton of calories, I intended to savor dinner after this.

We searched her floor until we found the apartment. I pulled out the LEGO keychain when we got to her doorstep. A decorative wreath, the fresh kind you can order from Maine, or Vermont hung on her door. I looked over the balsam green wreath dotted with brown and ivory accents, and scented with cinnamon sticks. This felt like an invasion of privacy. Something on the other side of this door could provide us the break we need. I stuck the key in, and turned it to open the lock.

Garrett suggested he go inside first, in case there was a problem. I thought it might be a good idea too, even though we were opening a locked door—a good sign in my book. I watched him walk inside.

He took one step and stopped. I nearly rear-ended him it happened so fast.

"What's wrong?"

He immediately put a hand up, and nodded a quick 'no' to me. I got super quiet then glanced over his shoulder and knew immediately why he stopped. The place was trashed. No indication from the outside, but inside it was clear someone had been looking for something they really wanted to find.

There were some intense moments of not knowing what, or who, might still be there. But seeming satisfied with his scan of the room, Garrett entered and pulled me closely behind him.

"My God, Chloe. What were you into?" I murmured as we entered.

The apartment was beautiful, except for the mess of files, papers, and couch cushions spread all over. I wondered if the local police knew about this. Why would a woman who allegedly committed suicide have this happen? Something much bigger was going on and we'd just stepped into the middle of it.

"Look at this place. There is no way she left it like this. Chloe loved order. This would have given her a heart attack." It wasn't a joke. She wouldn't have left it like this. There was never a hair out of place on the girl. She even organized her socks, so this could not have happened before she died.

"Looks like it, but we've got our work cut out for us. The police can't dig into a closed case unless they have something concrete. And this," he looked at the mess. "This could just be a case of a poorly timed break-in."

"Really?" I stood defensively. "How would they explain the television and artwork are untouched?"

"Hey, I'm not saying it isn't something more. I'm just telling you we're going to need real evidence before we ask the police to go looking for a killer. We need to be cautious. We don't want to accuse anyone, cop or coroner, of making a mistake just yet."

"Even if that's what happened?"

"Yes, even then. It'd be difficult for Cal to help if we had the cops on our bad side. Plus, it puts the bad guys on high alert."

"But they already know we're after something. I haven't exactly been quiet about investigating Chloe's death."

"Yes, and it's why you've got bad guys after you." Intensity flashed in his eyes. "But from what I've seen, they're only trying to figure out what you know, or scare you off. The longer we keep quiet, and build the case, the better."

"Stay low."

"Right. And figure out what Chloe is trying to tell you."

"Tell me?"

"You said it yourself. She called you about the case. Sent Tom Clark to give you the key. There's something you can do more than anyone else."

"Run into bad guys and brick walls?"

"Besides that," he chuckled. "Mattie, you have a lot to offer. Don't let your situation determine your value."

"Thank you." I softened, and took a deep breath. "I guess we'd better be thorough." I knew it was a long shot, especially, if public or elected officials were involved. Still, questions remained, like why someone powerful, and probably loaded with cash, was trying to cover up my friend's death?

"You take this part of the room." He headed to the other side of the room. "Look for anything out of place."

"You mean besides the tossed papers, and shredded couch?" I had to find something sarcastic to say to take the edge off. Danger hovered over this 'investigation' of ours. The fact that someone I knew was murdered scared me.

"Yeah, try to overlook those. You knew her. Look for anything out of the ordinary, and anything too ordinary. Something she may have tried to hide in plain sight."

"Great, so we'll be here a while."

"Plan on it." He picked up a lamp and put it on an end table.

My stomach grumbled. I snarled just a little, but shook it off, and dug into a pile of papers around her desk.

It looked like a tornado hit here. There was not a good starting place, so I decided to work my way from left to right.

The papers on the floor to the left of her desk looked mostly like household stuff. Appliance manuals, credit card statements, and electric bills.

The mess under her desk looked even less interesting. Rental policies and meeting notices.

On the right of her desk were some notes, but there wasn't much there either.

"Can I at least clean this up?" I asked Garrett who was checking out the living room.

"No, we need to leave it for the police."

"Okay," I huffed, frustrated. I decided to see if there was anything on her desk.

Most of the papers looked like more of what I'd found on the floor. Very few work files. Strange considering she lived and breathed work. Plus, the dock for her laptop was empty. Perhaps, whoever broke in took her other work files and computer. The bad guys could already have the information they wanted. How would we be able to do anything if it was lost?

While shuffling through the papers, I started to doubt our chances of finding anything in this mess, and sank into Chloe's desk chair.

I swiveled back and forth in a daze. Then I noticed a photo of us at the lake. You could tell we'd been on the lake all day—sun burnt smiles and oily ponytails. We looked happy, but it was slightly out of focus, and it later turned out to be a bad night for us all. I was surprised to see it taking up valuable real estate on her desk. It was the night Tab jumped me. Even though Chloe and Tab had a complicated relationship, I couldn't believe she would like the constant reminder of his cruel behavior. Maybe seeing him at his worst helped her stay away from him. Still, it seemed unusual.

I picked up the frame and looked it over. Six of us—Chloe, Tab, Patrick, Jos, Nina and me—posed with the lake house in the background. Other than Tab, I didn't know of anyone who might have been relevant to what's going on, so I flipped the picture around to examine the silver frame. That's when I noticed something on the back near the stand.

Three numbers, which looked like a date, but it wasn't the date the photo was taken. I remembered that one well. This date was off by a few months, although, it seemed vaguely familiar. I took a sheet off her flowery pink note stack, wrote the numbers exactly as she had, then stuffed it in my pocket.

When the frame was back in place, we continued to search the place for clues. If she'd left me a message on the photo, maybe she'd left others. I took another pass at her personal files. She kept a large monthly bills file with a logbook. There were a lot of bills: phone, gas, electric. We didn't have time to read everything, so I snagged that file and a couple others to review later.

Garrett and I worked our way through the Living Room and Kitchen, where the previous intruders had searched. There were some open drawers and cabinets in the bedroom and bath, but nothing stood out. Even the laundry room was a bust, so we locked up and headed back to the parlor.

Rain pelted the car as we drove. My feet hurt and my stomach was angry for not feeding it sooner. I needed to eat, change, and get warm.

The original plan had been to get home. I'd grab a hot shower while Garrett picked up dinner. He ended up on a call to Cal. That didn't bother me. What got under my skin was the text Tess sent. Whatever she wrote made him drop everything and run, which made me livid. We argued. Garrett told me what Tess said was important, and he had to meet her. What I heard was 'she's more important than you'.

He left. I sat there fuming for ten or fifteen minutes before the cold got to me. I was damp down to my bones and started to shiver. Garrett wasn't there to help warm me up. But I didn't need his help. A hot shower and whatever was stashed in my fridge would suffice.

I stormed off into the hallway and a noise stopped me in my tracks. It didn't sound like a normal-house-settling kind of noise. I took a second and considered my options. Head for the apartment, and I'm locked in, but possibly trapped. Head out of the house, and I have a shot at screaming loud enough to get someone's attention, if anyone was out in this weather. Either way, running felt like the smart move.

Everything remained still, except the thudding in my chest. I took a deep breath then ran for the door.

Just as I hit full stride, a Marvel Comic bad guy on steroids stepped in my way and I slammed into him.

The impact didn't appear to move him an inch, but it sent me flying. I landed on my ass. Hard. He reached out to pick me up with his meat hooks, but I scrambled through the viewing room door before he could get to me.

Once on my feet, I fled toward the front of the house. I didn't look back, but I could hear him slam open the door and bound after me. All the flowers and chairs from Chloe's service were gone, only the antique furniture and drapes that belonged to the room remained.

I pushed my way through the door to the front hall and bounced off an exact duplicate of the human cyborg chasing me. I fell to the floor, again. Then turned to get up and run, only I was too slow. Before I could get anywhere the first mammoth came up from behind and hoisted me in the air.

I struggled, yelled, and kicked air. It felt like the same beast that'd threatened me at the brick wall. He had me wrapped up tight all over again. I saw his arms and knew it was the same guy.

When I wouldn't stop wriggling, he asked his partner for an assist. Actually, it sounded more like a grunt. Just as the guy got close enough to reach for my legs, I nailed him in the groin. He flinched, turned purple, and fell to the ground.

The clone, or whatever you want to call him, dropped me to shield his family jewels, and I started to run. Before I could reach the front door, the first guy stuck his hand out and tripped me. I went head first into the carpet, and nearly sprained my wrist bracing for the fall. As I lay crumpled, I wondered if there was any way out of this. There was a sitting room to my right, a formal office to my left, and a giant door to freedom a couple feet in front of me. Great, if only the bad guys didn't have me pinned down.

"Ha-ha-ha! Very entertaining." The voice startled me. One of the goons must have received a signal, because he nodded at the figure. The big guy yanked me up by the hair, and restrained my arms, as Ruggiano emerged. "You like these guys? I call them Thor's Twins. It's catchy. Don't you think?"

Making up nicknames for the battering ram twins? This guy was seriously unstable. "What are you doing here?"

"You ask too many questions." Ruggiano nodded to one of the men and glared at me. "Take this nosy bitch downstairs. It's more private there."

Thor's Twins pulled out zip-ties, and went to work on my hands and feet. They shoved a white cloth laced with night-night juice over my face. I struggled and tried to jerk myself loose. About a second later, I passed out.

CHAPTER 21

Things looked hazy as I regained consciousness. It was cold and my body ached. I was tied up in the basement. I hated basements. This, I hated more.

A funeral home basement is about the worst place on earth to be when you're being held against your will. It's not like it was a cozy space with daylight windows, or a walkout. This was a place things went to be forgotten, or buried. At least it's how it felt with the 1950s washer-dryer set mocking me from a nearby corner.

No one was going to see, or hear me through the tiny covered windows. No one was going to pass by, because on nights we didn't have viewings, or meetings, no one bothered to come near the place.

My head swayed, and my eyes kept opening and closing. I knew Ruggiano was dangerous, but right now he flat out terrified me. I started twisting my wrists to break free, and searched for a way out. As it stood, there was none, except the rickety stairs behind the thugs holding me hostage. I shivered from the cold and my hopeless situation.

"I wouldn't be in this position if it weren't for that scum Sultan," Ruggiano said to one of his men. "And this one's as stupid as her father. Who is she protecting anyway?"

I tried to act passed out, but shock jarred my insides. What did Ruggiano have to do with my dad?

"Her family's been a thorn in my side for years. We deal with Sultan. Then we take care of her family."

The best I could do was blink off and on as if struggling to break a cobweb haze.

"What do you want?" I sounded drunk, but it helped conceal my fear. Whatever Ruggiano wanted was must have been important. Otherwise, he wouldn't be here. Although, he could be acting as brazen as the reports claimed.

"It appears you have something I need."

I thought of a dozen sarcastic comebacks, but decided against using any of them until I knew his intentions. This was not the time to get into a discussion of what he needed from a 'girl like me.' I kept cool.

"What do you mean?" I winced because talking with a swollen face hurt. A lot.

"I think you know exactly what I mean."

If he knew about the key, he must be connected to Chloe's case, and probably her death. If not, then I was in more trouble than I thought. But I had to find out. So, I tried to get him to tell me. "I'm not sure I know what you're talking about. Can you elaborate?"

"Tom Clark gave it to you at the viewing and I want it. Maybe you can tell I come from rough beginnings. Patience doesn't run in my family. And I think you know what kind of family I'm talking about."

"Capone or Corleone?" It was a dig at his mob-ness. He knew it, but studied me and bared his teeth. Maybe shooting off my mouth was not such a good idea.

My hands were tied so tight there was no wiggle room. My desperate wrist contortions only made things worse, and the strap dug deeper into my skin. Breathing hurt and the pain seared from having my hands bound behind my back so long. I needed to get out of here. I tried talking, actually reasoning with him, but could only croak out a weak appeal. He was in charge, and wasn't interested in listening. He wanted the stage all to himself. Speaking was a performance to him, like he held some imaginary audience captive, not just me. He moved closer. My gut clenched as the smell of his cologne mixed with the damp odor of the place. The single light bulb hanging from the grey ceiling cast his face with monstrous shadows. I searched the room for another way out. Nothing. Absolutely nothing came to mind. I braced myself, closed my eyes and thought, we all come from somewhere. Then he knocked me out. Cold.

I woke up and tasted blood. "Ouch!" It burned from my cheek to my eye. It couldn't be good to get knocked out this many times in a day.

"I gave you fair warning. Stop nosing around and give me what I want," he menaced.

One of the big guys yanked back my hair until I thought it might rip out of my head in one clump.

"Ow! Okay, I give!" I thought of how to cover. If we kept busy talking, maybe someone would find me. "He said he wanted to express his condolences to the family, but they were surrounded by people...all doing the same thing. I guess he had a work thing and needed to leave. He came to the office looking for help. He found me." My head hurt, it was distracting. "Can you tell Thor #1 to ease up? I'd hate to pass out before I give you what you want." Okay, not the smartest thing to say, but it worked. He loosened his grip on my scalp just enough for my face to fall back into place.

"Thanks."

"You were saying." Ruggiano wanted me to talk.

"The guy asked me to give Mr. and Mrs. Ellis an envelope. Said there was a note inside."

"What did it say?"

"I don't know. I didn't read it."

"Smart ass. What did Tom say about the note?"

"Tom wanted to tell them how much he respected Chloe. That he enjoyed working with her." I eyed him to see if he believed the story. "He thought it might help the family to know she was appreciated." It seemed plausible. Ruggiano could have bought it.

"Look, cookie. I've seen plenty of smart girls like you make mistakes. In case you haven't noticed, it never ends well." He bent down and got in my face. His thick brows furrowed above dark brown eyes. "So, I'm gonna ask you again. Where is it?"

I was angry, and possibly insane, because I started laughing at him. Hysterically.

"You think that's funny?" Ruggiano got mad. This time he had one of his goons try to break me. Thor #2 yanked my head back and squeezed my neck until I thought it would break apart from my body.

"Ow! Ow! OW!" I screamed. Something sounded like tearing, and there may have been a pop. I tried to force back tears, but the pain sizzled.

"No answer yet? Maybe you need the right motivation?" The goon squeezed harder. "Should we continue, or maybe we should find someone you actually give a damn about and hurt them?" Ruggiano smiled at my pain.

"No, wait!"

Ruggiano and the Thor Twins outnumbered me. There was no guarantee if I gave him anything that I'd live to see tomorrow. So, I had to stall.

"I'll give it to you, but I have to get it first."

Thinking on my feet, I told him it was in a safe deposit box. We'd have to wait to do the exchange until the bank re-opened. He looked at me for signs of a bluff, but I focused on the pain in order to block out the lie. He bought it.

"Go get it first thing. I'll arrange for one of my 'Twins' to pick it up."

"I will."

I studied Ruggiano this time. Trying to get a read on whether he believed me, or if he planned to end my life now. He looked undecided.

Ruggiano signaled for the guys to let me go. Either they were unhappy with Ruggiano calling them 'his twins' or they had no idea how to treat a lady. The brutes nearly sliced me open cutting the zip-ties off then pushed me onto the floor.

"You better not be lying, or I'll find you and really break you." Ruggiano liked threats. Probably made good on a lot of them, too. He kicked at my side, and began his ascent with his twins.

I curled up and sobbed. Only for a couple minutes, because my instinct to flee kicked in—before Ruggiano changed his mind and came back to finish me.

Panicked, I staggered up to my apartment, turned on the lights in every room, and called Cal. My bat was near my bed, so I grabbed it, curled up under the covers, and cried some more.

Garrett arrived ten minutes after my call. He tried to buzz me over the intercom, but I wouldn't respond.

"Mattie? Are you okay?" He waited. "Mattie?"

I couldn't speak. Too much had happened.

"I'm coming up," he sounded really concerned. He should be. What was he thinking running off to see Tess?

Knock, knock, knock, knock. I knew he was coming, but I jumped anyway.

"Mattie, are you hurt? Let me in!"

"Mattie," I heard Cal this time. He sounded calmer than Garrett. "Can you open the door?"

Instinctually, I shook my head 'yes' even though he couldn't see me. I pushed off the covers. My feet hit the floor. Everything felt so cold as I walked slowly out of the bedroom.

"Are you coming?" Cal used his relaxed tone.

"Y-yes."

"Okay, you're doing great. Just unlock the door and let us in, we're here to help."

By the time I got to the door, the bat was shaking in my hands. I turned the locks. They waited for me to open the door.

Garrett rushed in, but Cal gave him a look of warning. I felt wobbly.

The next thing I knew, I woke up in a hospital bed.

There was shrill beeping followed by a bunch of muffled sounds as my brain came to, then I was out.

I started to wake up, again. How'd we end up here? Bad guy images flashed like film bits, and I had to force my eyes open to make the pictures stop. My head throbbed. I hoped the doc would give me something stronger than an ice pack for this headache.

When the doc walked in and flashed a smile. My mouth dropped open. Maybe he didn't notice.

"Hi, I'm Dr. Maxwell." He extended his hand to shake mine. He lingered there a moment, and looked into my eyes. Okay, so maybe he noticed and was just giving it back to me, but he was young and good looking.

My doctor had dark hair and brown eyes, and looked like he could still be in med school. He flashed a light and looked into my eyes. I knew he was checking my pupils or something. I'd seen them do it to mom before, but it was so bright, I pulled back. He looked me over even after the light went out. I got the feeling he was trying to figure something out. Maybe he was surprised by my injuries.

Cal and Garrett brought me in, so they would have had to say something about my condition at check-in. Not sure if there was an "injured by a psychopath" check box on the admittance forms, but I'm guessing Cal had to tell them some version of the story.

"Says here you had a bad fall, is that right?"

"Yes." I hesitated, but figured it was best to play along.

"From a hayride," he sounded skeptical.

I hoped he didn't notice the corners of my mouth resisting a smile. "Thrown actually. I was thrown from the ride. Shouldn't have piled those hay bales so high, or let the horses go so fast."

Dr. Maxwell didn't believe me at all, it was obvious, but he didn't pressure me for the truth. "The good news is you don't have a concussion."

"The bad news?"

"You'll be bruised and sore for a while. You should get some rest the next couple days. Is there someone who can help you around the house?"

"Yes," I lied.

Dr. Maxwell eyed me. He tore off a prescription sheet and handed it to me. "Here's something for the pain. My number is on there too. If you have any trouble, or if you need anything, feel free to give me a call."

I thanked him.

Garrett came in just as Dr. Maxwell left. Garrett eyed the good doctor for a beat then turned his full attention to me. He sat at my bedside and gave me an overview of what he and Cal discussed. Cal had left for the police station. He planned to meet us later and take my statement. Cal was a cop, and I trusted his instincts. Even if it felt weird, I'd find a way to let him know about Tess and her texts.

Garrett promised to have a guard posted at the funeral home. If mom asked any questions, we'd tell her it was part of a security test. Garrett called it a concierge service they were 'looking into' for high-end clients, people who wanted extra protection during services and funerals. It startled me to consider a security detail, but I trusted Garrett.

Besides, I'd seen the guy the police brought to his kid's funeral in an orange jumpsuit and shackles—security might not be a bad idea.

Mom and I would act as helpful test subjects. They'd even pay us for our 'participation'. I sure hoped she didn't catch on.

The next item on the agenda was my mother. Garrett pulled out my phone. It had been in my purse, which sat beside an overnight bag he must have packed for my emergency visit.

After explaining my wounds were a result of a freak hayride

accident, and getting a recap of her day, mom reluctantly let me get off the phone. But only so I could leave the hospital to get some rest. I didn't want to keep news like this from my own mother, but we agreed it was best for her safety as much as mine to hide the truth. Mom offered to come back early, but Garrett assured her I was in good hands until she could return.

"Are you sure about this, Mattie?"

"Yeah, I'm fine mom. I love you. Say hey to grandpa, and Aunt Eileen." I tried not to cry after we hung up.

I really wanted to go to sleep and forget this ever happened. Instead, I sucked it up and asked Garrett to help me get home.

After the full wheelchair treatment, Garrett carefully lifted me to the car, and locked us inside. As we neared the parking garage exit, he stopped to talk. He stared for a couple seconds, which made my pulse shoot up and my cheeks flush, although I wasn't sure he could tell because of the bruises Ruggiano and his goons left on my face. Garrett pulled off to the side before we got to the ticket booth, and I caught the woman inside the booth shaking her head at us.

When I looked back, Garrett was analyzing me. Hair, eyes, bruises, and when he got to my mouth he leaned toward me.

"I need you," he whispered so intensely close my lips felt his. My eyes started to soften as I waited for his passionate kiss. "I need you," he said again, and brushed his lips gently across mine, "to stay out of trouble." My heart flipped. He sat back up into his seat and maneuvered the car to the pay window.

I caught the lady in the booth laughing. She handed Garrett a receipt and shook her poufy head of hair at me. Probably enjoying the show.

The turn signal indicated we were heading the opposite direction from home.

CHAPTER 22

Normally, I'd be thrilled to be in a hotel with Garrett. But I just couldn't get happy about it with all the pain and unanswered questions.

How did Ruggiano get inside the funeral home? Why did he want the key to Chloe's if he'd already broken into her apartment and tossed the place? Who was Sultan? And what did my father have to do with any of this?

Garrett hit the elevator button. He hadn't said much since we left the hospital. I didn't make much of an effort to talk either. The silence was nice.

We moved through the hallway. Garrett focused on the destination, and me, mindlessly following along wild with questions. He slipped the card into the reader and got a green light. My heart skipped a beat when I heard the lock click.

The hotel door swung open and we entered a spacious living area with a couch, large screen TV, end tables and lights. I walked in and sat my bag on the coffee table.

The door closed and latched into place. Garrett threw the deadbolt and did a walk-through. I accompanied him and sized up the sleeping quarters.

This was my room. Garrett had purchased an adjoining room to keep me safe, although, it also felt very intimate.

"Everything all right?"

"Yeah, just tired."

"Do you want to talk, or get something to eat?"

"I'd rather grab a hot shower and order room service, but thanks for the offer." I could hardly believe I was sending him away. A conversation, much less a relationship, was not going to work for me tonight. I needed rest, and to be alone to figure some of this out on my own. At least it's what I told myself. I was scared of taking things further with him when I felt so vulnerable. My life at this moment felt like equal parts confusion, exhaustion, and fear.

"No problem," Garrett said. "I'll probably unwind a bit. Just let me know if you change your mind. I'll be right through that door." He pointed to the adjoining door with the key card still in his hand. "Cal has to take your statement. But he'll come later. Is that okay?"

I nodded even though it hurt to move.

Garrett smiled sweetly and left.

I sat on the bed and stared at the door between us for a while. Would he come back? Did I want him to? I imagined Garrett walking through the door, pulling me into his arms and kissing me—not letting up until we both collapsed. I let the fantasy take over for a few minutes.

Channeling our chemistry warmed me until a cold blast from the air conditioner ruined it. "What on earth? Who turned on the air?" No one was there to respond. Annoyed, I turned the heater to high, and stomped off to the bathroom. Then I blasted water, adjusted it from freezing to scalding, stripped off my clothes and hoped for the best.

The water seared my skin. It felt good, but I shivered deep down. I stayed under the water hoping the warmth would reach my bones. My brain tried to analyze motives for murder, but gave up and wandered back to Garrett. I was warm in seconds.

Next up, clothes and food. On went stretchy pants, a tank, and a sweatshirt. I padded back to the bathroom to dry my hair and looked in the mirror. Everything about me screamed lonely girl about to throw back a $15 hotel burger and fries followed by a $7 piece of cake. Maybe I'd get some wine. Just then, someone knocked.

I walked to the door cautiously. The knock came again.

"Room service," the voice said.

I opened the door knowing it was Garrett. He looked me over. At least I didn't have on a housecoat with green gunk on my face, or curlers in my hair.

"You look like you could use a good meal." He wheeled in a room service cart loaded with food: fresh fruits, breads, and cheeses. But, it didn't stop there. There were crab cakes with remoulade, salad with shaved Parmesan, braised short ribs, and mashed potatoes, too. After the first cart, a hotel staffer pushed a second one right behind.

Desserts—jackpot! There were beignets, assorted cookies, and even a molten lava cake with chocolate sauce. My hunger was in overdrive. Suddenly, I was glad to have on my stretchy pants. I'd surely need them to enjoy this gourmet feast.

"My hero!" I couldn't stop smiling as I looked at the food and Garrett. He paid the guy who had wheeled in a third cart with ice water, soda, and even hot chocolate, then left, while I drooled over the food.

"Ready to eat like a queen?" Garrett gestured for me to sit at the table and placed a napkin in my lap to serve me. "My lady, shall we start with an appetizer?" He waved his hand over the crab cakes.

"But of course," I said, using my best fake French accent.

He laughed at my silly attempt. The tension of the day's activities eased and we were in our own little world for a while.

Later in the evening, the discussion shifted to what happened with Ruggiano. We could have waited forever, but it was necessary since Cal would be over soon to take my statement.

Garrett apologized for being pulled away by Tess. Remorse showed on his face. I had suspicions, but gave him the benefit of the doubt. He admitted her call was partly a ploy to get him alone.

It was painfully obvious Tess wanted Garrett back, and not one part of me wanted to see that happen. But the alternative could be Tess manipulating Garrett, or worse, protecting Chloe's killer. Garrett tried to reassure me it was one-sided affection. My head throbbed, so I changed the subject.

"Ruggiano and his goons were waiting for me. Inside." An involuntary shiver raced up my spine.

"They either picked the locks, or someone forgot and left a door open."

Or someone intentionally left the door open, something I didn't want to consider. It would have meant someone who had access to the funeral home—my home—couldn't be trusted. Garrett admitted he wondered the same thing. He planned to investigate, and handle the problem.

"Do you want to talk about what happened?" He was concerned I might need to get it off my chest. Here's a guy who brought me food and wanted to talk about my feelings. He seemed too good to be true. "I went to counseling when I came back from the desert. It was the only way to deal with what happened over there." Although he admitted to skipping a lot of sessions, the ones he did attend were "worth it," in his words.

If a big, tough soldier like Garrett could find the strength to expose the demons, so could I.

As I spilled out details, the fear of being captive resurfaced. My body reacted like it was happening all over again. I felt trapped and helpless.

We had to stop until Cal arrived.

Cal reassured me, over and over, this was not my fault. But he had this look of anger and sadness on his face as he interviewed me, like he connected with my pain somehow.

I managed to pull myself together long enough to explain what happened. How the guys caught me by surprise—they'd been waiting for me—and knocked me out. Cal and Garrett traded looks when I mentioned Ruggiano.

Cal told me he thought Ruggiano might come after me, but didn't think he'd show up in person. It shocked me more than anyone. Our best guess was he wanted to rattle me to the core—to scare me away from poking around. We discussed options, like pressing charges, but I knew my accusations weren't going to bring him down the way he deserved, so we scrapped that option.

When I told them Ruggiano mentioned someone he called Sultan, Cal stopped me. "Wait. Tell me exactly what Ruggiano said."

My eyebrows wrinkled up trying to remember the details. "It was something like, 'I wouldn't be in this position...if that Sultan scum,' or something like that."

"Explains the tattoo on the guy who jumped her earlier," Garrett told Cal.

"You mean the sword?"

"It's a scabbard," Garrett said. "Sultan's crew gets tattooed as part of their initiation. Steal something. Kill someone. Get a tattoo."

"So, Sultan is involved," Cal said.

While Cal and Garrett processed that information, I debated

telling them Ruggiano also mentioned my father. These two had my back, and I knew it. But my dad was such an unknown to me it gave me pause. "Can I have a minute?" It was more of a statement. I excused myself to the bathroom.

I closed the door and paced. Then stood and stared into the mirror. I wondered where I came from. At least, where the half belonging to my father's gene pool came from.

Pieces of our history flickered through my head, but it wasn't much. A time when my father spun me around and jiggled me until I giggled uncontrollably—then the long years without him. He'd left when I was young. Silence deepened over the years he'd been gone.

This wasn't helping. They were trying to help me. I had to come clean. I splashed some cold water on my face, patted it dry, and went back to tell them.

"My father," I blew out a deep breath. "Ruggiano said something about me being like my father. That he was protecting someone. I didn't understand what Ruggiano meant. But it might be something important."

The guys exchanged another one of those wordless looks that worried me. Cal quickly changed the subject.

"Sultan is an even bigger gangster than Ruggiano. Ever since Sultan came to town, everyone's paid him a percentage of their take on everything from girls to gambling and drugs. Or been killed."

"Um…" I probably looked dumb just standing there, but I didn't know much about gambling and casinos, much less guys named Sultan and Ruggiano, who may or may not have put a hit out on my friend.

"Ruggiano's crew, the East Street Boys, and a couple other gangs all pay up to Sultan. Word on the street is Ruggiano is jealous. He wants control. And he's setting himself up to make a play for Sultan's territory," Cal said it like I was supposed to know what it all meant.

Gang wars sounded dangerous, but how did Chloe fit into it?

"A power grab like that? Takes a lot of strategy, money and people. Perhaps, Chloe figured something out about Ruggiano that Ruggiano didn't want anyone to know. As for Sultan? The guys in vice say he's the big bad wolf. He'll dress up like your grandma, invite you for dinner then eat you alive."

"Yikes."

"Yeah, and Sultan is tied to the casinos. He's part of an

investment group pushing new casinos all over this area. I think if you want answers about the casino deal, he'll have them."

"Then I should go see him."

"You don't just go see The Sultan," Cal said. "It's too dangerous. Besides, he won't talk to just anybody. You need an intermediary, someone from the street who can help you get the intel you want."

"How do I go about getting one of those?" I kept after it.

"Mattie, it's too risky," Garrett chimed in.

"I got an informant who says Sultan is being cautious because he thinks Ruggiano wants to make a move. Sultan's already tight security was beefed up a few days ago. It's got everyone freaked."

"What can I do? I need information. I'll go see him myself."

"I'm telling you it's a bad idea." Garrett crossed his arms.

"Got a better one?"

"No." I could hear his teeth grind when he clenched his jaw. He was not happy, but I wouldn't back down. "This is the plan."

"At least let me go with you."

I thought about it for a minute. "Do you know him too?" As if Garrett knew all the mobsters in town. Maybe he did.

"Not personally," Garrett said. "But you're not going alone."

Neither one of us would budge. Garrett could go in and back me up. Sounded good in theory. But in reality, I knew we were going into a very bad guy's territory. I gave us a 50-50 shot at leaving alive.

There was no way I was going to tell my mom about any of this. She'd kill me for thinking up something so stupid. It felt stupid, but it seemed like our best option. Anyway, how bad could this Sultan guy really be?

"I can hear you," Garrett said. He couldn't. At least I didn't think so.

Cal gave his opinion. "It's risky. The Sultan used to be a henchman for Archie the Axe. And even Archie, named after an axe for Chrissake, thought the guy was nuts!"

"The look on your face says I can't talk you out of it. Can I?" Garrett softened up and tried his best to charm me out of it.

"Nope." I wanted him to use his charm on me, but not for this.

"Then I'd prefer to be there and help protect you—if it's even possible the way you rush at danger head-on."

"I'll think about it." I thought about it. "Okay. I may be crazy, but I know we'll probably get more answers if we're together. You can come as my back-up." Big, muscle-y, handsome, back-up.

"Oh, so now I'm the sidekick?"

"Hey, at least you're in the game," I joked back, which got a laugh out of him. Bringing someone strong like Garrett might be the only way the Sultan would let me live long enough to question him.

"Will you reconsider?" Cal asked.

"I don't think we have a choice." I told him. "Sultan's guys came for the key. Let's give it to them, and see if we can get some answers."

"Sultan's guys didn't hurt her when they came for the key," Garrett added. "I guess that's a good sign."

"You still need to be careful," Cal warned. "I'm not letting you two go alone. I'll be there when you go in, and waiting to make sure you both come out alive."

We didn't argue with Cal. Knowing he'd be there reassured me. This might actually work.

"Now, what about Ruggiano? He wants the key too," Cal said.

I thought about how to appease Ruggiano. "Maybe we can give them both what they want. I'll call Chloe's mom and see if she's got a copy."

"Okay, but why would they need a key when they could just break in?" It sounded strange to hear Cal talk about breaking the law, but he made a good point.

Someone, probably Sultan or Ruggiano, had already broken into her apartment. Why did these guys both still want the key? Maybe there was a third party who had broken in, I didn't know, but we had to find out. My head ran in circles then started thumping. I rubbed my temples trying to make the ache go away.

"Mattie," Garrett said. "You need to rest.

He was right, but it didn't make me happy to have to lie down in the middle of all this.

I'd have to tell Cal about Tess later. Garrett and Cal went next door to talk things over and I reluctantly went to bed.

My head throbbed until exhaustion won out. Then I felt nothing.

CHAPTER 23

Later that night I had the strangest dream. The native man I'd seen dusting bodies in the field before was standing near a bunch of slot machines this time. He picked up a bucket and poured rust colored paint over one of the machines. I reached out to touch the cool, wet paint as it flowed over the machines.

The man did it over, and over again, until the one-armed bandits looked like they were melting. He said something in another language right before the machines exploded. I ducked as millions of coins and bits flew past. The man noticed me, but didn't speak. He bent down and scooped up some pieces. They fell through his hands, but changed into a waterfall.

Water flowed into a lake beneath the man's feet. He shifted and showed me one remaining piece. It looked like Chloe's key. The man closed it in his hands, then cupped his hand over mine, and gave it to me. When I looked down, I didn't see the key, only the keychain. It broke apart and red ochre oozed from it. Before I could ask the man anything, I was jolted awake by a noise.

Only bits of dream remained when I sat up, so I curled back up and tried to get comfortable. I couldn't sleep. It didn't help that I had a gut full of food. Could my strange dream have been triggered by indigestion?

The left side of my head hurt, so I took a couple Tylenol, drank some water, and went back to bed. Around three o'clock my eyes popped open again. I lay there a while.

A small red light on the TV caught my attention, then I timed a green smoke detector light blinking every seven seconds. I observed vertical lines thrown against the wall a few feet away with each repetitive flash. On. Off. On. Off. Then I dozed.

When the digital clock read 5:39 am, I had to get up. My ears buzzed and my body vibrated like I'd been on a bender—only I hadn't. Unless you counted last night's banquet.

I'd worked through worse, so I got up and grabbed a shower. I needed the water to massage the places that hurt, too many to count. There were a few even the water couldn't reach. Still, the heat pelted my shoulders and helped wake me up.

I pulled my hair back, but tried to add some volume by blasting it with the hair dryer and hair spray. Although I felt kind of big-hair-country when it was finished, it looked pretty good.

I opened the curtains as soon as I was dressed. Dew coated everything—cars, blades of grass, lampposts, even the corner of my window. I pulled a sweatshirt on over my jeans and t-shirt, noticed a cloudy film on the in-room coffeemaker, and wished for a gourmet breakfast. I checked my phone for messages, texted mom and Jos, and watched the sun come up over the horizon.

Color flooded the sky and it hit me. I rushed to my messenger bag. Where was the key, I wondered? I shuffled through everything until I found it. My eyes scanned the keychain until I figured out our next move.

I threw the rest of my clothes in my bag, and double-checked the room for stuff I might have missed. When I felt confident everything I'd brought was going home with me, I rushed to the pass through door.

Garrett opened it before I even knocked. He held out a coffee cup. "Thought you might need this," he said, without passing judgment, and completely overlooking my zombie eyes and ten-foot hair.

"Thanks." I took the cup. "I needed this. Couldn't get much sleep last night, which would have really bugged me except I think the tossing and turning might have shook something loose."

"Really? Want to fill me in on the details?"

"Yes. But we need to make a stop on the way home." I tipped the cup and felt the sweet, hot coffee warm me as it went down.

Garrett looked me over as if deciding just how crazy I was today, but just smiled. Good, he's getting used to me, I thought, and we left.

It didn't take much convincing for him to let me drive his car. He was surprisingly comfortable handing over his keys considering his Maserati was worth more than some people's homes. I revved it to hear the engine grumble. Man, I could get used this, I thought then hit the gas.

We pulled up to one of the ritziest places ever built. Someone answered the speaker at the gate. I gave them my name, and they buzzed us in. Beyond the wrought iron, we travelled over the meandering brick paver drive with inset designs and a decorative border. It looked like a piece of art, same with the impeccably maintained landscape.

We parked at the top of the wrap-around driveway. A doorman opened more iron gates and let us inside the front doors.

The house had high ceilings, like over fifteen feet high, a double curved staircase, and luxurious appointments.

Our host dressed in a brown mohair sweater and cream pants reached out to hug me.

"Thanks for meeting us Mrs. Ellis," I said. "You remember Garrett McKenzie?"

"Yes, nice to see you both. You mentioned time was of the essence. Let's head upstairs."

Mrs. Ellis walked us up the elegant staircase capped with polished rails as big as joists. We turned toward Chloe's room. It had been five years since my last visit, but some things never change.

Her room was posh. Light turquoise covered the walls, and the large furniture was decked with white mohair throws and fluffy pillows. I nodded to Mrs. E, then went to the closet and dug around. Past the shoes, boots and bags were some brown boxes. One of them had LEGO SETS written on it. I pulled the box out and set it on her desk.

I lifted the lid off. Underneath some brick sets, she'd hidden a couple files. There were photos of a black-tie event, maps of pipelines, and notes about oil and gas usage. Underneath the files she'd left a notebook with numbers and the word 'Enlightenment' written on the inside cover. I pulled out the paper with the date from the photo on Chloe's desk. Under it, we found Chloe's laptop.

Chloe had been super paranoid in undergrad. She made back-ups of her back-ups because she lost a term paper—once. We came here, back when she was alive, and I remembered she stored one of her copies at home. I thought she meant a hard copy of some term paper, which she had, but she also kept a back-up library—on a back-up computer.

I fired up the computer then got out the keychain. I searched the LEGOs for the duplicate, which looked slightly different than the one I had.

I popped it apart to reveal a flash drive. It took a couple tries to realize Chloe had left the password 'enlightenment' in plain sight. I was able to unlock her laptop and find the file Chloe meant me to see. It was a land contract listed under a Michigan address. The same one on the paper Tom Clark gave me at her funeral.

When I double clicked the file, a list of names and dates came up. We'd have to figure out what they meant, but it was time to get to the Ruggiano hand-off.

"Mind if we take the whole box?"

"Sure, Mattie. What is all this about?" Mrs. Ellis questioned.

"Chloe went to a lot of trouble to hide this information. I think she was killed for it. I'm sorry, Mrs. E. I don't know much more than that. We have to go."

Mrs. Ellis looked shocked. We couldn't stay and explain, so I hugged her and started for the door.

"Oh, do you have the spare key?" It was vital to have it if we were going to give one to Ruggiano, and one to Sultan.

She nodded and pulled a key out of her pocket. She held my hand before she let the key go. "Be careful, Mattie. This isn't worth your life, too."

I reassured her we'd do our best, and we hustled out of there.

CHAPTER 24

Now that we had a duplicate key and key ring, we could pass off the one without the flash drive and files to Ruggiano's crew. But we'd have to get there first.

Good thing we weren't in my old beater, or we wouldn't have made it in time. As it happened, we almost missed the meeting.

He was an imposing figure, but I knew there were vulnerable places I could kick him if things got desperate. And if I had trouble, Garrett was nearby.

Thor didn't speak. He just held out his hand.

"Here you go." I dropped the key into his hand.

He looked at the key. Then nodded to me, and left.

Well, that wasn't so scary, I thought.

"We'll be in touch," he said over his shoulder.

So much for being off the hook.

When I got back to the car, Garrett asked me how it went.

"I gave him the key. He said they'd be in touch."

Garrett eyed me, knowing I'd said it too casually.

"What?"

"This was only to buy time."

"I was kind of hoping we were done with Ruggiano."

"If Ruggiano doesn't find what he wants, he'll be back. And even if he does, he might come back anyway. Just to toy with you."

I shuddered.

"Let's head home. We'll see if we can pull something off the drive and laptop."

We still had the back-up keychain with the flash drive. We planned to set up a meeting with Sultan under the guise of giving him the key dark-haired Zorro came to get.

I sort of spaced out running through scenarios for our next exchange. Once we pulled the data off the flash drive, we'd scrub it. I figured we'd add some dummy files back onto it, in case Sultan's crew checked the drive out during the exchange. Hopefully, giving him something would convince Sultan to share information about Chloe's case. I just hoped Ruggiano wasn't looking for anything more than the key, or else he and the twins would be paying another visit.

When I got outside of my own head, I glanced at Garrett. His eyes faced forward and he stayed quiet. Maybe he was working things out in his head, too.

It wasn't long after looking at him that I abandoned problem solving. There was a lot the two of us needed to work out. There was definitely chemistry between us. But did we want a relationship? What would happen if we tried being a couple and it didn't work? I worried about mom if things got messy between Garrett and me. I sighed. There wasn't anything I could do about it right now.

We remained quiet the rest of the ride and sorted through theories and feelings.

Although, I enjoyed more personal freedom while mom was gone, I had missed her. I was concerned about her health; concerned about people threatening me; and I really needed some motherly advice. So much was happening, I was glad she was coming home. But I freaked out seeing Aunt Eileen's sedan parked in the lot.

What would mom say when she saw my bruised face? What would mom say when she saw me with Garrett? These things worried me. On top of all that, we still had a killer to catch.

Garrett helped me out of the car. He paused before he closed my door. His deep blue eyes surveyed me.

"Don't worry," he said, and gave my hand a squeeze. "This is a lot to process. Your mom's going to ask questions. If you need help explaining, or time before we tell her what's going on between us, let me know. We can do whatever you want."

Between us. I liked the sound of it. But I had my doubts about rushing in and telling mom, "Hey, I know you were only gone a few days, but Garrett and I are a thing now." How would it sound? Would she be angry? Would it hurt our living arrangement? My left eye started to twitch running through the scenarios.

I wanted to be honest, but this was not the time to tell mom everything. She'd have enough questions about my accident. Garrett made a good point about waiting.

"Let's not wait too long, though." Garrett leaned near me to shut the door. "It's killing me not to kiss you right now." His lips grazed my cheek. From behind, it probably looked innocent, like he moved to close the door. But the heat from his movements told me otherwise.

Warmth faded as we walked inside expecting to see mom. Pangs of guilt intensified the pain of my episode with Ruggiano. My knees began to buckle. Garrett propped me up just as we opened the office door.

It was a full house—with some surprise guests.

"Mattie," Derek rushed up and hugged me, even before my own mother. Everyone stared. "I was so worried about you—"

Before he could say anything else, I started yammering. "It's nothing. Really. An accident at the farm...fell off a wagon," I laughed hysterically. "Wow, didn't actually think about that before I said it." Truth was, I hadn't thought about any of it, I just wanted to fill space, so no one would have a chance to ask questions. Unfortunately, my response drew suspicious looks.

"She's okay. Doctor cleared her for most activities," Garrett said.

My mom gave me a huge hug. It was so good to see her again.

"I missed you, mom."

"I missed you too, sweetie."

Hank told a joke to ease us through the public homecoming. The conversation shifted, and I felt we were safely past the questions, at least for now. Mom looked better. The blush in her cheeks made her look happy. A good dose of family bonding must have done wonders. We laughed when Hank said his punch line. Derek hung around until mom decided to head upstairs. Then he tried to say good-bye, but couldn't quite leave.

"If it's okay," Garrett spoke. "I'd like to review some information with Mattie."

Mom nodded. Aunt Eileen grabbed her bag and helped her upstairs. This left Hank, Derek, Garrett and me in the office.

Hank made an excuse to leave—something about seeing a man about a casket. Then there were three.

As soon as Hank was out of the office, Garrett ushered Derek toward the door. Derek turned back, rushed over, and kissed me quickly.

"I was really worried," he said, eager for a response.

I stood there dumbfounded. Although he seemed like a nice guy, Derek had the wrong idea about us. It was hard to figure out what to say to him, and I could feel Garrett getting angry.

"Are you afraid of what he'll think?" Derek asked me.

My brain hadn't formed the words yet. "What? Who?"

"Garrett. Are you afraid of what he'll think about our kiss?" Derek dropped it like a lead balloon, on all of us. I hadn't told Garrett about the kiss because I thought it was mostly one-sided, and wouldn't go any further. And because I was afraid of Garrett's reaction. Some part of me also felt IT's NOBODY'S BUSINESS!

Now, Derek had gone and spilled the beans, making it appear as if we had something going on, when we didn't. It was a sweet kiss. I didn't know if it there was anything else to it, but it hadn't compared to kissing Garrett.

"You don't mind if Mattie sees me, do you Garrett?" I turned all sorts of red, and was about to stop Derek's nonsense when Garrett spoke.

"If it's what Mattie wants."

I was ready to shoot my mouth off about making my own choices, but only stuttered a few words. Garrett left us alone in the hallway.

Derek seemed pleased before he saw the anger on my face. "What's wrong?"

"You had no right telling him we kissed—you kissed me! I don't know where you got the idea we're dating, but we aren't. Furthermore, if I'm going to be with anyone, it'll be a guy who doesn't try to railroad me for show."

"I'm sorry. I thought you felt something when we kissed the other night."

"I didn't. Now, stop talking about it."

"Are you sure there wasn't something there?"

There might have been something, but I didn't want to think about anyone romantically right now. "Please, just leave." I was irritated, and didn't have the time or the patience for this.

Derek's shoulders sank.

"Look, I'm sorry," it came out flat. "I've got too many things to figure out right now."

He walked out onto the stoop. I closed the door, leaned my back against the wall, and prayed for the last fifteen minutes to disappear. But my heart still ached, so I knew it hadn't worked.

I'd have to figure out how to patch things up with Garrett, and revisit whatever latent feelings were lingering from Derek's kiss. I walked toward the office when Aunt Eileen stopped me.

"Are you coming up? I hope we can visit a little before I head home."

Nothing seemed to be going right. My personal drama would have to wait. It would be smart to think about what I wanted to say to Garrett before I actually said it anyway. So, I followed Aunt Eileen upstairs. My hands lingered after I shut the door, thinking of him.

CHAPTER 25

Catching up with mom and Aunt Eileen lifted my spirits. No boy drama. Unless, you counted their attempts to get grandpa to keep his doctor appointments, and lay off the bacon.

I always saw grandpa as a strong man, because he was. But he was getting older, and had been more prone to accidents recently. I could relate, but I guessed he didn't have an evil thunder-god chasing him around town.

Eileen and mom explained they were able to get grandpa to his check-up. There would be additional trips needed to ensure he remained in good health. My aunt offered to do most of the shuttling, but it was obvious mom wanted to help as well.

I thought back to her recovery in the hospital. Cousins and old friends showed up to offer help and casseroles. Mom wanted to make sure grandpa knew he had a support system like that. We'd figure it out later, but I knew she needed to be part of grandpa's life more for herself than for him.

When my aunt left, she stopped me at the door. "Keep an eye out for your mom. She may seem well, but she needs rest. When we were at dad's appointment, she got short of breath a few times."

After seeing my reaction, Aunt Eileen reassured me it was okay, but the doctors had hooked her up to some machines just to make sure.

"They said she's fine, but the excitement from the move, and this stuff with dad has her stressed out. She needs to take it easy. Take care of her and let me know if you need anything." Aunt Eileen hugged me at the door and left.

I tried to put a smile on my face before I saw mom again. She'd know something was up if I hadn't. Judging by her expression, she knew something was off.

"Everything okay, Mattie?"

"Yeah, mom. Fine."

"You don't seem fine. Are you okay since the accident?"

"Yeah, it's just been busy here. I'm just glad you're back."

"Glad to be here...back home. Can I make you anything?"

"Let's just relax."

We looked over the apartment. Our photos on the walls, our magazines on the coffee table, and a family-made afghan draped across the couch—this was our home.

"I know it's not an ideal home, but it's ours," mom said. "Thanks for handling all the work while I was gone. I don't know what we'd do without this place."

I didn't handle it at all. Since we moved here, I'd complained about the place, and shirked most of the work. When mom needed to be with her dad, I'd come around enough to pitch-in, but was so messed up over Chloe's death and threats on my life, Garrett and Ryder had picked up the slack.

I didn't want to let mom down, but I felt like I had. She needed me. It was time for me to take responsibility, like a grown-up.

"I love you, mom." I hugged her tight.

"I love you too." Her embrace weakened. She was obviously tired. "Why don't you lay down? I've got class in a little bit, so I'll be busy for a while. We can catch up later."

She agreed then went to lie down. I put a blanket over her and she settled underneath.

"You know, I was worried." Mom ran her fingers gently over my bruised cheek. "I don't know what I'd do without you. Please try to be more careful."

"I will mom. No more farm equipment for a while." We laughed.

"Derek seems like a nice boy. I thought you might be interested in Garrett, but it's probably better you like Derek."

My heart sank. I didn't know how to respond. So I kissed her head, closed the door and left the bedroom. Hopefully, she'd get some sleep. It would give me time to figure out what to do next.

It was time for school. I grabbed my backpack and headed downstairs.

I was prepared to make a quick exit. Before I ran into anyone. It hurt to think of giving up whatever might happen with Garrett, but I had to consider mom, and our home. Those were the priorities, not my love life. Maybe I could act cool and skip the 'us' conversation. Thoughts rolled through my head. I jumped off the last step and bumped into him.

"Oh my gosh! You startled me."

"So, did you really kiss Derek?"

"You get right to the point, don't you?"

"Yes," he said, and walked toward the office. I went too, his expression intrigued me.

"Well, if you must know. Yes. But it was only because he kissed me."

"So, do you kiss anyone who tries kissing you?"

"No. No. Not what I meant." I blushed. He flustered me. When I stopped fumbling around for words, I noticed him grinning. Garrett was playing with me, but I knew why. Then I smiled. "Are you jealous?"

His jaw clenched and he moved closer to me, like a panther stalking prey. "Yes," he said firmly, then pulled me close. We engaged in an alarmingly amorous kiss, considering where we were. Mom was right upstairs, and anyone bringing flowers or dead bodies could walk in at any time. It was terrifying and thrilling. Once I stopped thinking, I really enjoyed it.

We enjoyed several minutes of passion. Enough that my lips buzzed long after we stopped. When the room came back into focus, I patted my hair into place and brushed at my shirt. Whew, nothing came off. If it had…Oh boy.

Garrett smiled. "You tempt me way too easily."

"Me? You started it!"

"I know, but it's because you make me lose control."

"Really?"

"Yes. I don't mean totally uncontrollable. I'd stop—if you wanted. But I want to get away from here and show you how I really feel."

"You mean that wasn't it?"

"It's a fraction of what I feel, Mattie. A fraction."

I shuddered to think how much more intense he could be, or if I could handle it. Then I remembered boundaries. We needed to set some boundaries. "Um, well, um. Class. I have to get ready for class—"

"Didn't mean to scare you off," he sounded hurt.

"You didn't. It's just that I, well. Maybe you did a little. But only because I have to consider our situation here." I looked around nervously. "Also, I'm not as um…experienced as you." Smooth delivery, my internal voice mocked.

Garrett chuckled. "You don't need to be anything other than who you are with me. We need to discuss what happens next, but I'm not waiting around to tell you how I feel. It's intense, but it doesn't mean we have to move fast. Whatever pace we set together is fine with me. As long as we can have an occasional lip-lock session like that one. And the one upstairs." He smiled his 1000-watt smile. "Promise we'll talk seriously about this, soon, and I'm good. Okay?"

"Mmm-hmm." It was all I could mumble.

"Didn't you say something about school?"

"Mmm-hmm. Wait. What?" I was totally distracted, but snapped out of it long enough for him to kiss me again before I left.

CHAPTER 26

Parking around campus was a challenge, but I managed to snag a spot in the same zip code. When I finally got to class, I shoved my bag under my seat, and took out my notebook and pen.

A dark-haired guy in his early twenties snuck in behind two girls, they were all late. He had on black jeans, a grey two-tone shirt and black Pumas. He had a blue book bag slung over his shoulder, pulled out his earbuds as he walked past me and took a seat in the next row. I couldn't place who he was—just that I recognized him from the lawyer's office—maybe a client?

The class listened for roll call. Then the professor rambled on about the syllabus and classroom guidelines. This left only fifteen minutes of real lecture time, but it didn't bother me. Something else had me distracted.

I kept feeling that there were eyes on me. It was enough I began to squirm. My pen moved across the notebook page, but the professor's voice faded in and out while I tried to figure out if someone was really watching me.

My roller ball dropped to the floor. I reached to pick it up and scanned the room as discreetly as possible. He was watching. The guy from Oxley's office. I analyzed him for a second before he smiled. I tried to relax and forced myself to return the smile.

Why was he watching me? It didn't feel like the kind of watching a guy does when he's attracted to someone, but more like he was analyzing me.

It was unusual for me to be so skeptical of people. But I'd become

227

defensive and edgy since the threats started. If I was going to endure interacting with strangers for an entire semester, or longer, I was going to need all the other problems in my life to go away.

I did my best to get through class. As soon as it was over, I bolted for the car. I didn't breathe until the locks clicked and the Hellcat rumbled. I felt safe again.

I'd promised to pick up supplies for Mrs. Jacobson, so I stopped by the art shop on my way over to her house.

Not realizing my speed, I zipped through errands, and ended up at her house a few minutes early.

There was an old Cadillac parked outside the house, so I took a spot at the curb. When the engine stopped, a man came out the front door. The way he and Mrs. Jacobson held hands gave the impression they cared for each other. He hugged her and left. She closed the door before I even got out of the car. She must not have seen me.

I gathered the bags and walked up to her door.

When she opened the door, she had a pink flush on her cheeks. She looked happy. I wanted to ask about her guest, but she spoke first.

"Over here, dear. Please put the bags in my studio."

"Sure," I said. "Do you need me to unpack them?"

"No, I'll make sure they're unpacked later. Would you like some tea?"

"Actually, I was hoping to get back and see my mom. May I take a rain check?"

"Of course. How is your mother?"

"She's all right. I think she needs sleep. My plan was to let her rest, and surprise her with dinner."

"That's very thoughtful. She's lucky to have you helping her."

"Thanks. I just wish I could do more."

"What do you mean?"

"If it were something simpler, like fixing a faucet or something, I could figure it out. But this is different. It's her heart that needs care, and I'm not sure what to do. I try to help, but she just tells me she's fine."

"When my husband, rest his soul, had his bypass years ago, the doctors give him a list of things to do, and some to avoid. Did your mom get something like that?"

"Yes."

"Well, maybe you should ask to review it with her again. It might remind her that you're there to support her, and she won't feel like she has to do it all on her own."

"Thank you, that sounds like a good idea. I'll ask when I get home. Now, about the supplies I picked up. Are you sure you don't need me to unpack anything?"

"I'm all set. Now, go and see your mother." Mrs. Jacobson helped me out to the door.

CHAPTER 27

After mom checked out, we had some hot tea and lemon cookies. It was hard to tell if her tired eyes were a carryover from her trip, or if she needed a doctor.

"Mom, is everything okay?"

"Sure."

It didn't sound okay.

"Now that you're home, let me know how I can help you rest."

"I will."

She was not usually this short with her answers. But before there was time to pry, the intercom buzzed.

"Mattie?" Garrett said, and started to flirt. I smiled, but my heart dropped when I saw mom's reaction. She knew.

"Um, I'll be down in a few," I cut the call short. It was just the two of us now.

Usually, I could read her face. But she remained calm. Too calm.

"Let's talk."

We shifted in our seats during a long, uncomfortable pause.

"What's going on?"

I wiped my damp hands on my jeans. "Mom, I can explain...I...we...it's complicated."

"How complicated?"

"Not that complicated, but still complicated."

"Mattie, you are an adult. But is this a good idea?"

"Which part?" It slipped out and I wanted to take it back.

"How many parts are there?"

"Well, ha, um…Just the one. I think."

"Are you two involved?"

"Depends, on what you mean by involved."

"Now is not a time to joke."

"Okay, mom," I said with the same frustration I'd felt at seventeen and she wanted to discuss boys. "I like him."

Her head sank as if this was a real problem.

"We're attracted to each other."

"Sweetie—"

"I know it's bad, mom. I'm not sure what it even means."

"It means you like each other. It's not bad to like someone, but it's something we need to discuss. Stanley frowns on rule-breakers."

"We didn't think about Stanley. It just happened."

"While I don't agree with everything Stanley does, I can see how he could get upset over this. Dating an employer is probably big time rule breaking in Stanley's book."

"We aren't officially dating. But mom, I don't want to mess this up. Any of it."

"I know," she huffed that exasperated breath only parents know how to make. "I'm glad you didn't think, and followed your heart. We just need to come up with a plan in case Stanley finds out."

"Thanks."

"You've had a lot of pressure on your shoulders to help me, and get back in school, and find a job."

"About that, I think I should drop my classes this semester. So I can help around here." It surprised me this came out of my mouth, but it was how I felt. Mom obviously needed more help than she let on she needed, our cash flow could use the boost. There was too much to sort out, class was an inconvenience.

"Mattie Harper, you will not drop out of school," mom was firm.

"Okay, but you need to let me help you more."

"Of course. We'll talk about ways you can help. But are you sure this doesn't have something to do with the handsome fellow that's working downstairs?" She had me there.

"Speaking of handsome, you better go find out what he wants."

I blushed, and we hugged. Sure it hurt to stand, and walk, but I did my best to fake it long enough to leave the apartment without mom knowing.

"Hey," Garrett said.

"Hey."

"Do you have some time to talk about our meeting with the Sultan?"

"Sure," I swallowed hard. "First, have you ever seen an older guy with Mrs. Jacobson?"

"No. Why?"

"Just curious. I saw a man leave her place today. They looked…close."

"Hmm. It wouldn't surprise me, I heard a couple old guys were hanging around trying to marry her for the money."

"Yikes, I hope it's not the case. She's a nice lady. I'll keep my eyes peeled though."

"Sultan?"

"What about him?"

"We need to prepare. He's not a man who casually 'meets' people. Unlike Ruggiano, he likes anonymity. And privacy."

"I take it, he's a hard guy to see."

Garrett eyed me a minute. I think he was figuring out what he wanted to say.

"Sultan is a powerful guy. He won't see just anyone. Cal was right. Even if he lets us in his place, there is no guarantee he's gonna let us leave there alive. The guy can't be trusted."

"Why are you telling me this now?"

"Because, I want to know if you want to back out."

"I can't. He might have information about Chloe."

"Do you really think he'll open up to you about her death?" Garrett shrugged. We both knew the answer was probably no.

"I'm the only one who'll know if he's lying."

"The guy lies for a living. Even you may not be able to read him."

"Sure, but I promised Chloe's mom. I have to try."

"Sounds like you've made up your mind."

"I have."

"Then let's run through it."

We spent the next hour prepping. He told me the story of Sultan's rise to power and that he had a reputation for eliminating any and all threats. He sounded as bad as Ruggiano. At least Ruggiano cared about himself more than business. A person stood a chance Ruggiano might trip up doing something brazen.

As far as I could tell, Sultan was only concerned with business, and wouldn't hesitate to eliminate anyone in his way. He had a knack for making problems and people disappear. The only reason he hadn't eliminated Ruggiano yet, was Ruggiano served a purpose.

Ruggiano had leverage on a lot of powerful people in the city, and beyond. He even paid Sultan a cut of his profits. Cal had told us a fight was brewing between them, but they were business associates for the time being. Cal's assumption was Sultan was biding his time before he took out Ruggiano, and took over the regional business. I wasn't sure if helping Sultan would eliminate Ruggiano, or if we wanted anything to do with either of them.

When we started looking around Chloe's files, we got stuck. Chloe had locked some documents. She must have known bad people wanted access. So, our plan to copy and wipe the drive was halted until Garrett called a buddy. Garrett apparently knew everybody. When his tech guru arrived, I recognized him from the gym.

He was the kid who'd been bullied. The one working on defense moves with crew cut guy.

After a closer look at his freckles, hoodie, baggy jeans, and Vans, I pegged him at fifteen, tops. He looked young and inexperienced, but it didn't stop him from working some real magic on the flash drive.

The boy went by the name Spade. He asked us a few questions, took a look at Chloe's files, and focused on the job.

Spade helped us transfer data to Chloe's spare laptop, and dummy up a bunch of important-looking, but innocuous files. I could have done it, but it would have taken me weeks. The way this kid was able to do it so quickly showed he had real talent. He could easily work for the government, or some tech company earning seven figures and stock options. And he was a nice kid too. Why anyone would want to beat him up was beyond me.

When he left, we got back to discussing the dangers of meeting Sultan. Garrett was determined to protect me, but all our planning for the worst was wearing me out.

"I need a break."

He didn't argue. He just stopped.

"It's probably time we see your mom."

"Us?"

"Is that what you want?"

"Yes. But, she already knows about us."

"What did she say?"

I told him about our conversation. And how I was concerned about Stanley because mom was concerned about Stanley.

"Let me worry about him," Garrett moved closer to me. "I want to know what you think."

"I think we have a lot to discuss. After we survive this meeting with Sultan."

"Agreed." He stood back and analyzed me.

"I don't want mom to know what we're doing. It might put her in danger."

"Cal can help protect her."

"I'm more afraid her heart couldn't take this. She'd freak if she knew I was meeting with mobsters searching for a killer."

"Got it. But you shouldn't get in the habit of keeping secrets. They have a way of hurting those you love. Even if you mean well." His voice trailed off.

I jumped when we heard the back door.

He left to see who was coming, and came back holding a bouquet of fresh flowers.

"Are you going to put them in the viewing room?"

"No."

"Why not?"

"They're for you." His jaw locked when he set them on the desk. His eyes were steel and angry. Something was wrong.

I looked for the card. He handed me a handwritten note on expensive cardstock. I searched his expression for answers, but found nothing. Unsure of what else to do, I read the note:

Dearest Matilda,

As truth seekers, our desire is to uncover the real story. I have your answers, and you have my information. Someone from my organization will contact you.

In the meantime, enjoy these beauties. They suit you better than dead ones.

Warmly,
Sultan

I dropped the note. Before I had time to process anything, Sledge and Manny came through the door. Garrett scooped the note off the floor and held onto it.

"And that's what I call male corpse enhancement," Manny nudged Sledge. "Get it?"

They laughed. Sledge stopped when he saw Garrett and me. Sledge turned to leave, but Manny shook him off, and walked over to me. Manny looked me over, which made Garrett really unhappy until I put my hand up.

"Can I help you?"

"I'm sorry."

It surprised me. Although Manny's voice sounded sincere, the look on his face said otherwise. It was the hungry for fresh meat look he'd given me before. My hands rolled up into fists, and Garrett moved into an attack stance.

"I think your hot and all, but Sledge told me not to come on so strong."

If that was his idea of an apology, it was lame. But there was too much tension in the room. If I didn't let this go, there would definitely be a fight. Odds were Garrett would take Manny in one punch. We had more bad guys circling, and I needed Garrett focused.

I decided to let it go. "It's not okay to scare people. But I accept your apology."

Sledge grabbed Manny by the collar and rushed him out the back. Smart move. Sledge knew as well as I did, they needed to leave before Manny said anything else.

Garrett came over and guided me into Hank's chair. I needed a distraction from my raw nerves, so I surveyed his desk. Hank was neat. It looked like the guy didn't do any work. But I'd witnessed how hard he worked firsthand. I guess that was part of the reason he was so good at his job. He knew where to find everything when he needed it. He also had big shoulders, which was vital in the funeral business. For a second, I wondered if he would help us smooth things over with Stanley—that was, if Garrett and I pursued this romance.

Mind still wandering, I noticed something unusual on Hank's appointment calendar. He wrote down important stuff—'It's easier to remember if I see it on paper,' he told me once.

Printed in small blue ink were the words 'Harper pre-need'.

I'd learned enough to know what a pre-need meant. An individual or a family might set one up, to begin the funeral planning process before a loved one died. It meant preparation. I assumed we couldn't afford a pre-need unless death was imminent, so I got angry.

When I slammed the kitchen door closed, mom jumped. She had papers spread out on the table. She was working on something.

"When were you going to tell me?!"

"Tell you what? What's wrong?"

"Why don't you tell me? Or are you going to lie some more?"

"Lie? Mattie, what do you mean?"

"I wish you and Aunt Eileen would have just told me!"

"Told you wha—"

There was a knock at the door.

"Is everything okay in there?" Garrett must have wondered what was happening, but I didn't have time to talk.

"No!"

"Mattie, don't be so rude." Mom hissed.

"Give us a few minutes, please!" She may have been right, but I was still mad. I stood there accusing her. "You're dying aren't you? The trip to grandpa's? Aunt Eileen's concern? The note on Hank's desk?"

"I'm fine."

"Mom, please don't lie. I'm a grown-up, tell me!"

"I'm FINE! While the move hasn't been easy, everything is okay. I wanted to see dad, but I may have overdone things a bit. Eileen probably wanted to make sure I rested. She knew you'd help. And the meeting with Hank is just exploratory. I wanted to learn more about pre-needs. It's really nothing."

"Why would you do that?"

"It's necessary. After the heart surgery, I vowed to get things in order in case anything worse happened. So it would be easier on you."

"Mom!"

"Mattie, please! Don't worry so much. I'm okay, just a little worn out. Call my doctor and ask her yourself."

She was right. Too much was happening, and it was starting to drive me over the edge. I heaved a sigh, and rushed to hug her. Such a hard squeeze can sometimes keep tears from streaking my face, but not this time. When I looked at her, she had her concerned mom face on. The last thing she needed was to have to take care of a grown kid.

"I'm sorry." I wiped my face with the back of my sleeve and

vowed to get it together.

"It's okay. A lot has happened."

Thank God, she didn't know the half of it. "I have a lot on my mind. Guess you can relate. Is there anything I can do?"

"No. But if I need help, I'll let you know. Now, how was school?"

"It was school. I think the class could be interesting."

She huffed at my vague answer, but let me off the hook. "Interesting is good. Keep at it, and you'll be finished before you know it." She always encouraged me to keep after things I wanted. "How is everything with Garrett?" She knew me well.

"He's fine. We're fine. I guess."

"You don't have to have all the answers. Have some fun. Be happy. Just be discreet until we can figure a way to tell the others."

"Thanks, mom. I love you."

We talked a little about the bills and the business. Then she shooed me downstairs to talk with Garrett.

I got to the office just as Tess was leaving. Garrett watched her go. And it burned. Every ounce of strength I had barely contained my tears. Instead of talking, arguing, or whatever, I turned and ran to the apartment.

Mom tried to ask me what happened, but I rushed past her. I grabbed my bag, my keys, and my jacket. I lied. Told her everything was fine. Said that I'd forgotten to pick up something for school, and I'd be back in an hour.

Garrett called when he heard me rushing out, but I didn't stop. As I got to my car, Millie appeared out of nowhere and stopped me.

"Where ya goin so fast?"

"Out."

"Seems to me, you leave a lot."

"So." I crossed my arms.

She huffed back. "I can see you're upset. If ya won't talk to him, how 'bout me?"

I wasn't in the mood to listen to Millie's or anyone's wisdom right now. "I'll think about it."

Before I could run out of there, she caught my arm. "Be careful. You can be stubborn, but no need to be stupid."

It didn't matter what she thought, I just wanted out of the place.

The door slammed when I wrenched it closed. I didn't care. I hit the gas and chirped the tires pulling out. It was dumb because someone nearly clobbered me. The Hellcat rumbled, and I sped away. No idea where I was headed.

CHAPTER 28

Downtown bustled. I snagged the first available space, got out, and beeped the locks.

After a frantic series of texts, first warning Cal about Tess, second to Jos who, thankfully, agreed to meet. She wouldn't be around for a while. I wandered aimlessly until I made my way to Fountain Square.

Chloe should have met me here. She should be alive, but she wasn't. Mom's health was fragile. Dead bodies came through the funeral home frequently. I knew life didn't last forever. But if I wasn't careful, mine would end sooner than expected.

It was foolish not to have asked Garrett about Tess, but it hurt too much to see him look at her that way.

Having grown up with one parent, I worked hard to be responsible and self-reliant, which made me wonder why I felt so sensitive. Before I analyzed my feelings too much, the water distracted me. My attention shifted to the murders.

The facts didn't quite add up. Why would three supposedly unrelated people end up dead, marked with the same red powder in some way or other?

The Coroner ruled the other two homicides. Cal mentioned the bodies were found in Ruggiano's territory with spear points, something called a buckler, and other artifacts belonging to the tribe involved with the casino deal. Could Ruggiano be sending a message, or was someone trying to send him one?

If the others were homicides, why say Chloe committed suicide? To hide the truth? To close the case and keep the police from investigating? Or because it was the truth? An answer I still couldn't stomach.

We needed to figure out how these people were linked. And we needed to do it out before the bad guys caught up with us.

My eyes darted around. Everyone looked suspicious. I stood out like total bad-guy-bait. Why hadn't I waited to meet Jos?

Someone touched my shoulder. I jumped up and took a swing.

"Whoa! Take it easy. I come in peace."

Relief set in even though my pulse still raced.

"I saw you here, and thought we might talk."

I wasn't excited to chat with my old flame, but it was nice to see a familiar face. So, I went along.

We walked around the square. Ethan apologized for being so distant the past three years. I admitted it was my fault too—my body relaxed as we cleared the air.

Jos sent a text. She was running late. There was time, so Ethan and I stopped for a drink. We joked about our lives, and before I knew it the second round of drinks were nearly gone.

"If I drink anymore without eating, someone will have to drive me home."

"I'm available for dinner." The way he said it was so playful, it was hard to say no. I only agreed to appetizers just to be safe.

We spent the time reminiscing. Jos showed up when he was finishing a story about his first 'real job'.

"Hey, girl."

"Jos!" I got up and hugged her. She eyed me with Ethan, so I felt obligated to give her the short version of how we got here. She gave me a look. I knew it meant she'd need the full scoop as soon as possible.

"Can I buy you ladies dinner?"

Jos was thinking about it when I stopped her. "Actually, we have some important things to discuss. Rain check?"

"Sure." Ethan paid the tab, shook my hand then left.

Jos didn't waste a minute jumping on that one once we were alone.

"A hand shake. Wow."

"Don't start."

"Don't start? How about you tell me what's going on. Why are you with him, and not Mr. Hottie?"

"Mr. Hottie—I mean, Garrett, had hands full with Tess when I left."

"So, you fell back into old habits with Ethan?"

"It's not like that."

"I remember how he charmed you into bed the first time. And how he conveniently cooled off when you took a job sophomore year. He wanted a girl on his arm, and found one, but she wasn't you."

"I didn't make much effort to keep things going."

"Yeah, but you didn't sleep with the first freshman who came along either."

"Jos, it's in the past."

"Are you gonna answer my question? What about Garrett?"

"Why don't you ask him?"

"Mattie, what did you do?"

"What?"

Jos knew me too well.

"I might have seen Tess at the funeral home. And I might have been so mad that Garrett watched her walk away that I might have stormed off, texted Cal, and you."

"What were you thinking?"

"I wasn't."

"Apparently not."

"What do I do now?" I sank onto a barstool.

"Go talk to him."

"I knew you'd say that."

"If you already knew, why'd you call me?"

"Moral support?" I smiled at her, and hoped she'd let me off the hook.

"You mean crutch. Nope. We'll talk once you've cleared the air with Mr. Wonderful." She nudged me off the stool and out the door.

Jos dropped me off by the car. I got inside. Jos waved, and drove away. She'd made it clear I had to find Garrett and apologize for storming off. I'd probably have to answer for telling Cal about Tess, too.

My life was a mess. I ran my hands over the steering wheel, but couldn't shake the guilt. Garrett deserved answers. He'd called in favors to help search for answers to my friend's death. He was the same guy who set me up with his mechanic to fix my car for free, and made sure I could borrow any ride I wanted. He was polite, and sexy. But he was also the guy Tess kept trying to manipulate—the same one who ran to her when summoned. My stubborn nature prevailed. I drove home determined to finish the investigation on my own.

CHAPTER 29

The next day I did my best to avoid Garrett. The funeral business was in full swing, so he was around the parlor, but tied up with meetings and funeral preparations.

It wasn't hard to avoid him once I figured out a school and job interview schedule that kept me away most of the day. The hardest part came when mom needed me home to give her a break, or run her to appointments.

Eventually, I told Garrett bluntly, "I have responsibilities." He got the message and stopped trying after that, either to give me space, or because he'd given up.

Mom, Mrs. Jacobson, studies, the job search, and my quest for answers kept me busy. Each day, I'd share breakfast with mom, straighten the kitchen then make myself scarce. I ran errands for Mrs. Jacobson, attended class, and studied at the library, where I spent more time researching possible suspects than actually studying.

I learned the allure and controversy of mobsters and casinos. Some mobsters claimed to promote order and protection; casinos boasted economic returns; but the studies I'd read concluded both increased violence and crime, which outweighed the benefits.

I'd witnessed the extremes Ruggiano was willing to go to get what he wanted. I resisted him and ended up in the hospital. Maybe he'd pushed Chloe, and killed her when she wouldn't budge.

Based on Chloe's files, he bought a large stake in the casino—worth zilch if it didn't get built.

There was a series of articles that ran in the Enquirer detailing some of Ruggiano's shady business dealings. One source was quoted as saying Ruggiano swayed a couple officials to vote in favor of the project by giving them hefty contributions. No one admitted to it, and no one wanted to testify, so he was never arrested. Slippery sucker.

The papers also ran photos of Ruggiano and the councilmen in question getting chummy at a charity fundraiser. The date surprised me. It matched the number on the back of Chloe's photo—the one taken at the lake. There was even a photo of the dead woman delivered to our door covered in red ochre powder.

I felt an adrenaline spike and searched every clip and news blurb Chloe kept related to the event. It was a benefit for the Children's Literacy Coalition. The same project Mrs. Jacobson had mentioned at tea.

Did she know Ruggiano? Did she have a mob connection? Did she know something about Chloe's death?

There were no direct links to Ruggiano in what I searched. So, I packed up and paid her a visit.

Mrs. Jacobson was surprised to see me. Even more surprised when I started grilling her about the Children's Literacy Coalition.

"I've contributed to them for years." She'd served us some tea and sipped hers.

"Are you close with any of the other members?"

"What do you mean?"

"I mean...well," I didn't know how else to ask, so I just blurted it out. "Do you know Rocco Ruggiano?"

Mrs. Jacobson was obviously startled by the name.

"I know his reputation." She broke my glance. Obviously hiding something. She seemed stuck for something to do other than answer me, so she signaled me to try the tea. I declined. Then she stood and indicated I should follow her, maybe to distract me. I warily followed.

We went from the living room to a solarium. A lot of windows meant a lot of light. Several easels held her paintings.

The painting in the center of the room wasn't huge, but the scene compelled me to come closer. It was the painting I'd seen her painting on my last visit.

Mrs. Jacobson stood at a rolling cart next to the easel and mixed a reddish powder with liquid from a squirt bottle, like it was as natural as breathing. She dipped her brush in the mixture and began to paint.

I watched her work. After a few strokes, she put the brush down to touch up a spot with her hands.

"It's beautiful," I said of the landscape.

She worked on the deep sky by the tree. "Thank you. I've been painting some version of this for years."

"Where is it?" I asked.

"A place far away." She sounded distant, so I didn't press her for the exact location.

"The colors are incredibly vibrant. How do you get it to look so real?"

"It's the red ochre."

What? Did she know about the murders? Could she be involved? "Where did you get the paint?"

"It's a lovely color from Old Holland. I've been buying supplies from them forever."

"Oh," I tried to sound natural.

"What dear?" She stopped momentarily and looked at me.

"It's nothing, really." I tried to figure it out, but I just couldn't put the pieces together.

"Many ancient people buried remains with artifacts. Some natives sprinkled red ochre powder over the graves as part of their burial ritual. It's quite fascinating." She smiled, briefly, studied my face then went back to painting.

"It sounds interesting," I told her, wondering if this old woman was killing off people, and sprinkling red pixie dust on their bodies like some kind of lunatic fairy.

"You should hear some of the stories I heard as a child. About the people that lived here long ago."

If she knew that I thought she killed those people, and it turned out to be true, I could be next. She could hardly walk, so maybe she had an accomplice. It was just the two of us now. My chances of escape were pretty good. I kept a sharp eye on the exit though.

"Well, one I remember most is about a young girl who fell in love with a native boy."

This sounded like the story Garrett told me. How much did Mrs. Jacobson know?

"She was a beautiful girl. Happy, sweet, and carefree. She had a habit of going off into the woods near her house and exploring them for hours.

One day she chased a bird far into the woods, where she came across the most glorious tree. She admired it, touched it and stayed by the tree until sunset. She realized it was late and started toward home. But, the light had faded and she got turned around.

The girl began to worry until a young boy came to her aid. He had dark skin, dark eyes and black hair. He startled her, but reached his hands out gently to help guide her home. After he brought her back to the edge of the wood, she asked him, "Who are you? How can I find you again?"

Of course, he didn't understand her language, so all he could manage to do was nod and smile. They met several times after that, and fell in love. Her fate had been sealed. Destined to marry a wealthy landowner, her father forbade her to see the native boy.

As some young women are inclined to do, she ignored her father, and went into the woods anyway. After being caught again, her husband-to-be broke off their engagement. Soon after, the landowner married her cousin.

The young girl was forced to live across the street from them, which she wouldn't have minded, except the landowner had his men cut down the trees and burn the woods." Something caught in her throat and she stopped.

"Are you okay, Mrs. Jacobson?"

There was a longing in her eyes. She told the story as if she'd been there. But it was well over a hundred years ago. No way she was alive then.

"Fine." She focused on the painting again.

What did this story, the mixed paints, and murders have to do with Mrs. Jacobson?

"If you ever find true love, Mattie. Never let it go. Don't take it for granted, or look for anything else, and if necessary, fight to keep it."

She was fiery, but I didn't have a chance to respond. The doorbell rang. I got nervous thinking her story was meant to distract me, which it did. Confused and nervous, I prepared to bolt.

"Would you get the door?"

For a murderer? No thanks!

As if Mrs. Jacobson sensed my unease, she tried to calm me with a gentle hand. Instead, I ran as fast as I could out the back door. On my way to the car, I noticed the old Cadillac that had been there before. It must have been her gentleman caller. I hoped they weren't evil killers, but I didn't stick around to find out.

Mrs. Jacobson knew where I lived, so if she had anything to do with the killings, we could all be in trouble. I needed help.

The only person I trusted with the details of Mrs. Jacobson's connection to Ruggiano, and her suspicious choice of paints, besides Garrett, was Cal. Cal was at a crime scene and temporarily unavailable, the dispatcher informed me.

Reluctantly, I reached out to Garrett.

I was on my way to meet him when a blue van came dangerously close to rear-ending me. The Hellcat had tons more power, so I hit the gas to outrun them.

I checked the rearview mirror, there was no van. Before there was time to celebrate the van sideswiped me. I tried to turn out of the spin, but the car was going too fast. It jumped the curb into someone's front yard and crashed into a tree.

The hit knocked me around good, but the passenger side door took the brunt of the damage. I was disoriented. Zorro, the guy with the sword, I mean scabbard tattoo was there. He and another guy grabbed me out of the car. The Hellcat was going to need bodywork, maybe a new passenger door, and plenty of paint. Zorro and his buddy put a bag over my head and shoved me into the van.

They drove and I bounced around in the back of a van that smelled like incense. I wondered if Zorro was a recreational user, or just a big fan of patchouli. The scent was cloying. So much so, I almost missed something that smelled like a bowling alley. I contemplated what that meant then the van stopped.

The men pulled me out, bag still on my head, and shoved me into an elevator. It sounded like we were in a garage, but it was muffled. I guessed by the chimes we ended up on the fourth or fifth floor.

Someone pulled the bag off my head. I was standing in an office fit for a king, or rather, a Sultan.

A familiar figure stood next to me facing the firing squad. I'd recognize those biceps anywhere.

When the bag came off, Garrett shook his head. He looked at me with a mix of pain and relief. I felt the same. It had been too long since we'd talked, but to make things worse, this was not what we'd planned when we agreed to meet Sultan. Without Cal as backup, it was just the two of us against an army of who knows how many guys in black carrying who knows how many weapons. I didn't have a good feeling about this.

"Ah, welcome. Welcome!" He surveyed us, probably wanted to see how we'd respond.

Even though we had no shackles, making a break would have been stupid. We needed information. Besides all they'd done up to now was take us by surprise, blindfold us, and bring us to Sultan's place, which was some sort of loft overlooking the city. Also, there were too many goons around for us to make a move.

I couldn't place exactly where we were, but if I had to guess, we were somewhere on the Covington side facing Cincinnati.

We were in a great room with floor to ceiling windows draped in decorator grey fabric that spilled onto the floor. The curtains were pulled back so we could see the view and a set of doors that led to a balcony perched above the river. It wasn't some dark, hidden lair. For that I was thankful. Light was a good sign. Wasn't it?

I caught a glimpse of Garrett. He looked like he was getting a lay of the land. I wondered if he could figure out a way to break us out of here.

"My apologies for the manner in which you were brought here, but one cannot be too careful these days." Hard to tell where he was from. I hadn't exactly traveled the world. He had a warm olive complexion—the wrinkles and paunch made him look about fifty— and he spoke with some sort of European accent.

He walked up to me.

"I've been wanting to meet you. And not just because you have some information that will help my business."

Garrett tensed. Sultan wagged a finger at him. "I'm glad to see you too, but let's not be hasty Mr. Mackenzie. By now, you've seen that you are outnumbered and outgunned. It would be a pity if anyone got hurt."

Garrett smiled as if he knew something I didn't, like how to deal with this guy. The tension in his shoulders remained, so maybe dealing with the henchman wouldn't be easy.

Sultan circled us before he took a seat behind a mahogany desk.

"Shall we start with you lovely?" He rolled his chair up to the desk, put his elbows on the armrests, and laced his fingers together under his chin as if he was waiting for me to explain the meaning of life.

I had no idea what to say, so I kept quiet, which wasn't like me at all.

"Why don't you tell us why you kidnapped us and brought us here?" One of the guards put on a set of brass knuckles, stepped forward, and punched Garrett in the gut. He let out a squeak of pain and doubled over. I rushed to help make sure he was okay.

Another guard stepped toward me. Sultan waived him off and he returned to his post.

"Kidnapping is such a harsh word. I'd like to think you're here willingly. My team has taken measures to protect me, the main reason for the secrecy."

Garrett couldn't stand upright, probably injured ribs.

Rage shot through me. "Can we get on with it then? We'd like to get out of here as quickly as possible." My tone was all business, so much so it shocked even me.

"Yes, yes. I can see why you like her." Sultan looked from Garrett to me. "Why don't we start with the files?"

"You nabbed me unexpectedly. What makes you think I have them on me?"

A flash of anger crossed Sultan's face. "Of course you have them. You wouldn't trust them to be anywhere other than wherever you are. I know enough about you to know that much."

I don't know what he knew about me, but he was right—up until the home invasion. I knew if we handed over our only leverage before we got information on Chloe's murder, or got out of here, we could kiss more than our leverage goodbye. I'd stashed the drive in a safe place. Garrett had no idea, and neither did Sultan.

"Of course, but you promised something in return."

"You're speaking of my note. I will oblige since you are my guests."

Sultan told us that Ruggiano came to him with a deal to fund a casino in Michigan. Sultan would fund the construction. They'd purchase the land using a shell company. Ruggiano would handle the grease the skids with the politicians, so the developers could finish in eighteen months time.

Sultan liked the plan, up until a land survey found a portion of the proposed site didn't belong to the tribe who'd agreed to let them build the casino. Five lots ran right through a corner of the planned high-rise.

The land survey was a point of contention. Until the land in question could be authenticated, or sold outright to the developers, the project stopped.

Sultan and Ruggiano agreed to buy out the owners—coax them to leave with the promise of more money than they'd ever seen before. When that failed, Ruggiano used threats until all but one family caved. The Sigos.

Although Sultan did not admit to knowing about the plan, he told us Ruggiano sent men to rough up the grandfather, Walter Sigo. Sigo spouted off something about the land being their heritage, and if they gave it up, they may as well have been dead.

This frustrated Sultan and Ruggiano. The latter hired a lawyer to threaten litigation against the family, tribe members, friends and employers helping Sigo.

Finally, Ruggiano paid off a bank manager to have the Sigo family evicted. It would have succeeded had it not been for Chloe.

Sultan explained that Chloe took on Sigo's case, and was dogged in her efforts to keep them on their land.

This sounded a lot like the Chloe I knew. Hard-working and determined.

"Sigo helped your friend get in touch with the money man responsible for buying up the properties, I believe he is your first victim."

Jimbo.

Garrett shifted uncomfortably.

"The girl must have been a real crusader," Sultan continued, "because she befriended this man and somehow convinced him to turn on Ruggiano. They compiled a list of all the people on Ruggiano's payroll: the business owners, politicians, cops, judges, and average Joes tied up in his illegal activities. They planned to share the list with the authorities in exchange for this money man's protection."

Learning this information made Chloe a target. Now that I had it, I was the target.

"The list your friend kept is the key to the kingdom. When it is mine, Ruggiano will no longer be necessary." Sultan nodded to one of his goons. "Neither will Sigo and his family." He said that last part under his breath, but I heard it.

"As for the other answers, look into the Brampton Corporation. That is where you'll find enlightenment." Sultan emphasized the word as if he knew it was Chloe's password.

It shocked me.

Sultan bared his sharp white teeth and I took an unconscious step back. Things were about to get worse.

"There's nothing to fear, as long as you have what I desire."

It sounded like a threat, a come-on, and all kinds of wrong. I looked around. He had nothing to fear. We were trapped in his lair.

I didn't know where we were, although he hadn't exactly hidden the view. I'd seen enough television drama to know getting a look at our captors, and their hideout, was not a good thing. We were still alive because Sultan assumed I had a flash drive stuck in my pocket. Once he had it, we'd be dead.

The guard who'd hurt Garrett approached me. He lifted up my arms and grinned as he searched me. His hands started low then traveled up my legs. He patted me down, thoroughly. Even squeezed my upper thighs and back pockets.

I stuck my chin out. "Get your feels in now, perv. I'm gonna break your hands the first chance I get."

The creep's smile widened.

"It's safe to say you searched her. Although, I'd love to see her tear you apart." Garrett gave the guy a death stare.

The guard took a step toward Garrett—

"Now, now. It's finished." Sultan got the guard to back away from us with a wave of his hand. "Did you get anything, besides her measurements?"

The guard shook his head. Sultan didn't like the answer. He stalked forward and studied me—I wasn't sure what he was thinking.

He suddenly pulled a syringe from his pocket and jabbed it into Garrett's arm.

Garrett flinched then dropped to the ground.

I ran to him. "Garrett? Garrett! Are you all right?" His eye went glassy. There was very little response when I shook him. I turned my attention to Sultan. "What did you do?"

"Only what was necessary. Now give me what I want."

"I told you, I don't have it!"

"Yes, but you know how to get it. Poisoning Garrett guaranteed you'd give me the drive."

"What did you give him?"

"A special blend of poisonous herbs. My supplier ensures me they're quite effective."

"You're insane!"

"I'm the bad guy, remember? I get what I want, or he dies." There was madness in his eyes.

Anger burned me up, but I had to save Garrett.

"I'll get it, but I need him, or whatever's left of him to help me."

"Fine." Sultan walked over and dropped the syringe in the trash near his desk. "I'll send along my guard Ivan to make sure you don't go to the police. Garrett has less than 24 hours to get an antidote, so you'd better be quick."

A guard helped me peel Garrett off the floor. We steadied him, so he could walk with assistance.

As we got near Sultan's desk, a plane flying by caught everyone's attention. We looked out the balcony. While the distraction was going on, I snatched the syringe from the garbage, and hid it up my sleeve, trying not to poke myself.

Sultan turned to back. "Do not disappoint me. More than just Garrett's life is at stake, Mattie."

I nodded and we left through the front door. No bag this time meant Sultan was didn't care what we saw. He expected to get the disk drive and have us killed.

CHAPTER 30

The ride was bumpy. Garrett panted, eyes closed, while we rode in the van. He was out of it, which forced me to come up with a plan on my own. The good news was we only had to overtake one guard. The bad news was Garrett couldn't move much, so I'd have to do it myself.

A few minutes after we left, the van came to an abrupt stop. It didn't feel like we'd been on the road long enough to get home.

The door slid opened. The grin on our captor's face was not at all innocent.

"Where do we pick up the disk drive?"

I'd already thought about our chances. We needed help. Going to the police station was too obvious. The funeral home was risky, didn't want him to hurt anyone else close to us. That left us with limited options.

I chose Chloe's. I knew where she lived, we'd just been there to search it, knew no one would be inside, and that the cops, meaning Cal, would likely check her place if we went missing. The security cameras outside the building, and in the foyer, were another plus.

I gave the address to the guard, but he didn't move. He just stared at me then looked at Garrett who was knocked out in the back of the van, and back at me.

The guy who'd patted me down pulled me out of the van.

I resisted as he dragged me along the side of the road until we got to a spot where grass met gravel.

"This is gonna be fun." He turned me to face him.

I knew this would end badly. I needed to do something, anything. Before he could shove me into the ditch, I jabbed the syringe I'd been holding into his neck. He yelled and grabbed at it. When he threw it to the ground, I used everything I had to shove the palm of my hand up into his nose. The crack sent him down, screaming in pain.

I ran to the van, jumped in the driver's seat, and sped off. As soon as I could glance back, I watched Garrett fighting to come to. He wasn't winning.

It was time to get help.

I parked the van near Millie's shop.

I called Cal then gave Millie the rundown. She studied the syringe, sniffed it with her eyes closed, twice.

Millie looked different here—in her element, a powerful force—more influence than she wielded at the funeral home. I watched. Her voluminous hair had been tied up in a head wrap of the same fabric as her dark-patterned dress highlighted with bronze threads that swept the floor.

It startled me when her eyes opened. Bulging and focused on me, as though they could see everything I'd ever thought.

Then as if she paid me no mind, she glided through a doorway curtained with hanging beads, her muumuu shifting as she moved. She was gone only a few moments before reentering the front of the store with a small vial. She handed it to Garrett. The liquid was a deep, dark red. Another potion. She had pretty good luck with potions, so I held back judgment. She peeled his eyes open and purred into his ears 'drink 'dis my boy'. He obeyed.

Garrett stumbled a bit when he threw back the potion, so we propped him up on a battered stool. Seeing him at the wooden counter, with strange plants and bits of God-knows-what-else stuffed into the jars behind him made the place look like some kind of voo-doo diner. 'Would you like an eye of newt soda? Or how about a toad stool shake?' Millie looked at me and chuckled. I shivered. Could she possibly know what I was thinking?

"That ought to last him da night, but it wasn't enough to bring him back."

"Bring him back?"

"Yeah, dis boy's gonna need more balm. He won't get better without it."

"Can't we just take him to a doctor?"

"Whoever poisoned him wanted him gone. Conventional medicine would only make it worse."

"He needs a few doses of dis." She held up a bottle of yellow elixir. She indicated he also needed more of the ruby red potion.

"I need to get up north and warn the Sigo family. Cal might be able to help, but Ruggiano has resources all over, and Sultan's men have a head start."

We watched as Garrett let out a small groan. "Can you keep him here and give him whatever potions or salves he needs?"

"I'm coming." He nearly fell off the stool. I helped straighten him.

"You need to stay here. Let Millie give you some medicine so you can get better."

"I don't have no more."

I stood stunned.

"My herbs need to be combined with more Balm than I've got. Where up north ya headed?"

"Tahquamenon Falls." Memories flooded my head and vanished as quickly as they came. "Sigo met Chloe up there. I think that's our best shot.

"You can harvest da plants at the falls. They'll be best near the water."

Garrett swayed.

"Better get him up there, fast."

If he didn't question her with his own life on the line, why should I? "How do we get there fast?"

"Cal can help." Garrett regained some color as he said it.

Millie gave me a ju-ju-to-go kit filled with vials, some herbs, and instructions. Then she handed me a small bible. "Keep dis with ya. Use the time to read Psalms. Try Psalm 16. It'll help protect you." She hugged me then pushed us out the door.

I contacted mom to let her know I'd probably be home late. Then, I called Cal. "Tell Garrett I'll get koala."

I had no idea how a cute and cuddly animal was going to help Garrett, but there wasn't time to ask Cal.

Cal instructed us. "Get to his car and meet me at Hogan. I'll send a link. Just open it and follow the map." He clicked off.

Garrett smiled when he heard 'koala', which made me feel, well uneasy, but more inclined to go along with this plan.

We got to the Maserati and Garrett gave me the keys.

"You should drive. I'll navigate and keep in contact with Cal. You aren't used to the com-link, and me giving you instructions would be too distracting."

Five minutes into the ride I finally breathed. The car ran great, Garrett held steady, and we headed toward Cal.

"About Tess," he said.

"Let's not do this now. You'll be fine."

"It's important you know what happened."

I didn't want details of what happened between Garrett and his ex-lover. Not now, not ever.

"She—"

"Garrett, please."

"Mattie, it's important."

I huffed, but let him speak.

"She was the one."

"Really? You're doing this now? Can't you just let me drive?"

"That's not what I meant to say. She was the one who sent the bodies to me."

And suddenly, air left the vehicle. I couldn't breath.

"The bodies were found near the river, in Ruggiano's territory. She was scared that he might be involved. He'd helped her when her family wouldn't and she thought she owed him. She wasn't trying to cover them up, just buy him some time."

So, Tess wasn't as horrible as I'd hoped.

"She knew I'd send them back and hid it from me, so no one would get in trouble."

"Then why tell you about it?"

"She didn't want me thinking she was covering something up. She wanted us to get back together."

"And?"

"Nothing. It's over between Tess and me."

"What about jumping the minute she texts?"

"She told me it was about your case. I did it to help you find Chloe's killer."

"What about the reports? Why didn't she note the needle marks on the other victims?" I changed lanes and noticed a black Mercedes do the same.

"She showed me her original notes. They were in there. She told me Detective Marlucci asked for the files. He may have had something to do with covering it up."

"Do you think someone is trying to frame Ruggiano?"

"Possibly. He wants fame, but he doesn't want to get caught."

"Garrett? I think someone's following us."

He looked back. "Move to the right lane." We moved. The car followed. "Now, move to the left lane." We moved. It followed.

Garrett faced forward with more color than he'd had in an hour, and let out a breath. "Let's see what they want. Increase your speed."

I pushed the gas pedal and watched as the speedometer moved up to 85, 90, then 95. The sedan closed the gap and rammed us. I struggled to hold the car steady, but managed to change lanes to avoid a minivan.

The sedan sped up and steered into the rear passenger side, which sent us skidding toward a semi. I gripped the wheel, eased off the throttle, and steered out of trouble. The way I'd practiced when mom insisted I learn to navigate icy roads before she'd even consider letting me take my driver's exam. They should make bad weather driving and steering out of a skid required for all drivers.

Garrett looked at me and smiled.

Noticing the car come up behind us again, I swerved to the fast lane, hit the gas, and put the semi between us.

I sped up until we were well ahead of the semi and changed lanes. Every move I made, the Mercedes followed.

They stopped trying to rear end us for several minutes as we increased speed to about 120 mph. We cleared traffic, but Garrett let Cal know we needed backup.

I moved to the right lane in case we needed to make an emergency exit, the Merc stayed on our left. A mile before exit 41, I glanced back at our pursuers. Blacked out windows made it impossible to see anything inside.

"Car!" Garrett yelled and grabbed the oh-crap bar.

I barely missed a truck. The Merc used the distraction to ram us in the left side. Already loose from me jerking the wheel to miss the truck, our car fishtailed. Foot eased off the gas, I tried to regain control when they hit us again. The blow shook my organs. Our car hit the shoulder, ran through an Adopt-a-Road bag, which sent garbage flying. We plowed through some grassy stuff and dove headfirst into a gulley where our car came to rest.

We were banged up, but the Maserati took the brunt of the damage. Probably totaled. I would have hung my head in shame, but Garrett came to the driver's side and yanked me out before something zoomed past us and hit the car. He dove and pulled me down with him right before the impact. Then an explosion.

We ran for cover and heard gunfire. Thirty seconds of rapid fire and it was over.

Cal rescued us, drove us to the airfield and presented the 'Koala'. My jaw dropped.

"Here it is. The AW119Kx, a single engine state-of-the-art machine equipped with a Garmin G1000H Integrated Flight Deck System, extra fuel capacity, luxury seating, and air conditioning." He eyed Garrett. "Better than that toaster we flew in the desert, and built in these United States."

I didn't know a helicopter could be sexy, but this one was all that and more.

Garrett grinned at the silver and black bird. "Our Indian Hills friend came through."

"Yup."

I stared.

"If you hadn't said Millie was involved, I'd have thought you were crazy," Cal said.

"It is crazy, but we've got our orders."

We boarded the chopper. Cal went up front. The engine started and blades rotated. It'd be noisy, but much quicker than driving, and able to land closer to the falls than a plane could manage.

We heard him over the speakers. "Buckle up and relax you two. We'll be cruising at about 140 knots before you know it."

In the time it took us to fly up north, Garrett started to look less like a corpse. I tried a half dozen times to search Brampton Corporation on my smartphone, I was able to read a blurb about the benefits of oil and gas exploration, and the first part of their annual report.

Something else Sultan said about Brampton had struck a nerve. My suspicions were confirmed when I remembered Chloe's notebook. She'd circled the word 'Enlightened' several times.

I copied some notes she'd written about the Sigo family into my phone. Someone from Brampton visited them after Ruggiano and his goons. I searched for the name then compared it to the board members. The second victim was on the board of Brampton. She'd visited the Sigo family as Jimbo's replacement, to extend them another offer.

Sigo mentioned he noticed an unmarked car, likely the police following her, not tribal authorities, when the woman left his home.

I told Garrett then launched into all the coincidences surrounding Mrs. Jacobson, Ruggiano, and Brampton. He laughed a huge belly laugh.

"There's no way she's involved. I don't think she would hurt anyone. Besides, she's not strong enough to have dumped the bodies."

"What about an accomplice? Or the association with Ruggiano?"

"Plenty of people were at the fundraiser, and even more know him personally. The charity might be a good place to look for other suspects."

Garrett leaned closer and held my gaze. It felt something like a spark igniting. My cheeks flushed.

"What make you think she would kill someone?"

"She's hiding something. And she uses the same kind of paint they found on the victims."

"Smart observations, but what's her motive? Ruggiano makes a better suspect. He's got a lot to lose, and he's proven he can kill."

"Maybe they're connected?" Something about Mrs. Jacobson and Ruggiano felt odd. We needed more answers.

Cal found a clear spot and set the helicopter down. He opened our door and I got out gingerly. Garrett had to help me out. The vibration had aggravated recent injuries, and my legs were wobbly.

The three of us got our bearings. We made a plan to head toward the falls together. Cal and I would help Garrett, only if he needed, as Garrett had insisted he was mostly fine.

Cal set us down on a small clearing, but we still had to hike a bit to get to the falls. Millie had insisted that the antidote would only work, if we got the plants that were by the falls. Something about the trees, and tannins in the water. I had too much to think about, so I trusted her, and just went with it.

I'd never seen the falls in person. We'd planned to, the summer

Tab tried to force himself on me. The lake house was a short drive from here—appropriately named, Paradise—and we thought it would be an adventure to find out why so many people considered this part of the UP God's country. Maybe the entire Upper Peninsula was Paradise. Hard to tell. After the incident with Tab, I headed home, never to see Tahquamenon Falls.

What I'd seen from the chopper was breathtaking, and from the ground, it looked even more stunning.

The place felt mystical, like elements beyond our earth resided here. It humbled me. I breathed in the autumn air—the scent of maple, oak, and rain. Already dressed in deep auburn and gold, the canopy shielded us from a light mist that had begun falling.

Cal told us we were less than a quarter-mile from the water. We trekked ahead hearing the falls as we approached. The place vibrated, giving off secrets in a low, mystical hum, which became amplified the closer we got.

Garrett took the lead, leaving me in the middle, and Cal at the rear. I squinted to see if I could get a glimpse of the water when a boom made me jump. We heard a gasp followed by a heavy thud. Garrett looked behind us, then at me and yelled. "Run!"

Confused, I stayed planted. It took me a second to figure out Cal had been shot. When it hit me, I followed Garrett's advice and ran toward the water. My heart pounded so hard and fast I couldn't hear anything but the thudding in my chest.

I sprinted past American Beech, Easter Hemlock, Yellow Birch and Sugar Maples—as I'd read in the information packet Millie gave me. Was I doing the right thing? Should I have stayed to help Garrett and Cal? What was I going to do when I reached the edge of the woods?

All I knew was Garrett had told me to run. And like a good soldier, I ran. Millie had given me a higher objective—find the balm and save Garrett. So I ran to save him.

My breath and footfalls were harder to hear closer to the falls. I gasped upon emerging from the trees. The water was powerful. Its reddish brown tint, like root beer streaked with rust, added more color to the landscape. There was no time to enjoy it. I pulled out a photo of the plant we needed and started searching.

Grass and wild things were fading. Part of the ground was littered with needles, so it took me a while to filter those out. Finding the specific seeds proved challenging because I was nervous and shaking. Millie told me to trim a three-inch section of root because the seeds might not be viable, and to gather some seeds, just in case.

I pulled out the jar Millie sent, unscrewed the lid, and bent near the ground. Using a pair of her clippers, I dug at a thin layer of earth a couple feet from the base of the tree until the roots revealed themselves. A gentle tug allowed me access to clip a section off. It went in the jar and I sealed lid. I placed the jar in a dry bag, sprayed the cut roots with something Millie gave me, patted some earth over them to help keep out insects, then scooped up some seeds.

I made sure to get extra knowing Millie could probably reanimate just about anything. Sultan was likely to come after us, and we might need them.

When all was finished, I closed the dry bag, and—

Someone knocked me down.

I moved to get back up, but whoever was there pushed my cheek to the ground and held me there.

"I came for you, Mattie," he cooed.

A little bile came up in my throat. "How did you find me here?" I tried to act like I had things in control, but I was terrified.

"You should know by now, I can find you anywhere." He enjoyed the threat.

"Please, you don't have to do this."

"Oh, but I do. You left us no choice."

"Us?"

Tab didn't respond. He looked in the direction of an observation deck—at no one— and applied pressure until my spine felt like it would snap.

"We finally get to see just how much you want me." He bore down and the pain in my back burned.

"I don't! Stop it!"

"Why don't you make me?"

I tried, but couldn't move or do anything. Garrett ran out of the woods and tackled Tab. They scrummed on the ground, but quickly shot up and stood to fight.

Tab swung. Garrett blocked him. Then Garrett threw a punch. They went back and forth, swinging and blocking. Every time Tab lunged forward, Garrett had a response, until Tab caught him with a body shot that took his breath away. I gasped. Garrett looked to see if I was okay, and Tab punched him in the kidney.

Tab watched Garrett fall. I grabbed a thick branch that littered the ground and ran toward Tab. I swung it like a bat. Tab blocked it with his right arm. Then with his left, he shoved me backwards.

Tab threw the branch toward the trees and reached for me. I moved to avoid his angry grasp. Not fast enough. He grabbed me from behind and lifted me off the ground. I struggled to break free, but couldn't remember training. Any of it.

Tab carried me to the water. I shouted for him to stop and pounded my objection on his arms. He kept going even after we left land for shallow water.

We were at the top of the falls. I saw the drop. He planned to throw me over. I had no idea if it would kill me, but roughly 50,000 gallons per minute of rushing water might drown me before I reached the bottom, or before I figured out which end was up. I fought, wiggled, screamed, and then by accident, head-butt him. It did more damage to my head than his.

"Crap!" he yelled.

"Ouch!" It felt like I broke my skull on his stupid head.

I had my bell rung, banging inside my head. Tab got mad as a hornet and pushed me down. He grabbed me by the neck. An icy shock pulsed from head to chest as he shoved me facedown under the water.

He was drowning me. I resisted, arms flailing, struggling to break the surface for a breath. I got hold of his plaid shirt and yanked. It didn't do anything, but I kept fighting. He brought me up once to yell something about being stubborn while I coughed up water.

His tirade was the break I needed. The impact and cold water must have shook something loose—I remembered something from the gym. I linked my hands and used the power behind both arms to shove my elbow into Tab's groin. It must have worked, because he squealed and let go. While he tended to his family jewels, I got up, soaking wet and coughing, and trudged through the water toward shore.

Just before I got there, Tab reached out and pulled me down. I faced the sky for a few seconds while he climbed on top of me. I'd seen that look on his face once before and I would do anything to stop him.

His eyes widened as he bent to whisper vile things in my ear. My fingers desperately stretched until they found a large rock. When it was in my grasp, I lifted the weight and hammered it into Tab's skull a couple times. He fell to the ground either passed out, or dead. It was hard to tell and I didn't care. The rock dropped.

I rolled over and a double barrel shotgun was pointed at me.

"Damn shame you made such a mess." The southern drawl was unmistakably Thibodeaux. So were the crazy eyes. He ordered me to get up. Instinctively, I looked back at Tab, still frozen on the ground.

"I'll deal with him later. Ladies first." Thibodeaux prodded me with the shotgun to move us closer to the tree line. "You look surprised to see me, Mattie."

Surprised? I was in shock. The man being groomed to take over the governorship of Louisiana had me hostage in Michigan's Upper Peninsula. "Did you follow us?"

"Those were my guys back there. They called when they saw you two heading out of the city. Ruined a perfectly good Mercedes, no thanks to you." He relaxed and let the shotgun hang a little low. He caught me eyeing it. "I wouldn't try anything if I were you. Most self-respecting southern gentlemen are taught to handle rifles at an early age."

"Most self-respecting gentlemen don't go around shooting cops and taking hostages. So, now that we know you're not respectful, or a gentleman, why don't you tell me why you're here?" I was wet, cold and my head felt like it would explode any second. I had no time to mince words.

"If I were my daddy, I'd backhand you. But I'm not my daddy. Guess you got lucky." He had an air of nonchalance that bothered me.

"Guess so." I waved my dirty, scraped up arms and sounded irritated.

He adjusted his grip on the gun to remind me of my place. "Answer my questions, and we can make this quick. How much do you know?"

"I must not know much if I'm standing here with you and your shotgun."

"My boy has a soft spot for feisty ones." He snickered. "Now, tell me what you know before I wake him up and have him beat it out of you. Or do whatever else is necessary to get you to tell me what I want to know."

My stomach turned sour. I didn't know if it would be that easy to wake Tab up, but I sure as heck didn't want to find out. The voice in my head was screaming 'Get out!' But he had a gun.

I stared at Mr. Thibodeaux and his gun. Images flashed in my brain. Brampton Corp. was a sponsor of the Children's Literacy Coalition. The company held a variety of assets, mostly concentrated in gas and oil. Then it hit me. He must have been one of Brampton Corp.'s shareholders.

Chloe had a map of oil pipelines in Michigan. Looked innocuous at the time, but then I remembered a terminal for Brampton Oil a short distance from the planned casino site. He didn't want the casino built; he was trying to stop it.

Along with the map, Chloe made notes about complaints of groundwater contamination. Apparently, there was an aging pipeline and the locals were convinced it had started to leak. A "guaranteed environmental catastrophe" she wrote. I assumed she was working on another case, but the cases were connected.

"You keep quiet much longer and I'm gonna get mad. You don't want to see me mad."

He was right. Tab had told Chloe stories about how mean his dad could get. She had seen enough of Tab to know the truth. It was one of the reasons she was so forgiving of his abuse. She would argue anger begets anger, and plead for us to show him sympathy, but it didn't matter when we saw her bruised and bleeding.

"You know you're not going to win the governorship when they find out you killed people."

"Killed people? I have plenty of people willing to do that for me." He shifted the gun to one arm and held up his hand. "I don't see any blood."

"I know you're guilty. There's dirty oil on your hands."

"Now we're getting somewhere. Tab thought she spilled her guts to you."

He meant Chloe and he was wrong. She hadn't told me a thing, but she wanted to before she died. Even after, she had me following the clues. It was taking time to put the pieces together—maybe something to do with all the bad guys chasing me lately.

Thibodeaux didn't look very patient, so I winged it.

"Sure. I know you're a shareholder in Brampton, and Brampton is big oil. Big enough they have a terminal station a stone's throw from the site of a new tribal casino. Problem is, the pipeline is old. If you don't get a new one in soon, you'll have an environmental disaster to clean up, which would be a political mess for you even as far away as Louisiana. You'd be the face of another catastrophe, people would be reminded of the gulf oil spill, and a bunch of angry voters would elect someone other than you."

Things started clicking. The land grab was as much about oil as it was about gambling. The maps in Chloe's files told me as much, seeing Thibodeaux cleared up why.

"If the build went forward, your new pipelines couldn't go in, and you'd be back at square one looking to patch old lines until you could find more land, make a new plan, and work through the bureaucratic red tape all over again."

"Chloe was right. You are smart."

How did he know anything about her other than what Tab made up? He must have read the questions on my face.

"How'd I know?" He smiled, just like Tab when he'd cornered his prey. "Since I can't let you walk out of here, I may as well confess," he leaned in and whispered, "I lied. There is blood on my hands. It was almost too easy."

By now he was grinning, so happy with himself. Happy over the death of my friend—a friend I should have been there to save.

"All I had to do was tell her how worried we were." Thibodeaux faked a sad expression. I wished I could knock the smugness right out of him.

"I told Chloe that Tab might hurt himself if he didn't get help. What really got her attention was when I said the family couldn't do it without her help. She agreed to meet with Tab's doctor and me. She was shocked when Dr. Avanti pulled out his needle." He got comfortable telling his story as though he'd staged the perfect murder. Thibodeaux disgusted and scared me. While he focused on his tale, I searched for a weapon and a way out.

"That man didn't come cheap, but he was happy to take my money. He needed it since he owed Ruggiano close to six-figures, which also made him the perfect mark. Doc wasn't smart enough to realize I paid him to kill those people, and had a trusted antique dealer ship him the artifacts found near the bodies, so I could implicate Ruggiano, but pin the murders on doc if things went sideways. See, I'm always thinking ahead." He tapped at his temple, like there was something up there besides a whole lot of crazy.

It was a double cross? How did he even know about the deal?

"I see the wheels are turning up there. There are people in my company that get paid to monitor my oil reserves. If something's gonna impact my business or my career, they let me know. It would have been nice if Ruggiano had done his homework ahead of time. Instead, he jumped in head first."

"So, use your influence and block the deal. Why make such a mess of killing people to frame him?"

"I made a better deal."

Another deal to get Ruggiano out of the picture? Who better to double cross Ruggiano than, "Sultan?"

Thibodeaux let out a short laugh. "It's mutually beneficial. Sultan wanted him gone, and I got to take out some mob guys and make money in the process. My new pipeline moves forward and Sultan's hands stay clean. No one would suspect me or my people, we live too far away to care, and the pipeline problems have been kept quiet. Sultan and I planned it so Ruggiano would take the fall."

If he was the one doing Sultan's dirty work then he must be here for more than just me. "You were the one dispatched to take care of Sigo?"

He searched my incredulous expression and responded. "It's gonna be the final nail in Ruggiano's coffin. It wasn't a secret he wanted to get rid of Sigo. When they find the family, there isn't a person on earth that won't think Ruggiano deserves the chair."

He told me his gruesome plans. And he sounded as though he'd enjoy it. After he finished with the Sigo family, he planned to end Sultan's reign.

"What about the list? You were going to double cross both of them?" I was in disbelief. Sultan gave up Thibodeaux, and Thibodeaux planned to take down Sultan. I guess 'No honor among thieves' also applied to psychopaths.

When he shifted his gun, I glanced at the ground and hoped I could reach the stick before he got a shot off.

Noticing my distraction, he shoved the gun barrel into my side hard enough I fell to the ground—right where I wanted to be.

"Get up klutz. Time for you to die."

I stared him down while my hands fumbled past dirt and leaves.

"Wait!" I needed time to find the branch. "What about the

powder? Don't you want my theory on it?"

"Why don't you *enlighten* me?" He settled his gun across his arms again.

"You didn't just want to take down Ruggiano. You wanted to hurt him for messing with your original plans." Apple didn't fall far from that tree—guess Tab inherited his desire to inflict pain from his dad. My hand searched while my eyes stayed on Thibodeaux. "You wanted to hurt him by hurting people he loved." The photo made sense. The reason it stuck out, the reason she hesitated when I asked her about Ruggiano was because they were protecting each other, hiding some sort of relationship.

The smug look on Thibodeaux faded.

"You knew he was watching out for Mrs. Jacobson. That's why he was at the fundraiser, and why she didn't admit knowing him. It would be dangerous if anyone found out. But you did, somehow, and saw her as an easy target. If Mrs. Jacobson had been accused of being involved in the murders, he'd have gone ape. You have no sense of decency at all. Do you?"

His shadowy glare terrified me. "All I had to do was get Tab to catch her no-good-wheelchair-pushing-cousin buying some weed. After that, the little scum brought me her special red ochre powder, no questions asked."

"No one would believe she could commit murder, she can barely walk." I secretly thought she could with an accomplice, but I was suspicious of everyone these days.

"I didn't need them to believe it. The evidence would force the police to bring her in for questioning where my people could do what was necessary to scare her into implicating Ruggiano. Dumb bastard thinks he's the next Capone. He's nothing."

Thibodeaux looked hungry for death. "Nothing. Just like you're about to be." He raised the gun barrel.

I rolled, grabbed the branch I needed, and jammed it into his crotch. He dropped the gun, shouted a few expletives, and grabbed himself. I quickly stood and swung the stick. He was bent over, but caught it with one hand and tried to pull me off balance. It brought me close enough he grabbed a handful of my hair. I swatted at him, and he started choking me.

I resisted, slapping at him as long as I could. My arms weakened and dropped. He dug in harder.

I watched evil spill into Thibodeaux's eyes as he squeezed the life out of me. I was fading. The thought of this no-good, greedy jerk getting away with murder pissed me off. His was not going to be the last face I ever saw.

My fighter awoke. I shoved my arms up, brought them back down over his arms, and broke his hold. Then I shoved the heel of my hand up into his face and broke his nose. He made a strange noise and grabbed for his nose.

Choking, I ran, got the stick, and hit him over the head as hard as I could. Then hit him again until he fell flat.

I moved away from Thibodeaux and fell to my knees. Hunched over and crying, I tried to force air into my lungs to stay conscious. It didn't work. Instead, I hyperventilated and got light-headed.

Just when I thought I'd pass out, a bronze-skinned guy dressed in a Grateful Dead t-shirt, jeans, and scuffed combat boots came out of nowhere. He laid a hand on my back for just a moment and my breathing calmed. The young man checked my assailant for a pulse.

The stranger reached out his hand to help me up. "Don't worry, he'll be out for a while."

I questioningly looked from my rescuer to Thibodeaux, then back.

"Seriously, nice shot. Name's Walt. I'm here to help. Now, let's get you up."

I knew Walt could have pretended not to notice the bludgeoned men, or left me stranded, but he didn't. I'd have kicked Thibodeaux while he was down, but it seemed a little over the top, so I reached my hand out for Walt and stood up.

A couple younger guys came from the trees and looked at Walt. He pointed toward Thibodeaux. "There are two. Get them out of here and clean up."

Walt helped me walk toward Garrett. I wobbled like a baby fawn, but I did it (mostly) on my own. "I came to warn your family. Instead, you came to my rescue."

"Lady, from what I saw, you saved yourself."

Something like appreciation or pride made me stand a little taller.

Walt helped Garrett come to with smelling salts. Except for some cuts and blood, Garrett looked pretty good for being kidnapped, poisoned, and beat. I was exhausted and looked like a drowned rat covered in dirt and leaves. Cold winds whipped over my skin like splintered glass. I suddenly wished for home, hot cocoa, and a warm blankie.

We walked further along to the place Cal had been shot. An old man with long grey hair braided halfway down his back was hunched over Cal. A small leather satchel hung at his side. The man pulled some root out of the bag and crushed it over Cal's gunshot wound. Cal winced. I let out a sigh. Cal was alive. He'd been propped against a tree and was breathing.

The old man had skin closer to coffee-with-cream. He said something in a language accented by clicking sounds and continued to patch Cal's shoulder. From the looks of it, he'd doctored more than a few wounds.

The old man stood to wipe his hands. When he turned, I let out a gasp. The tobacco skin, long gray hair, deep wrinkles around the eyes—it was the face from my dreams. *Who was he? How could he be here?*

Images flashed. There were dead bodies covered in reddish powder, the embankment, jackpot slots, and a bright light that blazed until I regained focus.

As if he knew what was going on inside my head, knew my questions, the old man walked over and spoke.

"You took long enough, bright eyes. We've been waiting for you."

"For me?"

The old man eyed me for a moment. "So we can get this man to a hospital." Then he winked as if there was some sort of secret we shared.

"I came to tell you Sultan's men were coming to hurt you and your family."

"Thank you for what you did to stop them."

It was good to know he'd be safe at least until the next group of assassins came.

On the walk back to the helicopter Walter Sigo and his grandson Walt told us about their land, the case, and Chloe's involvement.

"Some people don't care about the off-tribe casinos. We understand it can help make money for the tribe. But in our case, we know there are plenty operating, but there are dangers. We need to diversify operations, and must keep our council in check. Too many politicians and bad people are lining the pockets of our council. They're turning us against ourselves." Sigo looked irked, but he shook it off.

"When Chloe came to interview me. I told her the same thing. She was the only one who'd help us. The other lawyers got paid to leave us alone. I told her there were a few of our tribe who still opposed the deal. When I told her about the oil company that came sniffing around to buy up land right after the casino investors, she told me to keep these until I saw you."

The old man opened my hand with calloused fingers that had probably worked more than most people would in their entire lives. He placed a paper and a necklace in my hand. "Chloe gave specific instructions to give them only to you. She was afraid someone might kill her, but never stopped helping us. Make sure her killers are punished."

I squeezed my fist and looked him in the eye. "You have my word."

Pleased with my response, a smile crossed his crinkly face. Cal looked tired. It was time to leave.

The old man spoke to Garrett. "Teach her more than waving sticks and groin kicks. While effective, they will only delay death, not prevent it."

Garrett nodded a silent agreement. I thought I saw the edges of his mouth start to pull up into a smile.

"Cal will recover soon. You are welcome to stay and rest, but I can see she's already gone." The old man meant me. I didn't hear what he said next because I was already thinking about what I would tell Chloe's mom.

CHAPTER 31

We got back to the 'Koala'. A woman dressed like a hiker carrying some serious hardware exchanged words with Cal as Walt and Garrett loaded him, then me, into the chopper. Mr. Thibodeaux was cuffed and Tab had been restrained, but remained passed out on a stretcher. Walt and Garrett loaded the Thibodeaux men and we headed home.

Garrett took the controls. He was still weak, but in better shape to fly than Cal. I stayed by Cal and made sure he was comfortable and protected. Surprisingly, the guys slept most of the way, and with Garrett busy at the helm, I did my best to calm down as I turned Chloe's necklace around in my hands.

It was all too fresh, and I needed space to read the note, mostly because I didn't know if it would trigger anger or tears. This was not the place for a breakdown.

No matter, there was plenty of other stuff to figure out. How could I explain to mom what I'd been doing? What was next for Tab and his dad? Would Ruggiano and Sultan come after us? Too many thoughts fought at once. My head throbbed, so I watched out the window for a while.

When we got to the hospital, one of Cincy's finest took Tab away, still unconscious. Thibodeaux was met by more cops and his lawyer. A third person, a detective from the CPD, flashed his badge and took over when the deputy had trouble handling the lawyer. They took Thibodeaux downtown along with his posse to answer for his transgressions.

Chloe's killers would be brought to justice. I'd see to it personally.

Cal was admitted for observation. Whatever field surgery Walter Sigo did, was good enough Cal would recover despite the bullet's close proximity to a major artery.

Garrett was examined, and after ignoring the doctor's objections, left. I dropped him off. I would have stayed, but the poison was still a threat to him. I had to meet Millie. He needed sleep more than anything right now, anyway.

I raced over to Millie's shop with the seeds and roots I'd harvested.

"Did ya bring everything? Including the hair?"

"I did, but he thought it was a little too voo-doo."

"It's part of the spell."

"Spell?" Maybe Millie had magical powers.

"Did ya meet Sigo?"

"Yes, at the falls."

"Good. Ya needed to be there for the meeting to happen."

The meeting. Sigo. Then realization. I had the dreams about Sigo after taking Millie's potions. "But, how did you—"

"Get inside your head? It's a story for another day. Let's begin, we haven't got much time."

I was confused, but trusted her. Garrett trusted her, even if he didn't believe in magic. Truth be told, magic was something I wanted to believe in, but didn't know if it was possible.

"Okay. What can I do?"

"Ya need to crush these seeds ya brought back from the falls. Then ya need to add a vial full of the red elixir I made earlier and three drops of your blood."

"Excuse me. My what?" Garrett was right. She was into black magic, or something. I gave her the 'are you kidding me' look. She didn't blink, just used her fingertip and pretended to cut across her palm diagonally. I heaved a sigh. "Okay, give me something to prick my finger."

"Garrett's said you have a very trusting soul. It's a rare quality these days, but also a dangerous one."

"So, I don't have to slice my hand or dance over a boiling cauldron to save Garrett?"

"No, ya don't. But you will need more protection." Millie handed me what looked like an ancient pocketknife with ornate carvings on the wooden handle. "Be careful. It's old, and sharp."

When I touched it, the knife felt heavier than it should have. I could swear a surge of electricity shot through me. Things were getting out of control, but Millie hadn't let us down yet. Suddenly, a shock ran through me and I was back in a dream world. It must have been a hundred years earlier by the way everyone was dressed. Through a gun-smoke haze, I saw people, families, and natives running from something.

In a flash, the thing they were running from rode up on a horse. He jumped off and knocked me to the ground.

He pulled out his sword. I rolled, but he managed to cut through flesh near my shoulder. It hurt like fire. It was a small wound, but the blood came quickly.

Electricity surged and I nearly fainted. Millie stabilized me. I was back at her shop, confused about what happened.

Millie handed me a cloth to cover the wound. It cooled the fire and made my head feel better. Probably another magical thing I didn't have time to question.

Without any explanation, she mixed the potion, funneled it into an old apothecary bottle, and capped it with the stopper. She paused before she gave me directions.

"Ya take this directly to him, ya hear? He needs to drink this before the poison kills him."

I nodded. "Got it. Straight there, drink right away, or he dies." I said it calmly, but I was anything but calm.

"Ya need to drink dis one for your wound. And girl, admit you care. Tell dat boy how ya really feel. If you wait too long, he won't be the only one to suffer."

"But—"

"Go. We don't have time. Besides you're not ready to hear it all. Just go and save the boy. May the good Lord help ya both."

I took a step and turned back. "How did you know about Sigo?"

"Da spirits talk to me, girl." She cackled long and deep.

Were we in N'awlins? Maybe Garrett was right about the voo-doo thing. I couldn't ask because Millie pushed me out the door so fast.

Garrett was asleep sitting up in his office chair when I arrived. At least, I hoped he was sleeping. I went to put a hand on his arm and he nearly jumped when he woke up. But, he could barley move. If he'd had actual energy, he might have ended up out of his seat on the ground. Things looked very bad. He needed help, fast.

I held up the bottle, hoping it would work, but unsure if the potion could actually heal him. I sighed. "Garrett, she said you have to drink this."

"Unh," he grunted.

"Hey, you drink that one and I'll drink this."

He sat up and attempted to laugh.

"Why are you laughing? This is not funny."

"We have to play a drinking game using some red gunk an eccentric lady told us would keep me from dying. It sounds just crazy enough to work."

"She's an herbalist, and I feel the same. If we make it through this, you owe me a real drink. Now, it's late. Do it."

"Down the hatch," Garrett leaned back and drank.

I tipped mine back and let the potion slide down my throat. It felt odd, but it didn't taste overly sweet like I expected. It felt kind of thick, but was pleasant. Then I choked. Something like vinegar hit my taste buds.

Garrett had a coughing fit. I reached for a cloth. He waved me off and pointed to the glass. I gave him some water and he took a sip between gasps. It helped.

"That was awful."

"Not surprising, since I saw what she put in yours."

"Do I need to know?"

"No, but they do this kind of thing in the movies all the time."

"Movies, huh?"

He smiled and pulled me in for a kiss on the forehead. "Cal told me to keep an eye on you. Tab will be in the hospital for a couple weeks, but Thibodeaux made bail. We think he'll come after you. A security detail is on you and your mom 24/7, but be cautious."

I shivered at the thought. "Do you think Ruggiano or Sultan will come after us?"

Garrett handed me a note. "A messenger brought it over about fifteen minutes before you arrived." I opened the thick envelope and read the note:

Dearest Matilda,

After hearing of your recent trip north, my business associates and I have reached a new agreement. We will alter a few plans, but will continue our profitable partnership.

If it weren't for you, this new understanding wouldn't have been possible. We thank you for showing us a more fruitful opportunity could blossom.

I trust you'll accept this as a token of our thanks and friendship.

Warmly,

Sultan

He'd enclosed five thousand dollars cash. It would go a long way to helping mom and me, but there was no way I'd keep it. It was hush money.

"How do I send this back?"

"Let's show Cal. He'll help us figure out how to respond. I'll lock it up until we can meet him in person and discuss it. Get some rest. I'll be here if you need me."

"Do you want me to take you home, or bring you anything?"

He opened his lower desk drawer and pulled out a blanket. "Nope. I'm good. See you in the morning."

The light drizzle persisted. Fresh leaf piles were now matted heaps along the roadside when I looked outside. It was going to be a cold, wet night.

Mom needed help to get from the couch to the bedroom when I returned. I murmured something about a long day and needing to study, so she didn't ask questions. It bought me time. She was so tired, she barely moved while I gathered some dry clothes.

I washed up, changed into pink flannel PJs with fuzzy slippers, and made a quick dinner.

I took my plate along with a drink and got comfy on the couch. When the micro Mac and cheese was gone, I had an apple and some yogurt, followed by a couple cookies with milk. Being nearly killed made me famished. Food helped.

When I finally got comfy on the couch with my laptop, it was almost eleven o'clock.

My phone buzzed. I reached for it and noticed the note from Chloe stuffed in my purse. I'd get to it in the morning.

It was a text from Garrett: I've turned into a zombie and want your—brains!

I wrote: I'm partial to my brains, how about my body?

It was flirty, but felt right, so I sent it.

The bubbles on the screen flickered for a minute before his response came: Willing to negotiate a package deal?

I responded: Sure, but I'm a tough negotiator.

He responded: Counting on it.

Was it getting hot in here? On that note, I smiled and set the phone aside. I fought the urge to wander down and see him.

Now that I was alert, I spent the next couple hours going through the files and outlining what I knew for Cal and the CPD to review. Their analysis might come up with the same stuff, but it felt productive to do the work.

Shortly after two, I crawled under a blanket and passed out.

CHAPTER 32

When mom saw my note the next day, I'd been gone for hours. I told her I'd be doing a class project at the library, so she wouldn't try to reach me (no phones allowed), and to not expect me until dinner. I knew hiding was cowardly, but I'd talk through all this with mom after I got things done.

Sun peeked out from behind the grey hanging above, but the temps stayed cool. Since so much stress gripped my shoulders and chest, I planned to stop by the old gym Garrett had showed me, to shake off some bad energy.

Before I could go there though, I needed to take care of a couple things. As much as the Hellcat and I had bonded, she sacrificed a front-end to save me from a tree, it was time to get my car back.

I apologized to Dawes for the damage the Hellcat sustained—including the crumpled side door. He told me repairs kept him in business, and offered to let me visit her once she was restored to her original glory.

Bianca gave me the side-eye when I turned in the keys. She couldn't have been jealous of my Honda, but she sure acted like something was up.

Dawes shook his head when I left. I think he felt sorry for me, but he understood reality. And reality was I'd been through the ringer and I didn't drive an expensive muscle car with leather interior and 700 horsepower. I drove a crappy old rust bucket. One that had been fine tuned by a great mechanic, but still sounded like a dying chicken whenever I hit the gas, or turned, or tapped the brakes. So, after I saved the world, I'd get a good job, and maybe someday, I'd get a nice car.

Wind pushed my junker around the entire way to the Ellis house. Dread filled my gut, but I knocked on the door anyway.

I sat with Mrs. Ellis and told her everything. Someone brought coffee, cocoa, and cookies. We sipped, talked, and cried.

Knowing Chloe had not committed suicide brought her some relief, but with it came great pain. Nothing could bring Chloe back. We helped each other embrace the anger and sadness, and promised to stay in touch.

As much as punching stuff relieved stress, there was still residual anxiety even after my workout. It didn't help that I'd read Chloe's note.

In it, Chloe thanked me. She made sure to explain the silver etched necklace reminded her of our friendship—before Tab, when things became unbearable. She knew just what to say to make me feel better, but I cried anyway.

I toweled off, touched up my lips and eyes, and then changed into curve hugging jeans and a V-neck sweater. I got more looks on the way out than I had in my sweat pants, but no one said a word. It wasn't the kind of crowd that would have whistled or anything, but even if someone was tempted, the look on my face was enough to them keep quiet.

Garrett leaned against my old car as if it was a sports car. Lucky car.

"Ready to negotiate?" Garrett's thousand-watt smile beamed. My anxiety melted away. The poison was gone and he'd be fine.

"Are you ready?" I faced him with my hip near the driver's side door.

He turned to me. "I'm always ready."

Of course you are. "You look good for having been poisoned and all."

"Thanks, I think."

"You know what I mean."

"I do. Just making you squirm a little. Trying to get a tactical advantage. You look pretty good yourself." Garrett gently kissed my cheek. The heat between us made me want to...do so many things.

My heart pounded out of my chest as he moved closer. His lips brushed my neck softly and tingles surged through my entire body.

"I just want you to know I'm sorry."

A wave of emotion choked me up, but I managed a "Thank you."

"It's never easy to lose someone. I'm available anytime you need to talk."

"That means a lot." I tried to smile.

"Looks like I'll have to stick close to you though. Cal said Sultan and Ruggiano are cleared, and Thibodeaux is back in Louisiana letting his lawyer handle things, but I don't trust any of them to leave you alone."

I shook involuntarily. Garrett put an arm around me. His expression changed. "Do you want to go see her? She's good as new."

"What?" It was difficult to figure out what he meant.

He nuzzled my ear. "I'm talking about the Maserati."

I lightly punched his arm. "You're in big trouble. I thought your car exploded yesterday."

"It did. Dawes gave me a loaner. I should drive though, since you're so hard on cars." He laughed then looked at me earnestly. "Chloe was lucky to have you as a friend. You're smart, determined, and beautiful, and I want whatever trouble you'll give me."

He didn't pause to let me think or even respond, he just pulled me into a steamy kiss, and I knew we were both in big trouble.

ABOUT THE AUTHOR

Kristen Gibson is an author and freelance writer. Her work has appeared in numerous print and online publications. When not writing, she is most likely playing, biking, reading, or goofing off with her husband and children.

Visit the author online at
www.kristengibson.com
@KGwrites

26854223R00182

Made in the USA
San Bernardino, CA
06 December 2015